THIS NOVEL OF TRUE LOVE HAS

Sex in every style.

Murder in every mode.

Intrigue as intricate as filigree.

Pride, greed, vengeance, deceit, betrayal, and virtually every other sin that men and women can commit in all conceivable combinations.

Plus, of course,
A Happy Ending.

THE CRAZY LOVERS
a novel to be read for pleasure only

"A triumph . . . erotic show-and-tell . . . outrageously sexy!"
—*Newport News Daily Press*

"Savage and sensual!"—*Chattanooga Times*

"Fast and entertaining, with an unusual twist."
—*Wichita Eagle*

"An anything goes erotic saga."
—*Publishers Weekly*

Big Bestsellers from SIGNET

* Price slightly higher in Canada
† Not available in Canada

To order these titles,

please use coupon on

the last page of this book.

The Crazy Lovers

by
Joyce Elbert

A SIGNET BOOK

NEW AMERICAN LIBRARY

TIMES MIRROR

First Signet Printing, November, 1979

1 2 3 4 5 6 7 8 9

to Sam

The Crazy Lovers

eighteenth century, who had negotiated a alliance with the ... Iroquois tribe from which Mark was descended. After the first war, pretended the English ... were the

Part 1

The Lake—1945

1 &

I've always hated my mother, and I've always loved Harry.

Harry is my brother. I don't really understand what one relationship has to do with the other, and maybe it's got nothing to do with it, but even though I'm only twelve I think there's a connection.

Harry is thirteen and wonderful. No. Dazzling. Sexy. But it's a lot more complicated than that. Harry reminds me of that part in "The Member of the Wedding," when Frankie says that the reason she wants to go on the honeymoon with her brother and his bride is because they are "the we of me."

That's how I feel about Harry. We have a special kind of love, and if he married anyone else, I believe I'd die. So I guess it must mean I want him to marry me. And he's my brother! It's a sin against God to feel about Harry the way I do, anybody with half a head and even a little bit of religious training knows that. I know it, yet it doesn't seem to change my feelings.

There are three churches in the small town where we live. We go to the Presbyterian one, but I've spoken to girls who go to the others, Roman Catholic and Lutheran, and even though I tried to be very tactful, they all looked at me kind of funny. As though they knew exactly what I was getting at, so I pretended that I needed the information for an essay I was writing for my English class. I told them the subject was: "The Greatest Sin I Can Think of."

One girl, Sally-Anne, actually called me a damned liar right to my face. She was sorry for it later, though, boy was she sorry. I beat her up after school, behind the ice house, and she went home looking like an alley cat that's had a hard night trying to make out.

Sally-Anne isn't the first of my girlfriends I've beaten up. Basically I'm very shy and quiet, but every once in a while something will happen, somebody will say something that gets me mad, and I just go wild. Berserk. It's like I become another person, it must be my Indian blood. Sally-Anne once made the mistake of telling me that the other girls' secret nickname for me was "Crazy Squaw."

"If it's supposed to be so secret," I asked the dope, "how come you're telling me?"

"Oh, because of those airs you're always putting on. Like you're someone special. Better than the rest of us."

Sally-Anne had beautiful, long, wavy blonde hair at that time. She was very proud of her hair, so I got a scissors and cut it off to about an inch below her ears, all jagged naturally and weird looking. I warned her that if she ever told her mother who did it, she'd live to regret it, that the next time I'd scalp her. She cried and said I was the meanest person she had ever met, but since then I haven't had too much trouble with the girls around here. They're too afraid of me to start anything.

Little do they know that I'm afraid of a lot of things myself. Like just plain going to school. I'm always terrified when the teacher asks a question and calls on me to answer it. My heart starts to pound as I stand up, and sometimes even though I know the answer in back of my mind, I can't remember it because I'm so nervous.

Harry thought that what I did to Sally-Anne's hair was hilarious. When Harry and I were younger, we used to take off our clothes and pee all over each other. Why? I don't know. It seems so friendly. Then once I took his thing in my mouth and sucked on it for a while, like a lolipop, but instead of being sweet it tasted salty and strange. My mother would have a heart attack if she ever caught us. She loves Harry. She's never loved me, but I don't care.

False.

Not true.

I care like mad, still it doesn't do any good. That's one thing I've learned. Either someone loves you or they don't, you can't try to make someone love you even if it is your own mother. I want Harry all to myself. My mother doesn't love me and I can't have my father (Harry looks a lot like him), so I want Harry. It's as simple as that.

The reason I can't have my father is because he was killed in that awful war that just ended in August. I never forgave FDR for declaring war, anyway. I mean, I know he had to do it because of the Japs bombing Pearl Harbor. I'm not dumb and yet I don't exactly understand where Pearl Harbor *is*, despite the fact that our geography teacher has pointed it out to us on the big world map that rolls down. We all hate FDR around here. We think he sold out. He was born rich, and he sold out his own people.

"Betrayed them."

That's what my thin-lipped mother keeps saying whenever the subject comes up. Then she mumbles about states' rights and the federal government trying to take over everything, and how FDR was really a Jew-Commie lover, and things like that. Half the time I don't listen to her. I'm not interested in the Jews, the Communists, Hitler, Mussolini, and all that stuff that went on in Europe. Europe doesn't mean beans to me. It's a place on a map, like Idaho and Pearl Harbor.

Geography is strange. There's only one country in Europe that I'm fascinated by and that's Spain. It seems so romantic. I always think of Cortes as a flamenco dancer in tight pants, which amuses Harry no end. Harry is fascinated by Spain, too. Well, how can you help it?

When I think of Spain, I think of bright hot colors, like real purple and violent red and deep dark pink, not those washed-out pastel pink hats you see on the women around here when they go to church on Sunday. I'll never wear a hat like that. Pastels are very boring, and I've grown up in a pastel, gray and white world.

Yesterday was definitely not a pastel day, but before I get to yesterday I guess I've got to pinpoint where we live. It is important, no matter how you try to avoid it, isn't it? Well, just for the record we live in a house that my father built himself. It's made of logs and hand-hewn beams, and is situated on one of the most beautiful lakes you've ever seen in your life. It's a very long lake (about ten miles), and we used to have steamboats here less than fifteen years ago, before I was born. I'm sorry I missed them. I'll get into the whole steamboat and Indian business later, right now I want to get back to yesterday. And Harry.

I suppose I should describe him. Which is almost like describing myself, that's how much alike we look. I don't mean that he looks girlish or that I look boyish, I don't think either one of us does, it's just that, well, genes, they were teaching us the Mendelian ratio at school and I realized that unless Harry and I were mutants, we both had to have come out with black hair and the darkest brown eyes you've ever seen in your life. Because our father had black hair and the darkest brown eyes you've ever seen in your life.

And the science teacher (who's also the geography teacher) said that those are the dominant genes, as opposed to recessive—blue eyes and blonde hair, which sums up my mother's whole snotty English family. The English weren't the original settlers of Pilgrim Lake, even though they act like it. The Indians were. They came here about fifteen thousand years ago, my father's ancestors. But the English took all the land away from them in some peculiar treaty that nobody likes to talk about. Probably because they're ashamed of what they did.

So my father is dead. He died somewhere in the Pacific, bombing those damned Japs and one of them got him.

That's why yesterday is so important. Yesterday was the turning point in my life. And in Harry's, too, although he doesn't know it yet. You see, my father had been listed as missing in action for a year and we'd all just about given up hope. Not completely, but he wasn't on any of those lists they used to publish. He wasn't listed as a prisoner of war, so it was like one day he was there and one day we got a letter saying he had disappeared. Just dropped out of the sky, the way Glenn Miller did.

They don't actually use words like "disappeared" in the War Department, they've got fancier names, but what does it matter? I loved my father so much and then you get this crazy letter saying he doesn't exist anymore, or they can't find him, or they're not sure what happened, or something, and at the time Harry said:

"Don't give up hope, Alexis. You never know. He might be alive somewhere in the jungle."

"Or maybe he became a flamenco dancer, like Cortes."

"*That's no way to talk,*" my mother screamed. "*That's blasphemy!*"

"It was just a joke," I started to say.

I didn't get to finish the sentence, because my mother smacked me so hard across the face that I could feel tears come to my eyes. I held them back, though, I wouldn't give her the satisfaction of seeing me cry. She saw me cry a lot when I was a kid. She was always hitting me for doing something wrong, and she's gotten all the tears she'll ever get out of me, I can tell you that. Also, she never loved my father but now that he was gone she was playing the martyr, a role she's been practicing for years.

"This is no time for jokes," my mother said to me, much more softly now. "And besides, maybe Harry is right. Maybe your father is alive somewhere. Only God knows."

God and Van Johnson. I thought of a movie with Van Johnson when he played a pilot like my father, only he was dead, but he was flying around in heaven directing all those other pilots. A real flying angel. Thanks a lot, Louis B. Mayer, and that goes for Darryl Zanuck, and Jack Warner, and FDR (when he was alive), and the rest of the bigshots in this country, thanks for trying to make me believe in make-believe.

But I don't and I never will. I started going to the movies when I was very young. I'd cut school and sneak in the side entrance, and I say the hell with "The Wizard of Oz." I'm smarter than Judy Garland. I knew my father was dead before we found out for sure. Harry secretly knew it, too, because we think alike but I guess he didn't want to upset me, so he pretended. He should have known better.

Okay. Yesterday.

"I thank thee, Lord, for this bounty we are about to receive. Amen," said my mother.

We were just sitting down to Sunday supper (oxtail stew with sticky lima beans, some bounty), Harry, my mother, and me, when Mickey Rooney came riding over on his bike to deliver the telegram, dated October 14, 1945. My mother read it first and fainted. It seems they had found some gooey remains of my father, his teeth no doubt, and there was no question of it, so forget prisoner of war and forget missing in action. Dead is dead, and I'm glad FDR is even if it does sound unpatriotic. If it weren't for him and all his speeches about how he was going to keep us out of the war, my father would still be alive.

We had to call the doctor for my mother. Jack Benny was on the radio saying "Honestly!" to Rochester when the doctor arrived. He gave my mother some smelling salts and a stiff shot of whiskey, which she managed to choke down even though she hates the stuff. "Devil's poison," she calls it, because of my father's drinking problem.

Then she said something I'll never forgive her for.

"He was probably all tanked up, and that's why he crashed. And now I'm a widow with two small children to support."

Harry and I looked at each other, the same thought passing through our minds: the martyr strikes again. But Harry was always the sweet-talker, not like me.

"It's going to be okay, Mom." And he kissed her tenderly

on the cheek. "Alexis and I aren't kids. We can work at the store every day after school from now on."

"You already work at the store on Saturdays."

"Yes, but this way you can get rid of that dumbbell delivery boy, and save yourself eight dollars a week."

The sound of saving money always made my mother perk up. She was a real tightwad.

"You're a good son, Harry. A good boy."

She didn't look at me and I didn't look at her. All she could think of was:

1. Saving a lousy eight dollars a week;
2. Feeling sorry for herself;
3. And accusing a dead man, who couldn't answer back, that he'd been drunk when his plane crashed.

Then Dennis Day started to sing something on the "Jack Benny Show," and Don Wilson told us all the different things you could do with Jell-O.

"That's what we're having for dessert," my mother said, as though nothing unusual had happened. "Lime flavor. With peaches inside."

Well that was yesterday, Jell-O, Jack Benny, and Jap murder day in the Maringo household.

This morning my mother got up at seven o'clock just like always, and went down to the kitchen to make Ralston. I could smell its nauseating flavor from my bed. If there was one food I really hated it was cooked cereal of any kind, it made me want to gag. Harry hated it, too, even though Tom Mix and his Ralston Straight Shooters were crazy about the stuff. Harry and I listened to Tom Mix a lot, but we really preferred Jack Armstrong, who never tired of Wheaties, "the best breakfast food in the land." My mother, though, wouldn't have anything to do with Wheaties, not even in the summertime.

"Cold cereal is no way to start the day."

There was a tap on the door, and Harry came in wearing an old pair of my father's pajamas that my mother had shortened for him. He looked cheerful, almost happy.

"What are you so happy about?" I asked.

So he started to sing "The Army Air Corps Song": "Off we go into the wild blue yonder, flying high into the sun. Down they come zooming to meet our thunder, etcetera, give 'em the gun."

It was like making fun of our father, and I suddenly realized that Harry had never loved him the way I had, that he spent too many years being ashamed of Dad's reputation as the town drunk. Still, I couldn't get angry at Harry. I've never been able to.

"I just wanted to see how you are," he said.

"I'm okay."

He knew I wasn't, so he ruffled my hair. "See you downstairs."

The Ralston smell was getting stronger by the second, and pretty soon my mother called up, "Breakfast!"

I could hear Harry heading for the kitchen, but I wasn't making a move. I just lay there. A few minutes later, my mother marched in and wanted to know why I wasn't getting washed and dressed.

"Because I'm not going to school today."

"And why not?"

"I have a headache."

She felt my forehead. "You don't have a fever."

"I just have a bad headache."

She couldn't very well suggest that I take an aspirin because we didn't have any. My mother was so against medication of any kind that I'm willing to bet we had the barest bathroom cabinet in Pilgrim Lake.

"Try to get some sleep," my mother said. "You look like you've been crying all night."

"Is that a crime?"

For an instant I thought she was going to put her arms around me and kiss me, but I should have known better. My mother didn't subscribe to affection any more than she did to aspirin.

"There's some leftover stew in the Frigidaire, in case you get hungry."

Those were her last, warming words before she closed the door behind her to drive to work in her old Chevy panel truck. Mom's tough, all right, I'll hand her that. And besides she probably figures that if she doesn't show up at Ye Olde Family Shoppe (otherwise known as Maringo's General Store), her faithful clerk, Dennis, might decide to fiddle around with the cash register and we'd be out a couple of bucks.

"Planning on going to the movies today?"

It was Harry again. Now he had on an old woolly brown sweater, tan corduroys, and his favorite leather jacket.

"There's a new one playing, with Humphrey Bogart," he said.

I certainly had plans, but they didn't include movies.

"I don't feel so good. I'm just going to stay in bed."

"Adios, Alexis."

And then he was gone, too. So here I am at nine-thirty in the morning, still in bed, true to my word, the patch quilt pulled up to my neck and not an ache in my head. Just a lot of hot thoughts in my mind.

Like at noon I'm going to call Harry at school, before he goes to lunch, and tell him to come home right away. I won't say why. I'll simply insist. Then I'm going to suck him off again, while he plays with me. Yes, you heard right, Democratic Party Members, that's what we're going to do, your darling, innocent twelve- and thirteen-year-old offshoots of dead bomber pilots. TBMs.

Or maybe we'd do it anyway, even if our father hadn't died. Who knows? Not our mother, that's for sure.

There are mountains out there in the distance, they look so beautiful. It's only October now, but in a few months it will be cold and the mountains will be covered with snow. Snow is white and virginal and something terrific just occurred to me, something sexually terrific.

I'm going to seduce Harry. I don't think he'll resist. We've had enough of this groping, fooling around stuff, yes, that's what I'm going to do, seduce him. I believe it's known as sexual intercourse in the dictionary, which I read a lot. I've got another word for it. I'm going to screw my own brother. Oh, oh. What if I get pregnant and we have an idiot baby? But that's impossible. I've never had my period. I don't shave under my arms yet, although I've got hair down there. It's black and curly.

I wonder what it will feel like when Harry does it to me. I wonder whether it will hurt. I hope it does. I want Harry to hurt me good. Maybe it'll blot out the other hurt. Now what is the number of that sweet little stone school we go to? I've never dialed it before, but knowing my mother I'd bet my life that she'll have it listed in her personal telephone book under "emergencies."

Mom, for once you're on the ball. Because when I go downstairs in a couple of hours and look up that number and get Harry on the phone, and tell him to get his ass back here pronto, you can be sure of one thing: *this is going to be some emergency, all right.*

2

It was precisely eight-thirty on the dot when Louise Smith Maringo backed her 1938 panel truck out of the garage and headed for the store that had been in her family for three generations. Despite the fact that it was now known as the Maringo General Store, it was Louise's grandfather, Teddy Smith, who started it in the latter part of the last century when he owned his first vegetable and fruit farm, and when Pilgrim Lake still carried the original Indian name of Great Water.

After Louise's parents died in the devastating fire of 1933, the store automatically passed into her hands, she being their only child. She and Mark had been married for less than a year at that time, and Louise suggested they change the old, wooden, weather-beaten sign from Smith to Maringo.

"I think it would be more fitting," she said. "More appropriate, if you know what I mean."

What she really meant was that even though she had married someone of lower status than herself, she was going to defy the townspeople's disdain by this act of faith in her husband.

"Sure, honey," laughed Pilgrim Lake's bad boy. "Why in hell not?"

His nonchalant attitude confused and disappointed her. Louise felt she was making a very magnanimous gesture, a very sincere one, and it was only later that she discovered to her astonishment that Mark didn't give a damn. Not about the store, not about her, not about his child she was carrying, not about anything except the local fire water that passed for alcohol in those parts.

Louise now cursed as the panel truck suddenly stalled on the main road leading to the center of town. She checked the gas and temperature gauges. Normal.

"Damn."

She would never use that word in front of the children, but she was alone and nobody could hear her. Even so, she felt somewhat guilty about mouthing a curse word. After all, God could hear everything, couldn't he? That's what her beloved grandfather, Teddy, always maintained and Louise never doubted that he was right.

She put her foot on the starter, then on the gas pedal, and to her immense relief the old heap started up again. Still, it was unusual for a car to stall like that and she knew she should leave it at Buck's garage, just to make sure there was nothing seriously wrong with the carburetor or points. Another couple of dollars down the drain. Maybe she'd wait a few days before rushing off to Buck's and throwing away her money.

Louise sighed (if it wasn't one thing, it was another), and continued the three-mile drive to town. Although she had to look in the car mirror from time to time, she always avoided trying to look at herself. It was too painful. At thirty-three she was a drab, faded blonde with pulled-back hair. Her only concession to cosmetics was a bright red lipstick she bought for ten cents at the local drugstore; it was called Crimson Rose, and Louise felt that it helped perk up her otherwise bland appearance. In actuality, it created a startling, almost garish effect that she was totally unaware of.

"Here comes Crimson Rose," was the other shopkeepers' mocking reaction as they saw her get out of the Chevy each morning.

When Louise first married Mark, she used to curl her straight, pale lashes with one of those metal eye curlers and bravely apply a bit of medium-brown mascara. Then one evening when she was four months pregnant with Alexis, Mark came home drunk and told her that she looked like a silly kewpie doll who squeaked when you pushed its stomach. Although she had barely started to show, she had a terrible sickening feeling that at that precise moment Mark would have liked to push her stomach very hard indeed.

"Shit!" he shouted. "And double shit that I ever forced myself into this marriage mess."

"Please don't talk that way in this house. And there's no need to raise your voice."

"Yes, my dear." He bowed unsteadily from the waist. "My sincere apologies."

"Aside from me, Harry might hear you."

"Are you nuts? He's upstairs sleeping like a rock. Anyhow, do you think that a two-month old kid would know what *shit* means, even if he did wake up?"

"Children remember things."

"Kewpie doll."

Louise Smith Maringo never curled her lashes or used mascara after that. And although she hated to admit it to herself, she was ferociously jealous of her daughter's beautiful long, black lashes that framed her eyes, top and bottom, like an exotic fringe. Sometimes Alexis reminded her of one of those Latin movie hussies who used to be so popular back in the thirties. Lupe Velez or Dolores Del Rio. She wasn't sure which. She'd never gone to the movies much (except on free dish night), at least not to the kind of movie where the looser and more wanton the woman was, the more fun she seemed to have.

Fun was one commodity Louise had not seen too much of in her thirty-three years. Fun was for movie stars and rich people, like those who came to Pilgrim Lake in the summer months to take advantage of its fishing, sailing, and swimming facilities, or just to get away from the strain of big city life. Some came mainly to hike and camp along the trails that ran through the thick, lush forests surrounding Pilgrim Lake. Others were profesional bird-watchers.

But whatever their specific outdoor pleasure was, one thing seemed certain: they had plenty of money, and "C" cards for gas. Since during the war years "C" cards were only given to those people involved in essential industries, Louise suspected that the war-year vacationers were richer than those who used to come to Pilgrim Lake previously.

She always looked forward to the arrival of the wealthy city people, even if now and then a few of them did put on airs or try to talk slick, like that insurance executive from Hartford (could insurance be considered an essential industry?), who wanted to know how come she didn't stock any foie gras. Someone had told her that he and his family normally vacationed in the south of France each summer. Louise remembered smiling her best Crimson Rose smile at him and saying:

"I don't even know what that is, sir."

That made him laugh and he ordered a pound of her most expensive German sausage instead, and walked away looking happy and pleased with himself, as though he had just pulled off a great business deal. So had Louise.

Because it was the months between Decoration Day and Labor Day that the store more than tripled its normal income, and with Mark not around to drink up the profits Louise had secretly managed to stash away a small fortune. Within the four years that her husband was gone, she'd saved eight thousand dollars. That, combined with the five thousand her grandfather left her in his will, added up to a very tidy sum indeed. She invested part of the money in War Bonds and deposited the rest in a savings account in a nearby town, away from the prying curiosity of her know-all, tell-all neighbors in Pilgrim Lake.

Neither Alexis nor Harry had any notion of how much money their mother was putting aside, and she didn't want them to know. At least not yet. It might give them ideas that they were too good for the small town in which they had grown up. Louise suspected they already harbored such ideas, and if there was one thing she didn't want to do it was to encourage them any further.

Now that Mark's death was official and no longer open to question, Louise's most fervent wish was that when Harry graduated from high school, he take over as manager of the Maringo General Store. As for Alexis, well, Louise had plans for her too. Plans most befitting a girl with as much beauty, arrogance, and untapped seductive potential as Alexis had shown ever since birth. The thought of the two totally different sets of plans Louise had for her children made her chuckle, then she turned her mind to the day ahead.

(But as Alexis would say to Harry in Paris, many years later: "Don't you think it odd that in her will, she gave *you*, her favorite, a much rougher deal than me?"

And Harry would reply, with a twinkle of malice: "Oh, do you really think so?")

"Hello there, Mrs. Maringo."

A young, clean-shaven man wearing a starched, white cotton coat waved at her from the front of his combination drugstore, ice-cream parlor, and hamburger hangout which stood a few yards from her own equally impressive-looking store.

She waved back. "Good morning, Charlie."

Charlie's father had recently suffered a stroke, and Louise admired the way in which Charlie smoothly stepped in and assumed his natural, filial responsibilities. He was only twenty or so and enrolled in a local college, majoring in chemistry, when his father became paralyzed, but he had not hesitated for a second in knowing where his duties lay. Although Louise respected higher education, she respected something else much more: family solidarity.

Which reminded her that she had to contact her mother-in-law and break the terrible news about Mark's death. Juliana would probably collapse in grief, so it was hardly a chore that Louise looked forward to but what did that matter? A chore was a chore. Or as her grandfather would have said under similar circumstances: "What's it got to do with the price of maple syrup?"

Charlie smiled at her as she got out of the Chevy.

"Nice morning, isn't it, Mrs. Maringo?"

In a few hours the entire town would know that her husband had died a hero, and there would be notes of condolence, telephone calls, people stopping by to express their sympathy, and she would have to stiffen herself throughout it all. The bereaved, not-so-young widow.

"I'm afraid you'll only be seeing Harry for lunch today," she said to Charlie. "Alexis is home with a headache."

"I'm sorry to hear that, ma'am." He hesitated and she knew he was automatically about to suggest aspirin, but her antipathy toward drugs of all kinds was well known in Pilgrim Lake. "I hope she's better real soon."

"Thank you, Charlie."

One of Louise's few luxuries was allowing Alexis and Harry to order their favorite hamburger, french fries, and milkshake lunch at Charlie's place each weekday, since the small school they attended did not have a cafeteria that served hot meals. All it could boast was a cheerless room with long tables and benches, where children were able to eat the sandwiches and apples and anything else they might have brought from home.

Louise did not approve of that. She approved of hot lunches and ice cream, particularly since she sold Charlie all the ingredients that went into everything Alexis and Harry consumed. So, in a way, it wasn't such a luxury at that.

And then, after lunch, both of them would pop into Maringo's to say hello to her, kid around with the clerk and delivery boy, and take a fast peek at whatever goodies might have been delivered that morning. But most of all it was the glass-topped assortment of Nabisco cookies, and the huge keg of sauerkraut swimming in mysterious, aromatic, pickling spices that seemed to hold an eternal fascination for them.

No matter. Louise was just glad to have the opportunity to *see* them. Being a working mother, she considered it important to make contact with her children at some point during the day, even if only for a few minutes. Ordinarily she did not get home until after six, and at times the long separation made her feel she was not living up to her maternal responsibilities. Which made her feel guilty. Which was a feeling that a woman like Louise Smith Maringo did not like very much.

MONDAY-TUESDAY SPECIAL SALE!!

Dried lima beans—4 cents lb.
Target cigarette tobacco—5 cents pkge.
Nuco margarine—8 cents lb.
Fresh sugar doughnuts—10 cents baker's dozen
Silvercup—11 cents family loaf
Chipso—13 cents large box
Clabber Girl baking powder—14 cents
Loin pork chops—22 cents lb.
Sirloin steak—35 cents lb.
Ingersol pocket watch—95 cents

Louise could not help admiring the large, hand-lettered, red and white signs that just about leaped out of the front window of Maringo's. Each week she put ten strategic items on sale, reducing them by a couple of pennies, in order to entice Pilgrim Lake housewives who tended to delay the bulk of their marketing until Wednesday or Thursday at the earliest. It was amazing how effective the simple system turned out to be.

The Ingersol pocket watch, which she normally sold for a dollar, was very big among the teen-age boys in town and therefore it had become a regular on her weekly mark-down list. Harry told her that a lot of the boys would put aside part of their allowance for months to save up the necessary ninety-five cents to buy it at Maringo's special reduction price. Today she could expect about three or four of them to come marching in after school and proudly plunk down their money for the coveted timepiece.

"Good morning, Mrs. M." A tall, balding man held the door open for her. "I just hung the signs a few minutes ago. They look kind of swell, don't they?"

It was Dennis, a good-natured Irishman who had been her clerk since the start of the war. Because of a heart condition, the Army classified him 4-F. As far as Louise was concerned, though, he was A-1 with her when it came to efficiency, reliability, and honesty, three qualities you didn't run into so often.

"They look very nice, Dennis." In addition to putting up the signs, he hand-lettered them himself, and for no extra money than the twenty-five dollars she paid him each week. "Very nice, indeed."

"Thank you, Mrs. M. But I was wondering. Maybe instead of painting the products in red all the time, we should try another color. You know, just for a change. Like maybe bright blue."

She looked him straight in the eye, determined that she might as well start with Dennis as with anyone.

"If we change to anything, I'm afraid it's going to have to be black."

"Excuse me?"

"Mr. Maringo is dead. Killed in the Pacific. I only found out about it last night."

Dennis opened his mouth, closed it, then opened it again.

"I'm mighty sorry to hear that, Mrs. M. It's awful, a real tragedy. That makes six in Pilgrim Lake who didn't return. To tell the truth, I'm kind of at a loss for words at times like this. I don't know how to express my sympathies."

"You just have."

Her crispness confused him. She appeared so unemotional, yet what if she were only putting on a brave front?

"I realize this is none of my business, Mrs. M., but don't you think you should have stayed home today? Taken it easy, I mean? I'd be only too glad to look after things for you."

"You're very considerate, Dennis, but that won't be necessary."

"Are you sure?"

"I'm positive."

He felt more confused than ever. "As I said, it's none of my business but I remember how shook Mrs. Finnegan was when she lost her son in that Battle of the Bulge. She took to her bed for a week."

"Mrs. Finnegan is always taking to her bed." Louise had no use for lay-abouts. "I was just wondering how the sirloin will sell. Maybe I should have priced it at thirty-two cents instead of thirty-five. What do you think, Dennis?"

He stared at her blankly. "You know best, Mrs. M."

"You're right. Why give it away? Well, let me take off my coat and we'll get going. I certainly hope Land O' Lakes delivers that peanut butter today. We're running real low."

"We are at that."

Leaving a bewildered Dennis behind, Louise walked briskly toward the back of the store, where she hung up her tweed coat, washed her hands in the cracked basin, and put on the long, white butcher's apron she would wear during the busy day ahead. She owned several of these aprons and changed them only when they became too splattered with blood to be presentable. This one had a few blood spots on the front, nothing much, yet the sight of the blood made her feel dizzy, weak. She was suddenly afraid. But why? Of what? Blood-stains had never bothered her before this.

She drank a glass of cold water and reminded herself that in a few hours Harry would drop by after lunch, and that was a pleasant prospect, something nice to look forward to. Also he would be alone for a change, without Alexis, without his darling sister. Louise loved Harry so much.

Was that why she had never told him that Alexis was not his real sister? That the man who died in the Pacific was not his real father? But mainly, that she, Louise Smith Maringo, who loved Harry as she had never loved anyone in her life, was not his real mother?

The thought of ever having to tell Harry any of it made her feel dizzy all over again, and she drank two more glasses of cold water before she was able to face her first customer of the day.

3 ❧

Harry's Civics class was from ten to eleven, and of all the courses he took it was the one he liked the least. Ordinarily it just plain bored him to death, but today his degree of concentration was worse than usual.

"Harry, I asked you a question," he heard the teacher, Mrs. Conklin say. "In fact, I've now asked you the same question twice."

He looked up from the lined Big 5 tablet he was scribbling on, and to his surprise found that he had written the name "Alexis" over and over again. Some of the ink from the leaky pen had dripped onto his fingers, and he did his best to wipe it off on the handkerchief in his back pocket.

"Harry," Mrs. Conklin said, "I have asked you who is

second in command under the governor of New York State
and so far all I've heard from you is silence."

He could hardly wait for Civics to be over so he could get
to Gym, today was basketball day. "The attorney general,
Mrs. Conklin. I'm sorry, but you see—"

She did not let him finish the sentence, the bitch. He was
going to say that his father had just been killed, or rather that
he just found out about it last night and that that was why
he was daydreaming. Still it would have been a lie, a weak
excuse for his lack of concentration. Harry had not laid eyes
on his father for over three years, but the memory of dislike
for the man who drank too much, who mistreated his wife,
who avoided work at the store as often as possible, and who
obviously preferred Alexis to him was still very vivid.

The only thing that impressed Harry about his father was
his ability to get into the Army Air Corps as a bomber pilot
shortly after Pearl Harbor. Considering his father's bad
habits, it was a miracle he'd been able to pull himself together
long enough and hard enough to make the grade. But he'd
made it, and now he was dead. So in a sense, he died a hero.

Yet Harry could not forget his mother's words to the doctor
last night, that Mark Maringo really died as he lived: a bum.
It suddenly struck Harry why she said it. Because his father
only shaped up and volunteered to fight for his country in
order to get away from his family, which made Harry feel
even more bitter and disgusted about the whole rotten business.

The Seth Thomas clock on the wall, with its ornately scrolled
numbers, now pointed to six to eleven. In a moment a bell
would ring and the Civics class would file out, and Harry
would go to his beloved basketball practice.

Basketball was a thrilling reality. Harry played forward,
and last year had been high-point man against the neighboring
town's team. He sank four baskets and three free throws, for
eleven points. This year he would be even better, mainly
because now the eighth grade had a special coach from the
high school varsity team, Will Welchman, a regular guy who
knew modern basketball techniques, as opposed to Pilgrim
Lake's middle-aged gym instructor whose sports days were
long over.

"You have real potential, Harry," Will said a few weeks ago.
"Real possibilities, if you take the game seriously."

Harry understood what Will meant about possibilities: that
next term when Harry went into high school, he stood an
excellent chance of making the team there, playing with the

older guys, like Will himself, who was almost seventeen. Nearly four years Harry's senior. Five inches taller. And with twice as big a prick.

"I take basketball more seriously than any other crap they're trying to teach me in this place," Harry had said at the time.

"Good." Will was obviously pleased. "Because you've got natural athletic abilities. Natural is something you can't teach a guy, believe me. Technique, yes. Natural, no."

Suddenly the school bell sounded, signaling the change of classes. It was five to eleven. Harry put his writing tablet in the desk, the name "Alexis" reaching out to him almost as though she had directed him to keep her on his mind at all times. That wasn't hard to do. Because aside from basketball, Alexis was easily the most exciting prospect in Harry's life, which reminded him that after practice today he had a question to ask Will. A very special question. He hoped Will wouldn't laugh at him.

"Hi, Harry." It was Will, getting out of his tan pants and buttoned shorts. "You look kind of funny. Is something wrong?"

"My old man was killed in the Pacific. We just got the telegram last night."

"Hey, kid, that's tough. I'm real sorry. Are you sure you don't want to skip practice today?"

"No, it'll help get my mind off things."

"If you say so."

Harry forced a grin. "I say so, coach."

But it wasn't his father's death that was bothering him, it was the thought of Alexis at home in bed, alone. He knew what Alexis' pussy looked like, the black curly hair (why was it curly there, while the hair on her head was straight as a stick?), he had played with it enough to know. And she had done more than just play with him. She'd actually taken his prick in her mouth one night while their mother was asleep at the other end of the house, yet as hard as Alexis tried and as hard as he tried, no gism would come out of him. The feeling was a combination of pain and pleasure, and finally Harry asked her to stop.

"Doesn't it feel good?" she wanted to know.

"It feels terrific, but it hurts a little."

"Maybe it's my teeth. Am I biting you?"

"I guess that must be it. Let's do it again another time. I'm kind of sore now."

"Next time I'll be more careful."

She hadn't been biting him at all. Harry didn't know then what was wrong, but the incident with Alexis had happened sometime ago and since then he learned a couple of things from the other guys in town, and one of these days he was going to teach it to Alexis. One of these days very soon.

"Will, I've got a question to ask you." Harry decided to get it off his chest now, before practice. "Is it true that athletes have to stay away from girls?"

Will smiled with the knowledge of the older experienced man. "That's some question. What are you doing, Harry, getting a lot of it lately and worrying yourself sick?"

"I'm not worrying, I'm just asking." Harry had started to take off his sweater and corduroys. "The other day I was reading that prizefighters never bring their wives to training camp. And baseball players never take their wives on the road. Same with football players. So I was wondering, that's all."

"I wouldn't worry about screwing. I don't ever plan to give that up, and I'll bet that any top baseball player you can name has as many girls as he's got home runs. But you do have to take care of yourself, physically. I work out, run a lot, lift some weights, *and* get my share of tail. I've been getting my share since I was a kid no older than you. It's a habit that I have no plans to break, either. I can tell you that."

Will looked down at Harry's naked body. "You're hanging pretty good. You'll be getting it up one of these days yourself. I mean, unless you've already started."

"A little here, a little there." Harry wasn't about to admit that he was still a virgin.

It wasn't just Alexis' physical appeal that made him want her so much, it was that he loved her, they'd grown up together, had shared their entire lives. Harry realized that even though it was wrong, sinful, he loved Alexis in a way he could never love another girl. And the reason why he couldn't was very simple: he would never *know* another girl as well as he knew his beautiful, stuck-up, darling sister.

4

It was not until mid-morning that Louise found herself with a few moments' free time, and it was then that she resolutely decided to call her mother-in-law, Juliana, and tell her about Mark. It would be inhuman to put it off any longer.

At sixty-three and arthritic, Juliana Maringo continued to do the same work she had done since she was a healthy young girl. During the lucrative summer months this consisted of waiting on tables in Pilgrim Lake's most exclusive hotel, the Windsor, the very same hotel that Louise's parents used to dine at once a month before their unfortunate death, twelve years before.

Louise herself never patronized the Windsor. Not only had it become morbidly expensive, but she was horrified at the thought of being served a meal by her own mother-in-law. It would only emphasize the status difference between her side of the family and Mark's, and she had frequently begged Juliana to try to get a less servile job. But to no avail.

What was even worse, in Louise's eyes, was that during the long, nontourist season Juliana earned her living by cleaning people's homes. Her husband, Frank, had long ago drunk himself to death, leaving behind a legacy of unpaid bills and a clothes closet filled with empty Hellman's mayonnaise jars. The jars once contained gin, which Frank made during the grim, dry days of Prohibition. During his lifetime he'd been a dreadful source of embarrassment and humiliation to Louise.

As for Juliana, true she had to work, but as a common domestic for fifty cents an hour? Bon Ami, Oxydol, Spic and Span, and Johnson's floor wax. Those were the degrading mainstays of her mother-in-law's professional existence. But being of Dutch descent, Juliana saw nothing the least bit degrading about it.

"Everybody knows that Holland is the cleanest country in the world," she was fond of saying, "so I'm only doing what comes naturally."

"But you're not in Holland," Louise would reply. "In fact, you've never set foot in Holland. You were born here in Pilgrim Lake, and so were your parents and grandparents."

"Why stop with my grandparents?"

Juliana took pleasure in reminding Louise that her ancestors had landed in the New World not long after Louise's.

"That only proves my point."

"No, it doesn't. These cleanliness things are in the blood. It's the same with Indians and alcohol. They can't drink like other people, they go crazy. Poor Frank. He never did get that gin formula just right, he was always experimenting." Juliana laughed fondly. "That man spent a fortune on juniper berries. A *fortune*, I tell you."

At eleven A.M., after Louise had sold a plump stewing chicken (thirty-five cents) to one of her best customers, she motioned to Dennis to keep an eye out for the butcher counter in case someone came in while she was on the telephone. Juliana did not work on Monday morning, that and Sunday were her one and a half days off from cleaning up other people's dirt. The old lady invariably spent Monday mornings at home, cleaning up the dirt in her own tiny house. Pathetic, Louise thought, as she dialed the familiar number.

"Hello," Juliana said, after six rings.

"It's me. How are you?"

"I have a slight cold. Otherwise, I'm fine."

"You work too hard, Juliana. You should really cut down."

"Is that what you called to tell me?"

Louise cleared her throat. "Not exactly. But I was thinking —why don't you let me take you to lunch today? I'm almost certain that Charlie has his Swiss steak special on Monday, and you know it's one of your favorites."

"That's very generous of you, dear, particularly since you never eat lunch out. Is something wrong?"

"I thought it would be a nice treat for both of us. That's all."

"Nothing's happened to the children, has it?" A tone of alarm had entered Juliana's voice. "They haven't gotten into any kind of trouble, have they?"

"Alexis is home with a headache, if you call that trouble. I just want to buy you lunch. I feel extravagant."

"You don't sound like yourself, Louise."

"Meet me at Charlie's at noon. Please, Juliana. I insist. Now you be there."

"But I haven't waxed the kitchen floor yet."

"You can wax it after lunch."

"No, I can't. After lunch I have to go to Mrs. Finnegan."

"Then you can wax it this evening."

"I suppose so."

"Fine. It's settled. And whatever you do, don't wear your hairnet."

"I only wear it when I'm doing my cleaning. You know that. Are you sure you're all right, Louise?"

"Noon. At Charlie's."

Louise hung up before she blurted out the terrible story. It would be far too cruel to tell Juliana that Mark was dead, except to tell her in person, face-to-face. A husband, one daughter, and now her only son. Juliana had survived the three closest of kin, and Louise wondered how she was going to take the news of this latest death. Because in spite of Mark's bad ways he'd always been his mother's favorite child, as Harry was hers. Odd, that just now Juliana never even mentioned the possibility of something having happened to Mark.

"I'm going to have lunch with my mother-in-law in an hour," Louise told Dennis. "Next door, at Charlie's. I won't be too long. And the store's pretty quiet then, so I think you should be able to manage alone."

"I'll hold the fort. Don't you worry about it."

Dennis hesitated, realizing that it must be serious if his employer was paying for her own lunch. Customarily, she made a ham and cheese sandwich in the walk-in cooler and ate it behind the meat counter, then washed it down with half a bottle of milk.

"I guess the old lady doesn't know about Mr. Maringo yet," Dennis said.

"No. And it's not going to be any picnic telling her, either."

"I reckon it won't."

But Louise's mind had switched to business. "I've just come to a conclusion."

"Yes?"

Louise stared at the meat cleaver. "I'm sick of giving away chicken livers free. I don't think it's right. From now on, anybody who wants them is going to pay five cents a pound."

"I don't know, Mrs. M." Dennis looked doubtful. "People are kind of used to getting them for free, like soup bones and suet."

"Those are something else. You've got to give them away or there'd be a revolution. But you can make a whole meal out of chicken livers. Why shouldn't we charge for them? We're not Communists."

"I never thought of it like that before. Still, I've got to admit you're right as usual, Mrs. M. Do you want me to print up a sign? We can hang it in the window on Wednesday, after we take down the sale signs."

"I'd appreciate that, Dennis. Also, please do the lettering in black instead of red. Folks in Pilgrim Lake will understand about the chicken livers, once they find out I'm a widow."

"Sure they will. You need all the money you can earn. In a fair way, of course."

Dennis suddenly had a wild Irish notion. What if he wrote a sign saying:

IN MEMORY OF MY LATE, BELOVED HUSBAND
MARK MARINGO
WHO DIED FIGHTING FOR HIS COUNTRY
CHICKEN LIVERS WILL COST
5 CENTS A POUND
FROM NOW ON
LOUISE MARINGO

It was a notion that Dennis promptly stifled. Mrs. M. was not exactly well known for her sense of humor, to put it mildly.

"I hope you have a nice lunch," he said later, as Louise took off the stained butcher's apron and smoothed her knitted blue suit that had recently started to bag. "As nice as possible under the circumstances, I mean."

"We only sold one sirloin this morning," she said. "And two pork chops. It makes you wonder about people's sense of economy, doesn't it?"

Then she was off to meet her mother-in-law at Charlie's drugstore. It had been so long since she'd gone out to lunch that she felt almost obscenely exhilarated at the prospect, and it took an extra effort of will to force her face back into its usual dour expression.

"This is no time for gaiety or high spirits," she said to herself, praying that Juliana would be able to control her emotions when she learned of Mark's death. There was no telling how Juliana would react, though. She was totally unpredictable. A *fortune* on juniper berries, indeed! And Juliana considered it amusing.

"I'm meeting my mother-in-law for lunch," Louise said to a startled Charlie. "I see she hasn't arrived yet."

"No, ma'am. Would you like to sit near the window?"

Only one table out of the six was occupied. The bank manager and his teller were eating what looked like some kind of croquettes (ham? chicken? salmon?), and they both nodded politely to Louise. At the counter, Pilgrim Lake's postman was drinking a cup of coffee. He tipped his hat to her.

"A window table would be fine. How about that one?"

Louise indicated the table farthest away from everyone else, just in case Juliana broke down.

"What are the specials today, Charlie?"

"We've got Swiss steak, spaghetti and meatballs, and chicken croquettes. Everything's forty-five cents, including dessert. Rice pudding or tapioca."

"What about coffee?"

"That's five cents extra."

Louise knew that the chicken croquettes would be made from leftovers, spaghetti was dirt cheap, so the best bet was Swiss steak. She admired Charlie for charging five cents more for coffee. He was a good businessman, all right. She would leave him a dime tip.

"You've got to accentuate the positive, eliminate the negatime, latch onto the affirmative, don't mess with Mr. Inbetween," Bing Crosby sang on the jukebox.

"I believe I'll try your Swiss steak." Louise unfolded the skimpy white paper napkin and placed it on her lap. "And I'm certain that my mother-in-law will want the same."

"It comes with peas and carrots, mashed potatoes, and bread and butter, of course."

"Thank you, Charlie."

"My pleasure, Mrs. Maringo. Your son should be getting here any minute now. I'll bet he's going to be surprised to see you."

Louise did not consider the impertinent comment worthy of a reply, so she said nothing and Charlie went back to the kitchen to give the order to his cook. Then Louise spotted Juliana coming down the street. She was a short, stout woman wearing a long, gray velvet dress that she had bought back in the thirties. Over the dress she had on a darker gray cardigan which once belonged to her late husband. Her neatly clipped hair was gray, too. Only the string of pearls around her neck broke the uniform tone of color. The two women kissed each other on the cheek and Juliana sat down at the maple table facing her daughter-in-law.

"It's Mark, isn't it?" Juliana's gray eyes pleaded for rebuttal. "Just say yes or no."

"Yes."

"When did you find out?"

"Last night."

Juliana picked up her glass of water and drank half of it down in one fast gulp. "You should have called me right away."

"I thought it better to wait until morning."

"*Better?*"

"I thought if I told you last night you wouldn't be able to sleep."

"Do you think that that matters?"

"Maybe I was wrong," Louise said finally. "If so, I apologize. I was only trying to be considerate."

"I'm a good sleeper. I slept after Frank died. I slept after Kay died. I'll sleep tonight, too. Do you know why?"

Louise shook her head negatively, surprised by her mother-in-law's composure.

"Because if I don't sleep, I can't do my work. And if I can't do my work, I can't live. It's as simple as that."

Kay had been Juliana's daughter, Mark's younger sister, Harry's real mother. Louise only remembered her vaguely, because Kay was three years her junior. At the age of seventeen Kay ran away from Pilgrim Lake with a boy named Wilfred, a machinist from a nearby city. What nobody knew in Pilgrim Lake, except for Kay's immediate family, was that Wilfred had gotten her pregnant and she was too ashamed to have the baby in her home town.

Wilfred kept promising to marry her, but never did. However, he found a place for them to live in Rochester, which was far enough away to prevent gossip about Kay's condition from leaking back to Pilgrim Lake. Then in 1932 Kay died giving birth to Harry, and Wilfred placed his illegitimate son in an orphanage in Rochester, refusing to accept any parental responsibility whatsoever. In a letter to Juliana he simply said that he was sorry about what had happened but he couldn't take care of a baby by himself, and he was going to the Midwest to look for a better job. Juliana never heard from him again.

In order to save face, the story that Juliana circulated around Pilgrim Lake was that Kay had gone off to marry a nice young machinist from Rochester. The couple (Juliana said) were very happy, and subsequently moved out to Detroit where Wilfred had found a good job. Considering the economic situation in the United States, anyone who had a job at all, let alone a good one, was to be admired, envied. "Yes,

We Have No Bananas" and "Brother, Can You Spare a Dime?" were two of the songs that would continue to epitomize the plight of the nation for a long time to come.

"We've both had more than our share of family tragedies," Louise said.

"We certainly have."

"And yet, when I think back it all seems so unreal."

"Don't think back."

"Right now, I can't help it."

And sitting there in Charlie's drugstore, on a sunny October afternoon in 1945, the memories she had repressed for so many years jumped out of their careful hiding place to haunt her one last time.

5

As far as Louise was concerned, the whole tragedy had started in 1932, when she was away at college and, like a fool, like the naive fool that she was, went to bed with Mark Maringo and promptly became pregnant. It was the biggest mistake of her life, allowing Mark to seduce her, but what did she know then? Nothing. She was so young, so vulnerable, so plain. And he was so arrogant, so self-confident, so handsome.

She couldn't believe it when he showed up one weekend, unannounced and uninvited, at the small college she attended. It was to see her, he said.

"Me?" She stared at him, idiotically. "Me?"

"Sure, you. Why not?"

They were having tea in the visitors' lounge. She would always remember the old overstuffed chairs, the rose-flowered wallpaper, but mostly the other girls looking at her with envy.

"How did you get here?" she asked him.

"Hitchhiked."

The teacup shook in her hand. "Well. That must have been an experience. Where are you staying?"

"I've rented a room for the weekend, in town. I want to invite you to dinner tonight. And don't say you can't make it."

Louise could barely believe what was happening . . . this brash young man whom she'd seen around Pilgrim Lake for years but never once spoken to had hitchhiked such a long distance, rented a room, and was inviting her to dinner. And all out of the clear blue sky. Nobody had ever invited her to dinner before. It was easily the most glamorous, romantic thing she'd heard of.

"I'd be very pleased to have dinner with you," she said.

"Terrific. I'll pick you up at seven."

How could she have known then what his true motives were? That he was determined to improve his financial and social lot in life by marrying the girl whose father owned one of the most thriving businesses in Pilgrim Lake, as opposed to his own father, the laughed-at town drunk. How could she have suspected that he had a second motive as well, an equally important one, a much more devious one? She couldn't.

They went to dinner, they went to his rooming house, they went to bed. Despite the fact that he kept his socks on throughout the whole baffling, thrashing business, and his breath smelled of bootleg alcohol, Louise loved him in a way she would never understand. She loved him and was revolted by him. There was something cheap and thrilling and terrible about it all.

"I love you," he said.

Louise couldn't say anything. Two months later she found out she was pregnant.

"I'm going to marry you," he said.

Fortunately, Louise's parents were far too busy with their store to take time out to visit her, and weekly letters sufficed. As a result she was able to conceal everything from them until she and Mark were surreptitiously married by a justice of the peace one grim, rainy evening. It was only after the ceremony, when they returned to the rooming house, that Mark informed her they were going to have to adopt his dead sister's newborn son, Harry, and pretend he was their own.

Louise was sure she had heard wrong. "Dead? Kay? What are you talking about? What newborn son? Kay's living in Detroit with her husband. I should know. My mother writes to me every week."

"Kay's never been near Detroit. She died in childbirth in Rochester, and she wasn't married. That bastard Wilfred refused to marry her. So that means the kid is illegitimate. But that's not how he's going to stay, not while I'm still alive."

Louise could not digest this barrage of astonishing information, and as she sank into the room's only easy chair the springs creaked. Outside the rain had gotten worse. It hit the windows in heavy lashes.

Louise's astonishment was turning to anger. "You tricked me. You never said a word about any of this before we were married. You waited until now to open your mouth."

"I had to." Mark stretched out on the thin, cotton bedspread. "There was no other way. Besides, you're leaving out something."

"What?"

"You wanted to get married as badly as I did. There's no point in denying it."

"Of course I wanted to get married, but for totally different reasons. I wanted to get married because I'm pregnant and I'm in love with you. You wanted to get married so we could adopt your illegitimate nephew, and you're not in love with me at all."

Mark sat up, his eyes dark, threatening. "I never want to hear the word 'illegitimate' again."

"What if I refuse," Louise asked, "to go through with your adoption scheme?"

"I'll walk out on you and you'll never see me again."

To her horror, she knew that he meant it. She had to think fast. "Okay, let's say that we do adopt Kay's child. How can we possibly pretend he's our own, when we've just gotten married ourselves? How will it look?"

"Nobody in Pilgrim Lake knows we just got married. We'll say we were married over a year ago, and we've been keeping it a secret."

"A secret? From my own parents? Are you crazy?"

"No, I'm not crazy. I have my poor, dead sister's reputation to protect and that's exactly what I intend to do. And you're my wife, and you're going to help me."

"But what will my parents say? It's bad enough that I got pregnant before we were married, but I had that part sort of figured out. It's not the same thing as coming home pregnant, *and* with a one-month-old son besides. My parents will disown me."

"No, they won't."

"They'll never believe we were married over a year ago. Never. Not in a million years."

"They'll believe what you tell them because they'll want

to believe you." Mark seemed as blithely self-confident as he'd been the afternoon he showed up at her college, supposedly for one weekend.

"A premature baby is only a little white lie. What you're asking me to do is terrible, it's sacrilegious." But she was trapped and she knew it. "And even if my parents did believe this whole far-fetched story, what about our friends and neighbors in Pilgrim Lake? They'll never believe it."

Mark started to roll a cigarette. "Yes, they will. They wouldn't dare to insult such upstanding citizens as your parents by *not* believing it. Don't you see? It's all going to work out fine."

"No, it isn't." The tears that Louise had been holding back now rolled down her cheeks onto the collar of the demure dress she'd been married in. "It's a nightmare. Things like this don't happen in real life. Anyhow, why can't Wilfred adopt Harry? He's his real father."

"Because the son-of-a-bitch has disappeared. And even if he hadn't I wouldn't let a louse like that bring up my own flesh and blood."

Mark blew a smoke ring at the pasty ceiling. "Okay, it's settled. We're adopting Harry, but he'll never know he's adopted. Your parents will never know. And nobody in Pilgrim Lake will know."

"I'll know."

"That's right. You, me, and Juliana. We're the only ones who'll know. And when you give birth, the new baby won't know either because Harry will have been there before. So you see, this way when we adopt Harry both kids will be treated equal. A kid who's born illegitimate and remains illegitimate doesn't grow up right. It haunts him all his life. But that's not going to happen with my sister's little boy. He'll never suspect the truth, nobody will, and Harry will feel equal."

"Equal?" Louise shrieked, the tears starting to flow all over again. Equal, indeed! Because despite the fact that Mark's Indian ancestors on his father's side had landed in the area of Pilgrim Lake fifteen thousand years before, and despite the fact that his Dutch ancestors on his mother's side had been inhabitants of the community for two hundred years, they were still considered lower in status than Louise's family, which was of one hundred percent English origin.

For it was the Queen of England, in the early part of the

eighteenth century, who had negotiated a shrewd land deal with the naive Nemsi tribe from which Mark was descended. After the deal was concluded, the English (and later, the more crude Dutch) began to develop the rich surrounding farmlands, and as they did so the Indians realized that the contract they had unwittingly signed with "the blue-eyed people" meant they had deeded away their territory. Slowly, bitterly, but inevitably the Nemsis retreated to distant mountainous plains to start a new life for themselves.

Only a rare few, like Mark's great-great-great-great-grandfather remained behind. He had fallen in love with a Dutch girl named Margriet, and defying every tradition known to his proud people of unmixed blood, he married her. Then, in order to become assimilated into the white community, he changed his once-revered last name from Maringotop to Maringo, and began to denounce his honorable Indian heritage. . . .

"Things you say and do just thrill me through and through, I'm getting sentimental over you," the Pied Pipers sang on Charlie's jukebox, just as Charlie himself appeared before Louise and Juliana with two sizzling platters of Swiss steak. "Once I thought I could live without love, now I must admit love is all that I'm thinking of."

"I'll be back in a sec with the bread and butter," Charlie said.

"Family tragedies," Juliana mused. "Yes, we've both had our share. You having to adopt Harry. Then your parents dying in that terrible fire. My husband dead of drink. My daughter dead in childbirth. And now, Mark."

But to Louise's surprise, her mother-in-law was still calm and clear-eyed. If anything ever happened to Harry, Louise doubted that she would be able to take it as well as Juliana, in fact she knew she couldn't. And it was only then that she realized it was nearly twelve-thirty and Harry had not yet shown up. A premonition of fear shot through her. What was keeping him? Where was he?

"Well, they certainly serve generous portions here," Juliana said. "There's no denying that."

A moment later Charlie returned with dishes of bread and butter and the two women picked up their forks, and slowly, silently, started to eat the drugstore's steaming forty-five-cent luncheon special.

6 ❧

At three minutes to noon I took the book on Spain, went downstairs, carefully dialed our school's number, and asked for Harry Maringo.

"He should be in the locker room, changing after his gym class," I said to the school's lone operator, Miss Galant. "Could you please tell him that it's his sister, and it's important."

My heart was doing a tap dance, that's how nervous I was, nervous but more determined than ever that this was *it*, the day of reckoning or whatever you want to call it. I'd been lying in that damn bed of mine all morning, figuring how I'd go about seducing my brother, and I'm pretty sure I've got it all worked out. I don't think Harry would dare to back down, even if he felt guilty enough to die. I feel guilty too, but so what? We'll both feel guilty together, which any fool would know is better than feeling guilty alone, by yourself.

"Alexis?"

Harry's voice sounded strange and far away, unfamiliar, and then I realized why: we had never spoken to each other on the telephone before. Now it was like we were grown-ups, older, like Humphrey Bogart and Lauren Bacall in "To Have And Have Not," even though I don't remember them speaking on the phone in that movie. Harry and I weren't kids anymore.

"You've got to come home right away," I said. "It's very important."

"What's the matter?"

"I can't tell you on the telephone."

"Is something wrong?"

"Please, Harry. Don't go to Charlie's for lunch. Come home instead."

"Are you sick? Maybe I should go over to the store and let Mom know. If you're really sick, I mean."

The last thing in the world I wanted was for Harry to be within ten feet of the store, or of Charlie's, where she was liable to spot him. She'll spot him soon enough, if I know my mother, but it's not going to be in any place of business.

It's going to be right here in our own home-sweet-home. We have this bearskin rug in the living room, you see. It's real comfy.

"Just get on your bike and come home."

Then I hung up fast, afraid to say another word. I knew that Miss Galant had listened to the whole conversation. She's a spinster, maybe that has something to do with it, her curiosity about other people's lives, her lack of a man of her own, having to wait hand and foot on her mother, who's dying of cancer.

Well, I'll say one thing for Pilgrim Lake. There aren't any secrets around here, no skeletons in the closet, to quote my mother. I can see her right this minute, making the same ham and cheese sandwich she makes every day for lunch, gulping down her own bottle of milk. I never want to be like her: ordinary, habit-driven, boring. I'd kill myself first.

I don't know why my father married her to begin with, he must have been out of his mind. He was so handsome. I guess he had to drink a lot to blot out the mistake of who he married, that must have been the reason for his drinking. People laugh at us behind our backs. They don't dare do it to our faces because we've got the store, we pay our bills on time, we're respectable. I don't want to be just respectable, it's not enough. Harry doesn't want it, either. We both want more and we're going to get it.

You know what Harry and I want? What we've wanted all along? We want to be the summer people. We've talked about it a lot. We don't like being the townies, no matter how nice those rich tourists treat us every summer. *We* want to be the rich tourists and throw money around like it was just so much garbage. There was one girl this past summer, I'll never forget her. Her parents drove up in a long, black car, my mother said it was a Cadillac. She said it with admiration, no, with greed, because she knew she'd do a lot of business with those people. Or at least she sure was hoping to.

But the girl was about my age, twelve, and she was wearing a pleated white sharkskin skirt and a sleeveless little white sharkskin blouse that buttoned down the front. She was all tanned, and had colorless polish on her toenails. Her sandals were only a couple of bright green crisscross straps, and she had a bright-patterned kerchief on her head, it was green with pink and red dots.

The reason I'll never forget her was a lot of things. First of all, my mother would never let me wear white because it gets dirty so easy. And also I've never seen a young girl with polish of *any* kind on her toenails. I was fascinated by her. Jealous. The green sandals, the mostly green kerchief, and the la-de-da look on her face when she told me later, while we were swimming, that she had to be very careful about her ears because she'd had some trouble with them awhile back. I felt like pushing her face right into the water, even if she was telling the truth about her ears.

What she was really saying was that her family could afford to buy her two-piece sharkskin dresses that must have cost a fortune, not to mention covering her ears with silk kerchiefs that must have cost a fortune, too. She was saying she was better than me. And finally I did give her a fast dunk, making believe it was just a joke. I knew she wouldn't have the nerve to dunk me back. So I apologized and said I was sorry, but we all dunked each other here at Pilgrim Lake.

"But my ears," she said. "They're not supposed to get wet."

"You've got a bathing cap on." It was lemon yellow, the same exact color as her bathing suit. "Your ears will be okay."

She jumped out of the water at once, her colorless toenail polish glistening in the hot afternoon sun.

"I'd better go tell my mother about my ears."

None of us kids here ever wore a bathing cap, although Charlie sold them for the middle-aged women tourists, and they were expensive. Twenty-nine cents (Harry and I only get twenty-five cents a week allowance). My mother said it was because they were made of rubber, and rubber was scarce during the war. Expensive or not, I thought they looked ridiculous, I'd never go into the water with one of those dopey things on my head. Still and all I cried myself to sleep that night, remembering the way that white sharkskin dress looked against her even-tanned skin.

"Alexis?"

I hadn't heard the front door open. Harry was here, it was so fast that I couldn't believe it. He'd flown home, like our father would never be able to do now. I love the idea of airplanes, they can take you anywhere, make you free.

"I'm in the living room."

He walked in and I thought I'm as good-looking as Lauren Bacall, maybe better, certainly we're different types. And Harry. Even in that beat-up brown sweater and tan corduroys that must have been washed seven million times, he was as handsome as our father. But it's not just good looks, it's something *more*. Harry and I have it, so did Mark Maringo (that's

how I'm going to think of him from now on), our mother
doesn't have it and neither does Miss Galant, or most of the
creeps who live in Pilgrim Lake. I wish I knew a word for it,
the thing that makes Harry and me different, better, the thing
that sets us apart.

"You're still in your pajamas."

I was wearing the pink woolly pajamas that my mother
bought me last Christmas. She bought me that and figure ice-
skates. Harry got a Junior Race Flexible Flyer sled, which
he'd been dying for. I was happy about the skates and learned
how to do the waltz and the bunny hop, practically better than
any of the other kids. As for the pajamas, well, they've got
rabbits on them. I don't want to wear anything with rabbits
on it, I want to wear a dress like Lauren Bacall wore in "To
Have and Have Not," something slinky, black, revealing. I
don't have breasts yet, but I will and they'll probably be small.
That's okay with me. I just want to see something there.

"Of course I'm in my pajamas. I'm sick. What should I be
in? My regular clothes?"

Harry seemed very confused. Who could blame him?

"Alexis, I don't understand. What is it? Why did you want
me to come home? What's going on? What's happening?"

I'm not sure he said those exact words, it was a rat-tat-tat
kind of thing that came out of him all at once. I wasn't really
listening to what he said, anyway. I was listening to the melody
and that made me doubly nervous, because I could see that
Harry was.

"What's going on," I said, "is Spain."

"Spain?" Harry stared at me as though I were nuts. "Is
that what you got me away from lunch for?"

So I realized he was hungry, and his hunger had made him
mad. "Look, why don't I heat up last night's stew. There's
plenty left over. Mom said I could have it."

I went into the kitchen and turned on the stove. It was a
Tappan, and I remembered the strange story that Harry had
told me about jerking off one night with some of his friends.
Boys are so different, in my wildest dreams I couldn't imagine
doing anything like that with my girlfriends, even though I've
masturbated a lot by myself. Once I even used a carrot. I've
never been able to eat a carrot since, I pick them out of stews.

But the reason that Tappan comes into it is because when
Harry did it, jerked off, I mean, he said that the stuff that
came out of him hit the Tappan stove in the Millers' kitchen
where the guys were sitting around the table, competing with

each other to see who could make the biggest splash. Harry swears that one of the "p" letters on the stove was completely wiped out by his gism.

That's what he calls it: gism. Harry doesn't read the dictionary like me, so I know it's called sperm and frankly it scares me to death. What do I have to fight back with, physically? Still, its fascinating. And I can't possibly get pregnant because I haven't gotten my period yet. I must keep that in mind, it's very important. Otherwise I wouldn't be able to go through with what I'm going to go through with. And I'm going through with it, wild horses couldn't stop me, not now.

"How's the stew coming along?"

He was standing beside me and we were both facing the red and gold treetops outside. They always make me feel so sad, even though they're beautiful. Indian summer. The dictionary says that it's a period of mild, dry weather occurring in the United States and Canada in the late autumn or early winter, but it doesn't say why they named it after the Indians, after us.

"Why, Harry?"

"Why what?"

"The Indian summer thing. It's peculiar, isn't it?"

His voice was like when Pilgrim Lake becomes icy in January and February. "I don't know what you're talking about, Alexis."

That did it. He couldn't treat me this way, so cold and disinterested, just because he was hungry. I wouldn't let him. I was hungry, too. I turned the knob of the stove down from 450 degrees to 150, realizing that he couldn't see my hands. Harry didn't know it yet but we weren't going to eat any damn oxtail stew, and I wasn't going to eat him. We were going to fuck Indian summer.

"I was looking at some maps of Spain. That's what I've been doing all morning."

"Maps of Spain?"

As I've said before, Harry had always been as fascinated by Spain as I was, yet now it was like we had never mentioned the subject. We were standing only inches apart, but he was far, far away from me.

"Maps of *southern* Spain," I said.

"Alexis, why did you really want me to come home?"

"Because I want to show you something."

And then I did what I'd been rehearsing. I put my pink rabbit arms around Harry's woolly shoulders and kissed him right on the lips, soul-kissed him. It was so personal that I nearly fainted. We had never kissed before. It was like talking on the telephone, I felt really grown up. My mouth became all wet, so did Harry's. I couldn't tell which mouth was which, that's how mushy-together we were. So I pulled away.

"What's the matter?" he said.

"Come into the living room while the stew heats up. It's going to take a few minutes because I just got it out of the Frigidaire and it's cold as hell."

"I don't like it when girls swear."

I took his hand as we walked inside. It was moist. "But I'm not *girls,* am I, Harry?"

He had this queer, frightened look on his face. "No."

"I'm your darling sister, aren't I?"

"Yes."

"Say it."

He wouldn't look me in the eye. "Say what?"

"Say, 'You're my darling sister, so that makes it different.' "

"I'm hungry," Harry said. "I just got through with basketball practice and I'm starving to death."

"The stew won't take long," I lied. "I promise."

We were now in the living room. Harry sat down on the sofa that had been sagging for as long as I could remember, the springs were broken or something. But I was sitting cross-legged on the brown and white bearskin rug in the middle of the room. I felt like a real Indian, sitting that way. I can't explain it. I know my whole mother's family is English, and the Indian business with my father goes back generations and generations, and also my father was part Dutch, but it doesn't matter. Some things stay in your blood, like germs, if that's possible. I want to be beautiful. I see myself in a canoe.

"Where are the maps?" Harry asked.

He and I had seen maps of Spain before, but you couldn't tell all that much from them because Spain was always included in the map of Europe, it wasn't by itself. But recently I hitchhiked to the next town, where they have a large library, and I found bigger, better maps than anything we ever laid our eyes on at school.

These new maps were in a book on southern Spain (the only part of Spain we were interested in), and I stole the book under my jacket. I figured Harry and I needed that book more than any other people possibly could. To them, Spain was just some far-off place they'd never get to see in their entire, dull lives. But to Harry and me it meant a great deal more, or it would one day when we were truly grown up. What it meant was that somewhere in southern Spain, Harry and I could become the summer people at last.

"The maps are right here," I said. "They're in a book I've been keeping in my bedroom, but I brought it downstairs when I phoned you at school."

"Mom's going to be worried. About my not stopping in at the store to see her after lunch."

As though I didn't know. "She'll just think you dawdled too long at Charlie's and didn't have time."

"No. She'll figure something's wrong."

I had to get his mind off our mother and onto real life. "Look at this."

I went to get the book on southern Spain out of the old oak cupboard where I had put it. I knew that the glossy picture right on front of the book cover would grab Harry's attention right away, and was I ever right! It was a painting of a castle called Santa Barbara, in a place called Alicante. Through a kind of scooped-out, roundish archway you could see a lot of strange stone buildings built on different levels, a small-windowed room with a grate over it, a tunneled entrance that led . . . who knew where? And above the castle was a sky so radiantly blue it made Pilgrim Lake even in the summertime look like Alaska.

When Harry finally spoke, he said: "Where did you get this book?"

"I borrowed it from a library."

"Which library?"

So I named the nearby town. "I had to hitchhike to get there. I wanted it to be a surprise for you. Well, Harry, what do you think?"

He couldn't take his eyes off the castle. "I've never seen anything like it before."

"And there's more inside. More pictures, and maps that tell where the pictures were taken. I've read the entire book. Twice."

"Where did you say this castle was?"

"In a place called Alicante."

Harry opened the book, trying to find Alicante on a map. When he did, he said, "It's not so far south. There's a place called Malaga that's much farther south."

"Yes, I know, but it doesn't sound as interesting."

I had led Harry back to the bearskin rug, and I think he

was so dazzled by the painting on the front of the book that he didn't realize what he was doing, where he was, what he was saying, anything. But he kept on talking.

"On the other side of the map there's a place called Cadiz. That's pretty far south, too."

Then he named some more cities that were farther south of Alicante, but I knew that if he talked forever it wouldn't make the least bit of difference in the world because Alicante was where we would end up. I knew it as sure as I knew what was going to happen in a couple of minutes, and I knew both things were right: what we were about to do on the bearskin rug, and why we had to go live in Alicante someday.

The only difference between the two things was that I could hurry up the first, but I would have to wait awhile (how long, I wondered?) before I could hurry up the second. But I'd succeed. Scared and shaking as I was, I knew I'd succeed in both.

"What are you doing?"

Harry's fly on his corduroy pants had buttons on it, and I started to undo them. Underneath he was wearing his usual white shorts that were also buttoned.

"You know what I'm doing. Please put the book down. We'll look at it some more later on."

He laid the book next to us on the rug and just watched me as I removed his long pants and his short ones. Then I took off my pink rabbit pajamas in one second flat. All he had on was his sweater, but I was bare-assed.

"Harry, I love you so much. I want you to do it to me. I know you've done it to other girls, but I don't care. They don't count. Please. I know you know how. I don't know how. I'm still a virgin."

And then just as the smell of the oxtail stew started drifting in from the kitchen, my sweet darling brother said something I'll remember him for the rest of my life. Because he could have lied.

"No, Alexis. You're wrong. I'm a virgin, too."

"Then we'll learn together."

"I love you," Harry said.

We were starting to play with each other down there as we had in the past, but this was different. This time he was going to put it in me and I could hardly wait. Judging by the look in his eyes, and the way his breath was coming fast, neither could he. Then suddenly he stopped and just stared at me with his dark, flat eyes, and I saw him in the canoe too.

"This is a sin, Alexis. You know that. You're my sister. It's a terrible sin, what we're going to do."

"I don't care."

"Are you sure?"

"Sure I'm sure."

"This is what you called me home for, isn't it?"

"Yes."

And at last he smiled, really smiled, because deep down in his heart Harry didn't believe in sin any more than I did.

"It'll probably hurt," he said. "They say it hurts girls a lot the first time."

"I'm not *girls*. Remember?"

The smile was still on his lips, but it was his eyes that held me. "No, you're my little bitch sister."

"Besides, I want it to hurt."

There was a tomahawk on the wall, my father had hung it there a long time ago. I don't know where he found it. On the same wall was a picture of an English king. I don't know which one, he had a white ruffled collar. The only thing missing was a photograph of a windmill. But when Harry finally got hard enough to push it into me, I forgot about what was on the wall and what wasn't.

All I could do was close my eyes and think of Spanish archways and tunneled entrances that led to strange and mysterious places.

While Alexis was lying on the bearskin rug at home dreaming of mysterious entrances, her mother was trying to choke down the tapioca dessert at Charlie's drugstore, and thinking of hasty exits.

Louise Smith Maringo wasn't going to have coffee, not just because it cost an additional five cents but because she didn't have the patience to sit there one second longer. She simply had to get out.

"But if you want coffee, Juliana, you go ahead," she said to her mother-in-law, who had wiped her Swiss steak platter clean with the last slice of bread and butter.

"I could use a cup," Juliana admitted. "I've got Mrs. Finnegan to do this afternoon, and I need the extra energy. She's a messy person. It's a very messy house, I must say. Once when I got there, she hadn't even flushed the toilet."

"Please, Juliana. Not while we're eating."

"Sorry, dear. I know how upset you must be."

"Yes, I am. Of course, I am."

"Losing your husband." Juliana sighed, remembering the loss of her own husband, the inveterate bathtub gin-maker. "I understand how you feel."

Juliana didn't understand anything, and Louise had no intention of explaining that it was not Mark's death which was making her so frantic, it was Harry's unexplained absence. What had happened to him? Where was he? It was almost one o'clock and he hadn't shown up for lunch. Knowing how eagerly both her children looked forward to their hamburger and milkshake lunchdays, Louise could only suspect (no, *fear*) that something terrible had happened to keep Harry away. But what? An accident? Surely if that were it, she would have heard about it by now, Pilgrim Lake being the small town that it was. And if it wasn't an accident, what else could it possibly be? Louise signaled to Charlie.

"My mother-in-law would like a cup of coffee, and I'd like the check, please. I've got to go home immediately. I'm afraid something is wrong."

"Home?" Juliana said. "I thought Alexis only had a headache. It's nothing more serious than that, is it? You're not keeping anything from me, are you?"

Louise felt like biting her tongue for having announced her destination, for having aroused her mother-in-law's suspicions. She was amazed at her own, vague and unexplicit as they were.

"When I left this morning, Alexis had a slight fever. I'm sure she's all right, but I do think it best if I look in on her."

"You didn't tell me about the fever."

Louise silently pleaded with God not to punish her for this little, white lie. Hadn't she been punished enough in her lifetime?

"I didn't want to worry you, Juliana. You have plenty of problems as it is. But I know I'll feel better if I run home for a few minutes and see how Alexis is doing."

"Then you go ahead, dear. It will set your mind at rest.

Heaven knows, all you need now is a sick child on your hands. What with Mark gone and all."

Louise took a dime tip out of her purse and laid it on the maple table as Charlie approached with their bill.

"Excuse me, Mrs. Maringo." Charlie looked in confusion from one woman to the other. "I just heard about Mr. Maringo. I don't know what to say except that I'm very sorry, and you both know you have my deepest condolences."

"Thank you so much," Juliana replied.

So word had started to spread. Louise was not surprised. "Who told you?" she asked.

"The postman. Remember when you came in, he was at the counter, having a cup of coffee?"

"Yes, I remember." Louise stood up and automatically patted her baggy blue knit suit. "You haven't seen my son today, have you, Charlie?"

"No, ma'am. Now that you mention it, I haven't. It's sort of strange, his not showing up, I mean." He laughed nervously. "Maybe he's found a cheaper place to eat."

"Like where? The Windsor Hotel?"

Charlie flushed, said, "Excuse me," and walked off to wait on other customers.

"You shouldn't have been so hard on the boy," Juliana said. "He was only making a harmless little joke."

"I'm not in the mood for jokes today."

"Harry isn't sick, too, is he?" Juliana had turned pale. "Something's wrong that you're not telling me about, Louise."

"Harry is just fine. Relax. He must have decided to put in some extra time at basketball practice, that's all. You know how boys are. Now you have your coffee and finish your dessert. I'll speak to you later."

"Call me at Mrs. Finnegan's immediately if Alexis is worse. I'm her only remaining grandparent, and I have a right to be kept informed of these things."

Louise was becoming more impatient by the minute. "If Alexis is worse, I promise I'll call you."

"Good. And thank you for taking me to lunch, dear. It was most generous of you."

"My pleasure."

Louise's thoughts were flying, racing, soaring. She couldn't wait to get out of there and into her car. Thank God she hadn't left it at Buck's garage, it would probably be half-dismantled by now.

"Don't you work too hard, Juliana, you hear?"

Both women kissed each other on the cheek.

"I just do my job." Juliana's gray eyes stared into her gray coffee. "And I expect others to do theirs as well. I certainly hope that that lazy Mrs. Finnegan has flushed her toilet today. There's only so much a person can take, you know?"

Louise did not know. She did not hear. She could barely think, her heart was beating so fast. It was the worst fear she'd felt since she was two months pregnant with Alexis, and Mark had informed her they were going to have to adopt Harry. Alexis and Harry. Alexis and Harry. Alexis. Harry. The agonizing tune played over and over again in her head during the three-mile drive home.

It was broken by only one other thought: Juliana had become senile.

There was only a little bit of blood on the bearskin rug, not nearly as much as I had expected. Another thing I hadn't expected was how painless the first few thrusts were, the ones that broke the membrane, or whatever it's called.

Because after all the gossip I'd heard among the girls at school, I imagined that being de-virginated would cause a terrible, horrible hurt, a terrible, horrible wound. I remember Sally-Anne saying that when it did finally happen the first time, the girl screamed out like a wild animal, that's how much suffering she felt. Since Sally-Anne confessed to being a virgin herself, I asked her where she picked up this fascinating piece of information.

"From my mother, of course. Where did you think? And I guess she should know."

I realized now that Sally-Anne's mother obviously wouldn't know a roasted ear of corn from a plate of mashed turnips if one of them were to hit her smack in the face. Either that or Sally-Anne's father (the local plumber) was a heartless brute. Actually he looked like a mild, henpecked man the few times I'd seen him up close when he came over to fix our kitchen sink that was clogged with grease and gook. But what do appearances mean? Nothing, I now know, absolutely nothing.

My own mother's words on the forbidden subject were typical of all the rest of her wonderful nonadvice:

"You're too young to be asking a question like that."

"I'm twelve years old. I could get my period any day now. And as soon as I do, I'm a woman."

"Maybe in those medical books you're a woman, but if you got the curse tomorrow, you'd still be a young girl."

"I know some young girls who aren't virgins."

"Who? Which ones? What are their names? Are they friends of yours?"

"No, but I hear them talking at school."

"Disgusting!"

"What's disgusting? The fact that they talk about it or the fact that they do it?"

"Both. Both. Disgusting. Perverted. I don't want you to listen to anything they say. Walk away. Steer clear of those tramps."

"I do walk away. That's why I'm asking you. Because I don't want to ask them."

"Ask them what?"

"What it's like the first time."

My mother clamped her thin, Crimson Rose lips together so tight that they practically disappeared into her face. "When the time comes and you're grown up, you'll find out."

"Is that all you have to say, Mother?"

"It's no picnic. *That's* all I have to say."

"Is it really so bad?"

"Just behave like a lady, Alexis."

"Ladies wear white gloves and look like Olivia De-Havilland."

"You have a fresh mouth."

This conversation had taken place only a few months ago, and it was the last conversation we had on the subject. That was the end of it as far as my mother was concerned. Finished, good-bye, don't bother me, and behave like a lady.

"What's so funny?" Harry asked.

I didn't realize I had just laughed out loud until I heard Harry's question. He was lying on the rug beside me and his chest was naked. At some point he must have removed his sweater, but I don't remember when. The entire experience had been like a brilliant flashing dream, so fast, so vivid, so all-together that I couldn't separate the parts.

"It *is* a picnic, that's what I'm laughing about."

And then I explained what Mom had said to me.

"All that's missing is the fried chicken, potato salad, and Hire's root beer." I was still laughing. "Oh, wait. I forgot the ants."

Harry was watching me very closely, carefully, lovingly, I felt. Then he rolled over on his side and put his beautiful, hairless arms around me. We had just stopped making love seconds ago and he must have understood that I was still in a sort of daze, but he looked like he might be, too.

"Are you okay, Alexis?"

"I'm fine. I've never felt better in my life." It was true, about how I felt: grown up, proud, womanly. I had done it at last! "I feel great."

"I hope I didn't hurt you too much. I tried not to."

"It didn't hurt at all." I kissed his dark eyelashes, they looked just like mine. "Honestly, it didn't."

"But doesn't it feel sore inside?"

"Yes, a little. I don't mind, it's a nice sore. You made it."

He gazed down at the dark red splotch of blood on the rug, touched it with his finger, and kissed the blood off his finger. Now do you understand why I love Harry, why I will always love him? No matter what he does. Because I'm him, and he's me.

The mention of our mother pushed us apart. Even without her being there, she was an evil influence, coming between us, destroying the warm feelings we had about each other, killing them. Maybe someday I would be able to love my mother, but right now I hated her more than ever. And I was ashamed of my hatred, it wasn't a good thing. Then all of a sudden I started crying.

Harry came back to me, held me tight. "What's wrong, Alexis? What is it? Please. Tell me."

"I don't know." I was sobbing now, so unlike me. "I just thought of Dad. We'll never see him again."

"No. Never."

"It's kind of hard to get through your head. The word never. It's like 'impossible.' "

My tears were rolling down Harry's bare shoulder. His skin felt so nice and warm. I remembered my father's skin feeling like that when I was a little girl, before he went off to war. He used to tuck me in bed at night, not my mother, and once when I had a nightmare (it was lightning and thundering outside), it was my father who came into the bedroom and held me around, just the way Harry was holding me now.

They even smelled the same, my father and Harry, a fresh, clean smell like pine trees. We have a lot of pine around here in Pilgrim Lake, maybe it's crept into our bloodstream. Maybe I smell like pine, too. I never thought of that before. People don't know what they, themselves, smell like. How can they? They need someone to tell them.

"What do I smell like?" I asked Harry.

"You don't smell."

"No, I don't mean a bad smell. But what does my skin smell like? It must smell like something. Yours does."

"What?"

"Pine trees."

"Really?"

"Yes, I love the way you smell."

"I guess daisies," Harry said after thinking about it. "That comes the closest."

"Daisies are my favorite flower."

"I didn't know that."

"I thought you did. I've always loved daisies. I want you to know everything about me, Harry."

"I want to, too." He kissed my eyelids, I had stopped crying. "How did it feel when I . . . ?"

"It felt wonderful. I can't describe it."

"Try."

"It felt like a wave of something hot and hard had just entered my body. But it also felt like it belonged there. I want to do it again. Does that answer your question?"

"Yes."

"What did it feel like to you?"

"I was nervous," Harry admitted. "I wasn't hard enough. But Will says that one of these days real soon I'll be hard as a rock."

"Who's Will?"

"Will Welchman. The new basketball coach. He's a senior in high school."

"You're not going to tell him about us, are you, Harry?"

"I wouldn't tell anybody. It's nobody's business."

"Honest Injun?"

"Honest Injun."

That had always been our own secret joke. Now we had another secret to share, a much more serious one.

"Christ!" Harry sat upright so suddenly that my shoulder hit the rug. "I wonder what time it is. I should've been back in school hours ago, probably. And I haven't eaten or anything."

There was no clock in our living room, only in the kitchen. I had no idea myself what time it was, but unlike Harry I didn't care.

"Double Christ," Harry said. "What will Mom think? I mean, my not stopping by the store after lunch? She must be half-hysterical by now."

He started to get to his feet but I pulled him down.

"What's the difference? So you played hooky this afternoon. As for Mom, well, you know how she is. She's so busy with her Monday sales, She's forgotten about us. Money is the only thing that matters to her."

I touched him down there, he had practically no hair at all, whereas I had quite a bit. I wondered why that was. I wanted to make him hard so he could do it to me again. I was hoping he'd be slower and take longer this time. As though he were reading my thoughts, he said:

"Some gism came out of me before. It came out very fast. I couldn't help it. You felt it, didn't you, Alexis?"

"I felt something flow into me, yes."

"I don't want it to flow." He looked angry. "I want it to *fly*."

He started to kiss and gently bite my nipples. He was mine again. And the book of southern Spain was still next to us. I touched it with my free hand and looked at it as I looked at what Harry was doing to me and I to him.

"Remember the castle in Alicante?" I said.

He couldn't talk. He had taken my two flat breasts together into his mouth, as though they were one, and I could feel the sensation go deep down inside me, tingling.

"I'm going to have breasts soon, Harry. I want to have them for you."

Now he slid up and soul-kissed me on the lips. "And we're going to be the summer people, too. Aren't we?"

"Yes. I wonder how soon."

"It won't be long. Five, six years maybe."

Then he was hard enough to try to put it into me again. This time he did it more slowly, he was less nervous. I didn't want to close my eyes as I had before, I wanted to watch everything. Harry's eyes were open, too, and he was watching himself put it into me, he was looking downward now.

"Does it hurt?"

"No, it feels good," I said.

Then, wham, it was really in, and for a moment we just lay there locked together, not moving an inch. But slowly Harry began to move. I wanted to move with him, and I didn't know how or what to do, which way to move. Maybe he wouldn't want me to move, maybe he liked it better if I lay there perfectly quiet. It was all so mysterious, there were so many questions I had on my mind. My eyes were still wide open and the sunlight was pouring into the room, and I had started to wiggle a bit, and Harry was smiling at me as though I'd done the right thing, and then I saw our mother.

She was standing there, less than six feet away from us. Staring. We hadn't heard the old Chevy pull up outside. Harry didn't know she was there until he spotted the look that must have been on my face as my eyes met my mother's alone in combat at last. Harry stopped moving, like a wild animal that senses it's in danger. He opened his mouth to say something, but before it could come out our mother screamed at the top of her lungs:

"DEAR GOD IN HEAVEN!"

For some reason the smell of oxtail stew was very strong in the air.

Harry panicked when he heard Mom's voice. I will never forget the look of sheer terror on his face if I live to be a million. He became all soft inside me, took it out, and turned ever so slowly around to face the music.

"Mother." His voice was barely more than a croak. "What are you doing here?"

Frozen and stunned as she was, our mother managed to say:

"Put your clothes on, both of you. Immediately!"

I decided the hell with her, I wasn't going to move one inch. If she wanted me all dressed and respectable looking (like a lady), she'd have to dress me herself. But Harry got up and jumped into his clothes in three seconds flat.

"You bum!" she screamed at him. "You're as bad as your father. No. Worse. How could you do a thing like this? And to your own sister? Don't you know what sin means?"

Harry mumbled something about how sorry he was to have upset our dear mother this way. Maybe he was sorry, although I doubted it, but I sure wasn't. I was glad. Glad that Harry and I had done it, and glad that Mom had caught us doing it.

"*I said, put your clothes on, Alexis!*"

She sat down on the old oak rocker and looked like she was trying to rock herself into some kind of cold comfort. But it wasn't working.

"Here, Alexis."

Harry handed me my pink rabbit pajamas, which I tossed aside.

"Your brother might be a bum, yet at least he has some sense of decency left. At least he's got enough sense to cover himself up in front of his own mother."

"You gave birth to him," I said. "You've seen him naked before. I don't understand this business of covering yourself up all the time."

My mother's rage was really an interesting sight. You would have thought it was the end of the world, my being naked. Her eyes were popping right out of her head, like she'd never seen me naked before either. And poor Harry. He didn't know what to do, he looked trapped caught between two angry women, trapped and guilty. But I was the one who tricked him into coming home from school. I was the one who started the whole thing.

"It's not Harry's fault." I could stare my mother down now. "I phoned him at school and got him to come home."

"He raped you."

"No. He did not."

My mother looked from me to Harry.

"I didn't rape her," Harry said. "Honest."

"I seduced him," I said, feeling like Lauren Bacall all over again.

"What?!"

"That's right, Mother. If you want to call names and blame anyone, blame me. You've always blamed me in the past for everything. This time you'd be right for a change. Because

I'm the one who's responsible. I seduced my brother, and what's more, I'M GLAD."

"Wait a minute, Alexis." Harry didn't want me to take all the blame. "You might have started it, but I finished it."

By now my mother was beyond rage. In fact, she looked like she was going to faint.

"Both of you are disgusting."

"We love each other," Harry said, walking over to her.

"Don't touch me."

He stopped in his tracks, confused.

"My own children."

She must have repeated those three words I don't know how many times, over and over again. Then she said: "A bum for a son and a tramp for a daughter. That's what I have."

"Please, Mom." Harry said. "Try to take it easy."

"Take it easy? Is that all you have to say?"

"It won't ever happen again. I promise. I swear it."

"Liar. Your word will never mean anything to me after this. Liar. Degenerate."

Harry's face went black. "You're a dried-up old prune. That's what's wrong with you."

But she might as well have been deaf for all the attention she paid him. Her pale blue eyes gazed out at the lake, at the mountains, at the red and gold trees, although I'm not sure she saw any of them. I don't know what she was looking at. Maybe the remnants of Indian summer. I suddenly felt very sorry for her and I stood up. She started to cry and cover her eyes when something about me caught her attention. She was staring at my crotch. Then she shrieked out loud.

"Dear God, what has he done to you? Look! You're bleeding to death."

I looked down at myself, at where she was looking, and blood was gushing down my legs, a lot of blood, nothing like the little splotch that I'd left on the bearskin rug.

"You're hurt," my mother cried. "You're wounded inside. He wounded you."

I caught a fast glimpse of Harry's terrified face, of my mother's, but I knew I wasn't hurt or wounded. It was nothing like that at all. I had a funny taste in my mouth, I can't describe it because it didn't taste familiar. Then I started to walk toward her, bleeding on the floor.

"Mother, I'm all right. Harry hasn't done me any harm. It's finally happened. I've finally gotten my period."

She didn't hear me. She had slumped over in the rocker, her head resting on her blue knit shoulder.

"She's fainted," Harry said. "Like last night when she read the telegram."

"Call Dr. Deer."

While Harry was on the telephone I tried shaking my mother to revive her but it didn't work. The doctor arrived very quickly. He took her pulse and put his ear to her chest. Then he closed her eyes.

"Your mother is dead. Heart failure."

Harry and I stared at each other, unable to speak.

"You poor kids," Dr. Deer said. "Yesterday your father and now your mother."

I was wearing my pink rabbit pajamas again, and we had wiped the bloodstains off the floor (and off me) before Dr. Deer arrived. He shook his head.

"I just don't know what to say."

Neither did Harry and I, but something told me we were both thinking the same, exact thought: this was our first blood pact, but definitely not our last.

Part 2

Paris—1959

10 〜

It was Harry Maringo's first time in Paris.

"April in Paris, chestnuts in blossom," the old tune ran through his head over and over again, "holiday tables under the trees." Because, oddly enough, it was April, but he was not here on a holiday, far from it, he was on his way to a four o'clock appointment with one of the leading merchant bankers in the city, Ian Nicholson, a man he had never met.

Harry had never felt more anxious in his entire twenty-seven years, more committed, more nervous.

"Mr. Nicholson, I would like a line of credit for five million dollars to finance a three-picture deal starring my wife, Sarah Ames."

In effect, as crazy as it now seemed to him, that was what he would shortly say. But what would Ian Nicholson say in return?

"My dear fellow, I admire your courage, your—shall we call it—enterprising nature? I admire your wife's acting ability, I've seen her in several English films, you know. However, let's be realistic about this matter. Five million dollars? Why she's virtually an unknown property in America. And as for your own professional qualifications . . ."

No wonder Harry's hands felt clammy. He looked at his manicured nails as though they belonged to another person. Only yesterday he'd been having a haircut, shave, and manicure at Beverly Hills' most fashionable barbershop, Freddie's. Except that they weren't called barbershops in Beverly Hills. They were called hair stylists.

Freddie's was frequented by the famous, the rich, and that other group to which Harry belonged, the third, fringe group that hoped to join the ranks of the first two, and as quickly as possible. Perhaps when Harry did join, he would stop thinking of them as barbershops. Just the word itself conjured up memories of old Mr. Reilly, Dennis' father, with his gleaming bald head, cigar breath, and crude shaving mug held in an arthritic hand. You can take the boy out of Pilgrim Lake, Harry thought ruefully, but would it ever be really possible to take Pilgrim Lake out of *him?*

Although it was one of the oldest clichés in the world, it still remained an undermining one, and he pushed it away with the same brand of determination that had characterized his escape from the stifling confines of his small hometown and everything the town stood for. Alexis had been lucky. Thanks to their mother's will, she escaped early, she'd been shipped off to a fashionable boarding school somewhere in Switzerland while he, their mother's favorite, was expected to run the General Store in Pilgrim Lake for the rest of his life. Condemned to eternal mediocrity.

Even in death Louise Smith Maringo tried to cling to him, but he outsmarted her at last. Their steadfast, hardworking, reliable clerk Dennis now happily owned the store. Harry sold it to him for ten thousand dollars shortly after meeting Sarah and making his getaway. His mother must be rolling over in her grave, and Harry wondered what she would say if she could see him this very minute in his double-breasted, blue chalk stripe suit and jaunty carnation, his polka-dot foulard, his handmade crocodile shoes, Burberry raincoat, if she could have seen him lunching only a little while before at Laserre's, on steak poêlé Dumas and a flaming soufflé dessert, if she could have seen him check into the Hotel Lancaster last evening. The Lancaster was his wife's suggestion.

"It's elegant and discreet and the service is very personalized. And it's just off the Champs. You'll adore it. It's rather like Claridge's, actually."

Then Sarah stopped, remembering that Harry had never been to London, had never been to Europe, and before meeting her had never been much farther than a few hundred miles away from Pilgrim Lake. And only then because he finally won a basketball scholarship to Syracuse College.

"Well, you'll adore it nonetheless," Sarah amended. "Claridge's or not."

He kissed her because he liked to, and also to shut her up, for she had a habit of rattling. As usual her lips opened in moist, greedy anticipation. She had just returned home from a long day's shooting at the studio and still wore the riding outfit she had worn throughout a good part of this, her first, nearly completed, Hollywood movie.

Parisian girls, Harry noticed, coming out of his reverie, all seemed to have tiny waists, thin straightish legs, and small breasts. Yet despite their physical similarities each managed somehow to retain a style of individuality, to be different. He wondered what it would be like to make love to one of these girls with their rather hard mouths. He intended to find out, hopefully that evening after the business of the day had been completed. Again, the conflict bit at him: would Ian Nicholson go along with his adventurous scheme? Harry could not afford to fail. He could not afford to fail himself, but more importantly he could not afford to fail Sarah, who had placed so much faith in him.

"Ian Nicholson must be a rather odd sort," she had said, "to have spent so much time in France. You know how chauvinistic we English are, darling, how uncomfortable outside our own country. We can't bear to be away from the Palace Guards too long. Frankly, I'm homesick myself."

"How long has Nicholson been living in Paris?"

"Nine, ten years, I'd say. He's married to a Frenchwoman, very soignée, I understand. The main branch of his bank is in London, of course, but our Ian seems to be a bit of a maverick. Which is why I think you stand a bloody good chance of raising the money."

She had never laid eyes on the man she called "our Ian," although she claimed that her father did business with him some years back. Harry felt like a country bumpkin as he poured two glasses of 1939 Dom Perignon (the only vintage Sarah would drink) in their $125-a-day bungalow at the Beverly Hills Hotel. Sarah had insisted they stay there during the shooting of her movie, "A Pretty Kettle of Fish," in which she had the female lead. At first Harry was horrified by the hotel prices, but then he thought what the hell, it's her money, his ten thousand dollars having been spent within one year of their quixotic marriage. Yes, Sarah had the money, Sarah had the talent, Sarah had the connections. Sometimes he wondered why she married him, she could have had her choice of so many others.

"Because you're a super lover," was her reply. "And deep down, a super son-of-a-bitch. And both qualities appeal to me. You're also five years younger than I. A husband should always be younger. Well, a little bit anyhow."

He felt like a combination stud, houseboy, and kept man. The terrible part was that up until recently he enjoyed the feeling. Now it was beginning to arouse attacks of guilt within him. Lately he had trouble sleeping, and when he did finally fall asleep his dreams were heavy and weighted down with dark haunting figures, abstract riddles. Harry never wondered why he married Sarah, that was no riddle at all. She was easily the most intriguing woman he'd ever met in his life, except for . . . yet that was so long ago, another world, fourteen years since he laid eyes on Alexis.

Oh yes, their mother managed to separate them, but good, the bitch. The miserable, selfish, vindictive bitch. Her lawyers refused to tell him where Alexis was, and she herself had never written to him, not a word, not a postcard, not even after he married Sarah, a wedding that made minor headlines in newspapers around the world. Why not? Maybe Alexis was dead. The possibility made him shudder. He suffered nightmares on her account (or was it Sarah's?). His beautiful sister who looked so much like him, who *was* so much like him. No two women could be more dissimilar in appearance than Sarah and Alexis, and even after all this time Harry found it hard to believe that he would never see her again. It was not merely too cruel a possibility, it was unthinkable, morbid, beyond the law of human comprehension. Beyond decency.

"You're a million miles away," Sarah reprimanded him. "Come back. What are you thinking of?"

He would never tell her about Alexis, he would never tell anyone. Sarah was his wife and in his own way he loved her, but Alexis was his innermost, intimate soulmate. They could never truly be separated.

"I was thinking about you, sweetheart," he said. "You work so hard."

And as he handed her the champagne, she drew him over to the sofa she was lying upon. He made no resistance. One year of marriage had convinced him that blue-eyed, pink-nippled Lady Sarah Constance Ames-Maringo usually got her own sweet way in the end. And why not? Her father had been a fifth earl. She rarely spoke about him except to mention a family estate somewhere in Surrey, just as Harry rarely spoke about his own father except to mention that he'd been shot down in the war. Well, they had that in common, that and their lovemaking and their mutual ambition: hers to become an internationally known movie star, his to become the producer power behind the throne.

"Darling, aren't you going to sit down?" She appealed to the tall, athletic body she never seemed to tire of. "I'm so lonely. All those people milling around on the set, but it's you I think of."

Despite the fact that the sofa was huge (as was its twin on

the opposite side of the beige and brown room), he settled himself at her feet. He could smell her desire, it seemed to fill the air, envelope him in its perfume. Her eyes were half-closed as she sipped her drink, then she placed the tulip-shaped glass on an end table and slowly began to caress her breasts, a sight which she knew excited him, had excited him right from the start when they met at Pilgrim Lake where she had gone to recuperate in seclusion from what she then called, "a case of nervous exhaustion." It was to be, he later discovered, only one in a continuing series of mental breakdowns.

"Don't just sit there drinking your lovely champagne, darling." She had made her nipples very hard now and still would not stop running her hands back and forth across them, crisscrossing her hands, right hand now on her left nipple, left hand on right, delight on her lovely, greedy, insatiable face. "Do something, Harry. Help me a bit."

Harry placed his drink beside hers. What she did not know was that mixed in with his excitement was a kind of nervous revulsion as well. Large breasts had a magnetic but somewhat appalling effect upon him. He was riveted by the sight of them, he'd be the last to deny it, and still they continued to remain alien objects, threatening in their blatant demands: to be touched, to be fondled, to be kissed, to be sucked, to be bitten, to be spermed upon whenever he felt like it, because Sarah always seemed to feel like it, she did not tire easily of her habits.

"Help you?" Harry said. "But you're doing so well by yourself, Sarah. You're doing so very well, darling."

"Not as well as you do."

He placed a hand between her legs to feel the moistness. The floral curtains were drawn, the air conditioner was practically noiseless, and only one thin ray of late California sun slanted across the darkened floor, a ray of hope. Hope for what?, Harry asked himself. Divorce? Ridiculous. Yet it was the first time he wished he had never met this strange and demanding woman.

"I've had such a busy day," she sighed. "And I'm so bloody tired. I was out in the sun all day. And I want so badly to relax. Take off my boots, darling, will you? Later we'll order something extravagant from room service."

Obediently, Harry began to unfasten the tan gabardine pants and slip them down her rounded hips and firm, sturdy legs, her not-too-slender ankles, and the frankly wide feet. Her proportions were generous, she was a big girl, his little lady, and underneath the jodhpurs she wore skin-toned panties, garter belt, seamed stockings. He removed the panties and looked at the curly darkish blonde hair. There was quite a bit of it and it was shaved into a heart-shaped design. Harry had never quite gotten used to the sight of it . . . a heart-shaped bush was his ambivalent reaction the first time he saw it in the woods at Pilgrim Lake ("Let's go for a long hike," she'd said, "you're familiar with the area around here"), and it continued to remain his reaction: excitement sprinkled with distaste. He'd been to bed with a lot of women before Sarah, he'd seen and done everything, he thought, but nothing like this. As soon as he met her every other woman he had ever known automatically became obsolete, all except one.

"Now my suspenders, darling."

Suspenders equaled garter belt. He was starting to get used to the differences in their vocabulary.

"You're soaking wet," he said.

"I masturbated twice in my dressing room today. In between takes. Naughty, aren't I?"

He wasn't sure she was telling the truth. She often said things for shock effect. To tantalize. To fantasize. She was a hell of a good actress, there was no denying that.

A moment later she had begun to play with herself, parting the heart for Harry to see inside as he took another sip of champagne but kept his eyes on her, which was where she wanted them, needed them for her insatiable narcissism.

"That's better," she said. "Yes, that's much better, much much better. Aren't you going to join me, darling?"

Harry languidly reached his hands up to her breasts. They were free for him now, waiting for his touch, the very gentle breeze of a touch she had taught him to use, the teasing touch that would make her groan like a wounded bobcat until finally he would let his tongue go wild a bit, saliva glistening on each of her nipples as she continued to explore herself, her body now starting in on its rhythmic, spasmodic shake, Harry kissing, sucking, biting, until she made it through her first triumphant orgasm, and only then after she had done that and lay there still shuddering and shaking, did she allow him to remove his clothes and let the fun really begin. . . .

Five million dollars.

In plain old Yankee words it was a hell of a lot of dough, and his mind could barely grasp the numbers. Would the debonair (Sarah's description) Ian Nicholson politely snicker at the outrageousness of his request? And yet Nicholson had agreed to the meeting.

He turned silently down the long street flanking the gardens and entered the Rue de Rivoli with its deep, dark row of arcades.

The summer people. That was what they had promised each other they would be one day, he and Alexis, wherever she was, whatever she was doing, whomever she was doing it with. Another man could not separate them, just as Sarah hadn't been able to. Wives, husbands, lovers. In the long run other people didn't matter, they were only the means to an end.

11 ❧

Sometimes when I have the courage, I wonder about my life. Except that it hasn't been *one* life, not the way I see it, it's been a multitude of lives and I'm only twenty-six years old. God alone knows what the future holds in store for me: more disguises, more upheavals, different identities. Am I frightened? Perhaps. But curious, too. I've always been curious to explore the world. I was born curious, not like my mother, who died seeing so very little of everything.

"Chauffé, you're fidgeting!"

"I'm sorry, Madame. I won't move another inch, I promise."

It was late afternoon at the celebrated House of Madame Thérèse, and Madame was fitting a dress on me, chocolate brown velvet, precisely two inches below the knee. It was for the July showings and Madame was not happy with the dress, she kept pinning and repinning while I stood impatiently still, remembering that I was being paid very well by Parisian standards to do so.

"Someday I'm going to pin you somewhere tender if you don't behave."

"I wouldn't put it past you, Madame."

"Remember your place."

"Did you remember yours when you were my age?"

The minute I said it I could have bitten my tongue. If there was one thing Madame detested, it was being reminded of her age, which varied according to all the newspaper and magazine reports: she was anywhere from fifty-one to sixty-two. Nobody knew except Madame herself, who had been a notorious beauty in her time. No wonder she disliked her beautiful young models. We were a constant reminder to her of her lost youth.

Chauffé Nuwyler.

Yes, odd as it may sound, that is my name now. No more Alexis Maringo, whoever she was. And now I'm a couturier's model in Paris. Madame Thérèse vies with Chanel and Schiap as the leading genius-bitch designer in the high fashion field. It was Madame who gave me my new first name after discovering me at a seedy cafe on the Boul' Mich. First she said, "Don't just sit there looking pale and interesting," then she decided my name had to be changed, and then as if that weren't enough, she insisted I become a redhead. I didn't want to change my name, and I told her so rather heatedly.

"*Chauffé au rouge.* Yes, you're red-hot."

With that terrible smile of hers when she's mocking someone. So, since I was broke and working as a salesgirl at the Galeries Lafayette, not exactly the most stimulating or lucrative job in the world, I realized the time had come to think of my future.

"Okay," I agreed. "Call me Chauffé, if that's what you wish. When do I start work?"

"Stand up and let me see you walk."

I took a few brave steps. "All right?"

"Good. Very good. Most young girls don't know how to walk. They lead with their feet. You lead with your thighs. Still, you're rather on the tall side."

"Five feet ten."

"Then you'll be my tallest model. We shall have to fix you up a bit, though. I presently have two brunettes with straight hair. I can't afford another one. It's too boring."

"But my hair is one of my best features."

"*Oubliez-vous les cheveux.* You hide your face with your hair. We'll have your hair cut, dyed *rousse*, permed, then we shall see your face. And your face will become synonymous with my creations. For a short while, at any rate . . . a model's career is not a joy forever."

I tried to control my temper. That happened several years

ago and I still try to control it. One has to with Madame, she won't put up with nonsense from any of her girls (not even from Renée, her once-adored, ex-lover), it would be too threatening to the empire she created. Single-handed, she claims, but really with a lot of financial support from a lot of influential men, English, French, German, Italian, Swiss, yet she denies the accusations, the associations.

"I did it all alone," is her most frequently quoted remark. "Nobody helped me. Nobody gave a damn. I clawed my way up, if you will. Nobody gave me a sou."

Although I haven't lived in America for fourteen years and probably never will live there again, there are moments when I think I'm as American as apple pie, as Indian as my father's tomahawk, as English as Westminster, as Dutch as the Rijksmuseum. And at other moments I know that I'm muddled beyond belief in terms of national identification. Born in the U.S.A., educated in Switzerland, employed in France. I will not even mention my sojourns to other countries for fear of confusing myself still further.

"Do you think it's possible to leave your own country and get away with it?" I asked Eva earlier this morning as we were getting ready to go to work. "To leave and not be damaged by the consequences, I mean?"

Eva and I are roommates, she models for Madame Thérèse, too.

"Oh, I don't know. We *have* left, haven't we?"

"Yes, but you're engaged to a Spaniard and you're both saving your money so that when you marry you can return to Alicante."

"That's true."

"Then what you're saying is that even though you've left, you haven't really left . . . not in your heart."

"I suppose so."

Eva could be quite infuriating at times, yet we got along well. Probably because we were so different from each other and she took my up-and-down moods in stride, they weren't threatening to her, only to me. I never knew what to expect of myself next.

"You married your ski instructor," Eva said unexpectedly.

"Yes, when I was at that damned boarding school in Gstaad. Herr Nuwyler. *Der alte Scheisser*. Except he was young. What a bastard!"

"Doesn't he have a first name? You never mention his first name."

It was Kurt. "I prefer to forget it."

We were getting dressed. Our breasts were as flat as pancakes; our bodies so thin and angular that they didn't mean anything to either of us, they were pegs upon which Madame could hang her latest creations. There was an aura of asexuality about Eva and me that we ignored, pretended did not exist, although sometimes late at night when we were very tired, hungry, bored, restless, desperate, and found it hard to sleep we would make casual love. We were not like Renée, who openly, happily, admits she is a one-hundred-percent lesbian and can be very funny when recounting her various affairs with some of Madame's most illustrious clients (when Madame is not within earshot, of course).

Like the time Renée was having a fast soixante-neuf with a certain raven-haired comtesse, chez la comtesse, and the woman's husband, who was supposed to be at some important government function, came walking into the bedroom, took one fast glance at the situation and said:

"Oh, pardon me, ladies. I was looking for my liver pills." And just as promptly walked out.

Renée could have all of Madame's models in stitches whenever the mood struck her. She was so terribly funny about her exploits, so ribald.

We lived on lettuce leaves and were usually in bed by ten, all of us, all the girls who worked like dogs for Madame. Our weight was not allowed to vary more than a kilo in either direction or none of the clothes being fitted upon us at the moment would fit during the upcoming July showings. But we were paid well, the equivalent of forty American dollars a day . . . twenty thousand *anciens francs* a week. And our apartment cost twenty thousand francs a month, so it worked out very nicely in a way. Lettuce leaves, a lambchop with the fat cut off, Perrier water, one aperitif an evening. Really, that was what it amounted to. And other women who didn't know any better envied us.

"If he was such a bastard," Eva asked, "why did you marry him?"

"I was lonely. I was in an alien environment. I was the only American girl at that school. I was the only one whose parents weren't filthy rich. . . . In fact, I didn't have parents, they were both dead by then. He used to insist that I kneel on the floor before he'd make love to me. That I'd have to say, *Zu Befehl!*"

"What does that mean?"

"At your command," I said. "And so I divorced him."

"Men are all strange in one way or another when it comes to these things."

She sighed as she said it, her lovely face drooping a bit, as though in empathy for my unfortunate plight. Yet I suspected that she thought I was merely foolish, unworldly too, idealistic. Eva had very fine skin and great dark brown eyes upon which she was applying Arçançil mascara with precision care. I was shaving under my arms with equal precision.

"I will not have you arrive looking like scrubwomen!" Madame had once shouted. "You are a reflection of me, all of you. You will arrive looking elegant, made up. *C'est entendu?*"

It sure was and in a few minutes Eva and I would be made up, dressed in our deceptively simple black dresses, ready to take the metro to the Rue du Faubourg St. Honoré in the lovely 8th *arrondissement*. We lived in the 17th, just off the Parc Monceau, which was noted for its black swans. Unfortunately we could not see the exotic creatures from our balcony, we weren't high enough up. Now I was putting in my green contact lenses which Madame had insisted upon.

"I hate these damned things," I said to Eva. "But what can I do? She wants me to be a green-eyed redhead."

"It becomes you."

"It doesn't feel like me."

For some reason Eva was rouging her nipples. She only did that when she was meeting Eduardo. She said he liked them different colors at different times. Today was purple day. I guess he had to have something to make up for her flat-chestedness. He did it to her in the ass, she told me it was typical of Spanish men, they all enjoyed that.

"But do you?" I asked.

She shrugged her narrow, silky shoulders. "Oh, it doesn't matter. I'll be twenty-three tomorrow. I want to get married and get out of his awful business."

"Don't we all?"

"Sometimes I think you like it. I think you enjoy being recognized in public. I've watched you, your face tightens with joy when you spot someone who's spotted you. You can see them thinking, That's Chauffé, you know, Madame Thérèse's top model. Isn't she beautiful?"

It didn't bother Eva that she wasn't the top model, she showed absolutely no signs of jealousy. I was a bit jealous of her, though. She had my great dark eyes and my dark hair. She made me feel like an imposter. I was using the bidet now and since we only had one bathroom, Eva was peeing next to me.

"Happy birthday," I said. "We have no sense of modesty at all, you and I."

"Why should we? What we're doing are only natural functions."

But she hadn't grown up in Pilgrim Lake with the puritans. She'd grown up in Spain, land of my dreams, land of Harry's dreams, and she'd grown up in Alicante of all places! It was one of the wildest coincidences I have ever encountered. I still remember that book I stole from the library, the one with the picture of the Santa Barbara castle on the cover, the book, the *love* I had shared with Harry on that fateful afternoon.

And yet I pretended to everyone that I was an only child, even to Ian, whom I intended to marry as soon as he divorced that tenacious bitch, Paulette. Perhaps if Harry hadn't gotten married I wouldn't be in such a rush to do the same, but he went ahead and made an Englishwoman his wife. She even had a title: Lady Sarah Constance Ames. And an acting career. Their wedding was noted in *Time International*, in the "Milestones" column, and *Marie-Claire* ran a short piece complete with photos of the happy couple. She was a buxom blonde. He was so handsome that I just gasped when I saw his face stare back at me from the glossy magazine page. I have never felt so jealous in my life, so devastated, so abandoned, despite the fact that it was I who really abandoned Harry in the first place. By never writing to him from Switzerland, by cutting off all possible communication, by instructing my mother's lawyer to keep my whereabouts a secret from Harry, by trying to deny his very existence.

Even now it hurts to think of him too much, he brings back such terrible memories and such wonderful ones too. I force myself to forget. I tell myself that, like Alexis Maringo, Harry was yesterday. Children's games. That was all they'd been, that stuff we did to and for each other, infantile really. Eva had four brothers and two older sisters, and she was going to marry Eduardo, who worked as a waiter in the Montmartre. You would have thought she'd try to do better than a waiter, but like her own job his did not seem to mean anything to her either. I must say she was intriguing in her own quiet, self-contained, Spanish way.

Sometimes I wished I could share her quiet convictions,

yet I knew that at best it was a hopeless wish, at worst a kind of self-torture. I was a manufactured product, and she was the real goods. So I consoled myself with the thought that when she was fat and flabby and pregnant with her fourth child, I would still be slender and desirable, the much admired wife of Ian Nicholson, while her Eduardo would be chasing seventeen-year-old virgins and rolling in late at night to do it to her in the ass for the zillionth time. And Eva probably wouldn't even mind. She was very maternal, she would have gotten what she wanted whereas I. . . . What if she were right, and Ian did not divorce Paulette? *What if she were right?* I had invested two years in the relationship, I couldn't give up now, and I certainly wasn't getting any younger. The thought made me panic. At times I dreamed of killing Paulette just to get her out of the way.

"Chauffé, you can remove the dress now," Madame said. "I've pinned all I can. What are you doing this evening?"

"Meeting my lover."

"Too bad. I was hoping you'd have dinner with me. I don't wish to be alone."

There was a knock on the door and the maid came in.

"There's a telephone call for you, Chauffé. A gentleman."

Before I could reply, Madame said, "Get the gentleman's name and number and tell him that Chauffé will ring him back."

"But it might be Ian," I protested.

"You'll ring him back. Let him wait . . . don't be too eager."

"The trouble is, I *am* eager."

"All the more reason to conceal it. You have lovely breasts, lovely long legs, and when you leave here this evening I want you to wear the dark green mousseline de soie. It's one of my best designs, everyone tries to copy it. Be sure that he takes you to a brightly lit restaurant. You're a wonderful advertisement for me, you know that."

"Thank you, Madame."

She ran her hand down my back. "And you have a wonderful spine. They call me an old dyke too. But I'm not. I'm just a lonely, hardworking woman who has to compete with people like Fath and Laroche, Balmain and Mainbocher."

She never mentioned Chanel or Schiaparelli, her two female competitors. She refused to acknowledge their professional existence (just as she refused to acknowledge the affair with

Renée, or her bisexuality). Once when I said that I'd passed Elsa Schiaparelli's house on the Rue de Berri, Madame told me to shut up.

"Shocking pink, that's all that one knows. I don't want to hear about her and her one-color achievement."

I put on the plain kimono that all we girls wore in between fittings and looked at the clock on the wall. It was a very ornate gold beauty. The hands pointed at five to five.

"If I don't phone him back now, I might miss him, and I don't know where we're having dinner."

She patted me on the rear, one of her most infrequent but typically playful gestures. "If I had had a daughter, I would have liked her to look like you. Now go ahead and call your rich lover. I hope he takes you to Lucas-Carton."

"He'll probably take me to the Tour d'Argent."

And we both laughed since we both knew it was a restaurant for tourists. Ian and I wouldn't be caught dead there. Dead . . . murdered. I once told him that I had a dream in which I killed his wife. It was a lie, I merely wanted to see his reaction. Shock, fear. Men don't like violent women, they're terrified of them. I should have known better. But mixed in with the shock and fear was a kind of peacock pride, he was flattered (although he would never admit it) that I could love him so desperately I would dream of murder to reach my goal.

"Don't forget," he warned me, "Paulette is the mother of my child."

Mothers. Older women. They frightened me, made me feel like a young girl, like the twelve-year-old girl I'd been when my own mother died so suddenly. Blood was on my conscience. I never wore red now that I was a redhead. I never loved Harry. I think I'm frigid. Because I've *always* loved Harry.

"*Vite, vite!*" Madame said. "The telephone. What are you waiting for?"

"Yes, Madame."

I had nearly said, "Yes, *Maman*."

12 ✑

When Harry entered Ian Nicholson's private office at exactly four o'clock, he was simultaneously relieved and unnerved by the man he had come to see.

On the one hand, Harry was several inches taller than the merchant banker, which gave him an immediate feeling of increased confidence. But on the other hand, as Sarah had said, Nicholson *was* debonair with his continental suit (actually, it was from Savile Row), his impeccable English accent and easy, relaxed manner, obviously the result of having been sent to the finest schools, given the most expensive of educations.

"Eton or Winchester, no doubt," was Sarah's guess. "Followed by Cambridge."

Harry wondered if his own provincial background and free basketball scholarship to college could be apparent to this highly polished man. If it were, Ian Nicholson gave no indication of it as they shook hands.

"It's a pleasure to meet you, Mr. Maringo." Nicholson's handshake was stronger than Harry could have guessed. "I trust that your flight wasn't too terrible."

"Let's just say it was comfortingly uneventful."

"Smooth. Isn't that how you Americans put it?"

It was starting already, Harry thought, the battle between the old world and the new. The seller and the buyer. He wished he had gone to Harvard Business School. He wished his mother had never owned a smalltown general store. Dried lima beans: 4¢ a pound. He wished his father had been chairman of the board of General Motors instead of Pilgrim Lake's town drunk.

"Smooth is as good a word as any," Harry said.

"Please do sit down." Nicholson indicated a Louis XIV chair opposite his own gleaming mahogany desk. "Would you like something to drink? A scotch perhaps? It's become the vogue in Paris lately. The French think it's exotic for some strange reason."

"Probably because it's so expensive over here."

Nicholson smiled at the reference to money. On the surface he had a pleasant smile, pleasant but enigmatic. But then he

was the director of a famous bank, a shrewd man, somewhere
in his mid-forties, fairhaired and with a reddish blond
mustache, pale, almost watery blue eyes, everything about
his finely chiseled features diametrically opposed to Harry's
dark, volatile, sensual good looks. Harry tried to imagine the
kind of woman who would find Nicholson attractive. She
would not come to mind, but he felt certain there would be
a slew of them and the feeling made him uneasy.

"Or perhaps you would prefer a cognac. Coffee? Pick your
poison."

"Coffee and cognac, thank you."

Nicholson jabbed a button on his intercom machine with
the index finger of his left hand.

"A pot of coffee, please, Michelle."

Then he got up, walked across the room, opened the doors
of a tall cabinet and took out two cut glass goblets and a
bottle of 5-star Courvoisier. The cabinet was behind Harry
in a corner of the large office and he had not noticed it when
he came in. Now, half turned around in his chair, he saw
that it held many glasses and many different bottles of
alcohol. Everything from Dubonnet to Jack Daniels. Those
watery blue eyes of Nicholson's. Was it possible the man drank
too much? Sarah had not mentioned it. Nicholson returned
to his desk, poured a generous amount of cognac in both
glasses and handed one to Harry.

"Cheers," he said, just as there was a faint, almost in-
audible knock on the door. "*Entrez*."

An attractive girl in her early twenties entered, carrying
a filigreed tray upon which sat a tall white porcelain coffeemaker, two gold and white cups, a bowl of sugar, and two
demitasse spoons. Without saying a word she poured the
steaming black coffee nearly to the top of the cups and placed
a cup in front of each man.

"Will that be all, Sir?" she asked Nicholson in a softly
accented voice. Only once did she glance at Harry.

"Yes, thank you, Michelle."

Harry watched her leave as quietly as she had arrived, her
footsteps lost in the oval Persian carpet, her body desirable
even within the demure confines of its beige mohair suit, a
Chanel imitation. But the girl herself was another Parisian
original. They don't grind them out here like they do in
America, he was thinking. Each one adds a distinctive touch
of her own. In this case it was a leopard pin the girl wore, not
on the lapel of her jacket where it might be expected, but on

the half-belt of her suit in back. It was as though she intended to be noticed both arriving *and* departing. She was precisely the sort of girl Harry wanted to take to bed that evening.

"If you're as interested as you appear, it will cost you about ten thousand francs. Don't say I didn't warn you, *mon copain*."

Harry was certain he had heard wrong. "Excuse me?"

"It's the end of April, *fin du mois* time, as they call it in this delicious, practical city. She's bound to be a bit financially hard up."

"But she works for you." Maybe the jet lag had scrambled his brain. "I mean, she has a job. She's a secretary, not a—"

"Prostitute?" Nicholson had a surprisingly hearty laugh. "Of course not. Michelle comes from an excellent family in Lyon, her father is a distinguished lawyer. One thing has nothing to do with the other."

Harry felt like an idiot. He merely stared at the older man, waiting for clarification.

"There are many girls like Michelle in Paris, thousands probably if the statistics could ever be compiled. You see, we businessmen pay them only once a month. That's the custom here. We pay at the beginning of the month, and not too well at that, I'm somewhat ashamed to say."

"Are you trying to tell me that as a result of this quaint custom of yours, they have to supplement their income by going to bed with strangers for money?"

"They don't *have to,* but they all have rather expensive taste when it comes to clothes. You might even say they're all clothes crazy, and how can you blame them living as they do in the fashion capital of the world? I'd be willing to wager that right this moment Michelle has her heart set on a few frivolities for her summer holiday. The problem is that she's bound to be short of cash. You'll undoubtedly find her at a cafe near the Rond-Point after work, or if not her, another like her."

Harry swallowed his cognac fast, neat, in one unsophisticated gulp. Sophistication suddenly no longer interested him.

"Fascinating," he said.

"Don't look so shocked."

"But I am shocked. Why should I deny it?"

"No reason at all, my dear fellow."

"I'm not good at pretense. I'm too blunt. Too American."

It was the right kind of thing to have said, the right kind of tone to have used (forthright), exactly the right kind of challenge. He could tell by the slight narrowing of those watery blue eyes. To get what he wanted from Nicholson there was only one way to deal with him: on his, Harry's terms, Harry's turf. He would never win with this smooth English francophile any other way. Blunt, direct, small-town American. Naive. Vulgar, perhaps. Well that's what he was, that was his strength, and he was just beginning to feel it.

"I merely wanted to point out that girls like Michelle are perfectly respectable by our standards. Clean, too," Nicholson said. "But stay away from the Left Bank, you can run into trouble there. Okay?"

"Okay." Harry lit a Chesterfield. "I appreciate your concern, Mr. Nicholson, I really do. However I didn't come nine thousand miles to talk about broads." He used the word deliberately. "I came here to talk about five million dollars."

Bang. Right to the point. And Nicholson was caught off guard at last. It took him more than a moment to open his thin-lipped mouth.

"Five million dollars. It's an interesting sum. What, precisely, is your proposition, Mr. Maringo?"

No more of that "*mon copain*" crap. They were down to business at last. Harry blew a smoke ring at the cupids on the rococo ceiling and was about to answer the question when one of the two elaborate gold and white telephones on Ian Nicholson's desk rang. It was the one on his right. The private one, Harry figured, which wasn't used too often since the guy was obviously a southpaw. Reading backward, Harry noticed that the telephone on Nicholson's left, the hard and fast business one, had seven digits, the same as New York and L.A. The other, on his right, that he had just awkwardly picked up was blank, no digits at all. Clever. Obvious, but clever nonetheless.

"*Allo!*"

Pause.

"Oh, darling, I'm glad you rang back so soon." He turned to Harry. "Excuse me a moment." Then, putting his mouth close to the receiver, Nicholson said, "I was hoping you would. That woman you work for is a bloody monster. I'm sure she could have let you take my call earlier if she had cared to, the old witch."

Pause.

"What? *La communication est très mauvaise.* Oh, no time for that right now, Show-fay. I have someone in my office, a countryman of yours, as a matter of fact." He threw a fast wink in Harry's direction without losing a beat of the conversation. "The reason I called is because I won't be able to keep our date this evening. Now please, darling, don't throw a fit. It's not my fault. Well, I suppose it is, in a sense. Today is Jeanne's third birthday and I'd totally forgotten all about it. Do you see how beastly I am?"

Pause.

"I'll make it up to you, Show-fay, I promise. Have lunch with me tomorrow."

Pause.

"I know that you generally don't, thanks to the witch, but you can think up some excuse. I'd make it for tomorrow evening, but there's the Zurich business. Tell her you have to go to the doctor. Tell her anything. God, I'd love to strangle that woman. She's worse than the Beast of Belsen."

Pause.

"You will? Then you'll succeed, I know you, darling. Meet me at the Ritz Grill at one."

Pause.

"Too public? Oh, for God's sake. She *is* the Beast of Belsen. Very well, let me think. The Escargot-Montorgueil. And I refuse to accept no for an answer. I shall reserve a table upstairs, where as you know it takes an eternity to be served. That should teach the old witch a lesson or two. *Jusqu'a demain. Au revoir.*"

He replaced the receiver and sighed that universal sigh tacitly understood by all men, Harry being no exception. *Love, problems, an affair, is it really worth the trouble, the headaches, the risk?* Harry wondered who the lady in question was. Show-fay, with the accent on the last syllable. Harry had taken a crash course at Berlitz before leaving California and was trying to translate the odd sounding name into its logical French spelling but nothing he came up with made any sense.

Perhaps it was a nickname of some sort. But Ian had indicated that she was an American, so it doubly made no sense. Screw it. What the hell did he give a damn about Ian Nicholson's private love life?

"Sorry for the interruption," Nicholson said. " I had asked you what your proposition was and you were about to tell me when the telephone rang."

Sonny Liston might be saved by the bell, but not Harry Maringo. "I want to produce three movies starring my wife, and I need five million dollars to do it. I thought you might be interested in financing the project."

"Why not get a bank in your own country to finance it?"

"I don't own property in the States, I don't have any tangible assets. I'd have one hell of a time trying to raise five million dollars there. But I'll tell you what I do have: the best independent American distributor, a fine novelist turned scriptwriter, a director who's fed up with the red tape bullshit of the majors, and Sarah Ames."

Nicholson sounded dubious. "That's quite a package."

Harry sounded definite. "I think so."

"What about the script?"

"It will be a tragedy with a lot of laughs."

"Very amusing. What's the subject?"

"I don't know."

"*You don't know?*"

"That's right. He's thinking about it. He'll come up with something brilliant, he always does."

"Are you telling me that he hasn't put anything down on paper?"

"Not a word, and he won't until he sees a considerable sum of money. He's famous." Harry mentioned the writer's name. "If you've read any of his best-sellers or seen the last movie he did for John Huston, you wouldn't doubt his ability."

"I've read his books. He has an undeniable talent for black humor. But if we're talking about the same movie, frankly it wasn't very good."

"They cut out some of his most brilliant scenes. Now he wants final script approval."

"And he hasn't written a word." Nicholson sighed. "I must be mad to even discuss this venture. Who's the distributor?"

"United Artists."

Ian Nicholson opened a box of Upmann cigars, clipped off the end of one with what looked to Harry like a solid gold Cartier's cutter, and lit up. His eyes didn't seem so watery anymore, they were clear and bright now.

"I don't want to imply that you're a liar Mr. Maringo, but I find it a bit difficult to believe that UA would agree to distribute a picture without a script, starring an actress whose name and face don't mean a thing in the United States. Not unless her leading man is Marlon Brando."

"He'll be a French unknown."

"Then I find it impossible to believe. And without the United States you've got nothing, it's your primary market, that's where the money is. Foreign distribution would ultimately take care of itself, but without the United States . . ." He shook his head. "I've seen your wife in a few English films that Rank did, and in my opinion she's a very talented artist. But mention her name to any waitress in Chicago, and she'll look at you cross-eyed."

"Not after "A Pretty Kettle of Fish" is released, she won't."

"What's 'A Pretty Kettle of Fish'?"

"A high-budget movie being made in Hollywood this very minute by one of the majors, and Sarah has the female lead. The release date is set for September. Five short months from now."

"Who's your director?"

Harry named one of Hollywood's youngest, brightest, wittiest, who'd been nominated for an Academy Award only the year before. "He's directing Sarah in 'A Pretty Kettle of Fish.' "

"He *is* good," Nicholson conceded.

"Cuts his own film, too. Very important. We save time and money."

"I'm beginning to understand United Artists' interest somewhat better now. Where do you plan to shoot these movies?"

"Various locales in Europe. It's cheaper over here, in terms of crew. You don't have to pay those greedy Hollywood unions for overtime if it happens to rain on the wrong day. No dubbing either. It's too expensive, too complicated. We use subtitles. I'm here, Mr. Nicholson, for the very simple reason that I need a line of credit for five million dollars, which is what it will cost to make these movies. To make them right and promote them right, so we're certain to come out in the black. In fact, I need six hundred thousand bucks immediately. Otherwise we can't even get started."

The banker's eyes weren't merely clear now, they were hard and glistening. "How do you figure that?"

Harry took a very small white piece of paper out of his suit pocket and pushed it across the desk. Then he watched Nicholson scan the list of items that Harry had typed himself on an Olivetti rented from the Beverly Hills Hotel. He knew the list by heart.

$125,000 . . .	United Artists
125,000 . . .	director
100,000 . . .	studio rental
75,000 . . .	writer
75,000 . . .	Lake Como
50,000 . . .	pr agency
50,000 . . .	travel
$600,000	

"What's this about Lake Como?"

Harry was starting to enjoy himself. "Oh, that's where I plan to bring the principals together. That's where we'll have our introductory meeting. It's the best way to get people acquainted with each other, get them in the right frame of mind, get them to realize what a fabulous picture we're going to make."

Lake Como, in Northern Italy, had been Sarah's idea. Harry had never heard of it.

"We'll rent one of those palatial estates," she'd said. "It will be perfect. Motorboating, excellent food, snow-covered mountains in the background. It's very scenic, very posh, darling, just the thing to break the ice."

"I must admit it's an elegant idea," Nicholson said. "It's also a most expensive one."

"It will be worth every goddamn cent. I'm aiming for the Cannes and Venice film festivals, which draw the international Monaco crowd. You may think those festivals are circuses, but they get a lot of press coverage, a hell of a lot of publicity. You can't buy publicity like that."

"I seem to recall an extraordinary photo of Diana Dors taken at the Venice festival a few years back. She was in a gondola, wearing a mink bikini covered with diamonds that supposedly cost £125. My wife said it was the most vulgar thing she had ever seen and I had to agree with her, but still . . ."

"You remember it."

"Obviously. It was unforgettable."

"That's what I mean. Not that I'd ever let Sarah do anything so trashy, but she doesn't have to. Sophia Loren didn't have to. Still we'll be there and so will the *paparazzi* clicking away for all they're worth."

"You're very sure of yourself, Mr. Maringo, aren't you?"

"If I am it's only because I have faith in what I'm doing."

There was a long pause. "Before we go any further, I think we should discuss interest rates. As I'm sure you're well aware, we accepting houses charge a bit more than the joint stock banks. But that's why you're here and not at Barclay's, isn't it?"

Harry nodded. "You guys are more adventurous, you take more chances."

"Yes, we do. A bank like Barclay's wouldn't touch you with a ten-foot pole, if you'll pardon the expression."

"What rate of interest did you have in mind?"

"Ten percent."

The fact that it was three points above the going rate did not surprise Harry. He had expected it.

"What we're dealing with here is a very high risk venture. Very high risk." Nicholson seemed to relish the sound of the words. "Which is why there's another small matter to be discussed."

Harry doubted that it would be very small.

"This is all still conjectural," Nicholson said. "I'm not committing myself to anything as of yet, but if we do go ahead we'll have to form a holding company. The shares would be nominal, say one hundred francs apiece. But I'm going to want fifteen percent of those shares. Are you still with me?"

Harry nodded for the second time. UA wanted twenty percent of the gross profits of the movie, Nicholson was asking for ten percent interest on his conjectural loan, plus fifteen percent of the shares in a holding company that would in effect own the movie.

"At the point when your first film is successful, we will then sell you back our shares. . . ."

Nicholson continued to go on . . . Harry continued to nod. The message was loud and clear and pretty much what he had been prepared for, still now that it was being verbalized he felt queasy all over again. He should never have had that soufflé for dessert, it was burning a hole in his stomach. The hell with his stomach, it was his bank acocunt (the one that didn't exist) he should be thinking of.

Because even if Nicholson loaned him the five million, even if he successfully completed the first movie, even if he came up with a winner at Cannes or Venice, even if he turned out to be the first young American hotshot producer of the sixties, to get in on the ground floor of what was surely going to be a revolution in the film industry, even if he was a fucking genius and light-years ahead of his contemporaries, even if all that . . . would he end up with a dime in his pocket when it was all over? If he didn't, he would surely lose Lady Sarah Constance Ames-Maringo. And he couldn't face the prospect, he could face almost anything but that. She was his passport to a world he had long dreamed of.

Perhaps he never should have left Pilgrim Lake. At least he knew where he stood there, he didn't have to pretend to be anything he wasn't. Now pretense had become the name of the game, he had to watch his step every damned second. Perhaps he'd aimed too high.

"What do you plan to call this incipient company of yours?" he heard Nicholson say.

"Maringotop Productions."

"What's the 'top' for?"

"Where we're going to be."

"Touché."

"It also was my family's original name many years ago. I'm part Indian. The English screwed my forefathers, stole their land, raped their women."

"Sounds like you're here for retribution. I'd like to sleep on this one," Nicholson said. "Talk it over with my associates. How long will you be in Paris?"

"That depends upon you."

"I have to fly to Zurich tomorrow for a few days, but it occurs to me that while I'm there I might discuss your project with some people I know. Kill two birds with one stone."

"When can I expect to hear from you?"

"Today's Monday. I would say in about a week's time. Where are you staying, Mr. Maringo?"

"The Lancaster."

"I'll ring you as soon as I have definite word either way."

"I'll be waiting."

For what, Harry thought? To sign and be sold down the Seine? Brown eyes silently confronted blue, and blue eyes did not flinch. Was history going to repeat itself two centuries later? Or was it going to reverse itself?

As both men shook hands, each knew that the challenge was on. Neither could have possibly anticipated the macabre outcome.

13 ❧

"How nice to see you again, Mademoiselle Chauffé. How lovely you look. *Très chic*, as always. What can I bring you?"

It was my old waiter friend at one of the popular cafes on the Boulevard des Capucines, with his neatly pressed, shiny black jacket. I don't know why I decided to come here after work, since it was in the opposite direction from where I lived. It was in the direction of Ian's office, we sometimes met at this cafe and probably that was why I had gravitated toward it. Not because I expected to run into him, nothing as silly as that, I knew he'd be going directly home for his daughter's birthday dinner. But it made me feel closer to him, idiot that I am.

No wonder Eva frowned upon my relationship with Ian. I could see her viewpoint. Sitting here by myself at six-thirty, alone, on a lovely Monday evening, well, what sense did that make?

The thought of the long evening ahead depressed me. I didn't know what to do with myself. I didn't feel like going to a movie and I didn't know who to call. Because of Ian, I had stopped seeing other men long ago. Other women? I worked with them nine hours a day, enough was enough. Eva and Eduardo would be back at the flat now, she was cooking half a leg of lamb for them, she told me earlier, accompanied by *haricots verts* and *pommes frites*. Only Eduardo would be able to eat the *pommes frites*. Potatoes were strictly taboo for Madame Thérèse's models, although Eva once confided a disgusting secret to me. She said that when she cleared the table and went into the kitchen with the dishes (Eduardo, being a true Spaniard, considered kitchens outside his natural terrain), she would grab a few of the french fries, stuff them in her mouth to get the salty, oily, crunchy flavor of them, and then she would spit them out into the garbage.

"Here we are, Mademoiselle Chauffé."

The waiter placed a tall glass with the glistening red liquid in front of me, and next to it a syphon of soda water. There were three ice cubes inside the glass. Between them and the soda, the mildly alcoholic contents of the Campari would be sufficiently diluted to last me awhile. My tall red boring daily drink. Sometimes I switched to dry vermouth. It didn't matter. If I had more than one of either, I would have to cut out a crust of bread from dinner or I'd be over my calorie count. No wonder Eva secretly spits out potatoes.

"Are you meeting your friend here?" the waiter asked.

"I'm not meeting him anywhere, Jacques. He has family responsibilities tonight. I'll probably go to a bistro for dinner. *Oeufs sur le plat*."

"So beautiful," he sighed. "So alone. So unfair. Still, one never knows. You just might meet a more eligible man one of these days. It happens all the time."

More eligible for marriage, he meant. The cafe was packed.
I had taken the last table, someone cried out, "*Garçon!*" and
Jacques was off. Along the boulevard cars were going from one
traffic tieup to another, yet I never felt crushed in Paris despite
the masses of people, the incessant stream of automobiles, the
endless activity. Paris was like a garden to me, I loved it, and
yet I knew that I would not end up in Paris, it wasn't in the
cards. Paris was not the end of the line, it was just another
metro station.

A couple at the next table had recognized me, they appraised me with polite interest . . . my golden sable coat from
Revillon (Ian's birthday gift last November), my green silk
Madame Thérèse dress with her famous "T" trademark woven
into the cowl neckline. I always made sure to keep my coat
partially open when I was wearing one of Madame's designs,
so that her handiwork could be seen and identified. As a result
of this friendly advertising service I performed, Madame
made me a gift of one of her creations several times a year.

I was in the mood for adventure. I hadn't had an adventure
for so long. I was even in the mood to get drunk, eat *pommes
frites*, rip her green silk dress to shreds, call up Ian's wife and
tell her a couple of juicy stories about her darling husband's
behavior in bed.

"He might be impotent with *you*, Paulette . . ."

Then I'd make up a pack of lies, leaving out the fact that
Ian had trouble maintaining an erection very long. I would
pretend that with me he was a sex hero, Gilbert Becaud,
Gérard Philipe, Albert Camus. Oh yes, I was in a mad, wild,
Indian mood tonight. But I needed my beauty sleep, and since
Eva's bedroom and mine were conveniently separated by the
large salon, I could go home after my bistro dinner and get
into bed with a Colette novel that I'd read before. I would
make it through a few pages and then turn out the lamp, while
Eduardo fucked Eva in the ass and she dreamed about
retirement.

My body needed sleep after the long, exhausting day, but
my psyche needed excitement. I was in the wrong line of
work, that was for sure, marriage to Ian would be more like
it . . . deliciously late mornings in bed, with a maid to bring in
my café au lait and croissant, the morning papers, the mail,
my appointment book. Then she would draw a scented bath
for me. Just the enticing prospect made me ache with frustration. I felt like going to that new discotheque, Les Chandelles,
which was near my flat. I felt like mamboing away my frustra-

tion, picking up a faceless stranger who would later make fierce love to me. I didn't want anything tender tonight, I wanted to be an animal. We wouldn't talk, the stranger and I, we would dispense with words, our bodies would do the talking for us.

"*Pardonnez-moi, Mademoiselle, mais avez-vous une allumette?*"

I looked up at the tall, dark-haired man standing in front of me, holding a unlit cigarette in his hand. He wore a double-breasted, blue chalk stripe suit and spoke with one of the most self-conscious French accents I'd ever heard. His almost black eyes were staring into my fake green, his mouth curved into a familiar sensual smile, his intent as clear as the water in Pilgrim Lake in the summer. I could feel the blood rush giddily to my head, my feet turn into chunks of ice, my heart turn inside out. I did not think I would be able to utter a word. I was looking at my brother, Harry.

"*Une allumette?*"

"You know, a match." He spoke in English now, pointing to my lit Gitanes and his unlit Chesterfield. "If it's not too much trouble."

My hands were shaking as I fished around in my Hermes handbag for the book of matches imprinted "House of Thérèse." I handed Harry the matchbook and motioned for him to sit down. There was an empty chair next to me.

"*Merci, beaucoup.* Do you see the waiter?"

I gave Jacques the high sign and he came running over, sizing up Harry in one fast, knowing, French glance. For my matrimonial benefit of course. If only he knew he were sizing up my very own beloved brother, he would have died of sheer shock. That's what I felt I was dying of. It was impossible to digest, that after fourteen years of separation Harry should materialize in Paris of all places, and at my table, asking me for a match, *me*, the sister he once adored, de-virginated, and now did not even remotely, vaguely recognize. This lack of recognition on his part had a strange effect upon me, it was both an insult and an irresistible challenge. *How dare he not be able to see past my green contact lenses, and dyed, permed hair, and realize I was Alexis? How thrilling that he couldn't, how absolutely wild and delectable!*

"And what will Monsieur have?" Jacques asked.

"Scotch on the rocks, please."

"But certainly."

Jacques nodded with approval behind Harry's back.

"Is this your first time here?" I asked Harry.

"You speak English!" he said idiotically.

I didn't know whether to laugh or to cry. "I should. I'm American."

"No kidding. You don't sound American."

Didn't I? How odd. "What do I sound like then?"

"I'm not sure. Something foreign. Like you'd learned English as a second language."

I felt my confusion of identities loom up stronger than ever, and it was as depressing as ever. Maybe more so.

"That's very interesting," I said.

"Perhaps it's my imagination. When I saw you sitting here alone, well, I don't know, your clothes, I don't know what it was, I just assumed you were French." He hesitated, reappraising me. "But you're not French."

"No. Are you disappointed?"

"Of course not."

His emphatic denial made me certain that he was. After all, what kind of kick was there in picking up an American girl your first time in Paris? None. He could have stayed home for that. Home. Yet his wife was English. Lady Sarah Constance Ames-Maringo. The *Marie-Claire* article had said that although professionally she was known as plain Sarah Ames, in her private life she had chosen to retain her title and hyphenate it with her married name, a privilege afforded the titled English, Ian once told me. I wondered whether Harry was really in love with her. Even if he wasn't, he still made love to her just as I made love to Ian.

When I read about Harry's marriage a year ago, my determination to marry Ian had increased by more than leaps and bounds, by sheer gallops, that's how jealous and out-in-the-cold I felt. I knew that the only way I would ever be able to compete with her Ladyship was to have a husband of my very own, as contradictory as that may sound.

Compete? It was the first time I'd openly admitted to myself that I was still in the race for Harry's undivided love. I guess it was the sudden and unexpected physical impact of him this evening that did it, his presence had come as a violent blow to what I thought were my self-contained senses. Now they were scattered all over the place, as I realized that if it were the last thing I ever did in the world I was going to make love to Harry tonight.

"Are you on a vacation?" he asked.

"No, I live here. Paris is my home now."

"Oh, an expatriate. Where are you from in the States?"

"Expatriates went out with Hemingway."

Jacques appeared and placed the scotch in front of Harry, and Harry paid him for both our drinks. "Would you like another?" he asked me.

"*Mille grazie, signore—molto gentile—ma no.*"

"Spanish?"

"Italian."

French, German, and Italian (no Spanish). Those were the three languages they taught me at that wonderful school our wonderful mother chose for me, her motives being as bizarre in death as they always were in life. *Why*, I had asked myself, *mille volte*? Why did she choose to send me to an expensive, exclusive boarding school in Switzerland when she hated me so much? Perhaps that was why. She must have known how miserable and out of place I'd be there, and she was right. Whereas her legal bequest to Harry was that he stay put in dull, boring, no-future Pilgrim Lake and watch the store. One thing was for sure, she certainly had succeeded in separating us. For fourteen years, anyway. The last time I laid eyes on my brother we were both crying. I had never seen Harry cry before that. When we returned home from the funeral, accompanied by our grandmother, Juliana, she said:

"You poor children, you poor, darling children. Orphans. Whatever is to become of you? Do you want to live with me? But no, my house isn't large enough. Maybe I should come and live with you. You're both too young to live alone. I wonder what your dear, departed mother would have wished."

We weren't long in finding out. The next day our mother's lawyer came over to see us (we had stayed up all night, fucking), and read us the bad news. Even Juliana was surprised about the Switzerland part.

"What a strange will. Nonetheless, I'm sure she had her reasons."

My mother had stipulated that it was her "deepest desire" to have Juliana sell or rent her own home, and move into ours in order to look after Harry. And that's exactly what she did even before that wretched train took me away from Pilgrim Lake, away from the site of my most deeply engraved memories, away from my friends, away from Harry, away. At twelve years of age I had no parents, no hymen, and no home. How many other twelve-year-olds can make that scin-

tillating statement? As I waved good-bye at the train station,
Harry didn't say a word and neither did I. It was Juliana
who spoke:

"Take care of yourself, Alexis, dear. We'll all be together
again very soon."

Famous last words. Because I later received a letter from
her, a very sad letter in which she tried to point out (as
delicately as possible) that in my mother's extraordinary will
was a clause stipulating that I not be allowed to return to
Pilgrim Lake until I was eighteen and had graduated from
school.

I never wrote to Harry, not once, not out of respect to our
mother's wishes, heaven knows, but because it would have
torn me apart to do so. I couldn't stand the idea of being pen
pals with Harry, that would have been a hypocritical denial
of everything we meant to each other, a disgusting lie. At the
time I felt that my only hope for relative sanity was to try
to adjust, as best I could, to my new and alien environment.
Herr Nuwyler helped in that regard. Shortly after he started
to teach me how to ski, he started to teach me how to fuck,
even if I did have to kneel down at the side of the bed first
like a good little Lolita. But Herr Nuwyler was not Harry,
nobody was Harry except Harry.

I GOT NEWS FOR YOU, MOTHER DEAR, WHER-
EVER YOU ARE. WE'RE ABOUT TO DO IT AGAIN.
WHAT DO YOU THINK OF THAT, YOU MISERABLE
BITCH?

14

"By the way," Harry said. "What's your name?"

"Chauffé," she replied.

Show-fay. Harry nearly dropped his scotch at the sound of
the name. Was it possible? Could it be? Maybe it was a
common name for women in France. But she wasn't French,
and neither was the woman Ian Nicholson had been talking to.

I have someone in my office, a countryman of yours, as a matter of fact.

Those were Nicholson's exact words. Harry remembered them. And Nicholson had broken a date with the lady in question. This lady? It was too wild a coincidence and Harry didn't particularly believe in coincidences. He felt like saying, "Do you know Ian Nicholson?" but managed to control himself long enough to say:

"That's an interesting name. How do you spell it?"

"C-h-a-u-f-f-é. Accent acute on the 'e.' It means overheated."

"Are you?"

She smiled at him and for a moment he thought of Alexis. Their smiles were so very similar, they both had the same thin upper lip, the same full lower. Where was Alexis now? Right this very minute?

"Since you're American, how come you have a French name?"

"Actually, it was my employer's idea. *Chauffé à rouge.* She thinks I'm red-hot."

Nicholson's girlfriend was employed by a woman, the Beast of Belsen. The coincidences were getting not so coincidental.

"Then it's a kind of nickname," Harry persisted.

"Yes. You could say that."

"What's your real name?"

She smiled again. "I'll tell you later."

Through the golden sable coat he could see that she was small chested, the exact opposite of Sarah with her threatening nipples. Harry preferred women with small breasts, he often wondered what happened to Alexis in that department. At twelve she had no breasts at all, from the waist up she could have been a boy. Sometimes Harry wondered what that meant about *him.* He had considered the possibility that he might be a latent homosexual, then discarded that terrifying possibility. No, he hadn't married Sarah for her breasts or to prove that he was a true, red-white-and-blue American heterosexual. He married her because he liked her accent, her title, her Englishness, her money. What a snob he was at heart. He was even impressed by Chauffé's obviously expensive coat. Had Nicholson given it to her?

"Are you in Paris on business?" she asked.

"You guessed it."

"Let me guess the business."

"Okay, but first are you sure that you won't have another of whatever it is you're drinking?"

"Campari. No, thank you. I have to watch my weight. I'm a model, you see."

"Who do you work for?"

"Thérèse."

The Beast of Belsen? It was starting to seem weirdly possible. Thérèse was world-famous, and everyone had heard stories about what a bitch she was.

"I'd like to go to bed with you," Harry said.

She did not flinch. "How strange. I was thinking the same thing."

Harry was speechless. He couldn't believe his own good luck.

"I know a place," she said.

"Yours?"

"No, we can't go there. My roommate has invited her boy-friend over for dinner tonight. It would be too indiscreet."

"Then what kind of place?"

"It's a hotel for lovers, a *mueblé*," she said. "And since we won't stay the entire night it will cost about seven thousand francs for the room."

Eight dollars? What kind of dump was she taking him to?

"Is it clean?"

"You Americans." She was laughing openly now. "Is that all you can think of? Is it clean? Does it contain garlic? Am I going to be gypped, poisoned, mugged? It's too ridiculous."

"I don't enjoy being laughed at. It doesn't amuse me. Besides, you're American too."

Her face clouded over, she seemed to trail off. "I'm sorry. I didn't mean to be insulting. Really, I'm sorry. What's your name?"

"Harry."

"You're very good-looking, Harry."

"You're beautiful."

It was only when she stood up that he realized how tall she was. About five feet nine or ten in stocking feet, he would imagine, deducting three inches for her alligator heels. Sarah was only five feet six, and he was about to be unfaithful to her for the first time since they'd gotten married. He knew he should feel guilty, but he didn't.

"We'll have to find a taxi," she said. "It's not within walking distance. It's over in the 17th."

In the taxi he held her hand. Her skin was very soft, her

perfume tantalizing as hell (Thérèse's *Les Fleurs*?). He couldn't wait to see her without clothes. She would have long, long legs and lovely small, firm breasts. Which would be her favorite position? And what about contraceptives? Maybe she was only planning on soixante-neuf. She had said nothing about money for herself, only for the room, and that was re-assuring to Harry because he'd read somewhere that all call girls, prostitutes, etc., invariably told you how much it would cost in advance. On the other hand, perhaps the *fin-du-mois* types operated differently. Ian Nicholson should have told him about that. Damn it, what a crucial piece of information to have omitted!

Harry had never paid for sex in his life and he was proud of that. In Pilgrim Lake he was known as the local stud. He doubted if there was one hometown girl he missed getting into the sack with, in certain cases they all but dragged him. And at college it was a cinch, all the coeds were dying to hop into bed with the guys on the basketball team. If he'd been good enough to become a pro, he would have had women crawling out of his ears, he'd heard all the wild sex stories on that score. But somewhere in his junior year something happened to dampen the enthusiasm that was necessary if you wanted to go into the big-time, professional grade.

"Not roughness, not brute strength," he remembered the college coach, saying over and over again, "but endurance, speed, and stamina. Those are the keys to success in basket-ball."

However it was exactly roughness and brute strength, he then realized, that appealed to him. One of his classmates (who learned it from his father) taught him karate and after that Harry just plain didn't give a damn about sinking goals, points, scores, any of it. He was tired of dribbling, passing, shooting, guarding, and maneuvering. Most important of all he was tired of the inevitable teamwork that basketball en-tailed. He far preferred the lone, individual, on-your-own style of the art of karate self-defense. It suited his personality.

So after he graduated, it was back to Pilgrim Lake and the Maringo General Store. And more girls. And then Sarah showed up . . .

"Here we are," Chauffé said.

After Harry paid the driver, he noticed the discreet gray-stone building that was obviously their destination. On one side of the wall was a small bronze plaque which read: Résidence Françoise. That was all, no flashing signs, nothing showy to attract attention, no cheap giveaway clues here. Had he walked past this nondescript place by himself, he never would have guessed that it was a hotel for lovers. A hotel. And they weren't carrying any luggage, not even an over-night bag, nothing!

"We don't have a goddamned suitcase between us," he said.

Chauffé pushed a buzzer. "Relax. They wouldn't let us in if we did."

A petite, middle-aged lady with gray hair combed into a tight bun opened the door and looked at them without seem-ing to look at them. Harry suspected she was so adroit at sizing up people that one flash of the eye was all she needed. And yet she was as ordinary in appearance as the building itself, as pedestrian and unspectacular as his Dutch grandmother, Juliana, when she had been in her mid-fifties. (He still kept in touch with Juliana, who strongly disapproved of his mar-riage to Sarah. *That English actress hussy*, was Juliana's first reaction to Sarah and despite her subsequent silence on the subject, Harry suspected that that continued to be her stub-born, unshakable opinion.)

"*Bon soir, Madame, Monsieur*," the gray-haired woman said.

"*Bon soir, Madame*," Chauffé said, taking her aside.

The woman led them into an open, grillwork elevator and pulled a lever that indicated they were going to the fourth floor. When they got out, they followed her down the corridor silent except for a flicker of laughter, followed by a muted female cry, to a room at the end marked "Marie Antoinette." She unlocked the door and handed the key to Harry. It was the first door he had ever seen anywhere in his life that did not have a knob on the outside.

"*A bientôt, Madame, Monsieur.*"

And she was gone, her longish black dress reminding him of nothing so much as a stealthy black cat creeping off into the labyrinths of the night. Harry turned his attention to the room and was agreeably surprised by what he saw, no, more than surprised, he was impressed, titillated. A huge bed with freshly scented, flowered sheets, a mirrored headboard, mirrored ceiling, three silk-papered walls, the fourth wall (opposite the bed) revealing an enormous mural of an 18th century couple cavorting in a bucolic setting. There were sheep and shepherdesses in the background, the latter with staffs in their hands.

"Let's hang up our clothes, shall we?" she said.

Harry turned around to find that Chauffé had already taken off her coat and dress and was standing before him now in a low-cut black lace bra that fastened in front, sheer black seamed stockings, and the skimpiest of black garter belts. Her black silk panties, fringed with lace, lay on the floor beside the bed. She still wore her black alligator, three-inch heels, and her sparse pubic hair was jet black. He must have been staring more than he realized because she said:

"No, I'm not a natural redhead as you can plainly see."

The fact that she dyed her hair did not disturb or disillusion Harry, not after mingling with movie people for the past year, but something else definitely did disturb him and he had no idea what. His heart began to race in a way that he associated with fear, imminent danger, like just before he was about to get into a fight with one of the guys in Pilgrim Lake.

"Our clothes," he said. "Yes."

There was a bathroom which he mistook for a closet before realizing there were no closets here, only some hooks on the wall. No wonder Chauffé had told him that suitcases were not necessary. The bathroom contained a toilet, tub, shower, sink, and bidet, as well as an assortment of freshly laundered towels and washcloths. This was no whorehouse, no dump. *Where the hell was he?* He removed his jacket, shirt, and foulard, and hung them on one hook, then took off his socks and shoes, and lastly his trousers and shorts, which he hung on a second hook. Sarah once told him that there was nothing more ludicrous than an undressed man still wearing his socks and shoes.

He moved toward Chauffé and gently touched the front clasp of her brassiere, through which her small breasts were visible.

"May I?"

"Please."

There was only one hook on the clasp and it yielded instantly. He placed the brassiere on the wall hook over his polka-dot foulard. He liked the sight of the two unnecessary pieces of clothing one on top of the other. Then he came back behind her and cupped her breasts in his hands, knowing that she could feel his erection against her lovely firm ass.

"That's nice," she said.

She lay down on the flowered sheets and he saw her twice,

once on the bed and once in the mirrored headboard. The double vision was exciting, but something more than that, something . . . his heart started to race again, or hadn't it ever stopped? He began to kiss her breasts. The nipples were not pink like Sarah's but light brownish, café-au-lait. Beneath the scent of her perfume was a familiar musky fragrance that he knew only too well, too intimately, it was too frightening, too stimulating for comfort. His breath sounded like wild gasps in his ears, as harsh and uncontrolled as the hurricane that Edith Piaf was singing about. Chauffé lifted up his head with both hands.

"I'd like to take my shoes off," she said.

"I'll do it."

"Thank you."

As he bent down to remove her shoes, he could feel her doing something else up there at the head of the bed, but he did not look back to find out what it was until he had taken off her alligator shoes and pushed them inches away from him. It was only then that he slowly turned around to face her. Gone were the glittering green eyes, magically replaced by eyes as dark and black as his own.

"Hello," she said. "I'm Alexis."

15 ❦

Harry stared at her, then at the two tiny green plastic contact lenses lying on the nightstand where Chauffé—his mind was racing as fast as his heart now—*Alexis* had placed them, while he'd been removing her shoes. All she wore now were her black stockings, attached to the tiny black garter belt. When he could finally speak, his voice sounded more like that of a frog than a human being.

"I don't believe it. It's impossible. But it's true. You *are* Alexis. Things like this don't happen. And it's happening, Alexis. Chauffé. I don't know what to call you."

He had lost his erection.

"Alexis." She suddenly looked very tired, as though the

masquerade of identities had gotten to be too much for her. "Alexis. Please, Harry—Alexis."

In later weeks, months, years, he would only remember the conversation that followed in jumbled bits and pieces, a verbal kaleidoscope of multihued revelations, irreconcilable nonsequiturs, hateful jabs, and the most tender of loving exchanges. For who knew where to start, and how? The years of separation had been so long, so painful, so silent. It was that very lengthy, painful silence which now catapulted brother and sister into a desperate attempt at reconciliation.

She seemed perfectly calm. He felt as though he were drowning. "What the hell are you doing in Paris?"

"I told you, I live in Paris now. I've been living here for five years."

"Why Paris?"

"It seemed the logical choice after the rigidity and discipline of Switzerland."

"So you've been in Europe all this time."

"Well, yes. Where did you think I was?"

"I didn't know. How could I have known? You didn't write to me, not once." He felt foolish, childish. "Not one letter in fourteen years."

"Please, Harry, don't make me feel even more guilty than I already do. I wanted to write, you have to believe that, but I couldn't bring myself to do it."

"Why not?"

She shook her head sadly. "Because it made no sense. Not for either of us. I knew it would just make matters worse if I wrote, so I decided to try and forget you."

"And?"

"I succeeded up to a point. I went on with my life. That's what people do. They go on. You went on."

"But did you really forget?"

"No. Did you?"

"No."

They looked at each other in the flesh, and then at themselves in the mirrored reflection on the ceiling.

"You're different," Harry said. "I mean, you're the same but there's a difference and I'm not referring to the red hair or those contact lenses. It must have been the school. The people you met. Europe. The languages. You're so sophisticated. I feel like a hick in comparison."

"I don't want you to feel that way," she said, fourteen years too late. "Besides, it's not true."

"It's true and you know it. I'm still a guy from a small American town. You could be from anywhere."

"But I'm not from anywhere," she pleaded. "I grew up in Pilgrim Lake, too. Do you think you can get rid of your roots so easily?"

"You seem to have."

Instinctively he had hit her most vulnerable point: Alexis, the imposter. "You make me feel like a fake."

"*Au contraire*, my darling. You carry it off very well. Congratulations. You even fooled me, your own brother."

"You're being cruel, Harry."

He *was* being selfish, cruel. She was right. After all, how did he know what nightmares she had gone through since the last time they'd seen each other? How could he read her heart? That was what bothered him the most. She'd escaped him, forged ahead, survived, prospered. And yet beneath the pulled-together façade, he sensed that she was miserable.

"Are you having an affair with Ian Nicholson?"

"Oh, my God." She was clearly dumbfounded. "How did you find out? Who told you?"

"You might say you did. I was in his office this afternoon when you telephoned—"

"In Ian's office?"

"Yes, on business. Naturally, I only heard his end of the conversation, but it was enough. He kept calling you Chauffé, and then when I met you at the cafe . . . well, it's an odd enough name you must admit. Also, he indicated that you were American."

"It's too crazy." She covered her face with her hands. "It's plain nuts."

He realized that she was crying and he started to cry, too. They were twelve and thirteen again, saying good-bye at the railroad station, only this time the hurt went much deeper, it had lasted that much longer, festered quietly for so many years that it now ravaged them both in its eruption.

"Are you in love with your wife?" Alexis asked.

"Yes. No. It's hard to explain. It's different. It's not like you and me."

She wiped her cheeks with the back of her hand, an old childish gesture. She was so pale. "Nobody can ever be like you and me."

"I love you."

"Still?"

"Always."

And he began to cover her face with kisses that were so tender, they both trembled. It was like kissing your twin self.

"Unreal. It's totally unreal," she kept repeating.

"No, it's real. We're together again."

"It's too late."

He sighed. "I know."

Now that he had admitted defeat, she looked at him accusingly. "You could always get a divorce."

"I don't want to."

To his surprise he realized it was true. As much as he loved Alexis, he did not want to divorce Sarah.

"But you're not in love with your wife."

"Are you in love with Nicholson?"

She did not answer. She did not have to. His answer spoke for her as well: *Yes. No. It's hard to explain. It's different. It's not like you and me.*

"I assume Sarah isn't with you this trip."

"It sounds so strange to hear you say her name."

"Is she or isn't she?"

"She's in California, making a movie."

"Thank God. I don't think I could have stood it if she were in Paris right now." Alexis fell back upon the mound of pillows with a soft moan. "It would have been the last straw."

"Why don't you take off the rest of your things and get under the covers? You're trembling."

"Yes."

She undid the garters that were holding up her stockings and dropped both stockings and garter belt on the heavily carpeted floor. In her haste she had ripped one stocking. Her fingernails were long and painted a shimmering shade of coral. Harry remembered them when they were short and bitten and colorless, but his sister was grown up now, she was twenty-six, and he'd missed watching her make the transition from a girl to a woman. It was a loss that could never be recouped, and he silently cursed their mother for the cruel deprivation she had inflicted upon him. No. Upon *them.* Because Alexis had been deprived as well. He wondered if she felt it as keenly as he did.

There was only one way to find out. By making love to her.

But even as he started to caress her, Harry realized that he was not doing this in order to find out whether Alexis had missed him as much as he'd missed her all these years. Who the hell was he kidding? Himself, for Christ's sake! His own dumb, deluded self. But definitely. His motives for making love to his sister were not so cool and investigative as he would have liked to believe, as it would have flattered him to believe.

He was not *testing* Alexis about their relationship.

Hardly.

It had taken fourteen years of separation for Harry to now admit to himself—for once and all—that there was nothing, *nothing* he would not do for Alexis. Except the one thing he couldn't do because of their close blood ties: marry her and give her children. But aside from not being able to marry her and give her children, he was at her disposal as he'd been ever since she was born—nine months after him (their father might have been a drunk, but he was a horny, potent one).

"Oh, Harry."

Her orgasm surprised him, he had not expected it. He hadn't expected the fierceness of it. She writhed and twisted and moved away from him, while still holding on to him (or was he holding on to her?). He had never felt a woman shake like that, it was a series of convulsions really, and he was respectful of her autonomy at that moment, for even though he had started her shaking and moaning, she really no longer needed him. Her own body had taken over, taken her away from him, was giving itself pleasure after pleasure, and Harry could only watch in admiration, awe, and resentment.

He wanted her to want and need him as badly as he did her. At all times! About everything! He wanted her to be dependent upon him, to say:

"Oh, Harry, I do need your help."

Instead, she was just saying:

"Oh, Harry . . ."

Meaning, I'm coming all by myself, thanks for the trip, amigo, I hope you have a good one too.

His own orgasm, minutes later, was mild and unsatisfying. When he came with Sarah, his head felt like it was going to fly off, but did that make him love Sarah more than Alexis? No. Decidedly not. For he *had* Sarah. Emotionally, sexually, in every way imaginable. Alexis would always elude him, have stronger orgasms than he did, be a stronger person than he was. Harry wanted to be strong, too. Important. He desperately wanted to be important to the only human being in the world who really mattered to him: Alexis.

Afterward they kissed and hugged like children, sat up in bed, and began to talk. About the past. There were so many things Alexis wanted to know.

"What happened to the Maringo General Store?" she asked.

"You remember Dennis."

"Our faithful, devoted clerk?"

"Right. Well, he owns the store now. I sold it to him about a year ago, after I decided to marry Sarah and move to the West Coast."

"Are you sorry?"

"Do you mean about the store or about marrying Sarah?"

"Both."

"No. Not at all."

She flinched, was quiet for a moment. Then she asked, "Juliana. Is she still alive?"

"Yeah she's alive and still cleaning houses, if you can believe that. She's one tough old lady, but she's very hurt that you haven't written to her in so many years. She was afraid something had happened to you. An accident or something like that. I was afraid, too. At times I thought you must be dead."

"God knows I've wanted to kill myself often enough. It's a miracle that I'm not dead. Did you really worry about me, Harry?"

"A lot. More than a lot."

"If you'd wanted to find out where I was, Juliana would have told you. She knew the name of the school in Switzerland. You could have made her tell you."

"I tried. She wouldn't say. She kept repeating that that's the way our mother wanted it. You remember how stubborn she could be. Then when you left school, you disappeared. Nobody knew where you were. It was cruel of you, Alexis. Juliana's been worried sick for years, she couldn't trace you. It was as though you'd fallen off the face of the earth overnight. Why did you do it?"

"I told you, I wanted to forget the past. It's as simple as that. I wanted to make a whole new life for myself, and I did. I became a new person. Chauffé Nuwyler." She sunk even more deeply into the pillows. "I was married in Switzerland. And divorced."

It took minutes for this latest revelation to sink into Harry's brain, and when it did it only served to reinforce his acute sense of loss. In the fourteen years of their separation, his sister had led a multitude of lives that he would never truly know about no matter how much he interrogated her. Nuwyler. He would not ask about her mysterious ex-husband. What good would it do?

"Do you have children?"

"No," she said. "I was very careful. I knew the marriage was a mistake right from the start. I'd rather not even talk about it."

Harry was relieved that she hadn't had a child. Now he understood why he had not protested more strongly about Sarah's reluctance to bear children. The only woman he wanted a child with was Alexis, and that was out of the question. Something told Harry that the two of them would spend the rest of their lives childless. It was a sad and bitter realization.

"How serious is your affair with Nicholson?"

"Very serious."

"For him, too?"

"Don't be cute, Harry."

"I'm being protective. It's my brotherly privilege. I don't want to see my little sister get hurt."

"She won't. She will marry the man."

"Is that what you really want?"

"Yes."

Harry was more disturbed than he would have thought possible. "I see."

"Are you shocked?"

"Why should I be?"

"Because I'm here in bed with you."

"We were in bed *first*," he bitterly reminded her.

She stared at him from another world of bearskin rugs and red and gold treetops, and a lone tomahawk on the living room wall.

"Ian will get a divorce and then he and I will be married."

It was as though she had memorized the line and recited it now without conviction or hope, mainly to convince herself that it was true.

"Is that what Ian said?" Harry asked.

"More or less."

"You're lying, Alexis. You always were an unconvincing liar. But I've met your Ian. He doesn't strike me as the sort of man who's planning on an imminent divorce. I think he's quite content with the situation exactly as it is. Who wouldn't be? The wife and the girlfriend. It's every guy's deepest fantasy."

"I hate his damned wife. I'd like to kill her."

Harry was about to dismiss this last remark as the cliché reaction of every frustrated girlfriend, but there was a look on Alexis' face that he had seen once before, many years ago, right after their mother keeled over and died before their eyes. The look was a combination of sheer animal triumph and sheer human contempt. He had never forgotten it, he never would.

"Don't kid around, Alexis."

"I'm not kidding." She looked at him slyly.

Harry tried to keep his voice light. "You can't just go ahead and kill a woman merely because you want to marry her husband. The very fact that that's what you want makes you the number one suspect. The police would nail you in a second."

"In other words I have the perfect motive?"

"Right."

Alexis smiled at him from her sea of pillows, the flowered sheet pulled up to her chin.

"But you have no motive at all. Do you, Harry?"

What he had been longing for a few minutes ago was finally coming true. She was asking for help at last.

"*Do you, Harry?*" Alexis repeated.

She was giving him his chance to be important. On a Résidence Françoise silver platter.

16

As soon as Harry got over feeling needed, important, and essential to Alexis' future happiness, he started feeling uneasy. Very uneasy.

In fact, for the slimmest of moments he tried to convince himself that he had heard wrong, that surely he was misinterpreting her insinuation. But he knew he wasn't. He understood only too well what Alexis was saying, what she wanted him to do, and he was both cold with fear and hot with the desire to please her, to prove his inestimable importance to her. But he had to tread carefully.

"I not only have no motive for killing Nicholson's wife,"

he replied, "I have a perfect motive for probably being the last person in the world to want to kill her."

"Why is that?"

"Because I'm trying to get Nicholson to finance a motion picture project of mine. That's what I was doing in his office this afternoon. Trying to raise five million dollars."

"That's a lot of money."

"You bet it is."

"What did Ian say?"

"He didn't. He's going to think about it and call me next week."

"So it's up in the air whether you get the money or not?"

"I'm afraid so."

Alexis was not smiling now, she was plotting, scheming.

"The police would never suspect you. You're above reproach. Just think of it from their standpoint. You're happily married to a lovely film star. You're a well-dressed American businessman, not some doped-up beat poet. And best of all, you *need* Nicholson. His goodwill. His respect. And as you just said, his money. Why would you, of all people, want to murder his wife?"

"I wouldn't. And I don't."

But Alexis was so caught up in her own scenario that he might as well have been talking to the wind.

Harry was starting to feel intense stirrings of excitement. To be able to pull off a premeditated murder and get away with it was somehow thrilling beyond words. It was crazy but it was thrilling. And that he would be doing it for Alexis' sake, for his beloved sister, only added to the excitement. The fact that he was considering the cold-blooded murder of a woman who had never done him any harm began to seem quite irrelevant.

"How old is she?" he asked.

"About forty."

An older woman. That appealed to Harry. He would use one of two karate methods, depending upon how she was dressed. A shirt, a jacket, a robe, something with lapels, that was a cinch. Otherwise it would have to be the three lethal chops. Both methods were guaranteed to kill, even if she were some kind of amazon.

"She's petite," Alexis said. "Small-boned. Slender. A typical Parisian type."

"Not too strong." Harry got out of bed and began to pace

up and down the beautiful, decadent, dimly lit room. "A pushover," he said at last.

They talked further. It was a plan Alexis had obviously had for a while.

Harry was thinking. "Ian said he'd be gone for a few days."

"That's right. He'll probably be back in Paris either Thursday night or Friday."

"That means I'll have to do it tomorrow or Wednesday."

Alexis tried to stifle a yawn. "I guess so."

That she could be so casual about such a crucial matter while he was still reeling with apprehension, excitement, self-importance, and nerves, only highlighted the difference in attitude that lay between them. He longed to be as casual as she. On the other hand, he would be the one taking all the risks. . . . And yet he was going to do it. He was going to murder her lover's wife, so that she could be free to marry him! Greater devotion hath no brother, Harry thought, both amused, perplexed, and horrified by his own ambivalence, his own altruism. Perhaps it wasn't altruism at all, perhaps he was setting the stage now for a future favor from Alexis.

The next day while Alexis and Ian were enjoying an aperitif upstairs at the Escargot-Montorgueil and holding hands, to the delight of their waiter, while Harry was picking on a trout soufflé in his suite at the Lancaster and talking to Sarah at the Beverly Hills Hotel (five A.M. California time), Paulette Nicholson was eating a cold meat and salad luncheon at home with her daughter's nanny. Three-year-old Jeanne was seated between them, reluctantly swallowing vegetable soup.

Ian was saying things like: "Chauffé, you have no idea how much I detest leaving you right now. You seem so down. But I'll be back in a few days and then we'll go someplace splendid and celebrate."

Alexis was saying things like: "Madame will murder me

when I return three hours late, but just being here with you is worth all her miserable wrath. I'm going to miss you terribly, darling."

Harry was saying things like: "The bastard has to go to Zurich on business, so the whole deal is being delayed. Not that I expected an overnight miracle, but this means my hanging around Paris longer than I intended."

Paulette was saying things like: "It will be nice to spend a quiet evening at home for a change. I'm so tired of the opera, the ballet, the cinema, the theater, the *world*."

Rose, the English nanny, was saying things like: "Now, Jeanne, eat your vegetable soup and wipe your mouth." And to her employer, "Yes, Madam, a quiet evening would be nice."

Above the three-year-old's head, the women smiled at each other in conspiratorial anticipation.

A few minutes later the *bonne* entered to clear away the dishes and bring in a dish of fresh fruit and coffee for the two women and a strawberry custard for Jeanne. Unlike Rose, the *bonne* did not live in. She arrived at the apartment on the Avenue Foch each morning at seven to prepare breakfast, lunch, and dinner for the four members of the family, Rose having been brought over from London shortly before Paulette was due to give birth.

Ian had insisted upon an English, Norland-trained nanny for his child despite his wife's objections. At the time Paulette failed to see why a Frenchwoman would not suffice, but Ian had been adamant on the subject. As much as he admired the French way of life, he could be astonishingly stubborn when it came to certain matters, Paulette had discovered.

Astonishingly insensitive, too.

Paulette recalled their wedding. First they went through a civil ceremony in Paris, and then it was agreed to have a formal church ceremony in the south of France, where Paulette's parents owned an old chateau situated in the wilds of the Dordogne valley. This was beautiful but undeveloped countryside, totally unlike the glamorous Mediterranean coastline, the only part of southern France Ian was familiar with. He seemed strangely remote as Paulette's parents made preparations for the lavish affair, with many of the wedding guests invited to stay at the chateau over the weekend.

The house was in a flurry of activity. There were four bridesmaids, a dressmaker doing last minute alterations, uncles, aunts, cousins, several hired maids as well as the *bonne* from the family home. Everyone was in a pitch of excitement, everyone except the bridegroom, who sat in the salon reading the *Financial Times*. Ian was the very epitome of English sangfroid. He looked as though he had wandered into a household of strangers and was forced to stay a few minutes while waiting for the local mechanic to fix his car, which had broken down on a nearby road. That was how detached and disinterested he appeared to be. It was an image that Paulette was not likely to forget.

Just as unforgettable (although for totally different reasons) was Paulette's initial image of Rose Pye, when she first arrived at the Nicholson household to assume her duties as nursemaid for the baby soon to be born. Although Paulette was due to give birth any day, she had managed to retain her usual aura of chic throughout her pregnancy. This was accomplished by gaining only five kilos, and paying strict attention to her clothes and toilette.

Paulette was then a worldly thirty-seven, Rose an unprepossessing twenty-three. In her round felt hat with the brim turned up, and plain navy dress and coat, she reminded Paulette of a washed-out, bloodless old maid. Still, her references had been excellent. Paulette sighed and showed the young girl to her room, which adjoined the nursery, at the other end of the huge apartment from the Nicholsons' own bedroom.

"This is very nice," Rose said, surveying the simple, spotless, spartan room that contained a washbasin in one corner, an armchair and wardrobe in the other, and a single bed freshly made up. A connecting door led to a primitive cupboard of a bathroom. "Very nice indeed, Madam."

"I hope you'll be comfortable."

"Oh, I'm sure I will."

"Perhaps after you unpack you'd like to see the baby's room. You might have some suggestions."

"Yes, of course. I won't be long, Madam."

Paulette could see why not. The girl had brought only one medium-sized suitcase with her, very new, very shiny, very vulgar.

"Is this your first time abroad?"

"Yes, Madam, it is." Rose crossed the room to peer out the curtained windows. "But as I said in my letter, my French is fluent. I've been studying for months."

It was only then that Paulette realized the girl had a slight limp, which she managed to camouflage quite ingeniously.

Paulette admired her effort. At the same time she could not help wondering whether the limp was the result of something like polio or whether she was born that way. Her own morbid fears of giving birth to a defective child were calmed somewhat by the sight of Rose's infirmity. Although Paulette did not consider herself a superstitious woman, she felt that this crippled girl was sent to them as a good omen, an assurance that the Nicholson heir would be born strong, healthy, and physically flawless.

Several days later, that is exactly how Jeanne Jennifer Nicholson was born.

Rose's nights off (when she was not babysitting) were infrequent, but she never complained. The boys who came to pick her up seemed nice enough in their student clothes and their inevitable motorbikes, and Rose was as carefree in her dress then as she was careful during working hours. The fact that her baby's nurse led a double life would have disturbed Paulette were it not for Rose's impeccable professional training, and she had to agree with Ian that when it came to caring for Jeanne, Rose could be trusted implicitly. As for her nighttime forays to the existentialist cafes that had begun to crop up on the Left Bank . . . well, reasoned Paulette, the girl was young, curious, and entitled to her recreation. She certainly worked hard enough for it.

Still, Paulette could not help but feel a pang of jealousy when she saw the solemn daytime Rose transformed into a glowing creature of the evening. At first she thought it was merely Rose's youth that she envied. Only after Rose had been with them for about a year (and Ian had started his affair with that Swiss model who worked for Thérèse), was Paulette able to admit to herself that her feelings toward Rose were far more complex than she had imagined up until then. But being a woman of tact and practicality, she waited for the right time to find out whether despite Rose's incessant stream of boyfriends, her sexuality might not be so single-minded as it appeared on the surface. Aside from frightening the wits out of the girl, the last thing she wanted to do was lose her services as a nanny.

Paulette need not have worried. Rose turned out to be as much of a treasure in bed as she was outside it, and ironically (Paulette thought, lingering over her luncheon coffee) the first time they became lovers had been during a business trip of Ian's to Zurich. That dull Swiss city. That beautiful city. It would always hold a special place in Paulette's heart, and she realized that she was looking forward to tonight's love-making with as much zest as she had two years ago. No. *More*.

Jeanne stopped eating her strawberry custard. "When will Daddy be home?"

"Daddy will only be gone a few days. He'll be back home by the weekend. Now please finish your dessert, then go and wash your hands. Rose will fetch your coat."

"I'm tired of going to the Bois all the time."

The two women exchanged glances. One of the main reasons for the daily park outings was to give Jeanne enough exercise so that after her supper and six o'clock bath she would be tired enough to go to sleep early. A diluted glass of red wine with her evening meal was another help. Without the fresh air and the wine, Rose once said she suspected that the over-active little girl would stay awake half the night, keeping up the rest of the household. Paulette heartily agreed. It was not easy being a mother for the first time at the age of thirty-seven, and now that she was forty her patience had grown shorter.

She and Ian had tried unsuccessfully for ten years to have a child, when at last the miracle happened. And yet, despite his joy and pride in fatherhood, it was shortly after Jeanne's first birthday that he started the affair with that model. Paulette even knew her name: Chauffé Nuwyler. One of the salesgirls at Balmain had been thoughtful enough to tell her. Ian had no idea that Paulette knew anything about the affair and like a typical, practical, upper-class Parisienne she certainly did not intend to confront him with her knowledge or, much worse, cause a scene. Most businessmen had mis-tresses, and like Paulette, most wives feigned ignorance. In the end, after Ian tired of his girlfriend, he would come back to her. Husbands usually did. The only problem was that as a result of her own affair with Rose, she wondered whether sex with Ian would ever be the same again.

They would make love tonight in the bed she shared with Ian. Once Jeanne had woken up after a bad dream and wandered into the connecting room, where Rose usually slept. Not finding her there, she began to cry and run toward her mother's room. Fortunately the lovemaking had ended minutes before. Rose was once more wearing her cotton robe, Paulette was wearing one of her many handmade nightgowns, and the two women were smoking a cigarette and sipping Armagnac. Paulette was in bed, Rose was seated on the chaise longue, as a distraught Jeanne came running in, tears flowing down her cheeks.

"*J'ai eu un mauvais rêve*," she cried, "*et Rose n'était pas dans la chambre à coucher!*"

"That's because Rose couldn't sleep, so she came in here to talk to me," Paulette said, taking the child under the quilts with her. "Would you like to sleep here with me for the rest of the night?"

"Oh yes, Mother. Can I?"

"Of course, darling. And you won't have any more bad dreams, I promise."

"Can Rose sleep here too?"

"I think that Rose would like to go back to her own room."

"Yes, I would," Rose said. "Thank you for the Armagnac, Mrs. Nicholson, and for our little chat. I feel much more relaxed now."

"What did you talk about?" Jeanne asked. "Did you talk about me? Or were you talking about Daddy?"

"We were talking about you, precious," Paulette said.

Jeanne cuddled up to her mother. "I like it when people talk about me. Can I go to sleep holding your ruby necklace? You know how much I love it."

Paulette's eighteen-carat pigeon blood ruby, suspended on a diamond chain, was Jeanne's favorite toy. It had been Ian's anniversary present to his wife the year before. The ruby cost the equivalent of two hundred thousand American dollars, the diamond chain twenty-five thousand dollars. To Jeanne it was just a pretty, sparkling plaything that she liked to hold.

Paulette now put on her leopard coat, getting ready to go to her three o'clock facial appointment. She hoped that tonight would be quiet and peaceful. Had Jeanne barged in ten minutes earlier that other time. . . . Paulette shuddered to think of the consequences, then promptly pushed the subject out of her mind. There was no use in being gloomy on such a lovely day, and what promised to be an even lovelier evening.

"Can I have an ice cream in the Bois?" Jeanne asked her nanny as they went out the door.

Paulette did not hear Rose's reply. She was looking at her leopard coat in the mirror and wondering whether she should have it remodeled for the winter. But remodeled to which style? It was something to think about, and she made a mental note to talk to the people at Revillon. Then, because she had a sense of humor, she laughed to herself and at herself. Half the world was blowing up, America was sending monkeys to the moon, the Algerian mess seemed worse than ever, and Queen Elizabeth would not let her sister marry a commoner.

And all I'm concerned about, Paulette thought, is whether or not to have a fur coat remodeled!

She sprayed herself generously with Jolie Madame and decided that all things considered she was a damned lucky woman.

18 &

At nine-thirty that evening Harry wandered into an elegant flowershop on the Champs-Elysées and asked for two dozen long-stemmed yellow roses. Alexis and he had spent the previous night at the *mueblé* making love and making Harry's accent sound as though he came from some provincial hole in the wall in France.

"You certainly won't be taken for a Parisian," Alexis said, "but neither will you be taken for an American. Not if you practice your new pronunciation."

The salesgirl at Les Fleurs Majestueuses looked at the poorly dressed young man, obviously wondering how anyone with such cheap clothing could afford more than a small bunch of wilted violets.

"They are for my mother in the hospital," he explained. "The doctors say there is no hope."

"*Mes regrets, Monsieur, mes regrets profonds.*"

"*Merci, Madame.*"

As she went to get the roses it occurred to Harry that in his black turtleneck sweater and black cotton pants (borrowed from Eva's boyfriend, Eduardo, without his knowledge), his cap and dark glasses, his frayed fleamarket raincoat, not even his own mother would have recognized him. He paid for the flowers in coins, rather than notes, as though he had been conscientiously saving them for just this sad occasion. Then he adjusted the sunglasses so that the salesgirl could not see his tear-stained eyes, and in a slightly choked voice thanked her for her compassion.

"*Pauvre jeune homme*," she murmured to herself as Harry shuffled out on a pair of scuffed, gum-soled shoes he had removed earlier from a clochard sleeping along the Seine.

It was drizzling and the air smelled dank and unpleasant. The salesgirl had wrapped the roses carefully so they would be protected from the weather, and Harry decided to walk up the Champs to the Nicholsons' apartment. Alexis had described the building on the Avenue Foch and the layout of the apartment itself in infinite detail. She once spent a night there when Paulette, Jeanne, and the nanny were visiting Paulette's parents in the south.

"There's a huge oak door at the entrance," Alexis said. "You press a bell on the left and the concierge will ring you in."

"Even if she doesn't know who I am?"

"Yes, because once you get in there's a small courtyard with her apartment on the right. She'll open a window to look at you. But she's a lazy old thing. All you have to do is say you're delivering flowers to Mrs. Nicholson and make sure that she sees them. That's why yellow is better than red at night. It's more visible."

"Then what?"

"She buzzes the Nicholsons' flat to indicate that somebody is coming up. But there's no kind of intercom, so she can't speak to Paulette. As far as the concierge is concerned, you're merely a delivery man from the florist. The sight of all those long-stemmed roses will impress her, believe me. Particularly if you say they're from Mr. Nicholson. She wouldn't dream of stopping you."

"Okay, that sounds logical enough. But why would Paulette let me in? Wouldn't she just take the flowers at the door, perhaps give me a tip, and say goodnight?"

Alexis grinned. "That, my darling brother, is for you to figure out. Now if you go there about ten o'clock, they'll long have finished dinner, the child will be asleep, and the only problem I can foresee is that Rose, the nanny, might still be awake. But as I said before, her bedroom is way at the opposite end of the apartment from Paulette's."

"When the concierge rings up to the Nicholsons, where is their buzzer located?"

"In the hallway."

"Then isn't it possible that Rose might hear it?"

"Anything is possible. But if you get there too late, when Rose is sure to be asleep, it would make the concierge suspicious. Rose is just a chance you'll have to take."

"It seems to me that I'm taking an awful lot of chances for reasons I don't even understand."

Alexis pulled him down to her and wrapped her arms around him. "Of course you understand. We're going to be the summer people, remember?"

"This certainly seems like an odd way of going about it," Harry said, as they began to make love again in the Marie Antoinette Room at the Résidence Françoise. . . .

Now, as he stood before the huge oak door and pushed the bell that the concierge would answer, he wondered whether he was truly out of his mind. Because he didn't feel nervous. That was the strange part. He felt almost inhumanly calm and detached. Perhaps it was partly because of his disguise. His black hair was hidden beneath the cap, his black eyes by the sunglasses which he wiped off now. The drizzle had turned into a windy rain and all he looked like was a poor, underpaid delivery chap out on a wet evening. In his cheap clothes and bedraggled appearance, anyone with half a conscience would feel sorry for him.

The bell responded and Harry walked through into the inner courtyard, which was pretty much as Alexis had described it. She had not said how dark it would be. The only light seemed to come from the concierge's *loge*, all the tenants in the building apparently having drawn their drapes against the damp night air. A woman's face peered out through a partially opened, rain-streaked window.

"*Qui est là?*"

Her voice was like gravel.

"I am delivering flowers for Mrs. Nicholson in apartment five," Harry said, carefully speaking in the rural accent he had practiced with Alexis the night before.

"*C'est un peu tard pour les livraisons.*"

"Yes, I know it's late but the flowers are from Mr. Nicholson."

He held up the long package with the top part of the florist's wrapping paper removed, so that the yellow roses could be seen by the concierge. He doubted that in his dark clothes she could see much of him, except in the most shadowy of outlines.

She made a shrugging motion. *"Très bien."*

Then she slammed the window shut as though the entire business was not worth her time or concern.

So far, so good, Harry thought, covering the roses with the wrapping paper. The elevator was similar to the one at the Résidence Françoise, a bit on the rickety side compared to its streamlined American counterpart, and for a second Harry felt like a bit actor in a French movie trying to remember his few paltry lines.

There was only one apartment on each floor and as he got out of the elevator and pushed the bell to number five, he automatically glanced at his watch. It was nine minutes to ten. The suspense as to who would open the door was killing him, but he was prepared for the possibility of its being Rose. He hoped to hell it wouldn't be, but he was fully prepared all the same.

Alexis had told him there was a peephole through which the occupant could look to see who was calling. Harry held the bunch of flowers in front of his face, waiting. No one responded to the ring, so he rang again. And still there was silence on the other side of the door. A terrible thought occurred to him: what if both women had retired early and could not hear the buzzer? He remembered Alexis saying that Paulette was an insomniac and took sleeping pills. With her husband away, she might have decided to make an early evening of it. As for Rose, there was always the chance that she was one of those women who slept like the proverbial dead.

What if nobody came to the door at all?

Resolutely Harry pushed the bell again, praying that he would not awaken the Nicholsons' little daughter. That would be just about all he needed. It was his first tremor of nerves since he started on this devilish mission, on this miserable rainy evening. Just as he was about to give up hope, he heard a woman's faint voice ask who was there. He repeated the same florist delivery line that he'd given to the concierge a few moments ago. There was a momentary hesitation before the door to apartment five finally opened.

The woman facing him was definitely Paulette, he knew that from Alexis' precise description (which she obtained partly from Ian, but mostly from Madame Thérèse, who once met Paulette socially and hated her for patronizing her competitor, Balmain). Petite, short curly brown hair, hazel eyes, a small cleft in the chin. It all fit except for one thing. This woman who was reputed to be the epitome of chic was now in a state of total disarray, her silk lapeled robe only loosely (hurriedly?) sashed, her hair tousled, no slippers on her feet, eyes wide with terror. But of what? Of whom? A nondescript delivery man? Harry suspected not. Something didn't add up.

Then he realized that she gave off a fragrance which pervaded even the scent of her heavy perfume. Harry knew what that fragrance was, he had encountered it all too often in his philandering life. S-E-X, in capital letters. Paulette had been making love with someone when he interrupted them in bed. That accounted for her disheveled appearance, her obvious fear, and yet afraid as she was she had been more afraid *not* to answer the bell. But why? Harry didn't know, yet it was apparent that fear—and fear alone—had caused her to come to the door without even bothering to put on her slippers. Her toenails were painted a pale shade of pink and carefully pedicured. Somewhere inside the apartment was a man, her lover whom she had invited over for the evening, knowing that her husband would be in Zurich.

A man! It was the one possibility that Harry had not been prepared for, and he tried to think fast. A small man? A large man? A *frightened* man who was lying now in a bed that belonged to another man. Frightened men could be dangerous. A man whom Ian was having followed? That could account for Paulette's fear, that she was being watched by someone Ian had hired. She must have panicked at the sound of the doorbell, afraid that if she didn't answer it her guilt would be more firmly established than if she did. Stupid of her, Harry thought, she should have pretended to be asleep.

Harry stepped in and handed the wet bouquet of roses to Paulette. "Your husband wanted to make sure that you received them this evening."

"My husband?" She sounded as though she didn't have a husband, or at least not one who was in the habit of sending her roses. "How very odd." Then she seemed to pull herself together. "But how very nice."

The door closed behind Harry. He could hear no sounds coming from anywhere in the large, dark apartment. It was strangely, eerily, still—which meant that he must work even faster than he had planned, but the job shouldn't be too difficult. It was a stroke of good luck that her silk robe had lapels on it.

"Well, thank you for the delivery," Paulette said. "It's a bad night and you look cold. You should go home. You're shivering."

"No, Mrs. Nicholson, it's you who are shivering."

At his words she drew back, the sash of her gown coming undone, revealing a slender, pale, well-cared-for body. A stream of something wet dribbled down one shapely leg. Semen. Or saliva. It was too dark to tell. And Alexis had known nothing about this adulterous affair, had suspected nothing. But then, why should she? Why should Nicholson admit to his mistress that he was being cuckolded by his wife? No, the man's pride would be too great for that, his sense of humiliation too vast. Too bad for me, thought Harry, that this unexpected event should have occurred.

"*Un pourboire*," she said, frantically looking around at nothing. "I have some francs in my purse."

She did not get two inches away when Harry struck the first painful blow, his right hand straight and rigid hitting her smack beneath the nose. Her eyes blinked wildly in loss of vision as involuntary tears flowed from them. Blood poured from her nostrils. The second blow, as soundless and rapid as the first, caught her below the chin, right on the thyroid cartilage, and Harry could have stopped there if he had the time. She would fall to the floor and in a few minutes edema would set in, causing her to choke to death.

But he did not have the time, there was a much faster way, a much more efficient and foolproof way. Grabbing the lapels of her robe, he pulled them as hard as he could in crisscross direction, and with his heavy knuckles turned inward he reached and pressed the two carotid arteries on either side of her slender neck. The action smothered her scream and stopped her heartbeat.

Paulette Nicholson was dead. Harry looked at his watch again. Less than three minutes had elapsed since he'd entered apartment five. He took her pulse just to make absolutely certain that his mission had been accomplished. There was no doubt about it. Dead as a doornail, with two dozen yellow roses strewn around her body, a fitting funeral homage from an anonymous admirer. And not a fingerprint on her.

"*Mon Dieu!*"

Harry spun around at the sound of the startled female cry. Out of the bedroom that Alexis had indicated was the master one came a naked woman, limping, screaming, hysterical.

"Who are you?" she shouted in French. "What have you done? What do you want?"

It was too late to bolt out the door now. The nanny had seen him. Even in his careful disguise he could not afford to take chances, not at this crucial point. He stood there looking through his dark sunglasses as Rose knelt down beside the dead body of her employer and began to sob.

"But who are you?" she kept repeating. "Why have you done this terrible thing? Were you hired by Mr. Nicholson? Or is it money, jewelry that you are after?"

Those were the last words Rose Pye would ever utter. She was somewhat harder to kill than Paulette because being naked made it impossible to use the relatively easy crisscross lapel method. However, since she was in a prone position to begin with, he did not have to use the first two karate blows or try to knock her down. What he did have to do was get her pinned in an intricate stranglehold position (that his friend at college had taught him very well), which incapacitated movement of either her arms or legs, and administer one lethal karate chop aimed directly at the carotid artery on the right side of her neck. The right side just happened to be more convenient because of the position she was in. No matter. One side was as effective as the other. Dead was dead.

Then Harry walked swiftly into the Nicholsons' bedroom and grabbed the first piece of jewelry he saw. It was Paulette's ruby pendant which Jeanne had been playing with only a few hours earlier. Stuffing the pendant in the pocket of his flea-market raincoat, Harry headed for the door leading out of the apartment, stepping carefully around the lifeless bodies of the two women who lay sprawled on the Persian carpet only inches apart.

As he put on his gloves and turned the knob to let himself out, a small figure in a dainty nightdress emerged from a room far down the long hallway. Jeanne rubbed her eyes as though she had just awakened from a terrible nightmare and could not distinguish dream from reality. By the time she began to scream at the top of her lungs, Harry was out the building and strolling down Avenue Foch, whistling to himself.

19 ⌒

"Paulette and the nanny?" I said. "I can't believe it. What a shock that must have been for you."

"Shock isn't the word for it," Harry said. "I thought Paulette had some guy back there in the sack, which was scary enough, but then to see this naked woman come limping out of the bedroom, to realize who she was, what they'd been doing together . . . well, I was totally unprepared. And you never had a clue?"

"Never."

We were in my bedroom and Harry was changing from Eduardo's clothes to the suit he had left with me before going to Avenue Foch. I still couldn't believe that he had done it, killed Paulette, and all for my sake (the killing of Rose was strictly incidental and didn't count). It was the most flattering thing I could conceive of: that someone would love you so much he'd actually go out and kill for you, despite the immense personal dangers such an act entailed for himself. Although as I had reassured Harry the night before, he'd be the last person in the world the police would ever suspect. That is, unless he didn't get out of my flat pretty soon.

I don't know what perversity made me talk Harry into wearing Eduardo's sweater and trousers when he killed Paulette. It was so risky. Maybe that's what appealed to me, to Harry, also. We both love risks, dares, the high-wire act.

"It's twenty to midnight," I said to Harry. "You'd better hurry. And don't forget to use the back stairs going down."

Fortunately the building I lived in wasn't fashionable enough to afford a concierge, but the last thing in the world either of us wanted was for Harry to bump into one of the other tenants. That's why he had used the back stairs when he'd come over earlier to pick up Eduardo's clothes and leave his own clothes with me.

"What are you going to do with the rest of this stuff?" he asked, indicating the cap, raincoat, shoes, and sunglasses.

"Don't worry. You've done your part. I'll do mine. You just go back to the Lancaster and whatever happens don't phone me. Not here, not at work. You do understand how important that is, don't you? That we have no further contact with each other for the time being?"

Even though I did love Harry as I would never love another man, it still did not stop me from anticipating my future life as Mrs. Ian Nicholson. It was as though one thing had nothing to do with the other, odd as that may sound.

Harry took me gently by the shoulders. "I want to make love to you so badly—right now! But we have to be practical, don't we?"

"Yes, darling, we do."

Then we kissed a long, desperate, unpractical kiss that burned itself into our very souls, branding us for each other forever. Because I knew now, as I had known when I was twelve years old, that with Harry and me it would be forever no matter how many separations there were, no matter how long those separations lasted. We didn't want to be separated now, but we didn't have a choice. Our lives weren't ready for the final coming together, not yet, and things like that— timing, rhythm, whatever you call them—can't be pushed or rushed. It's as though they have a mind of their own and if you don't swim with the tide, well, you drown. That's what it amounts to. I knew it and Harry knew it, and the terrific, the *ecstatic* part was that we didn't have to talk about it, we both knew we knew.

Because when you belong to someone the way Harry and I belong to each other, it's not necessary to discuss certain matters, least of all the most important ones. Those are the ones you know in your heart. And I feel sorry for people (probably 95 percent of the world, if not more) who will never experience the sheer intensity of what Harry and I have. It's beyond love, in a way. It's mystical and yet it's awfully real. Maybe it's supernatural, the kind of total identification that Harry and I share. And maybe it can only happen if you've known each other right from birth.

"Okay, I'm off," Harry said, combing his hair back into the shape of its obviously expensive cut. "Take care of yourself, Alexis. I hope things work out as you want them to."

"Do you mean with Ian?"

"Yes."

"I hope they work out for you, too. With Ian."

"He certainly seems to be the central character in both our lives, doesn't he?"

"Only at the moment," I reminded him. "We're the central characters."

Harry appraised me in my rust-colored peignoir, my face clean of makeup, my curly red hair held back by the sash of the peignoir.

"You'll make a beautiful bride," he said.

"And you'll make three highly successful movies."

"Do you think Ian will agree to finance my project?"

"Yes, I know he will. I wonder when we'll meet again," I said.

Harry grinned, all forgiven. "And *where?*"

Then he was out the door and I was alone with the remains of his murderer's disguise. The first thing I did was slip on my antelope gloves and carefully fold Eduardo's sweater and pants and put them back in Eva's bureau drawer where she always kept them. The pants were still wet from the rain but they'd be dry by morning, and besides neither Eva nor Eduardo would have cause to suspect that they had ever left our flat.

Then I took a large pair of kitchen shears and began to cut up Harry's cap, raincoat, gloves, and shoes into very small pieces. The shoes were so old and worn that except for the heels they weren't much harder to cut than the other stuff. I put all the pieces into a plain brown paper bag, threw the sunglasses in with them, and hid the bag on the floor of my wardrobe closet behind the yards of long silks and chiffons and taffetas and velvets that represented my free collection of Thérèse originals. Tomorrow I would dispose of the bag.

The next morning I put the bag inside one of Madame Thérèse's carrier bags. Eva was too hung over to work. I set off alone for the metro station fifteen minutes earlier than usual. Instead of getting off at my regular stop, I waited until the train had gone two stops farther and then I hopped out along with the rest of Paris on its way to work, scurrying, hurrying, half-asleep people who would not come to life for at least another hour. And amidst the bored, sightless mob I removed the brown paper bag and dropped it in the nearest ashcan at the corner of some nondescript street.

"I still can't believe they're dead." I was playing my act to the hilt with Madame pretending to have just heard about the murders on the news.

"You'll have to wait a decent amount of time so as not to be condemned by our pious, hypocritical society, and then, Chauffé, you will legally become Mrs. Ian Nicholson. And I'll have to find myself another model. Oh well, *c'est la guerre*. Where do you think you'll live? Do you think you'll stay on in Paris?"

I knew that Ian would never want to remain in Paris after this, and I loved it so, this beautiful, charming, romantic city. He would probably want to return to London.

The day passed uneventfully. I telephoned Eva at noon as I had promised, and she sounded as zonked out as when I'd left her that morning.

"Ian's wife and the nanny have been murdered," I told her. "Can you believe it?"

But even that startling piece of information failed to break through the barriers of her hangover. "That's terrible," was all she said on the subject. "Could you please pick up some aspirin when you come home this evening? My head is killing me."

"Sure."

I bought a large bottle of aspirin on my way back to the flat, and I also bought a copy of the evening newspaper. The double murder had made the front page, complete with a large photograph of a bewildered, sobbing Jeanne and two small inset photos of Paulette and Rose. DEUX FEMMES BRUTALEMENT ASSASSINÉES! screamed the *Paris-Soir* headline, going on to say that the motive for the killings was still undetermined and that although the police had not ruled out robbery, neither had they ruled out the possibility of it being a crime of passion.

Mr. Ian P. Nicholson, director of the famous merchant bank Nicholson et Cie., cut short a business trip to Zurich, said *Paris-Soir*, and flew back to Paris when informed of the tragic news earlier in the day. He was working closely with the Police Judiciaire to try to provide them with clues as to why anyone would want to kill his lovely socialite wife and his daughter's English governess.

There was no hint in the newspaper that the two women were engaged in a lesbian act just before the killer struck. And yet, according to Madame, it was mentioned on the radio. Odd. Neither of the victims had been sexually molested or raped by the killer, who posed as a florist delivery boy, the paper emphasized, and there were no fingerprints anywhere. "A very professional job," concluded the paper's reporter, almost in homage to Harry's handiwork. "A very baffling case."

"Ian telephoned a few minutes ago," Eva said, as I came

into her bedroom. "He said he'd ring you back within the hour."

"How did he sound?"

"Very upset, but trying to control it. The English, you know. And very eager to talk to you."

"He must be in a state of shock," I said, as the telephone in the salon began to ring. "Excuse me, it's probably Ian."

It was.

"Chauffé, darling . . ." His voice was all knotted up, constricted. "It's the most incredible nightmare. I've been with the police half the day and I still can't believe it. Who would want to do such a ghastly thing?"

Why was everyone asking me? "It's obviously the work of a maniac."

"That goes without saying."

"I can't tell you how sorry I am, Ian. Where are you calling from?"

"Home, darling."

"Don't you think you should be more careful on the telephone? Under the circumstances?"

"What do you mean? I certainly didn't kill them. What do I have to be careful about? Oh, my God." He was quietly weeping. "Do you know that the bugger stole a very expensive ruby pendant of Paulette's? But the police don't think that robbery was his real motive. They think it was just a smoke-screen."

"For what?"

"Jealousy. A jealous lover."

"Whose lover?"

"Either my wife's or Rose's."

"But I don't understand. Even if one of them did have a lover, what would he have been jealous about?"

"Oh, my God," Ian said again. "It's worse than you can imagine. Paulette and Rose were having an affair, and this madman found out about it and went berserk. At least that's the cops' theory so far. That's why they're not buying the robbery motive."

"Paulette and Rose? But the newspapers didn't say anything about it—at least *Paris-Soir* didn't."

"I know. The press is cooperating with the police for the time being, to leave out the homosexual angle. The police feel it will make their job easier if the killer thinks they're just looking for a jewel thief. I didn't know about the affair myself."

I hesitated to tell him about the radio broadcast Madame had heard that morning. He was upset enough at it was.

"How is Jeanne?" I asked finally.

"The doctor gave her a mild tranquilizer, and I've hired private nurses around the clock. Jeanne's still in shock. She woke up just as the bugger was leaving the flat. Thank God she didn't wake up before then. He might have killed her too."

"I really don't think we should talk much more on the telephone, Ian. For your sake."

There was a long silence. I didn't know whether he was crying or merely sitting there in his lonely apartment, a man whose life had collapsed around him overnight, a desperate man, an angry man, an agonized man, a man who in his grief had nobody to turn to right now but me.

"I want to see you, Chauffé."

"I want to see you, too, but I think it would be wiser if we waited a little while. The police are bound to have you as a suspect on their list. For all you know, they've tapped your phone."

"I don't give a damn. I'm innocent and I want to see you." He hesitated. "I love you, Chauffé. I never realized how much until this very minute."

"I love you, too."

We made plans to meet for dinner at my place the following evening. It would be the first meal I had ever cooked for my future husband, and I wondered what to make.

20 ❧

After I hung up, I decided to make something to eat for Eva and me. It would have to be an omelet as we were low on groceries. But for a change I had no appetite. Usually I'd be starving at this time of day, now my stomach felt queasy. I'd been thinking a lot about Harry, what he was doing, how he was feeling now that it was all over. Did he have any regrets? I didn't.

Eva was not very hungry either. I mixed two tall Campari

and sodas and brought one into her bedroom. She was still reading the newspaper, but had progressed to page seven.

"Hair of the dog," I said. "Drink it down, and no back talk. It will give you an appetite."

It was when she turned the page that I saw the small caption near the bottom: ENGLISH ACTRESS INJURED ON MOVIE SET. Staring back at me was a picture of Harry's wife, Sarah Ames, whose face I remembered from a couple of movies she'd made for Rank.

"Give me that."

To Eva's amazement, I snatched the paper out of her hand. According to *Paris-Soir's* news service, Sarah Ames had been violently thrown down a hill by her horse during the last scene of the movie she was starring in, "A Pretty Kettle of Fish." She was rushed to Cedars of Lebanon Hospital, where a team of specialists diagnosed a severe spinal injury and remained doubtful whether Miss Ames would ever walk again. Miss Ames' director could not account for the bizarre accident. He was quoted as saying that the horse, the same one Miss Ames had ridden throughout the making of the film, had been specifically trained for camera work and that Miss Ames herself was an experienced equestrienne. The article ended by stating that she was married to her American manager, Harry Maringo, currently in Paris on business.

"What is it?" Eva asked, her eyes intently upon me. "You've turned white."

I mumbled something about Ian being involved in an important financial transaction that concerned Sarah Ames, and how this would be the end of it.

"Poor Ian," I added. "It's as though fate is conspiring against him. He's getting it from all sides, and all in one day."

"You really do love him, don't you?" Eva asked, moved by my compassion.

Little did she know that it was Harry for whom I was holding back my tears, not Ian. He wanted so badly to produce those three movies starring his wife, now he had nothing. I wondered what he would do after he returned to California.

"Of course I love him. Why do you think I've been with him the last two years? It's not much fun having an affair with a married man."

"Perhaps I've misjudged you," Eva said. "You're not as hard or self-centered as I always imagined. Please forgive me."

"There's nothing to forgive."

Then I went into the kitchen to start whisking eggs for our *omelette aux fines herbes*. But I could not whisk away my concern for Harry and his future. It seemed so very bleak. I felt very sorry for him. So did Ian, as it turned out.

"He was an enterprising chap," Ian said the next evening over the *blanquette de veau* I had made for dinner. "It's a bloody shame his wife's career is finished. I had decided to lend him the money he wanted. I thought it would be an exciting venture, something out of the ordinary for stodgy old me."

"You're not stodgy, darling."

"The police don't think so either. They've been having me followed since yesterday. One of their plainclothesmen is across the street right now."

My heart started to beat faster. "I knew we should have waited awhile, I told you that, Ian. I knew it wasn't safe for us to meet so quickly."

"Safe? What can they prove? That because of you I hired someone to kill my wife and my daughter's nanny? Ridiculous."

"Then why are they having you followed?"

"I suppose they have to check out all possibilities, however remote. That's their job."

"So they haven't made any progress on the case?"

Ian put down his fork and wiped his mouth. "No, darling, and I doubt that they ever will. They don't even have a physical description to go on, other than the killer's height and the fact that he spoke French with a provincial accent. That's all the salesgirl at the florist's could tell the police, and she was the only person who really saw him. All the concierge saw was a bunch of yellow roses and a man standing in the shadows."

Within less than twenty-four hours of the crime, the newspapers had begun to refer to it as "The Yellow Rose Murders."

"When is the funeral?" I asked.

"Tomorrow."

I shivered. "It's all too horrid."

"Try not to think about it. And we won't talk about it anymore. In fact, let's never talk about it again for the rest of our lives."

The whistling of the kettle interrupted our conversation. I went into the kitchen and poured boiling water into the coffeemaker, hoping that the resultant brew would be strong enough for Ian's taste. We were having an orange tart for dessert. I should say, Ian was having it. Murder or not, I was still watching my waistline.

Part 3

St. Moritz—1974

21 &

My marriage to Ian is a quiet disaster.

The only reason it's quiet is because Ian is English and he doesn't like scenes, outspoken conflicts, hand-to-hand, mouth-to-mouth combat. He considers those too vulgar. Instead, his methods consist of subterfuge and hypocrisy, mean verbal darts, and the most insidious kind of emotional blackmail.

"Last month's statement from Harrods was, shall we say, a bit excessive? I notice you seem to have developed a rather strong attachment to a certain department of theirs. The Designer Room. Isn't that what it's called, darling?"

As though he didn't know.

"I didn't realize that my fondness for the Designer Room had gotten out of hand," I said, sipping decaffeinated coffee. "I'm sorry. I'll be more careful in the future."

Knowing Ian, I would not put it past him to cut off all my charge accounts without a moment's warning. "To teach you a lesson," is how he would phrase it, smug in his moneyed omnipotence.

"Please try to remember," he now sighed, "that despite what you may imagine, I do not—*repeat do not*—possess an un-limited supply of wealth, Alexis."

He stopped calling me Chauffé as soon as we were married and had moved to London. I think that the name, being French, was too closely associated in his mind with the murder of Paulette and Rose, and everything he wanted to forget about Paris. It had also been my *demimondaine* name before I was elevated to the respectable social status of being Mrs. Ian Philip Nicholson.

"I said I would be more careful in the future," I reminded him.

"Thank you."

We were having breakfast on our balcony overlooking the lake (now frozen), at the extravagant Engadine Hotel in St. Moritz. Ian insists that I join him for breakfast promptly every morning, despite the fact that I am half-asleep, irritable, and cannot stand the smell of kippers, all of which he is well aware of. My old dreams of late, leisurely breakfasts in bed—when I was a model in Paris—have been squashed by the tyrant Ian has become.

When I was his mistress he treated me with loving care, undoubtedly because he was afraid of losing me to another man. Now that I am his wife, his behavior has changed into a kind of feudal possession which I've discovered is not uncommon among upper-class Englishmen of Ian's generation.

Do this, don't do that, go here, don't go there, behave the way I tell you, remember who's boss. . . .

Still, I put up with his insufferable commands because we live very very well and I wouldn't know what to do with myself if he should decide to trade me in for a younger woman. The fact that I dislike my husband, at times despise him, is not as important as my frantic financial dependence upon him.

Money money money.

And yet it wasn't just his money that had intrigued me in Paris. I genuinely cared for Ian then, loved him as much as I'm capable of loving any man except Harry. . . .

". . . snow conditions appear to be superb," I heard Ian say, with genuine enthusiasm in his voice.

Snow conditions, merchant banking, and sex chains (plus a few leather and rubber aids). Those are the only things that can make that bastard I married become enthusiastic. Yet sexually, his enthusiasm is more begrudging, resentful. Ian cannot forgive me for being one of the few women who is able to drive him out of his erotic mind. He hates the hold I have over him in bed, but he needs it as badly as he needs his smelly kippers in the morning.

However, I decided not to let my husband get me down, not on a beautiful, sunny, clear winter day like this, a perfect day for skiing. Actually, Ian was right about the snow conditions.

To a nonskier, snow is either white slush which he can happily live without for the rest of his life or else it's pristine, pure, and poetry-making. But to skiers on a time-limited, money-extravagant, Christmas holiday, as Ian, Jeanne, and I were, powder snow is what dreams are made of. And that's exactly what we have today in glamorous, jet-set, overpriced, scenically perfect, bitchily-dynamic, super-snobbish St. Moritz, where the Engadine Hotel leads all its alpine rivals as regal pacesetter.

"Do you want to hear an interesting definition of St. Moritz?" I asked my husband and stepdaughter, neither of whom appeared terribly curious. "Somebody described it as the international playground of the aristocracy of Europe and the moneytocracy of America."

"Not badly put," Ian said, looking up from his kippers and eggs, "except that it conveniently omits England's role in making St. Moritz what it is today."

"What does England have to do with it, Daddy?" Jeanne asked.

"Just that if it hadn't been for some misguided but stubborn English lord, we might not be sitting here right now, at least not under these opulent conditions. His name escapes me, but back in 1865 he made a famous bet with Johannes Badrutt, the hotelier, that London was warmer in the winter than St. Moritz. Badrutt, whose heirs now own the Palace Hotel, took him up on the bet and won. Hence, winter tourism began before the end of the nineteenth century, and the English—I hasten to add—were the first to convert that to their own invention: ski holidays. Before the bet was made, people only came here during the summertime."

Jeanne seemed singularly unimpressed, almost bored (who could blame her?), as though she had more pressing matters on her mind. And I suspected I knew what they were. Her device of appearing bored whenever her father tried to impress her with his knowledge frequently worked on Ian, who sought his daughter's approval, her love, much more than he sought mine, which he mistakenly took for granted. Still he forced himself, despite himself, to be strict with Jeanne when the occasion demanded it.

"What St. Moritz really is," Jeanne said, buttering another croissant with honey, "is just a load of crumbs held together by their dough."

I laughed, Ian frowned, and Jeanne shoved the dough into her small, eighteen-year-old mouth, unaware of the pun. Yes, my stepdaughter is a very grown-up, headstrong girl, who according to Ian resembles her late mother to an almost uncanny degree. Having never met Paulette, I wouldn't know. All I can remember is the vague description I received from Ian and the much more detailed one from Madame Thérèse: petite, short curly brown hair, small-boned, a dimple in the chin. What they both had omitted was the incredible smile, which (assuming Paulette possessed it, too) transformed a merely pretty girl into a startlingly dazzling one. And knowing this, Jeanne was selfish with her smiles, she doled them out at careful strategic intervals.

Like right now, a few minutes after her sarcastic denigration of this Swiss *Wunderkind*, she was trying to sweet-talk her father into letting her go to one of the smaller hotels after dinner, the Alpina, rather than join us at the plush Prince Regent's Club . . . the Engadine Hotel's gift to countesses and shahs, movie stars and trillionaires, oil sheiks, playboys and potentates, dukes and duchesses, elegant ex-call girls from Berlin who had become famous industrialists' wives, la crème de la crème of international society, as well as lesser figures who didn't mind shelling out fifty dollars for a bottle of scotch to rub shoulders on the gleaming, ebony dance floor with people they had only seen photos of in magazines like *Paris Match*, *Vogue*, *Harper's & Queen*, and *Die Elegante Frau*.

"Why do you dislike the Prince Regent's Club?" Ian asked his daughter.

"I don't dislike it. I mean, it's okay for you and Alexis, but you're older. I'd rather be with people closer to my own age. Is that so unusual, Daddy?"

Smile. Dazzle, dazzle.

Ian finished his last kipper which, thanks to the crisp mountain air, did not smell as bad as within the confines of our dining room in London.

"What you mean," he said, "is that you'd rather be with that phony Scottish rock singer whose group is at the Alpina."

"Tom's not a phony and neither is his group," Jeanne protested. "They've played successful concerts all over Europe and England for several years now. Just before coming to St. Moritz for Christmas they played at Manchester's Belle Vue and the Bournemouth Winter Gardens—"

She stopped, realizing that her father and I were staring at her with surprise.

"And where did you unearth this interesting information?" Ian asked. "I was under the impression you had only met Tom that one time, when Alexis and I were with you. Or have you managed to sneak off and see him behind my back, and despite my distinct wishes?"

"No, Daddy, I am not a sneak and there's no reason to sound so medieval. The reason I know the cities they've played in is because I happened to run into the drummer yesterday afternoon, when I went ice skating."

We'd been in St. Moritz one week to the day now, and Jeanne had made the acquaintance of her hero that very first evening. Ian agreed to go to the Alpina because he wanted to please his only child. I'd gone to please Ian. The situation rather amused me although I tried not to show it. Jeanne's sudden infatuation . . . Ian's refusal to budge an inch . . . my own lack of concern about either of them. To me, Tom McKillup was just another nice-looking, semitalented young man, trying to make it in a very competitive business. That was all. Little could I have guessed the enormous importance he was to play in all our lives within a very short space of time.

Jeanne shifted in her chair and addressed her father. "I don't understand how you can be so unfair, so prejudiced. You've only met Tom once, for three seconds. How can you pass such harsh judgment?"

"And you only met him for a few seconds longer than I did. How can you be so enamoured of someone you know nothing about?"

"I just thought he was . . . nice, talented, sincere. And yesterday the drummer filled me in a little about the group. He's from Edinburgh, too. They all are, Daddy. That's why the group is called Castle Rock. Castle Rock is where Edinburgh originally started, it's supposed to be an extinct volcano now. The drummer said it's very high up, hundreds of feet above sea level, and you can see really beautiful views from it."

Ian meticulously wiped his lips, as I had seen him do nearly every morning for the past fifteen years. Except that today he used one of the Engadine Hotel's napkins, which had the same loosely woven, silvery initials on it as the bed linens and towels: EH. The ingenuity of the weaving was that it gave the illusion of a high degree of glasslike brilliance, very similar to that of the long, frozen lake nestled down below in the Engadine valley, in southeastern Switzerland.

"Did the drummer, by any chance, tell you about Tom's background?" Ian asked. "For instance. What is his father's line of work?"

Jeanne put her cup of Ovomaltine down so hard on its saucer that it shook. "Honestly, Daddy, is that all you ever think of? Money? Position?"

"I consider it a perfectly reasonable, perfectly acceptable question under the circumstances."

"*What* circumstances?"

"That at the age of twenty-one, you will be a very rich young lady, by inheritance. *Those* circumstances."

Jeanne was trapped and she realized it, but there was no way of wiggling out of this one except to tell a lie. Knowing Ian and his access to private investigative sources, she was far too smart to try and deceive him.

"Very well." She sighed theatrically, as though it were quite hopeless, nobody understood her, least of all her own father. But her attractive suntan seemed to whiten a few shades as she replied: "Tom's dad owns a pub. Okay? Now are you satisfied?"

"I might have known," Ian said.

His own tan was a light bronze mask that hid many facial lines, making him appear much younger than his fifty-nine years. Even at that age my husband is still a handsome, imposing man. I've noticed women looking at him on the slopes, on the ice skating rink, in the swimming pool, in the lounge at tea time, in the dining room, on the dance floor.

Of course at the Engadine everybody looks at everybody else, first to see if they're super rich, or celebrities of some kind, or just plain infamous-in, for whatever reason. But even though they cannot place Ian in any of these convenient categories, their glances often continue to linger moments after the identification process has failed them. They seem to feel he is someone important. So does Ian.

And although I find him personally repugnant, I have to admit that he is much more striking looking than in his younger days. His blondish-gray hair and brilliant blue eyes, his erect bearing, his insufferable self-confidence only serve to emphasize the insolent demeanor that so many women consider irresistible. Today would be no exception, I could see that.

Ian looked his very best in a sapphire blue, polo-necked cashmere sweater, navy blue, anti-glis, expertly fitted Bogner trousers, his three-toned blue anorak slung over a chair waiting to be put on and zipped up as soon as breakfast was finished and the slopes beckoned. Once on his way he'd wear Testa's woolen visored cap that had seen him through many other St. Moritz ski seasons and smartly showed it.

"They may not be the Bay City Rollers or The Who," Jeanne was saying to her father, "but they're not exactly poverty-stricken either. Why in Manchester alone, Tom earned more than two thousand dollars in one week."

"Money per se is not the issue," Ian replied. "Especially money that's determined by the public's notoriously fickle nature when it comes to rock groups. So kindly refrain from quoting any more vulgar figures to me."

Jeanne who had a one-hundred-dollar-a-day room, down the corridor from our own sumptuous five-hundred-dollar-a-day suite, quickly replied:

"I know what you're going to say, Daddy. Breeding. Social status. Good schools. Ancestors. All that jazz. That's why you disapprove of Tom. Because he's not upper class, not *our* class."

"Precisely." Ian honored her with one of his rare smiles. "Now if you're quite finished, let's take the hotel's helicopter to Corviglia. Then we can go by cable car to Piz Nair and ski down the East side to Marguns."

"If you want to know the truth, I prefer Gstaad. So does David Niven," Jeanne said, maliciously. "It's homier than St. Moritz."

Ian's patience was starting to wear out. "You don't seem to realize that most girls your age would give away a year of their lives to spend a Christmas holiday like this. Besides, the slopes at Gstaad can't begin to compare with what we have here. So kindly stop being so damned chauvinistic merely because you go to school there, and let's get on with it."

"*Went* to school there," Jeanne corrected him. "I've graduated, remember?"

Ian said something in reply but I was no longer listening to them, I had tuned them both out. I didn't want to be reminded of Jeanne's exclusive boarding school is Gstaad, since ironically it was the same school my mother had insisted I be sent to when I was only twelve. Jeanne and I have eaten the same delicious cream pastries at the same sidewalk cafes, learned to ski down the same *pistes*, learned to finally feel at home amidst the cuckoo clock charm of Gstaad's woodsy chalets. The only thing Jeanne had wisely *not* done was to marry her ski instructor, who, she recently told me, was an Austrian despot but a master of the exhilarating, daredevilish *Schuss*.

"You should see him *zoom* down those slopes," was Jeanne's admiring comment on her instructor. "The son-of-a-bitch is so good he can even keep his legs glued together and still look like he's going ninety miles an hour."

I had told Ian earlier that I would not be skiing with them this morning, perhaps I'd join them this afternoon, I wasn't sure, and to my surprise he accepted my statement without the fuss I thought he would make. Perhaps he was mistaken enough to imagine that although I was an expert skier, the sport still held bad associations for me—even after all these years—as a result of my disastrous marriage to Herr Nuwyler. If that was what Ian chose to believe, it was fine with me, I didn't care. But my real reason for dropping out today had nothing to do with my first husband. No. It had to do with my first (and only) love, Harry.

"From Marguns, we'll ski to Trais Fluors," Ian said to Jeanne. "Then to Marguns again."

Things were going exactly as I hoped they would.

"What do we do at Marguns?" Jeanne asked listlessly.

"Take the lift up to Corviglia and have lunch at the club."

"Okay, Daddy."

"Right. Put on your anorak, get your equipment, and let's be off. Time is running out. It's going to take us at least two hours to get to Piz Nair."

Piz Nair was the highest mountain you could ski from on the side facing south, just under ten thousand feet. But both my husband and stepdaughter were excellent skiers, so I wasn't the least bit worried about them, merely relieved that they would be miles away from where Harry and I would be.

22 ◠

I had received a strange postcard from him three months earlier. Although it was not the first communication Harry and I had had since Paris, it was definitely the most serious and unusual; surely the most provocative.

In the early sixties I had met Harry in New York for a stolen week of intimacy and lovemaking. That week sticks out vividly in my mind because it was such a precious, leisurely, continuous stretch of time, a time for filling each other in on what had happened to our lives.

"Sarah is paralyzed from the waist down and always will be," Harry had said. "Also, her personality has changed. She's grown hard, nasty, cheap. She controls the pursestrings. I've got a small checking account, running-around money, that's all. She seems to feel that that gives her the privilege of treating me like a well-paid male nurse. And I guess it does. She's insufferable."

"We're both in the same boat. We're both living off other people's money, people we don't love, can't even stand most of the time. We've sacrificed everything for financial security, but the trouble is we can't actually get our hands on the money. It's doled out to us like our allowance when we were children."

"I thought that the life Ian could offer you was what you wanted," Harry said.

"So did I, at the time. But it hasn't worked out that way. Don't you understand what I'm saying? I'm miserable."

"Why don't you leave him?"

"For the same reason you don't leave Sarah. I've gotten used to an easy life. I'm trapped. Where would I go? What would I do? Get a job as a model again? I'm too old, too spoiled."

Harry gazed at me. "Your hair isn't red anymore, or curly."

It was almost as though he wished it were, or that I still had fake green eyes, anything to dispel the undeniable fact that with my natural black hair we looked more alike than ever, that I was the sister he had always loved, once killed for, could not forget.

"What are you doing in New York?" I asked him.

"Writing a novel."

"A novel?"

He laughed. "Yes, it's about Hollywood, the inside story. I'm trying to make some damned money, trying to become financially independent, trying to break away from Sarah. . . ."

But he hadn't broken away; the novel had been a flop.

After that week in Manhattan, Harry and I continued to meet briefly, nervously, fleetingly, both of us afraid of being found out by Sarah and/or Ian. We never spent more than a few hours together, and every time we parted it was with a renewed sense of pain and regret . . . regret that we had to leave each other once again, pain because we knew it would be another year before we'd be able to snatch a few cherished hours out of our highly structured lives, away from our possessive marriage partners.

Our meetings, sketchy and dangerous as they were, always took place in London hotel rooms. There was no way I could justify another foreign trip without arousing Ian's suspicions, and since Sarah had started to visit her father at his Surrey estate every spring, Harry managed to zip down to London by telling her that he had an appointment with his tailor. Of course this meant he actually had to find a tailor and spend some of "our" time on fittings to eventually produce a new suit, hacking jacket, whatever.

Even though it was easier for me to get away (I was out for the afternoon, "shopping"), I grew to hate the anonymous hotel rooms (we never went back to the same one twice), the blank-faced hotel clerks, the hurried lovemaking, the rush to get dressed, get out, go our separate ways. And yet, if it hadn't been for these meetings, as agonizing and frustrating as they were, I don't think I could have gone on with my marriage. Harry said the same thing about his marriage the last time I saw him, each of us agreeing that the passing years only made our lengthy separations that much harder to bear.

"It's brutal, being away from you," Harry had said, choking down a fast whiskey from room service. "It makes me hate Sarah twice as much. It makes me crazy. But if I didn't see you even once a year, I think I'd crack up altogether."

We were in a small hotel in Chelsea then. I remember that it had blue and white floral wallpaper, and that it was raining.

"What are we going to do?" I asked, realizing that I invariably asked the same question, and that Harry invariably replied with the same terrible answer—in one form or another.

"I don't know, but I'll think of something. We can't go on like this. It's not human."

This past spring, Harry did not send the usual note informing me of his arrival date in England. Ordinarily that would have been his first note. The second would specify the day we could meet, the time, the name of the hotel, and the name under which he was checking in. But neither note arrived.

I went to the "poste restante" counter at the main post office in Trafalgar Square several times a week, from the end of March to the end of May, only to be told there was nothing for me. Finally one day just as I was about to give up hope, the clerk handed me a letter from New York. It was from Harry, of course, and it was brief. All it said was that he and Sarah would not be coming to England that spring and he would keep in touch.

I was confused, bewildered. Keep in touch? *When? How?*

I cursed Harry for not being more explicit in his letter as to how long I would have to wait before hearing from him again. I cursed myself for never having broken the love-bond with my brother. I cursed Ian and Sarah for keeping us apart. I cursed the world for being unfair.

So I waited . . . and waited . . . and then one morning this past September when I wasn't thinking about Harry at all, a note arrived at home. Ian had left for the office and my daily cleaning woman was late. Harry's note was so brief that I still knew it by heart:

> DARLING:
> Imperative that you and Ian be in St. Moritz over Xmas. Will meet you *alone* on the slope at Sala-strains, near the ski school, on Saturday, December 22nd, at 11 A.M.
>
>   Love
>   HARRY

I now looked at my absurdly expensive, jeweled Grima watch. It was a few minutes before nine, which meant that I had better get moving . . . bathe and change into my orange salopettes and orange anorak quilted in black and white. With them I would wear my favorite black cashmere polo.

At the age of forty-one women become nervous. Fifty is beckoning with all the loss of youth that ominous age implies. The odd part is that I could not conceive of turning fifty, it seemed too absurd, too cruel. In my mind's eye I would always be a young girl in her twenties. But I was not a young girl any longer, Jeanne was a young girl and I hated her for it. She had gotten her period yesterday, she informed Ian and me, and said she felt lousy, cramps and all that.

I would never feel lousy that way again, because even unbeknownst to Ian I have not menstruated for a year now. Yes, the much dreaded change of life has begun. Perhaps if Ian and I had had children I would not care so much, I might even be relieved to get rid of the awful thing, month after month. But we haven't had children. A gynecologist I saw several years ago believes it's because of the abortion I had after I returned from New York City, impregnated by Harry.

"It was badly bungled," the gynecologist said, upon examining me. "If you want children as you claim you do, why didn't you go through with the pregnancy? Particularly since abortions were illegal in England in 1963. Unless you left the country, you were probably operated on by a disqualified doctor."

"Yes, I was."

The gynecologist shook his head, mystified.

How could I tell him that I was *dying* to have the baby, but it would have been my brother's? How could I explain that even though I never considered my relationship with Harry unnatural (it was my relationship with Ian that seemed unnatural), I still was unable to ignore the old taboo against incest and what it might ultimately lead to: a physically or mentally defective child?

I shuddered at the mere thought. What I wanted was a beautiful baby of Harry's, a living, breathing reminder to me of how much Harry and I loved each other. But it was too much of a chance to take. Genetically, the cards were stacked against me.

Ian, naturally, does not know about the abortion any more than he knows about my menopausal condition. I don't want to tell him that I'm no longer fertile, I'm ashamed of the fact. I don't know why I'm ashamed, but I am. I wonder if I'll tell Harry. I've always told Harry everything, and he's done the same. We don't keep secrets from each other, we never have, and yet I'm afraid to tell him that I can no longer bear children. Maybe I'm afraid that he'll no longer love me or find me attractive. Anyhow, it's not imperative that I tell him right away.

And as I got up to draw a bath in our eight-foot, sea green marble tub, I wondered again what was so imperative about our being in St. Moritz. What exactly did Harry have in mind? But I had a sneaking suspicion that I knew. Sarah's father had died of a stroke shortly before I received Harry's note (the English newspapers had carried the story of the Earl's death). Which meant that Sarah was now a very rich lady in her own right. And I remembered Harry's words to me, first in New York and then over the years, when I asked him if he ever considered killing his wife.

"All the time," was his repeated answer. "But she doesn't have enough money yet. She won't until her father dies."

And now the old boy *was* dead. It was a chilling thought, it was a thrilling thought, one that wouldn't leave my mind as I slipped out of my satin peignoir and nightgown and sank down into the delightfully scented tub where I intended to luxuriate for awhile before I put on my ski clothes and went to meet my unscrupulous brother at Salastrains.

23 ⌾

Just before leaving the hotel, I put Arosana suntan lotion on my face, adjusted my Perillat flip-up white goggles, took my initialed Kneisel skis and poles, and started out on the long icy walk to the terminal above Schulhaus Square. From there I would queue up for the blue funicular that would take me (and about sixty-five other squashed passengers) to Chantarella, the little train's first stop up the mountain.

The main trouble with St. Moritz, I thought, as I passed Scheuing's Sport Shop the outside of which was lined with various brands of skis, all in brilliant vibrant colors, was that it took so damned long to reach the slopes. Because after I got off at Chantarella, I still would have to walk about twenty minutes or take a horse-drawn sleigh to Salastrains.

Salastrains!

It was where the rank beginners went, which undoubtedly was why Harry had chosen it. I had told him over the years that Ian was an experienced skier, and no experienced skier would be caught dead there. The low slopes were strictly for novices, children, and fumbling classes at the local school. Salastrains also boasted a very large outdoor restaurant for those who wished to sunbathe, eat bratwurst, and drink *grog mit rum*. The restaurant was invariably packed with expensive people of varying ages, swathed in *über* alpine finery of every description.

There was an aggressive quality about St. Moritz which I loathed and yet was fascinated by. Everyone looked so sleek, so arrogant, so self-satisfied, so *rich*. I often wondered how they looked back home in their own surroundings. That was another strange quality about the place: it seemed to have the knack of bringing out the potential dictator in most people. They shoved, pushed, refused to apologize, were just plain rude in showing little or no concern for anyone else. Yes, it was a real cornucopia of blazing ego-power worthy of the demented Third Reich.

I was finally in the funicular, crushed between a handsome ruddy-looking Germanic couple in their sixties and two French girls wearing sable jackets and ingeniously patched blue jeans, surely the *prêt-à-porter* work of some highly paid international designer.

I suspected that the majority of people in my car would not be getting off Chantarella but going on to the next stop, Corviglia, where the slopes tended to attract many intermediate skiers . . . Corviglia, where in a few hours Ian and Jeanne would be having lunch at the celestially exclusive Corviglia Club. It was about as easy to become a member of the Corviglia Club as it was to talk NASA into letting a civilian walk on the moon, yet Ian had managed it. At times my husband acted as though he were a combination of Gunther Sachs, Henry Ford III, Aristotle Onassis, and the Shah of Iran all rolled into one. No. Not acted it, *believed* it, which was even worse.

And yet in bed he was astonishingly passive, masochistic, needing not just chains and whips but some of the most esoteric sexual devices the English are notorious for.

But then most of them marry proper Englishwomen, unlike my husband, who wanted me to have my nipples pierced and gold rings put on them (a custom going back to 1899, I have been told), which I refused to do. So then he ordered a silver lamé leather corset for himself from a specialty shop in Mayfair (£120), and a few jars of Norwegian Heather Honey to smear on my vagina. After I got through beating the shit out of him, he was only too happy to lick the honey off me as a reward for his delirious punishment.

Of all the men of different nationalities I've known, the English are surely the kinkiest in their blatant desire for pain. They've been spanked by their nannies and caned by their headmasters to such a degree that their asses are in a perpetual state of heat.

"*Scheiss!*" the German in the car said to his wife.

They were arguing about something or other, but I didn't feel like listening. The sheer sound of the German language never fails to remind me of Herr Nuwyler, so I turned my attention to the view from the window of the funicular and it was truly sparkling: all those craggy white mountain ranges, all that clear, clear sky, dots of dark fir trees, dots of orange, yellow, red, green, blue *things* zigzagging downhill, not people at all, just beautifully hued mechanical toys. It's an incredible sight, unforgettable. No matter what anyone says, no matter what my own reservations are, there is no place in the world like St. Moritz. It creates its own dynamism, its own supercharged electricity. Everything about the place is geared for ice-cold seduction.

But my meeting with Harry, when it finally came about less than half an hour later, was as hot as the sun shining overhead. I spotted him first, he'd gotten there ahead of me and was standing (as he had specified in his note) next to the ski school, watching the instructor take his pupils, one by one, down a shallow slope without their poles.

"Flex your knees," the instructor, a weatherbeaten man, kept repeating. "Keep your body tilted slightly forward. Relax!"

Every pupil appeared absolutely terrified, but down they went, sprawling, some falling, some shakily managing to make it to the bottom with their dignity intact, some laughing.

"They look funny, don't they?" I said to my brother's back.

Harry wheeled around at the sound of my voice. "*Alexis.*"

He was wearing a Western-style, two-piece ski suit and anorak, all in blazing red with black shoulder stripes. Even his polo sweater was red, just like the one he had on when he opened the door to his brownstone over ten years ago in New York to find me on the threshold. I had not seen him wear that sweater since. For our clandestine meetings in London hotels he always wore a suit, shirt and tie. I imagine Sarah would have found it inappropriate for him to go to his tailor in anything less formal.

"Hello, Harry." My voice sounded strange in my ears, choked. "I don't know what to say. I've missed you."

"I've missed you, too. Sarah was ill. That's why we had to cancel our trip to England this past spring. I'm sorry."

"What was wrong with her?"

He brushed off my question with a kind of nervous irritation.

"It doesn't matter. She's a hypochondriac. If it's not one ailment it's another. Now that her father is dead she can't forgive herself for not having seen him one last time. I can't forgive her for ruining my chance to see you. I knew you'd be waiting, wondering . . ." Then his grim expression was replaced by the smile I had always loved so much. "You look fabulous, Alexis. You never seem to age."

"You look fabulous too."

But it was a lie. Even through my dark sunglasses I could see that since our last meeting he had definitely changed. There were lines on his face that smacked of dissipation (perhaps they had not been so noticeable in the shadowy hotel rooms). They reminded me of other lines on another face that I also loved once: our father's face. And I knew instantly that Harry now drank more than he should, just like our father used to. I could only conjecture how long Harry's excessive drinking had been going on, how bad it was, how he felt about it, what—if anything—*I* had to do with it. Or was I flattering myself? I didn't think so. Then our voices overlapped.

"Where is Ian?"

"Where is Sarah?"

We both laughed, but it wasn't amusing. Instinctively we took each other's gloved hand, just as we used to do when we were kids in Pilgrim Lake, the town's outcasts, with only each other for solace and support. At the ages of forty-one and forty-two, we were still like children, still clinging to each other, and it was as though everything that had happened to us since our cruelly enforced separation those many years ago had never happened at all, did not count, meant nothing whatsoever, because we were caught in a time machine, Harry and I, a machine that would not allow either of us to move forward, no, not even by one rotten inch.

"Ian is skiing with Jeanne," I said. "They're probably at Marguns or Trais Fluors. They're miles away from here."

"Oh, so Jeanne is along, too. She must be quite grown up by now. Let's see . . ."

"She's eighteen."

We silently acknowledged the fact that the only time Harry had ever laid eyes on Jeanne was the night he killed her mother and governess. Jeanne was three years old then.

"We're having a cozy little family reunion this Christmas," I said.

Harry's sardonic tone even outweighed my own. "I can imagine."

"Jeanne just graduated from school. She'll be going to university next month."

"It's hard to believe that so much time has gone by."

"Wasted time," I reminded him. "You still haven't mentioned Sarah's whereabouts. Or are you here by yourself?"

"Hardly. Sarah is in the mineral baths back at the hotel. Her private nurse is with her."

"Which hotel?"

"The Engadine."

"Coincidence. That's where we're staying."

Harry smiled again, his eyes hidden behind dark goggles.

"I know," he said, giving my hand a reassuring squeeze.

But I felt myself pull away. "You know? How?"

"I had a hunch that the elegant Engadine would be Ian's choice, so I checked with them before I made our own reservations. They said you were booked for the fifteenth of December."

I began to get a tight feeling in my chest. "Yes, we arrived a week ago."

"We arrived late yesterday afternoon."

"I'm surprised I didn't see you at dinner."

"Sarah was very tired. We had our meal sent up to the suite."

The tight feeling was getting worse. "Harry, why is it so important that you and Sarah be in the same hotel as Ian and me?"

"Because we're all going to become great friends," my brother said in a tone of voice I knew only too well. It was the same tone he had used back in Paris, at the Résidence Françoise when he agreed to kill Paulette. "Great, great friends. I want you and Ian to be at the Chesa Veglia at tea-time today. Shall we say around five-thirty?"

The Chesa Veglia, which was opposite the famed Palace Hotel, was a small, rustic, very popular restaurant, particularly between five and seven P.M., when all the après-ski people came in to drink the local brandy or scotch or an interesting mulled claret called *Glühwein*. It was also possible to order any number of delicious regional food specialities if you were hungry.

"What's happening at the Chesa Veglia?" I asked.

"Sarah and me. We'll be there."

"And?"

"Either Ian will recognize me or I'll recognize him."

Obstacles and problems rushed into my head. "That could be awkward, dangerous," I said. "I'm not supposed to know you. There's not supposed to be any connection between us, because of . . ."

"Paulette?"

"Yes."

"You won't know me. I won't know you. Don't worry, Alexis. Just leave it all to your brother."

"Ian doesn't realize I have a brother. I told him I was an only child."

"That's funny. I told Sarah I was an only child, too."

"I also told Ian that my maiden name was Storms. He asked me about it after we were married."

"Storms," Harry mused.

"I had to tell him something, and since you showed up in Paris that time I sure as hell wasn't about to say Maringo. Ian would have remembered that was your name."

"What about your old passport?"

"It had been changed to Nuwyler. I became a Swiss citizen during my first marriage to that miserable ski instructor."

Harry sighed. "At least you had an expensive Continental education. Look what I got stuck with. Yes, Sarah knows that my parents owned the town's general store. She didn't care. What does Ian think your parents did for a living? Or did you tell him the truth?"

"Don't be an ass, Harry. Ian thinks my father was a distinguished lawyer, and my mother was beautiful and loved to entertain. Pilgrim Lake's most gracious, most charming hostess. I made up a whole new set of parents for myself. I figured it would give me a certain cachet in Ian's eyes."

"You always were a terrific liar," Harry said with admiration.

24 &

When Ian returned to the Engadine at five o'clock after two exhilarating skiing sessions (one in the morning, one in the afternoon, with a break in between for a long, hearty lunch at the Corviglia Club), he was pleased to find Alexis in a much more relaxed and receptive mood than she had been in when he left her that morning at breakfast.

Jeanne had gone directly to her room to change her boots and deposit her equipment, and Ian said he would ring her as soon as he and Alexis had decided where they were going to go for a drink.

"Hello, darling," Alexis said, looking up as he came in. "Did you have a good time?"

"Super. Conditions couldn't have been better. Really great."

She smiled a genuine smile for a change. "I'm glad."

"And what have you been doing with yourself all day?"

She was stretched out on the velvet chaise longue, an Agatha Christie book in her hand, opened to what appeared to be the last few pages.

"Reading another Miss Marple murder," she replied.

Ian knew from fifteen years of married experience that his wife never read the Poirot books—for some reason she hated the little Belgian detective—and he also knew that when Alexis started a Miss Marple book she read it in one sitting, all the way through.

"Because otherwise I lose the thread of the story," was always her explanation.

Ian took off his ski boots and put them outside the door to be polished for the next day. "Then you haven't gone out at all?"

"No. Decadent of me, isn't it?"

"As long as you've enjoyed yourself, darling. That's all that matters. That's what St. Moritz is for. To do exactly as one likes."

He poured himself a large scotch, neat, from the mahogany bar and drank it down in a couple of fast swallows. It felt good, warm, it seemed to go directly to his toes and linger there, tingling. Then he lit the fireplace and stood with his back against it, his feet sweating from the day's exercise inside his thick black socks. He would not put on other socks until after they returned from their après-ski drink, and he changed for the evening; if he did that now, he'd have to remove all his clothes and it was not worth the effort, only to put them back on again. It was hardly *echt* to go out at this hour in anything but your ski clothes, it simply was not done.

Unless, like Alexis, you hadn't been skiing at all. She was wearing a lovely white cashmere polo, while wool culottes, and heavy white-ribbed tights. Her lips were colored in her favorite shade of burnt orange. When they left the hotel, she would put on her long, red fox boots that matched her equally long red fox coat, and on her head a kelly green suede cloche into which she would stuff her ebony hair. Alexis always told him what colors she was wearing, as being color blind himself, he tended to perceive everything except red and blue as varying degrees of gray.

He knew how hard she worked at mixing and matching and rematching until every detail was just right. Once in

London when they were late for a dinner party, she asked him to fish out her jade earrings and he accidentally came across a three-page handwritten list that Alexis had compiled. It consisted of every piece of clothing she owned and the various ways in which they could be worn. It was that kind of perfection Ian admired about her. It was her cool air of evasiveness that he despised. For despite their many years together he still did not understand the woman he had married. Perhaps that was why he'd never left her. Like Alexis, Ian too loved a good mystery, but he preferred his in the flesh, not bound between the covers of a book.

"Shall we go down to the lounge for a drink?" he asked. "I told Jeanne I'd ring her as soon as we decided where to meet."

"The lounge?" Her huge dark eyes seemed to drift off, away from him, away away, he was forever losing her attention. "Oh, darling. I'd like to get out for a breath of fresh air."

"The Schweizerhof? It's a nice little walk from here. Do you good."

"But you can't stand the Schweizerhof. You said so just the other day. It's too—what expression did you use?"

"Too bloody modernized."

"Yes, those were your very words. Well then, how about the Cresta Bar at the Steffani?"

Ian bolted away from the fireplace as though a flame had just shot up his ass. "*With Jeanne? Are you out of your mind?* If there's one place that Glasgow rock and roll singer will be at this time, it's the Cresta Bar."

"Edinburgh," she replied, her eyes wandering to the mountains, which she told him now appeared to be a darkish-blue color, rimmed in pink. "He's from Edinburgh, darling."

"I don't give a shit if he's Rainier's first cousin from Monaco. I don't like the smell of the whole damned business, don't like it at all. And I do wish you would try to back me up. It would help you know, if you agreed with me. Verbally, that is."

"Why? Jeanne never listens to anything I say. She never has."

"That's because you never say anything to her. Anything of importance, I mean. You don't try to discipline her in any way."

Again, those eyes fleeing out the window. Was she bored? Depressed? Irritated? Ian knew she had gone through the change of life, but feigned ignorance, realizing that she did not want him to know. In the last few years he'd begun to attribute her sudden changes of mood, her vast silences, her tacit reproaches, her stubborn insomnia to the fact that she no longer felt desirable as a result of that damned menopause. But he desired her as much as ever, that was the ironic part. In fact it occurred to him right now, standing shoeless on the Engadine mohair rug (a minor fortune) that he didn't really feel like going anywhere for a drink, he felt like making love to his wife. The Gucci bag in one of their three huge closets was just waiting to be reopened and have its sexual paraphernalia taken out for the fun to begin.

"Alexis?"

She recognized the change in his voice, he could see the recognition in those usually inscrutable eyes of hers, and now he could hear the change himself. He had never heard it before. There was a pleading, cajoling tone that had not been present previously. For some reason he felt compelled to repeat it.

"Alexis?"

She threw back her head and laughed at him. "No, darling. Not before our après-ski drink. *After*."

She was right, of course. Like changing one's clothes, it wasn't *echt* to make love at this particular hour. He'd been lying to himself earlier when he said that was what St. Moritz was for: to do exactly as you liked. Perhaps some people were able to, but not Ian Philip Nicholson, who followed the rules (tradition, tradition!) whenever he possibly could. Besides, it would be nice to put on his fur-lined boots, his sheepskin jacket, and show off his tall, beautiful, implacable wife. And then a great idea struck him. Why hadn't he thought of it before?

"I've hit upon the perfect solution and I refuse to take no for an answer," he said. "About where to go for our little drink. And actually, since we're going, let's get started. I'll phone Jeanne while you finish dressing."

She made one of her Alexis-bored faces. "Don't tell me. The bar at the Kulm."

"Wrong."

"The Monopol?"

"Doubly wrong."

Alexis sighed. "Okay. I give up."

"The Chesa Veglia. It's so expensive that that phony rock singer from wherever he's from won't have the money to show his face in there."

Then he picked up the telephone and asked the operator

for his daughter's room. What he did not see was the sly smile playing on Alexis' burnt orange lips as she obediently began to stuff her hair into the green suede cloche that suited her to a double-t.

The Chesa Veglia, which resembled a little alpine chalet, was one of the most chic après-ski spots in St. Moritz. Even now at only five forty-five, it was more than half full. There were long gleaming wooden tables and benches, and the waitresses wore traditional Swiss costumes of dainty white blouses with puffed, beribboned sleeves, embroidered vests that stopped just beneath the bustline, and gayly colored dirndl skirts. Each one had an immaculate white lace apron over her skirt and a cheerful smile on her face as she dispensed trays of drinks to her robust, healthy-looking customers, who were engaged in spirited conversation (in a variety of languages) and much good-natured laughter.

"I see a place for three," Jeanne said, "Right opposite that woman in the wheelchair."

Ian scanned the wood-beamed room until he spotted a blonde in a wheelchair. The sight of any disfigurement always made him kindly disposed toward the unfortunate sufferer. Ian prided himself on his good health and physical fitness and had nothing but sympathy for those less lucky than he. Alexis, he knew, reacted just the opposite way; any form of illness or deterioration revolted her, she was so terrified of growing old, and he noted now that her face was an impassive mask as though she were trying to conceal her distaste.

"Daddy, don't you see who I mean?" Jeanne said. "She's wearing a mink coat and talking to that dishy dark-haired man."

At close range the blonde woman in the wheelchair appeared to be much older, faded, more shriveled than she had at a distance. The luxurious mink was wrapped tightly around her so that no portion of her body was visible. Ian was surprised by her well-bred English accent.

"I'll just move my chair back a bit." She glanced behind her to make certain that nobody was in the way. "There, now. That should do it."

After Ian, Alexis, and Jeanne had slipped into their seats, the dark-haired man made a motion to help wheel the woman forward again, but she was too quick for him (years of experience, Ian thought ruefully), and a moment later the five of them were ensconced in a cozy semicircle.

"Thank you, Madam," Ian said. He gave the dark-haired man a perfunctory smile.

The woman was drinking scotch and there was a gravelly tone to her voice, but her eyes were a clear, piercing blue. They seemed to dominate her haggard face. Ian suspected it had once been quite beautiful.

"This little chair is most versatile," she said. "If only it could climb stairs, I'd be all set."

The dark-haired man in the blazing red ski suit spoke for the first time. "That's what you have me for, sweetheart."

"Oh, you're American!" Jeanne gushed. "Like my stepmother."

Harry and Alexis looked at each other, politely acknowledging the land of their mutual birth.

"Is this your stepmother?" Harry asked Jeanne, who it seemed to Ian had not taken her eyes off the handsome stranger since they'd come in. There was something oddly familiar about the man, something Ian could not place.

"Yes, I am," Alexis said. "My name in Alexis Nicholson . . . my husband, Ian . . . my stepdaughter, Jeanne."

"I'm very pleased to meet you. This is my wife, Sarah, and my name is Harry Maringo." He drained his pear brandy and looked around for the waitress. "This brandy is damned good stuff. Very warming after a day on the slopes."

Ordinarily Ian would have launched into a skiing conversation, but his mind was sidetracked at the moment. *Maringo.* It certainly was an unusual enough name. An ex-business associate or client? One of Alexis' art gallery friends? Someone he'd been briefly introduced to at the Corviglia Club a few years back? A name in one of Agatha Christie's Miss Marple books which he sometimes read a few pages of to put him to sleep?

It was of no consequence. It would come to him sooner or later. Right now he needed a scotch. In spite of his sheepskin jacket and fur-lined boots, his feet were cold again. When the waitress finally arrived, smiling, Ian ordered a glass of *Glühwein* for Alexis, a hot *citron pressé* for Jeanne, scotch for himself and Mrs. Maringo, and another pear brandy for her husband.

"My round," Ian said when the drinks appeared. "Cheers."

"Cheers," the others repeated, raising their glasses.

Again Ian noted that Jeanne seemed fascinated by Harry Maringo, who was old enough to be her father. Maybe she's just a born flirt, he thought. After all she is half French, it's supposed to be in their blood. Still, he didn't like it, not one bit. He would have to speak to her afterward. She was all but undressing Maringo with her eyes, then taking off her own anorak so that the upper portion of her body could be clearly seen. It seemed to Ian that she thrust forward her breasts just to make certain they did not go unnoticed. A glance passed between him and Alexis, who was as stony-faced as she'd been that morning when he left her to go skiing. In contrast to Alexis, Jeanne appeared bright, eager, glowing.

"Tell me, Mr. Maringo," she said. "Where in America are you from?"

To Ian's astonishment, Alexis began to choke on her drink. . . .

25 ❧

"It went down the wrong way," Alexis managed to say after a minute. "Ian, could you please get me a glass of water?" The color was gone from her face.

"I'll get it," Harry Maringo said. "I'm on the outside."

When he returned with the water, she sipped it slowly until her breathing was normal again and her color had returned.

"Are you all right, darling?" Ian asked. "Do you want to leave?"

"No, I'm fine. Honest."

Two couples at the next table had begun to quietly sing something in German. The Chesa Veglia was now filled to capacity with expensively clothed, attractive-looking people, enjoying themselves. How pleasant it is to be here, Ian thought, warm at last. When they returned to the hotel, he and Alexis would make love, then take a brief nap, bathe, and change for dinner. He was starting to feel the pangs of hunger already, lunch being but a dim memory. The Enga-dine was internationally famed for its high standards of cook-ing. The chefs there were consummate artists. He was hoping for *rôti de veau* or a nice *poussin* on this evening's menu when he heard Jeanne say:

"Oh, Mr. Maringo—you never did answer my question. About where you come from in America. I hope I'm not being too inquisitive, but you see I've never been to America myself and it fascinates me."

"I'm from a little town in upstate New York. I don't think it would fascinate you at all."

"Why is that?"

"It's very small, very provincial, very insignificant. I doubt that you could even find it on a map. It's called Pilgrim Lake."

"Pilgrim Lake," Jeanne mused, stirring her drink. "It sounds romantic."

Alexis looked up, her huge eyes filled with surprise, bewilderment. "That's strange. I come from Pilgrim Lake, too."

"You're kidding," Harry Maringo said.

"No, not at all. That's where I was born. That's where I grew up."

"So she did," Ian said. "She's mentioned the town to me on several occasions. But what an odd coincidence."

"It most certainly is," Alexis agreed. "Uncanny."

"We probably went to school together." Harry gazed at Alexis curiously. "What was your maiden name?"

"Storms."

He tapped his fingers on the polished wooden table. "Storms. Storms. Wait a minute. Was your father a lawyer?"

"Yes." Alexis had turned pale again. "Yes, he was."

"And he was a pilot, and shot down and killed in the war."

"That's right. But how could *you* have known . . . ?"

Ian had never seen Alexis so caught off-guard by anything. Ordinarily she was the soul of composure, if not ice. Again, he had the strange sensation of having met this Maringo chap before. But where? When? Through whom? Perhaps he merely looked like someone he'd once known.

"You see, I remember your family very well," Harry Maringo was saying to Alexis.

"You do?"

He laughed self-consciously, modestly. "It's not so unusual, really, your father being a well-known lawyer and then a war hero. Surely you must have realized that in a town as small as Pilgrim Lake, your family was very much looked up to, respected, admired, whereas mine . . . to put it as bluntly as possible, we were from the other side of the tracks. That's probably why you don't have any recollection of me. But if you'll excuse my saying so, Mr. Nicholson, I must confess that I had a schoolboy crush on your wife ever since we were kids."

"You did?" Alexis said. "I'm sorry, but I can't seem to place you at all."

"No, you wouldn't. You didn't know I was alive. A lot of the other boys had crushes on you, too. You wouldn't look at any of us. I can't say now that I blame you. We must have struck you as a bunch of ruffians."

Ian was pleased that his wife had been the object of masculine admiration at so young an age. More, he liked the reason why: because her family was on a higher social level.

Harry went on, addressing Alexis. "I even remember your mother, she was so lovely and she always wore perfume. From time to time she would come into our store herself. She invariably bought the most expensive cuts of meat, the choicest delicacies, well, as choice as we had. She was a real lady but it was seldom that we had the pleasure of serving her, since it was usually your maid who did the marketing."

"Store?" Alexis said.

"The Maringo General Store in Pilgrim Lake. My family owned it."

Alexis honored him with a patronizing smile. "Of course. Now I know who you are. You sometimes delivered groceries on your bicycle."

"That's right. I did often deliver groceries to your home until your mother died so suddenly." Harry's expression saddened. "It was a terrible shock to all of us that she passed away at such a young age. You must have been about eleven when it happened."

"Twelve."

"And then you disappeared from Pilgrim Lake. Bang. Just like that. There were rumors that you'd been sent to school somewhere in Europe. Is that true?"

"Yes. Switzerland."

"Darling," Ian cut in, "you should be flattered that even as a little girl you made such an indelible impression on Mr. Maringo. It must be very flattering indeed."

"It is." Alexis had retreated to her ice-bound self once more. "But frankly I'd like to drop the entire subject. It all happened so long ago. It's all so painful to be reminded of past history."

"Of course, of course," Harry said quickly. "How stupid

of me to have brought it up. I guess I got carried away when I heard that you were from my own home town. I apologize for my insensitivity, Mrs. Nicholson."

Alexis vindicated him with a queenly nod, then began to look around the room with an air of impatience, irritation, and Ian suddenly felt sorry for this nice Mr. Maringo who had put his foot into it. The chap obviously led a hellish life, starting from childhood. And it couldn't be much fun having an invalid for a wife, no matter how much he loved her. He watched now as Maringo took his wife's gloved hand in his own and softly began to massage it, then kissed her on the forehead and asked if she wanted another scotch.

"I'd adore one," was her reply. "Thank you, sweetheart."

"Your wish . . ."

It was touching to see a couple so devoted to each other, *genuinely* devoted, Ian thought with a twinge of confusion. He did not really understand that kind of closeness, despite the fact that he loved Alexis in his own way. His way was carnal, not romantic; fetishistic, not intimate. He had his particular sensual needs as certainly all English gentlemen did, and he would indulge them whenever he damned well felt like it. Such as instigating that delicious affair with his French secretary, Michelle, shortly after he and Alexis were married, the only mistake being that he had thrown it (and all the interesting details) in Alexis' face.

"She's better at fellatio than you are," he had told Alexis.

"She let me attach pumps to her breasts before we fucked," he had told Alexis. "As a result of the pumps—they're the kind that are used to extract extraneous milk from nursing mothers—her bust measurement went from thirty-four to thirty-six. She's not flatchested like you."

"She cut off some of her pubic hairs and smoked them in a pipe," he had told Alexis. "Then she cut off some of mine and did the same thing."

"She tied up my penis with my old-school tie and let me suffer for an hour while she squeezed my testicles and then slapped them with a long rod," he had told Alexis. "It felt bloody damned good. She took me across her knees and spanked my ass until it bled. I came three times."

And after Michelle he answered a variety of Soho ads couched in coded sexual language, particularly the ones that contained references to caning.

He told Alexis all about those, too. She never forgave him.

"Daddy." Jeanne was tugging at his sleeve, the way she

used to do when she was a child and demanded attention. "You haven't heard a word we've been saying. The Maringos are booked into the Engadine, too. Isn't that super?"

Ian could not imagine what she was getting so excited about until he realized that her attraction for Harry Maringo was still going strong. He had never seen Jeanne like this before. She was quivering at the mere knowledge that she happened to be staying at the same hotel as the object of her sudden affections. That it was a large hotel, with over three hundred accommodations, did not seem to occur to her or make any difference in her ill-concealed zeal. From the fervent expression on her face, anyone would have imagined that she and Maringo were sharing the bridal suite.

And yet only that morning all she could talk about was the Scottish rock singer. So she was fickle, too. Maybe that was a good sign. At least with this Maringo fellow she would get no encouragement, which was more than Ian could be sure of with Mr. Rock and Roll. Ever since they'd entered the Chesa Veglia, Maringo had discreetly but firmly pretended not to notice the salivating glances Jeanne kept throwing in his direction. The fact that the man had a wife did not appear to deter Jeanne for a moment. If this was the kind of deportment they taught them at that school in Gstaad, Ian was delighted that she would soon be going to university where more serious business awaited her.

"How long will you be staying in St. Moritz?" Ian asked the Maringos.

"Just through the New Year," Sarah Maringo replied. "Then we return to Guilford."

"That's a pretty part of the world. Have you always lived there?"

"No, we were in America until very recently. You see, my father died a few months ago and left me . . . I should say, us . . . his estate. It's quite lovely, isn't it, Harry?"

Maringo kissed his wife on the cheek. "It looks like a million dollars to a poor, smalltown boy like me, sweetheart."

A million dollars. Five million dollars. Something clicked in Ian's mind, something that went back to his days in Paris. Of course! That was why Harry Maringo seemed so familiar. He was the brash young American who'd come to see him about borrowing five million dollars to finance a wild-schemed but intriguing motion picture deal.

Ian's mind was racing now, putting the pieces together. He shifted slightly in his seat to get another view of Sarah

Maringo, who would naturally have been the once-famed English actress, Sarah Ames, sexier though, more curvacious.

It was hard to believe that this shriveled, middle-aged woman in the wheelchair and that vibrant, quicksilver blonde movie star were one and the same person, and yet there could be no doubt about it. It was fifteen years since she'd been thrown from that beastly horse during the shooting of a Hollywood picture. As Ian knew only too well, a person could change drastically within fifteen years. He certainly had. Maringo had changed, too, his face was harder, it spoke of much suffering and pain. Ian wondered what he was doing with himself these days in terms of work, but did not feel on familiar enough ground to inquire.

Still, he was interested, curious. Guilty? Nonsense, he told himself. It was hardly his fault that he'd been unable to finance Maringo's five-million-dollar business venture, it was implausible, impossible after Sarah Ames, *Lady* Sarah Ames (it was all coming back to Ian now) became paralyzed following her unfortunate accident, and could not star in her husband's proposed movies. What a tragedy for them both, Ian thought, his emotions more stirred than they had been for a long time. What a damned bloody tragedy! Then he realized that Alexis was whispering something in his ear. There was a note of urgency in her voice.

"Let's go back to the hotel and make love."

Ian could not have been more surprised if she had announced that she wanted to ski naked down the north side of Piz Nair. Nor more pleased. Excited. He was starting to get an erection already.

"I'm afraid we have to be pushing along," he said somewhat sheepishly to the Maringos. "At my age I can't afford to miss my daily nap, not if I want to do a bit of nightclubbing after dinner. It's been a pleasure meeting both of you."

He and Harry Maringo shook hands. "Which club do you frequent?" Harry asked.

"The one in the hotel. The Prince Regent's. It's as good as any of the others, and a hell of a lot more convenient than walking on icy paths over to the Palace. In fact if you and your wife are in the mood, why don't you join us there for a drink?"

"That's very kind of you," Harry said. "We'd love to, wouldn't we, sweetheart?"

Sarah managed an enigmatic smile above her glass of neat scotch. "It's a splendid idea. Particularly since I've enjoyed meeting you all so much." Her glance sarcastically included Jeanne, whose eyes were still glued on Harry. "So very, very much."

"Right," Ian said. "Shall we say about eleven? Eleven-thirty? I'll book a table in my name."

"We'll be there," Harry said, waving good-bye.

"*J'adore le Prince Regent's Club,*" Jeanne giddily announced as the three of them emerged from the warmth of the Chesa Veglia into the cool, clear, mountain air. "I want to come, too."

Ian stared at her in disbelief. "But only this morning you said—"

"—that it was for older people?"

"Yes."

"Well, I've changed my mind, Daddy. Why should *I* run after *him?* Let him come and find me if he so interested."

"I assume you mean your indigent Scottish rock singer."

"He's not indigent, but that's who I mean."

Alexis was chewing her lips, a rare nervous gesture. She could not have missed noticing Jeanne's vulgar display of interest in Harry Maringo, and it obviously disturbed her. She must realize, as Ian did, that Jeanne's change of heart toward the Prince Regent's Club was due strictly to her anticipation of seeing Maringo again. Perhaps Alexis cared more about Jeanne's welfare than he had given her credit for, Ian thought, linking arms with the two women he loved most in the world, the two women he least understood.

"*J'adore St. Moritz,*" Jeanne sang. "*Comment elle est belle!*"

26 ❧

When we got back to the Engadine, I was steaming.

So was Ian, but for different reasons and in a different way. He was sexually steamed up about my lovemaking suggestions, whereas I was steaming mad, angry, infuriated, and more jealous than ever of my stepdaughter and her flirtation with Harry at the Chesa Veglia.

It was the last thing in the world I would have predicted, that Jeanne would find my brother so attractive and, even worse, make such an obvious display of herself by flaunting her attraction before all of us. That was the real reason I had urged Ian to leave: I could not stand the sight of Jeanne's behavior. The fact that Harry pretended to ignore her lascivious attention did not fool me for a second. Just as I wasn't fooled by his lovemaking charade with that wretched-looking wife of his. He sure could put on a good act, though, which was why I felt so frightened now. What if, behind his careful pretense, Harry *was* sexually drawn to Jeanne?

I thought of them in bed together, with him caressing her supple, eighteen-year-old body, and it made me sick with jealousy. I doubted that Jeanne was a virgin, there was too much know-how in her calculating brown eyes. At her age she would be tremulous in response to an experienced man's lovemaking, and if Harry was anything he was experienced with women. He would experiment with Jeanne, he would try everything until he got it just right and drove her up an ecstatic wall. I could almost hear her moans and shrieks just as I was very soon about to hear my own.

Surprised? Why?

Ian's brand of lovemaking appeals to me from time to time. Not always, though—I have to be in a certain mood, I have to be angry about something or someone, and thinking about Harry and Jeanne was rapidly changing my steaming anger to steaming desire. I am interested in the subject of tenderness, when it comes to lovemaking, because it is only with Harry that I am able to be tender and, more importantly, at the same time more sensual than with any man I have ever known.

With Ian I am something else, something different, an animal, barely human. I sink low. Ian might have my body, but Harry has my heart. Even now as I took off my ski clothes and neatly hung them in the bedroom closet, I was getting ready for Ian's strangely impersonal brand of sex. He was getting ready, too . . . ready for me to torment him by not using the belts, whips, and chains in our Gucci suitcase, at least not until he had totally satisfied me. Then he would beg. Good. I enjoy seeing him reduced to a pleading caricature of a man, it gives me pleasure, I like to laugh at him. He has humiliated me so much, in so many ways, in the past, that my desires have become twisted and I recognize this twist in my nature to my horror, happiness, and regret. I think that when I was very young, I might have been a nice girl, sweet-natured, idealistic, but my mother cured me of all that with her wretched cruelty. And now I have become cruel like her, the last person in the world I ever wanted to emulate.

"Two tinseled Christmas trees dripping with crystal icicles," Ian said, undressing rapidly. "One in the sitting room, and one in here. The Engadine thinks of everything, doesn't it, darling?"

"The concierge must have installed them when we were at the Chesa Veglia."

"It's a nice touch," Ian said, as he took off his *Bunterhosen.* "Thoughtful."

Thoughtful, too (for five hundred dollars a day) was the second fireplace in our Chippendale, gold and marble bedroom. Two Christmas trees, two fireplaces, two tall tapering candles on either side of the huge, inviting bed. Then I realized they were electric, fireproof, practical. Yes, the Engadine certainly did think of everything.

"The Swiss are the most thoughtful people in the world," I said. "And probably the most ingenious. They've created a thriving, solvent country around their thoughtful hotels."

Ian murmured something about the low interest rates in Switzerland and then asked: "Aren't you having a lovely Christmas, darling? That's why we came here, you know. To enjoy ourselves."

I thought of Harry. "I'm enjoying myself."

We were both naked now. I was the same height as Ian, but Harry was taller than I. What was he doing this very minute? Making his way to little Jeanne's room? I doubted that he would risk such a move, it was too chancy, he wouldn't be such a fool. Outside it was dark pink, lights glistened from distant villas, and the frozen lake below was barely visible, shadowy, soon to be bathed in moonglow, but not yet.

"Why don't you switch on the candles?" I said to Ian, who promptly obeyed.

The room took on a rosy, seductive sheen as I lay down on the sweet-smelling sheets and smiled at the man I had married. For a moment he was confused. Or pretended to be.

"Aren't you going to—?"

"No," I said.

He had a semierection as he visualized me beating him

with any of the whips, chains, or leather belts we always traveled with.

"But I thought—"

"Maybe later," I said, slowly starting to spread my long legs.

He stood at the foot of the bed, watching me, knowing that if he didn't do what I wanted I wouldn't do what he wanted and it would drive him crazy. He really had no choice because he could never force me when it came to sexual matters, only when it came to financial ones. I had to be strict with Ian if I was to retain my financial prerogatives. If I did what he wanted too often, he would lose respect for me and cut me off at any one of a number of London's more luxurious shops.

"What are you waiting for?" I said. "Get into bed."

"Right."

He lay down beside me, his blue eyes moist, his scotch-scented breath heavy as he tried to kiss me. I wouldn't let him. Kissing was too intimate. I bit his lips as warning, which he immediately understood.

"Are you excited?" he asked.

"Not yet." It was a lie; sadomasochism always excites me. "Why should I be? What have you done?"

"Nothing. But you know that I want to excite you. I love it when you get excited, darling."

He was lying on my right side and he put his left arm around me, grabbed my left hand and pulled it back so that I could not move it. His grasp was very firm. He knew I liked the pretense of being prisoner, captive. Then he started to pat my vagina with his other hand, very softly at first, pat pat pat, then slightly harder PAT PAT PAT, until he was slapping, not patting, but it didn't hurt, it felt good, and I was getting wet inside.

"Keep it up," I told him.

All the time that I was enjoying this, I hated him. But hatred breeds its own kind of thrill and I knew that I would have an incredible one-after-another series of orgasms, and I would then hate him even more. I always saved my love for Harry. I could be tender with Harry, never with Ian, who equates tenderness with weakness.

"That's enough of that," I said, referring to the slap-pats.

"Are you sure you don't want more?"

"Positive."

"All right."

He put a finger inside me, his mouth on my left nipple. I would let him keep this up for as long as possible, because the longer he had to wait for his own reward the more he would enjoy it, and I could have him at my mercy, which is precisely where I wanted the son-of-a-bitch.

"Does it feel good?" he asked.

I was soaking. "It feels terrific. Don't stop."

"No. You know I won't."

But then, minutes later, he did. "Turn over on your tummy."

The English are still back in grade school. They are forever using words like "tummy" and "buttocks" and "spank" and "cuddle."

"I'm going to spank you on the buttocks," Ian said in a little boy voice (his business associates should hear the great man now). "How many do you want? Ten?"

"That's too much." My own voice was as icy as the lake below. "Five will do."

The blows stang pleasurably. I happen to have very tough Indian skin or he would be hurting me. I'd never let Ian hurt me, physically. That was my domain when I got going with him later on.

"Do you like it? Do you like it?" he kept repeating as his delicate hand crashed across my ass.

"Yes, but it's enough. Now I want to come."

I turned over on my back and let him start to stimulate my clitoris again. His left hand brushed gently, back and forth, against my left nipple. I was suspended in air, weightless, bodiless, and yet all body, and then I felt the familiar taste in my mouth which always heralds my orgasms.

"Oh, don't stop, don't stop, don't stop . . ."

I might have been screaming, I might have been whispering, I honestly don't know, because once I started to come I did not know what I was doing or saying. The orgasmic waves swept over me in swift, relentless succession, there seemed to be no end to them. I bit Ian's shoulder and cried out again for him not to stop until I was finished writhing and shaking. It seemed to take forever, but probably only a few seconds had passed when I was able to open my eyes and focus upon him. He had a full erection now, and the entire room smelled wet and steamy and sticky.

"Touch me," he said. "Squeeze my testicles."

He was too gentlemanly to say "balls."

"Squeeze them hard."

"I don't want to. I'm afraid you'll come right away."

"I won't. I promise."

I just laughed at him as I got out of bed and went into the

bathroom to wipe off some of the wetness. It was uncomfortable being all that wet. And besides, I needed to regain control of the situation if I were to go through with the rest of our customary sex ritual.

"I think I'll use the brown belt," I said when I returned to the bedroom and headed for the closet with the locked suitcase. "You know, the skinny brown one."

His voice was barely audible. "Whatever you say, darling."

On the other hand, I was so damned mad at Jeanne's flirtation with Harry that I instantly changed my mind. Ian's ass was thick, he could take a few chains tonight without bleeding, providing I didn't hit him too hard. The only reason I felt concerned about his bleeding was because I'm afraid of going too far, and then I might not be able to stop the bleeding for quite awile. After all, we couldn't very well appear at dinner with blood staining my husband's impeccable trousers, now could we?

"What are you doing?" he asked, when he heard the rattle of various chains coming from the now unlocked suitcase.

"Changing my mind. Turn over on your stomach and stay there."

I took the chains (and the brown belt, for good luck) and went back to bed where Ian was lying flat down on his stomach, as instructed. He had a rather interesting habit of lifting up his ass a bit, in blissful expectation.

"Keep your eyes closed," I said. "And *wait!* Do you understand?"

Did he ever! He shut his eyes tight and shivered slightly, not knowing when the first blow would come, not knowing exactly where, not knowing how hard it would be. That was part of the overall excitement for him, not knowing. He couldn't see me but I was sitting straight up, in a sort of yoga-Indian position, my legs crossed, a chain in one hand and the brown belt in the other. I felt very composed and authoritative about it all.

"Are you ready?" I asked.

His answer, "Yes, darling," was half-muffled in the Engadine's exquisite linen sheets.

"Good," I said.

Then I just sat there, motionless, smiling to myself, trying not to think of Harry, only of Ian. I knew the routine by heart, although to keep it from becoming a deadly bore (after all, we had been married fifteen years), I tried to vary things as much as possible. Rhythm and timing. Those were the variations. A second? Five seconds? Five minutes? Slow? Hard? Hardest? Or just a *tingle* of punishment? He never knew when I would strike, or with what degree of strength. Once when I was in a particularly good-natured mood, I forced him to wait (silently) a full thirty minutes without moving a muscle. He came that time with the very first stroke. But we couldn't afford thirty minutes this evening, not if we were to bathe, dress, dine, and meet Harry and Sarah at the Prince Regent's Club.

"Say it," I said.

He hesitated, but only for a moment. "Hit me."

"Hit me, *what?*"

Now there was no hesitation. "Hit me, *please.*"

"Please, *what?*"

"Please, darling. Please don't torture me like this."

"Why not? You deserve it, don't you?"

"Yes, yes. I deserve to be beaten. I'll take my punishment quietly, just don't make me wait too long."

I shoved a pillow underneath him so that his ass was raised even higher. He was practically whimpering now.

"Please, please."

The crack of the brown leather belt was first, the sound zinged through the starlight silence of pristine St. Mortiz, and next came the deliciously loud clank of my gold Cartier chain belt as it hit Ian first on one side of his ass, and then as he waited in respectful silence (because he knew that if he opened his mouth I'd stop altogether and let him jerk off into the tinseled Christmas tree while I finished my Agatha Christie book, unconcerned), I let him have it on the other side. Then I started doing it very fast, alternating between leather and metal, thinking of the French summation of this peculiar pleasure: *le vice anglais.* I stopped abruptly and asked Ian how it felt.

"Better. Much better, now that you're punishing me for being so bad."

"Turn over."

When he did I could see that he was trying to suppress his panting. I touched his penis, which was very hard and slightly wet.

"Naughty boy."

"I can't help it. Some of the semen just comes out when I'm aroused. I'm very close to orgasm."

"Not yet."

"Whatever you say."

I gently slapped his penis a few times with the belt, holding back the chain, upon which his eyes were fastened.

"That feels marvelous," he said. "Do it again."

"No. You've had enough for one evening."

Alarm spread over his face. "I haven't! You can't stop now!"

I pretended to think this over. "Oh God, you really have misbehaved yourself, haven't you?"

"I've been very, very naughty," he admitted. "Please let me have my full share of punishment. Please, darling."

"It's just that I don't want you coming this way. I simply won't have it. I want you to come inside me. Is that clear?"

"Yes, yes. I'll come inside you, I promise, but please spank me one more time."

My laughter was genuine. Genuinely cruel, that is.

"Only *one* more time, Ian? Is that what you're saying?"

"Yes yes yes yes yes yes."

He was lying, of course. After one more time he'd want one more time, but he wasn't going to get it. I was going to get the natural Alaska lynx hooded coat, maxi length, that I'd recently seen advertised in Harper's & Queen (about £13,000) and there was only one way to get it: not to let Ian get his. At least not the way he wanted it. Sexual intercourse meant zero to him, but I liked it, and after all my concerted effort I felt that I deserved it.

"Very well," I said finally. "I'll do it one more time. Hard."

"Thank you."

Zap!!!!

"Oh Christ," he said, squirming with pleasure. "Do it again, I'm *begging* you."

In response to his plea I threw both leather and metal on the swirling Persian carpet and said, "Okay, you son-of-a-bitch, now get on top and fuck me!"

He had no choice. So he did as he was told, came very quickly, very intensely, shuddered for minutes afterward and moaned about how marvelous I was, how absolutely and positively thrilling to be with. . . .

Somewhere far in the distance a churchbell chimed. It was eight-thirty, time to bathe and dress and make a respectable entrance in the grand, crystal-chandeliered dining room of the eminently respectable Engadine Hotel. I was debating which gown to wear—the beaded chiffon St. Laurent, or the crepe, camisole-top Bohan—when I heard Ian say:

"If you won't use the whip and separator, will you strap me to the bed later on? I promise not to make a sound."

My answer to Mr. Nutsville was not to make a sound myself. But just to show that I was not entirely heartless, I did allow him to lick my toes, which he did with great salivating skill until I kicked him away, minutes afterward.

I had decided upon the St. Laurent.

27 ∽

Harry hated Sarah's flesh. It made his own crawl. And tonight she was wearing sleeveless yellow silk evening pajamas which revealed her thin, sagging arms. Ordinarily she wore long-sleeved clothes, and as he pushed her wheelchair into the ebony confines of the Prince Regent's Club he could only wonder (as he had so often in the past) what in hell he was doing still married to this wraith of a woman. His only consolation was that he wouldn't be for much longer.

"Good evening, Sir." The maître d' was at Harry's side. "Do you have a reservation?"

"Yes, we're meeting a Mr. and Mrs. Nicholson. They've booked a table in their name."

The maître d' had to use a small flashlight to scan his reservation list. A band was blasting away and couples were gyrating with frenetic energy on the packed dance floor. The walls and ceiling of the Prince Regent's Club were comprised of huge smoked mirrors, and the only light came from the small, pine scented candles on each table. Harry was amused to note that many of the beautiful people were wearing sunglasses nonetheless.

The entire scene was like an exotic fashion show set to rock music, with just about every conceivable night-shining outfit represented, from Oriental-styled brocades, to couturier jeans studded with jewels, to the barest of panne velvet plunging necklines, to silver harem suits. Harry had never seen so many good-looking women in one room in his life, and that included the days when he and Sarah lived in Beverly Hills and were on the movie star party route.

"If you will kindly follow me," the maître d' said with a small bow. "Your friends have not yet arrived, but I see that there is a reservation for five. I believe Madam should be comfortable here."

It was a large circular table which could easily have accommodated eight people, but there were only four chairs strategically placed around it. Nicholson had, no doubt, explained to the maître d' about Sarah's wheelchair taking up extra space. The table was set back from the dance floor, which also appealed to Harry. Very few people would have to pass by Sarah.

"This will do just fine," Sarah said to the maître d', who responded with another short, Prussian bow. "Could you please have a waiter bring us a bottle of Haig and Haig Dimple, Perrier water, and ice."

The maître d' turned to Harry for confirmation. Harry nodded in agreement, inwardly fuming. When Sarah wasn't putting on her submissive sweetheart act, she loved to give the orders. She loved strangers knowing that it was she who controlled the pursestrings in the family.

"Well, I assume that *Miss* Nicholson will be with us this evening, since the reservation is for five," she said to Harry after the maître d' had disappeared. "I hope she manages to restrain herself more effectively than she did earlier today. The flirting little bitch."

Harry tried to be offhanded. He was not in the mood for an argument. "She's just a kid. You know how they are at that age. They flirt with every man. It's a silly game with them."

Harry patted her cold hand as though to assure her that she had nothing to worry about with him, her ever faithful husband. Actually, he was proud of how deftly he managed to ignore Jeanne's attentions. He felt certain that his diplomacy had not gone unnoticed by Ian Nicholson.

The thing that bothered him was Nicholson's apparent lack of memory of their ever having met in Paris fifteen years before. True, it was a long time, but still it struck Harry as strange. Had he made so little an impression on the merchant banker that day? If so, he must rectify that now by acting devoted to Sarah, polite to Alexis, rejecting of Jeanne—but in a protective, avuncular way.

"I wonder if I should remind Nicholson that we once met in Paris," he said to Sarah. "What do you think, sweetheart? He really seems to have forgotten."

"I'd like to forget it, too. That entire movie project of yours, and why it failed to materialize."

"I'm sorry. I didn't mean to stir up unpleasant memories." It was almost as though she blamed him for the horse accident. "Anyhow, here comes our scotch."

As the waiter approached their table, she said: "And, Harry, darling, do try not to drink too much tonight. Lately you've begun to smell like a distillery. Even some of your clothes reek of alcohol. It's quite disgusting."

God, but he felt like strangling her right this moment in the plush Prince Regent's Club. She was a bitter old nag, and he had taken her damned abuse for far too long. No wonder he drank to excess. It was the only way he could blot out her incessant demands, insults, and humiliations, and manage to retain any sanity at all.

"Well, here they are," Sarah said. "And Little Miss Finishing School is with them in a perfectly tarty gown."

Actually they made a striking, colorful threesome, Harry thought, ignoring Sarah's comment about Jeanne's dress, which suited her sexy young figure very well. It was a fire-engine red maxi with spaghetti shoulder straps, and it was obvious that she was not wearing a brassiere. Ian had on an impeccably tailored, double-breasted, midnight blue tuxedo with black satin lapels and buttons, and Alexis—lovely Alexis—wore a floating lime chiffon with a beaded top.

In comparison Sarah looked dowdy and washed out in her pale evening pajamas which had no discernible style: the bodice just hung on her, now that her breasts (like much else about her, physically) had shriveled since her accident. No wonder she was jealous of Jeanne's youthful suppleness.

"Roederer Crystal?" Ian asked Alexis and Jeanne, both of whom nodded in agreement just as the rock group came to an abrupt stop.

"And I was about to ask Mr. Maringo if he would dance with me," Jeanne said, ignoring her father's flash of disapproval.

"I'm afraid I'm not very good at this energetic form of dancing," Harry replied, lying. "Age, you know."

To his irritation he heard Sarah say, "But you're excellent at it, sweetheart."

She was always testing him. If he danced with Jeanne, he

would never hear the end of it afterward; if he didn't, she would make him appear to be an ungracious liar before the Nicholsons. There was no way to win with her, which was why he had to kill her.

Or rather, why Alexis had to.

As far-fetched as it sounded, he had an eerie intuition that once he hit upon the right way to go about it, he and Alexis working together could pull it off. He knew now that he could count on her full cooperation. Her very compliance with his request to meet in St. Moritz had been encouraging, but after their little talk today he was more reassured than ever. Her initial nervousness about bringing Ian to the Chesa Veglia, with all the implications that entailed, was quickly dispelled when Harry urged her to trust him, to have faith in him.

The point was that Alexis *wanted* to trust him. She was as eager to get out of her stultifying marriage as he was to get out of his. And although she was not unaware of the risks involved, she was intrigued by the prospect of adventure, dare, and, more importantly, the forbidden lure of their being together in the near future. He understood Alexis. After all, they were brother and sister, the closest of blood relations. In the long run their minds would always work in the same cunning, ruthless fashion.

"Do you ski, Mr. Maringo?" Ian Nicholson asked.

Harry was taken back. "If I didn't, why would I be in St. Moritz?"

Sarah looked contemptuous, Jeanne looked bored, Alexis looked embarrassed, Nicholson looked sympathetic.

"I can see, then, that this is your first time here, Mr. Maringo."

Harry was starting to feel uneasy. "Yes, it is."

"Nothing to be ashamed of, you know. It's merely that many of the St. Moritz habitués come here solely for après-ski pleasures, which is why they can dissipate their energies dancing and drinking the night away." Nicholson had barely sipped his expensive champagne. "They don't have to get up early the next morning to put in two hours on the slopes."

Harry repressed the urge to take another slug of scotch.

"I see your point, Mr. Nicholson, but I happen to be an enthusiastic if not very accomplished skier."

"You must take lessons in that case. There's an excellent instructor here. His name is—"

The name was drowned out by the wail of a tenor saxophone, playing the opening bars of "All the Way." The rock

band was gone and another older, more conservative one had
taken its place. Jeanne immediately perked up.

"Now surely, Mr. Maringo, you can't refuse me *this* dance."

To Harry's surprise Nicholson laughed with what seemed
like genuine amusement. "My daughter is incorrigible, I'm
afraid. But if you can bear it, why not have a dance with
her? If you don't, I daresay that I'll be forced to and I'd
much rather sit here enjoying the company of these two
lovely ladies."

Jeanne had already gotten to her feet, and now that he
was being given the green light by her father, Harry did the
same, making a jovial gesture of surrender. At this point he
would have danced with King Kong if it were sanctioned
by Ian.

Besides, Jeanne might turn out to be of some value to him
in disclosing information that he could use later on when they
all went back to England and he mapped out his murder plan.
As eager as Alexis was to cooperate, he did not want to
press her on the subject of her marriage, Ian's peculiarities,
weak points, soft spots. He was afraid of arousing Alexis'
latent fears by too much probing.

                    When somebody loves you . . .

The words of the old song were being softly sung by an
attractive female vocalist as Harry took Jeanne in his arms
on the shiny black dance floor. The smoked mirrors seemed to
enclose them in a fog of intimacy, which he tried to resist
and Jeanne tried to encourage. Her body in its revealing red
knit gown pressed against his maroon dinner jacket and dark
trousers. He could feel her nipples, her belly, her thighs, her
young girl's legs practically entwine him in tantalizing, teasing,
seductive embrace.

He made an attempt to extricate himself, but her grasp
was stronger than he would have imagined. Besides, the last
thing in the world he wanted was to get into an overt struggle
with her while others in their party looked on. He could
only hope that they were seated too far away and the room
was too dark for them to perceive the degree to which Jeanne
was physically biting into him.

"How would you like to make love to me?" she said.

Harry was startled by the bluntness of her approach.

"Don't you think I'm a bit too old for you?"

"No. I think you're sexy as hell."

"I'm also married as hell."

"So what? I don't care."

"But I do," Harry said.

"You can't be serious. You must play around."

"It so happens that I don't, but I assure you that if I did it wouldn't be with someone young enough to be my own daughter."

"You sound stuffy now. Like my father. Anyhow, I don't believe you. You're too dishy to remain faithful to a crippled wife, so who are you kidding?"

"Nobody," Harry said, thinking that if the circumstances were different he'd fuck her on the spot and probably enjoy every minute of it. "I'm not kidding a soul, least of all you, but I should imagine that you'd have a boyfriend close to your own age. You're a very pretty girl."

"I'm also pretty terrific in bed."

To his embarrassment, Harry could feel himself getting an erection. "If you're so terrific in bed, you must have a boyfriend telling you so. Or are you in between acts at the moment?"

Happy to be near you . . .

Jeanne's movements faltered, then she regained her composure and her voice took on a new note of defiance. "Since you put it so quaintly, there *is* someone I'm interested in but my father objects to him. Violently, I might add. You don't know my father."

"What don't I know about him?"

"What a snob he is. How suspicious he is. How distrustful."

"Distrustful?"

Jeanne was still clinging to him, but Harry felt it was out of despair now, not desire. "My father would distrust any man I became interested in, if he weren't upper class."

"And I gather your boyfriend isn't."

"He's not my boyfriend, at least not yet. We only met last week, and since then Daddy has been practically chaining me to his side. He's afraid that Tom would exploit me financially."

"What does your friend Tom do for a living?"

Jeanne gave Harry a look of utter disgust. "Now you sound just like Daddy."

"I don't mean to, although I must say I can appreciate your father's feelings."

"Can you?" Disgust had turned to bitterness. "Can you, really?"

"I think so." Harry had a hunch he was onto something. "But I can also appreciate yours, and I'd like to help if you'd let me."

"Then make love to me."

"I don't understand. You just said—"

"Yes, yes." Jeanne was becoming more impatient by the second. "I *am* interested in Tom. He's wonderful. He's the lead singer and guitarist for a rock group working here in St. Moritz over the holidays. Tom is really talented, terribly attractive, and it's not as though he's penniless. His group has played concerts all over England and Europe, they've made records, they earn money, they'll probably become as famous as the Bay City Rollers. But try and tell that to my father."

"I still don't get it. If you're so wild about this Tom fellow, whatever his last name is, why do you want to go to bed with me so badly? What I mean to say is, if your father objects to someone like Tom, just think how he'd feel about someone like *me*. I'm twenty-four years older than you, and I have an invalid wife to boot. Your father would consider me a total bastard and Tom a godsend in comparison."

"His last name is McKillup." Jeanne was smiling now, a strange conniving smile Harry had never seen before. "That's the whole point."

"What point? That his name is McKillup?"

"No, you idiot. I'm trying to bring my father to his senses. If you would only have a fast affair with me, it might open Daddy's eyes. He might just realize that by denying me Tom, he's driving me to even more catastrophic extremes."

"Thanks for the compliment."

But Jeanne seemed oblivious to his sarcasm. "You don't realize how critical a situation it is. My father has threatened to cut off the money I'm supposed to get when I turn twenty-one if I associate with Tom or anyone like him. He told me so today when we were having lunch at the Corvigla Club. My father is a medieval maniac. He always has been, not just with me. With Alexis as well. And before Alexis with my mother."

Harry could not believe his ears, yet despite her desperation the girl seemed perfectly serious, earnest.

"What do you mean?" he asked. "What do Alexis and your mother have to do with it?"

"Plenty. Everything. Oh, you don't understand my father!"

"I'm trying to."

"To tell the truth, it's not just the upper-class part. It's the fact that my father has a very jealous and possessive nature when it comes to the women who are closest to him. My mother was murdered when I was very young. I don't know whether you're aware of that."

"I read about it somewhere," Harry said.

"I really believe that's when it started. When my mother was murdered." Jeanne seemed lost in her own world of sad and painful memories. "You see, the murderer was never apprehended, they never found out who he was, how he got into our flat, but they have their theories. A lot of good theories do. Still, they have them."

"Who's 'they'?"

"The French police and my father. At the time it happened the police were convinced it was a crime of passion and so was my father. For that matter, he still does. But there's a catch, as you Americans say. My nanny was murdered by the same man. So the police couldn't decide who the crime of passion was about, who was having the affair: my mother or Rose, the nanny. One of them was and that's how they believe the murderer got in. Either my mother or Rose innocently let him into the flat. Or possibly he had a key of his own and let himself in."

"If that's true, why would he kill them both?"

"I'll get to that in a second, but the main point is my father is *positive*, absolutely *positive*, that it wasn't the nanny who was playing around. He thinks my mother was cheating on him, that she was the one who opened the door that terrible evening. You see, Daddy was in Zurich on business, so the coast was clear."

Harry was startled. No. Stunned. Shocked.

Years ago when Alexis came to visit him in New York City, she said that Ian distinctly disagreed with the French police's theory . . . that he believed the murder had been committed for motives of profit, for the ruby necklace. And furthermore, Alexis had said that Ian felt sure it was the nanny who was having the affair, not Paulette.

Since then they had never discussed the murders again. It was not just that the subject was extremely unpleasant, there was also the time factor: their hurried lovemaking in a variety of London hotel rooms barely left them with the few precious minutes they needed in order to hold each other close before they had to get out of bed and put on their respectable clothes, their respectable faces. Still, Harry had never forgotten what Alexis said about Ian's theory of the two murders. And that theory clearly contradicted what Jeanne was now saying.

Harry could hardly move his feet to the music, that was how bewildered he now felt.

One of them was lying. Either Alexis or Jeanne. But which one? And why? What reason would Jeanne have to lie? Alexis, on the other hand, had always been a very good liar.

And how foolish of him to give Sarah the pendant. It was a vainglorious moment—a weak attempt to prove she wasn't the only one who could bestow gifts. It was upstairs this very minute in Sarah's jewel case. What a fool he'd been to have ever given it to her! Worse than a fool. Crazy. Insane. Plain nuts. Thank God she hadn't worn it tonight.

"I still don't understand why this man would kill two innocent women. Assuming he came there to keep a romantic appointment."

"I think he dropped in unexpectedly. They didn't know he was coming. And I further think that he found my mother and my nanny in bed together. Or realized that they had just been in bed. So he killed them both in a state of jealous rage. Then he stole a ruby necklace to make it look like theft was all he had in mind from the start."

Harry's heart was starting to thump. "Why would you think that your mother and Rose were sexually involved?"

"I have my reasons," Jeanne said flatly, mysteriously.

"Then you don't believe your father's theory: about your mother having a lover? A male lover, I mean."

"A lover, yes. Male, no. Even though I was only three years old when the murders took place, I have strange memories of—I don't know how to explain it, but I have memories, impressions of there being a relationship between my mother and Rose that went beyond the normal professional one. Children are more intuitive than they're given credit for. Their minds aren't so cluttered with outside rubbish."

"I don't follow you."

"Children are closer to their instincts than adults. They might not understand those instincts at the time, but they remember them years later and can often piece them together, make sense out of them. So even though my father was on the right track that there was another person in my mother's life, he was on the wrong track about the sexual identity of that particular person."

Now Harry was really nervous. "If your mother was only involved with Rose, as you believe, then who was the man who killed them both? Do you think it was a boyfriend of Rose's?"

> But if you let me love you
> It's for sure I'm gonna love you
> All the way
> All the way . . .

"Possibly it was someone Rose knew," Jeanne said, applauding lightly as the song came to an end. "And possibly it was some nut who didn't know either woman but had seen them around and desired to go to bed with one of them. That's what bothers me. The murderer could just have been some anonymous sex fiend. There's something I've never understood about the entire business. Something very odd indeed. Something that doesn't quite add up."

Harry didn't like it, he didn't like it at all. The girl was too shrewd, too uncannily perceptive. As they started to go back to their table, Jeanne said:

"As a result of my father's suspicions, he's never trusted another woman since. Not Alexis and not me. I'm convinced he's hired a detective to have both of us followed. He thinks my mother made a fool out of him, and he's not going to let Alexis do the same, and he's not going to let me do the same either. He wants to possess us both. Don't you see what I'm saying?"

Her voice had risen to an hysterical pitch, drowned out only by the even greater noise in the nightclub. "My father is an irrational, jealous man, I tell you. It's awful! I can't get him to see reason when it comes to Tom, and I can't turn to Alexis for help because she couldn't care less. In fact, I have nobody to turn to except you. If only you would play along."

"By making love to you, you mean?"

"Yes, goddamn it, yes."

"I'd like to oblige you, but if your father is as possessive as you claim, I don't think it's a very wise idea."

Jeanne's face turned into an ugly dark scowl, frightening in its frustrated anger. "You're like all the others. All those so-called grown-up dumb bastards. Afraid of going out on a limb. Afraid to take a chance. Afraid. At least my poor mother had courage. I don't care if she was having an affair with Rose, she was doing what she wanted to, which is more than can be said for the lot of you bloody hypocrites."

To Harry's surprise she began to cry. "If only my mother were alive today. She would understand my problems."

"Please don't cry." Harry put an arm around her trembling bare shoulder. "It's probably not as bad as you think. Your father is only trying to protect you."

"Oh, bullshit. Tom is a nice guy, a decent guy. I don't have to be protected against him. It's people like you and your wife, Alexis, and my damned father I have to be protected against. That's who."

So Ian was a jealous, possessive man. This particular fact fascinated Harry more than anything else Jeanne had said. His fears were starting to dissolve and thoughts were starting to form in his mind, constructive thoughts. . . . Someone new had now entered the scene, someone Harry had not yet met, but who might prove strategically important to his plans.

"Where does your friend Tom play? Which hotel? I'd like to hear him if he's as good as you say."

"He's better than good. He's sensational. He and his group, the Castle Rock, are at the Hotel Alpina. As I told you, Tom is the singer and lead guitarist. Give him my love if you do go over to see him."

"I'll do that," Harry lied.

They were back at the cozy table for five. Harry was stunned to see how quickly Jeanne had stopped crying now that she was confronted by her father's dreaded presence. So she really *was* afraid of him (as Alexis undoubtedly was), Harry thought, more interested than ever in Jeanne's description of Nicholson's ominous personality. Harry held her chair while she sat down and smiled at the others.

"Mr. Maringo is a very smooth dancer," she said.

Alexis was drinking champagne, Sarah was drinking scotch, but Ian Nicholson was not drinking at all. His cold blue eyes confronted Harry.

"Mr. Maringo is also a very smooth businessman," Ian said. "We met years ago in Paris. I just remembered. I believe it was in 1959, or am I wrong, Mr. Maringo?"

"It was 1959, all right," Harry replied. "And please call me Harry."

"Oh, I will. I will. Providing you agree to call me Ian."

"It's a deal."

The band started to play "It Was a Very Good Year."

28 ⌒

Harry and Sarah had arranged for adjoining bedrooms in their seven-hundred-dollar-a-day suite at the Engadine. Sarah's room had twin beds, one of which they decided would be slept in by her nurse of many years, Miss Stark. Harry would sleep in the other bedroom, alone, except when Sarah wanted to make love. Then she would be moved into his bed for what Harry dreaded as "the arduous experience."

Since they had only arrived in St. Moritz late last evening, Sarah was tired and content to be left alone (to Harry's vast relief), but back now after a boozy few hours at the Prince Regent's Club, his wife was starting to utter those whimpering sounds that Harry understood only too well.

Alcohol always made her feel erotic. It had the exact opposite effect upon Harry, and since he'd been drinking so heavily for the last few years, Sarah's complaints about his marital responsibilities were becoming more and more frequent, more and more nagging, more and more unbearable. To cap it all off, she had lately begun to talk baby talk whenever she was in the lovemaking mood.

"Oodn't you like to fucky little Sarah?"

They were still in their evening clothes in her bedroom, and Miss Stark was reading the latest issue of *Woman's Journal* in the sitting room, with the door discreetly closed. Middle-aged Miss Stark had been with them long enough to know what to do, when to do it, and when *not* to.

Although she struck Harry as a weird neuter lady with no discernible interests other than the care of Sarah and the reading of every English woman's magazine on the market, he was forever thanking God for her being in their employ. In an emergency or semiemergency, he knew he could always count on Miss Stark and tonight was going to be no exception.

"Yes, Sarah," he said as calmly as possible, "I would like to make love to you, but first I've got to go out for some air. Take a fast walk. I'm suffocating from all that smoke and lack of ventilation in the club. Can you wait up for me? I won't be long."

She pouted like a child. "Oodn't you like to give little Sarah a kiss before you go?"

He dutifully kissed her on one withered cheek and promised to be back shortly. Then he put on his black suede and leather coat over his evening clothes and told Miss Stark that Lady Sarah was exhausted.

"Please give her several Valium shots as soon as I leave," he said.

Miss Stark nodded. She understood. Sarah would think the injections were for the pain she continually suffered, or thought she suffered. Harry had never been sure how much of the pain was imaginary, how much was real, and he didn't give a damn. Just so long as the bitch was knocked out when he returned from his true destination: the Hotel Alpina, where Tom McKillup and his group were playing.

"I'll take care of it," the nurse said.

"Thank you, Miss Stark. I don't know what we would do without you."

Then Harry walked out of the suite, down the red carpeted corridor, down the elevator, and off into the nearly two A.M. moonlit beauty of St. Moritz. He hoped that Tom's group had not quit for the night. It was a long time since he'd wanted to meet anyone so badly, he thought, as he walked with careful precision along the icy path that led to the Hotel Alpina.

He remembered passing the Alpina yesterday, when he and Sarah were being driven from the train station to the Engadine. The reason he remembered the Alpina (as opposed to other hotels they had passed) was because of a stunning blonde standing beneath the hotel's canopy. She was wearing a long, golden seal coat and seemed to be waiting for someone.

She reminded him of how Sarah used to look in the old days when she would have been waiting for him and he would have been anxious to get there. Now he was anxious to get somewhere else, *to* someone else, but he was afraid to walk any faster for fear of slipping on the treacherous ice.

Black. Except for the sliver of a moon and a dazzle of stars illuminating their favorite sites, it was black all around him, as black as his hand-tailored overcoat. Black pine trees, black mountains, black chalets, but it was a velvet kind of black, all-embracing, all-encompassing, all-forgiving. It gave Harry courage, led him to believe that Tom McKillup and the Castle Rock would still be going strong when he arrived at the Hotel Alpina.

And they were.

A desk clerk directed him downstairs to the Alpina Grill

Room, which was a restaurant at lunchtime and a discotheque at night. Five young men in kilts and argyle knee socks were blasting away at drums, guitars, and electric piano, but one was standing in front of the others, playing guitar and singing

> I saw the boys play rugby today
> I saw them on TV
> With the sound turned off
> With my love turned on
> With my head turned high.

The boy who was singing looked as though he were in his mid-twenties. He had sandy hair, not too long by current youth standards, a square jawline, an upturned nose, and (like Jeanne) a spellbinding smile. A huge glittery sign on the wall behind the group said: CASTLE ROCK—EDINBURGH'S FINEST.

Still wearing his coat, Harry sat down at an empty table for two and looked around him. There were stained glass windows, dark ceiling beams, hanging lanterns, curtains in swirling patterns of red, beige, and green. It was a pretty place, pretty Swiss, pretty typical, but the customers were definitely on the young side, which was not typical at all for hyperexpensive St. Moritz. When the waitress came over, he asked her for a Cresta Starkbier, and also how much longer the group was going to play.

"Soon they will be finished." She appeared tired. "*Gott sei dank!*"

At the other end of the room was a bar. Harry had just noticed it when the waitress returned with his beer. Seated at the bar was the same blonde he had seen last evening standing beneath the hotel's canopy. At least he could have sworn it was the same one, wearing the same golden seal coat, only it seemed to him now that she was considerably older than he had imagined at first. One of the lanterns played upon her face, and it was not the face of a beautiful young girl but rather of a fortyish woman who had once been a beautiful young girl. Again he thought of Sarah. With sadness, bitterness, disgust, but most of all with resentment.

Harry took a sip of the good German beer and realized that the blonde's eyes were firmly, unswervingly fixed upon Tom McKillup, who was winding up his rugby, love, and drug's song with a resounding wail. There was an expression in the blonde's eyes that Harry recognized only too well: desire, lust, call-it-anything-but-do-it-to-me-baby. . . .

Would Tom? Harry wondered. Did he? The possibility that Tom might be attracted to older women went beyond Harry's even highest hopes. It would make his own plans that much easier to carry out, providing of course that Tom was receptive to them. Harry took another sip of the beer just as the song came to an end, and the drummer and piano player walked forward to join the three guitarists in homage to the audience's enthusiastic applause.

Still, it was a small audience, a small room. If Tom and his group were as terrific as Jeanne claimed, why were they playing at a modest hotel over Christmas rather than being on a whirlwind tour of England or America? Not being a follower of rock bands himself, Harry had no way of knowing how famous (or un-famous) the Castle Rock were, what their potential was, whether they had set recording dates. But he intended to find out.

Several young girls rushed toward the bandstand, their main object of admiration being Tom McKillup, who signed autographs and kissed one girl on the top of her head, smiling all the while that appealing, tantalizing smile. Even in a kilt and argyle socks, there was no denying Tom's strong sex appeal. It was a boyish kind of appeal. James Dean and Donny Osmond came to mind. Young women would swoon (did anyone still use that word?) over him, older women would feel maternally aroused.

Harry felt aroused himself. He would definitely prefer going to bed with Tom McKillup than Sarah who, he hoped, would still be dead asleep when he returned to the Engadine. Little did Sarah know about the number of homosexual affairs he'd had over the past years, little did she guess.

Sometimes it even surprised Harry that he had turned to men for sexual gratification, but not really. Sarah was so insanely jealous of other women that men turned out to be much safer bets, and for some reason she never seemed to suspect that many of the "chaps" (Sarah's darling word for them) Harry frequently brought home to dinner were men he had been in bed with only hours before.

Or perhaps she did suspect but found the situation less threatening, and consequently it was never discussed, never brought out in the open, for which Harry was bitterly grateful. It was one of the few things he *was* grateful to Sarah for, one of the very few, since he did not like to think of himself as a homosexual. Circumstances had forced the arrangement upon him, that was all.

The five members of Castle Rock had left the bandstand and dispersed. Harry was just about to stand up and approach Tom McKillup when he realized that McKillup was brushing off the cluster of girls who still clung to him and was rapidly approaching the blonde at the bar.

"She's probably his mother," he heard one of the young girls say to another.

"He certainly fancies his mother!" the other replied.

They were English and stoically accepted their fate, trooping out of the Alpina Grill Room, dejected but being brave about it all. As they left, they were debating the merits of the next day's skiing conditions.

But Harry was focused on McKillup and the blonde, who kissed the rock player on the mouth the minute he reached her. It was a slow kiss and one that made Harry certain that an intimate relationship existed between the two of them. Damn it! He wondered how long it had been going on, how serious it was. Probably just a holiday romance and she probably had money, which would appeal to McKillup.

The only thing Harry knew about rock groups was that they invariably came from poor families, like prizefighters. Providing they had the respective talent, these were two of the professional avenues of escape to a world they otherwise could never dream of entering—a world of wealth, success, acclaim, and the pick of any woman (or man) they wanted.

A wooden bird in the cuckoo clock above the bar announced that it was two o'clock. That same little birdie secretly announced to Harry that Tom McKillup was one of those people who found both sexes equally appealing and would not hesitate to indulge his desires if and when an attractive situation presented itself.

Harry stood up, decisively belted his six-hundred-dollar coat, and went to find out if that little birdie was right.

29 ⤟⤟

Two evenings later, Jeanne Jennifer Nicholson was trying to decide what to wear for dinner and later for the Christmas Eve Gala that she was definitely not looking forward to. All those multilingual, middle-aged sophisticates, eating and drinking and smiling and small-talking it up. What a bore!

She went through the row of evening clothes in her closet, fingering each one absentmindedly. That was a bore, too, this constant dressing for dinner, the jewelry, the makeup, the matching accessories, and now her hair and fingernails freshly done at the Engadine beauty salon (*membre du syndicat haute coiffure française et coiffure artistique suisse*). But despite those lofty credentials, the stylist had given Jeanne the hairspray treatment before she could stop her. Jeanne hated the sticky stuff and brushed it out as soon as she went up to her room.

Now, standing there naked, she decided upon the rust vampy Biba with the high neckline and balloon sleeves and her chocolate brown satin slings and purse. That should keep Daddy and Stepmommy half-happy, which was more than they deserved. Biba's dresses were always tacitly sensual even when there was hardly any flesh showing, but at least Ian could not berate her for "looking like a tart" as he had the other evening when she wore the red maxi with spaghetti shoulder straps and her tits visible for one and all to see. He certainly would not be able to say anything like that tonight. She would even wear a brassiere. How respectable could you get?

It was still too early to start dressing. She walked to the huge window and watched snow descend upon the village of St. Moritz. Somehow it did not seem like real snow, not here in this sleekly packaged, make-believe world. She tinkled the crystal icicles on the Christmas tree that sat next to the window, and sang "Rudolph, the Red-Nosed Reindeer" off-key at the top of her lungs.

Nothing happened. Nobody complained.

"*Viva Biba!*" she shouted at her nonaudience.

Then she collapsed on the scented bedsheets and burst into tears. But even as she wept, she could not help wondering whether they were real tears or just another bit of appropriate theatricality. *Lovely, lonely little rich girl cries her heart out in the chic stage setting known as St. Moritz*. Well, why not? Maybe she was catching the disease, too—she'd been exposed to it for nine days now, the disease known as pretension, phoniness.

Yet somehow she did not think so, she was too critical of the people around her to be like them. If she were like them, she'd be happy now looking forward to the evening ahead, not dreading it, not feeling that everyone was against her. Jeanne wiped her eyes on the pillow cover, sat up, and hugged her small naked body to herself, remembering Harry's rejection two nights ago at the Prince Regent's Club.

That had definitely been the last straw, the crummiest kind of betrayal, because the fact was that she didn't give a damn about going to bed with him and she couldn't even have *that*: what she didn't want, but needed in her campaign to shake up her father and make him see (as she had told Harry) that Tom would be a godsend in comparison to him.

No, it was Harry who pointed out that charming fact. What difference did it make who said it? It was true. She felt weak in the knees just thinking about Tom, and unless she sneaked off behind her father's back and went to the Alpina she would have little chance of running into him anywhere around here.

The fact that Tom didn't do any of the things that people who came to St. Moritz normally did only made Jeanne more interested in him than ever—as she had done them all with the exception of the Cresta Run, the perilous toboggan slope. The Cresta Run was unique to St. Moritz, there was nothing like it at any other ski resort anywhere else in the world. The only thing that amazed Jeanne was that it existed at all, being as spectacularly dangerous as it was. She had gone up to the starting place above the Kulm Hotel early yesterday morning to see what the big action was all about.

A lot of men of different nationalities, wearing crash helmets, huge goggles, leather knee-and-shoulder pads, and boots with sharp toe spikes were lined up ready to get on a skinny aluminum toboggan that was roughly four feet long. Then, at the microphoned command of the English Air Vice-Marshall, each would be launched, one by one, headfirst down a narrow icy path with treacherous turns until he reached Celerina, about three-quarters of a mile away in the valley. That is, if he were lucky enough to get there intact.

And the toboggans were merely sheets of aluminum (they

didn't call them "skeletons" for nothing), and the only way the driver could try to prevent himself from injury or death was to move his body to the right when he wanted to go right, left when he wanted to go left, backward to slow down a little, forward if he wanted to go oven faster than the average speed of eighty miles an hour. If he really panicked and wanted to eliminate himself from the competition, he could cut his spiked boots into the icy path and stop altogether, but according to one entrant, an American, that was known as "chickening out."

It hardly surprised Jeanne to discover that the Cresta Run had been founded by the English. Being half-English herself, she understood the mad stoicism that characterized the Anglo-Saxons and could produce a competitive "sport" in which men risked fractures, bleeding faces, broken collarbones, broken backs, and God knew what else, just for the praise of a few compatriots and a crowd of adoring girls who would be waiting for the daredevils (the American had proudly explained) at the Sunny Bar of the Kulm when it was all over. Drinks and lunch were then in order. Plus quite a bit of screwing afterward, Jeanne imagined, particularly for the victorious hero of the day.

But even though Jeanne acknowledged the part of herself that was English, it was the French part she identified with—one of the many reasons that up until last week she dreaded going to King's College in London, starting next month. The mere thought of it had made her sick. She would have much preferred going to school anywhere on the Continent rather than returning to bloody boring England—her father's idea of course. He was hoping that when she graduated from King's College she would get a job in the Foreign Office and eventually marry some nice young diplomat and take her place in proper society.

The only reason Jeanne hadn't put up more of a fuss was because in a few years' time, with her language background truly perfected, she could also apply for a job at the United Nations in New York, the EEC in Brussels, or possibly the European Parliament in Strasbourg. They all needed interpreters. But after meeting Tom McKillup her feelings about going to university in London had changed considerably.

Jeanne stood up and went to the window again. It was still snowing, more heavily than before, and if it continued like this tomorrow morning there would be deep powder snow, which she loved. It took an expert to ski in deep powder, and that she was thanks to all those hours of practice on the mountain slopes of Gstaad.

Yes, she was a top-notch skier, a top-notch language student (French, German, Italian, and Spanish), and a virgin at eighteen. Probably the last eighteen-year-old virgin left in the Western world.

The only reason she had never gone to bed with a man was because she had never wanted to. The temptation simply was not there until she met Tom. At times her lack of sexual desire bothered her terribly. For one thing it didn't seem very French of her to be so uninterested in lovemaking and she often wondered if there was a physical reason for it, a glandular imbalance or something.

Secretly she suspected that the real reason had to do with the murder of her mother and nanny when she was only three. She still remembered the shadowy figure of a man dressed in black fleeing from their apartment and leaving behind the dead, naked bodies of the two women she loved most in the world.

The small travel-alarm clock next to the bed pointed to nine-fifteen. Jeanne decided to start getting dressed leisurely, since dinner would be served at ten. Alexis and Ian were probably downstairs at the bar right now, enjoying cocktails with the Maringos. The two couples seemed to have hit it off to a remarkable degree, because her father, who ordinarily was English-cool toward strangers, had suggested last evening that they share the same dining table for the remainder of the holidays, and the suggestion was enthusiastically agreed to by Harry Maringo with an acquiescent smile from his pathetic wife.

"That would be lovely," Sarah said, the expression on her face belying her words.

Jeanne knew that Sarah Maringo was jealous of her and it struck her as ironic. Harry was not her type, she could never be attracted to a man with dark hair and dark eyes. Again she remembered the shadow of a stranger who had murdered her mother and Rose. He seemed so dark, the night was so dark, the apartment was dark except for that thin stream of light coming from her parents' bedroom.

No. Dark men like Harry Maringo might appeal to other women, but certainly not to her. What was more, she didn't *like* him. He was too smooth, too glossy, too mucho-macho for her taste. And yet such was her desperation about Tom that she even went so far as to boast to Harry about how terrific she was in bed. If anything, she was scared stiff of being pretty terrible when the crucial moment presented itself.

And it *was* going to present itself, she thought with stubborn conviction as she slipped a beige stretch bra over her head and adjusted it around her small breasts. She wondered if Tom liked small breasts.

The first and only time she met Tom was not quite by sheer chance. Her father had been so anxious for her to have a good time over the holidays that when they arrived last week he agreed to take her to the Alpina Grill after dinner. Naturally Alexis agreed to go too, Jeanne thought with contempt. Alexis would agree to fly to Mars if Ian suggested it, just so long as he didn't take away any of her precious charge accounts or cut off her ceaseless supply of fur coats. Alexis was a fur coat freak. She easily had more than ten of the most luxurious fur in her vast and coveted collection. The night they went to the Alpina she was wearing the beige chinchilla.

The minute Jeanne laid eyes on Tom she became dizzy with desire. She had never understood groupies, those fanatic girls who followed rock stars all around the world, who screamed and yelled and sometimes fainted during the actual performances. At best Jeanne considered them foolish, at worst idiots.

But when she heard Tom sing and play guitar, she began to get an inkling of what it was all about, she began to feel the excitement he engendered. There was a magnetism about him, an electric force she had never encountered in her life, an aura of energy and glamour that made her instantly decide he would be her first lover. When the Castle Rock stopped for a break, she rushed up to the bandstand before either Ian or Alexis could restrain her.

It was the first time she had ever done anything like that, and she knew her father would be mortified. She knew, but she didn't care. The only thing she cared about at that precise moment was to talk to the sandy-haired young man with the green eyes, who sang so poignantly, to touch him, make him aware that she cared, somehow make him care too.

"I think you're marvelous," she told Tom as he stepped down. "Really great."

He grinned, pleased. "Thank you very much."

"You probably hear it all the time, but I don't go around saying things like this all the time." She felt hopelessly inept, banal. "I've never even spoken to a professional musician before."

"That's okay. We don't bite."

She took his hand. It was very warm, reassuring. "I'm with my father and stepmother. Over there." She indicated the shadowy table with a look of despair. "Do you think you could bear to join us for a drink? Please say yes."

"I'm afraid I can't. It's against house rules. We're not allowed to mingle with the guests. Sorry."

"But surely just for a few minutes. . . ." She was desperate, she couldn't lose him now. "Please. Couldn't you break the rules this one time?"

"Honey, I'd love to but the management would have my neck."

He had called her honey! She felt weak, dizzy, giddy. If anyone had told her she could feel this way about a man she'd just met (and a man in a kilt at that!), she would not have believed it, she would have said it was corny. But there was nothing corny about the way her heart was beating, the way her mouth felt dry. Then, out of the corner of her eye, she saw her father staring at her with dismay while Alexis just sat there smiling her Greta Garbo smile.

"I want to see you again," Jeanne said quickly. "I have to see you again. You can't imagine how important it is. You have no idea—"

"Hey, honey, calm down! Don't get so excited. It's not the end of the world. Where are you staying?"

"The Engadine."

He whistled softly. "V-e-r-y good. Daddy must be loaded."

She decided to overlook this indiscreet reference to her father's financial position. "Will you call me? At the Engadine? I'm in room 406. My name is Jeanne Nicholson. What's yours?"

"Tom McKillup."

"Will you call me?"

"I'll try," he conceded, "but time is pretty tight between now and New Year's Eve. Frankly it's going to be difficult. Do you live in London?"

"Yes. I mean, I will be as of next month. Why? Do you live there too?"

"If you consider it living, we travel so much. But London is home base. We have a flat in Fulham, the group and I."

"That's marvelous. I start King's College in a few weeks." At that moment she could have smothered Ian with kisses for talking her into it. "Our flat is on Mount Street and we're in the telephone directory. Nicholson. But surely you don't have to wait that long. You must have some free time during the next two weeks. Why not call me tomorrow? We can go skiing."

"I don't ski," he said with an apologetic smile. "Can't take the chance of breaking any vital parts, not in this business."

She was about to ask him what he did do besides melting girls' hearts at the Alpina Grill Room when she saw Ian approaching them, his lips compressed in stern disapproval.

"Oh, Daddy." She tried to keep her voice light, casual, but she was trembling. "I'd like you to meet Tom McKillup. Tom, this is my father."

The two men shook hands. Jeanne was not unaware of the number of girls trying to reach Tom's side. But they were remarkably well behaved, despite the fact that most of them waved pieces of paper for his autograph. Like children, Jeanne thought, feeling more sophisticated by the minute.

"It's a pleasure, Mr. Nicholson," Tom said easily.

Ian frowned. "I'm afraid I have a very impetuous daughter. I apologize for her behavior. And now if you'll excuse us, Mr. McKillup, we must be leaving. I'm certain that your other fans won't object." He shot a look of disdain at the group of eager girls. "Delighted to have met you."

Before Jeanne could say another word, Ian led her away and then she and Alexis were being bundled out the door like refugees fleeing an invasion. All sense of Jeanne's sophistication promptly vanished.

"*Really, Daddy!*" was all she could say once they were out in the sharp night air of St. Moritz. "*How could you?*"

"It was easy. I do not enjoy seeing my daughter make a public spectacle of herself over some randy rock singer. I saw the way he grabbed your hand."

Alexis snuggled into her chinchilla and characteristically said nothing.

"Tom did not grab my hand. I grabbed his!"

Ian did not speak. It was as though he considered the conversational possibilities beneath him. And yet he loves me, Jeanne thought as they walked back to the Engadine in uncomfortable silence.

Growing up without a mother had affected Jeanne in ways she herself was not aware of. In certain practical matters it had matured her beyond her years, forced her to become more independent, but in other matters it had robbed her of the intimate rapport she needed in order to develop emotionally as a woman.

Jeanne knew that Alexis' mother had died suddenly when her stepmother was twelve. What she did not know was how similar she and Alexis were beneath their respective façades. Her father's second wife had never been much more than a phantom figure to Jeanne, a beautiful, icy, gold-digger of a ghost, and while it was truly difficult to despise Alexis, it was equally difficult to like her.

But now as Jeanne sat before the dressing table mirror, putting on makeup, her thoughts were not on Alexis, they were firmly fixed on Tom. Would he call her before they all left St. Moritz or wouldn't he? That was the exasperating question. She didn't really expect him to, she merely prayed that he would.

"Prayers are messages relayed to God by angels," Rose had once said.

The possibility that he might be in love with someone else suddenly occurred to her. Why hadn't it occurred to her before? Tom might be dreaming about another woman this very minute, just as achingly as she was dreaming about him.

It was Jeanne's first taste of the unfairness and anxiety of love, and she didn't like it, not one bit. She felt a sense of helplessness that unnerved her, made her realize there was little she could do except wait.

Tom was indeed dreaming of someone, and if Jeanne had known who it was, she would not have been merely unnerved, she would have been dazed by the identity of that person. For it was someone she knew, someone she would be sharing the same dinner table with very shortly, someone she did not like.

30 ❧

The dining room at the Engadine Hotel was rich, regal, chandeliered. Freshly cut flowers sat in slender crystal vases on each table, silver shone, damask serviettes glowingly touched impeccable lips, philodendron leaves wrapped themselves around pillars that supported the baroque ceiling, and two huge Christmas trees stood at either end of the room, all tinsel and glitter.

Waiters hovered for the flick of a command from one of the diners, they hurried silently on thick rosy carpeting to fulfill those commands, they smiled, they nodded, they listened. But above all they watched the occupants of the three hundred or so velvet-covered chairs, who in turn ignored everyone and everything except the dishes placed in front of them, the wine poured into their glasses, the people at their immediate table, whose pearl and emerald and diamond jewelry vied with their own in flashing brilliance.

Jeanne couldn't help it. She thought of the starving masses in India, delighted not to be one of them, annoyed with herself for arriving fifteen minutes late. At the very last second, just as she was about to leave her room, she collapsed into another crying jag and as a result had to do her makeup over again. She hoped nobody in her party would notice how red and swollen her eyes were, but she needn't have worried. She realized that as soon as she spotted the four of them.

Why, they're all smashed out of their bloody minds! was her immediate stunned reaction. Even Alexis, who rarely drank more than an occasional glass of wine, seemed loaded to the gills and was giggling inanely at some remark that Sarah Maringo had just made. To look at the two couples, anyone would assume they'd been the closest of friends for years.

"Darling," Ian said, as the waiter seated Jeanne in the empty chair between Alexis and Harry. "Where have you been? We were starting to become concerned. In fact, I was just about to ring your room."

But before Jeanne could reply, he waved a hand and said, "Never mind. You're here and you look lovely. Very lovely, indeed. Well go on, eat your caviar. We've had ours."

The menu before her said: *Caviar Sevruga d'Iran.*

She dipped a silver spoon into the tiny black pearls, spread them on a toast point and took a bite. It was delicious. The wine steward filled her glass with champagne, then refilled the other classes.

"Cheers cheers cheers cheers!"

It sounded like a singsong tribal chant. Jeanne wondered how much champagne the four of them had consumed in the bar earlier. Quite a bit, judging from their flushed and foolish faces. People who drank never realized how silly they appeared to people who didn't, Jeanne thought just as Harry Maringo began to tell an anecdote about his and Sarah's halcyon days among American movie stars.

"When we were living in Beverly Hills, there was a famous movie actress, a lesbian, whose constant companion was a smelly Afghanistan named Louis. The actress and Louis went everywhere together, she was never seen without him. He even came to the set when she was filming. . . ."

The story seemed to go on forever, but Jeanne stopped listening after the first few lines. Something else had caught her attention: Sarah Maringo's ruby necklace. Jeanne's mind flashed back fifteen years and fluttered there, remembering the ruby necklace of her mother's that she used to play with when she was a child in Paris, the necklace that had been stolen by the murderer of the two women.

Jeanne had seen other ruby necklaces since then, but they never reminded her of the one that belonged to her mother, as Sarah's did. There it lay against the poor woman's shrunken bosom, the huge red oblong stone glistening on a diamond chain. Jeanne could still remember how it used to feel in her hands, warm and comforting. She put down her caviar spoon, suddenly frightened by the specter of evil.

Harry Maringo was winding up his movie star story and everyone at the table laughed in unison when he said, "And that's how Louis became Louise!"

Ian was the first to notice that his daughter was the only one not laughing. There was a strange expression on her face.

"Is something wrong, Jeanne?" He gazed anxiously at her across all the silver and crystal and china. "You've turned very pale. What is it, darling?"

"Sarah's necklace."

"What about it?"

"It looks exactly like the one that Mother used to own."

An uneasy silence descended upon the table until Ian spoke. "Which necklace was that?"

Jeanne knew of course that her father was color blind, but she also knew that red was one of the two easiest colors for him to distinguish (the other being blue). He would realize that Sarah was wearing a ruby, he could easily recognize the oval shape, see the flashing chain of diamonds. He *should* remember, or had he somehow managed to erase it all from his mind?

"The ruby necklace," Jeanne said. "The one that was stolen the night Mother and Rose were murdered. Surely you can't have forgotten it, Daddy. You gave it to her."

Sarah Maringo shuddered, her hand automatically going to the pendant around her neck. "Your mother murdered . . . I had no idea . . . I never would have worn it tonight . . . oh, you poor child, I'm so sorry!"

Ian was torn between reprimanding his daughter for her bad manners in bringing up such an unpleasant subject and trying to comfort her because of the anguish plainly written all over her face. She was obviously reliving an old nightmare. He himself had blotted out that nightmare a long time ago.

"Jeanne," he said gently but firmly, "you're putting Mrs. Maringo in a very awkward position. It's hardly her fault that she happens to own a piece of jewelry which resembles one belonging to your late mother. I think we should drop the entire subject immediately and get on with our dinner."

"But it doesn't just resemble it!" Jeanne protested.

"What, precisely, do you mean?" Ian asked, starting to lose patience.

"*I mean, I think it's the same one!*"

At which point their waiter appeared with the second course of what everyone (rapidly sobering up) felt was going to be an interminable dinner. The second course was cold Norwegian lobster with a choice of sauces.

"Don't be ridiculous," Ian said to Jeanne. "It merely looks like the same one."

"No, I don't think so."

"For God's sake, you were only three years old when your mother died. Use your head. What can a three-year-old child possibly remember?"

Jeanne put a dollop of mayonnaise on her lobster, despite that fact that she had lost her appetite. "That it was an eighteen-carat pigeon blood ruby."

"You don't remember that," Ian said, choosing the hot butter and truffle sauce. "It was something you must have heard me mention years later."

"Perhaps." Jeanne accosted Sarah Maringo. "Well? Is it?"

"Jeanne!" Ian could not believe his ears. "Have you gone quite mad? I want you to apologize to Mrs. Maringo at once. Do you understand?"

"I don't see what there is to apologize for. I was merely asking a simple, factual question."

Sarah squeezed half a lemon, through a wrapping of cheesecloth, onto the cold lobster. "Don't upset yourself, Ian. Your daughter has a good eye. This does happen to be an eighteen-carat pigeon blood ruby. It was an anniversary gift from my husband."

Everyone's gaze turned to Harry, the only person at the table who had dispensed with sauces and was actually eating the lobster.

"Correct," he said. "I gave the necklace to Sarah on our second wedding anniversary."

"If I'm not being too impertinent," Jeanne said, "may I ask you where you bought it?"

"You *are* being impertinent," Ian cut in. "It's none of your bloody business!"

"I bought it in Beverly Hills," Harry said. "From Van Cleef and Arpels."

"And how many years ago was that?" Jeanne asked.

"Fourteen."

"You see, Daddy?" There was a look of triumph on Jeanne's girlish face. "It could easily be Mother's necklace, which was stolen fifteen years ago, passed through a maze of illegal hands, and then was legitimately sold to Mr. Maringo. It's not impossible."

"Reputable jewelers like Van Cleef and Arpels do not deal in stolen merchandise," Ian said, becoming more angry by the moment.

"But what if the firm didn't know it was stolen? I tell you, it's Mother's necklace. I know it!"

"I consider this conversation to be in extremely poor taste." Ian drained another glass of champagne, but the bubbles seemed flat. "I fail to see what you're trying to accomplish. But just for the sake of argument, let's assume that it is the same necklace. So what? What does it prove, except that Mr. Maringo bought it in good faith? What is your point, Jeanne? This is Christmas Eve. We're supposed to be enjoying ourselves, not digging up the grisly past."

"Don't you think it's a weird coincidence that of all the people in the world who might have bought Mother's necklace, it should turn out to be someone sitting here with us tonight? The odds must be about twenty million to one against it. Or more."

"Maybe Mr. Maringo never bought the necklace at all." A sardonic note had crept into Ian's voice. "Maybe he murdered your mother and stole her jewelry. What kind of odds would you give me on that?"

"This is beginning to sound like one of those devious Agatha Christie plots," Sarah said. "Too unbelievable."

"Oh, do you read her too?" Alexis asked. "I'm a devoted fan. Particularly of her Miss Marple books."

"I prefer Poirot myself, despite his nasty pretentiousness."

"Now who's being grisly," Jeanne said to her father, "talking about Mr. Maringo and murder?"

But to her annoyance neither he nor the others seemed to be listening to her. Sarah and Alexis were solemnly discussing the respective merits of Jane Marple versus Hercule Poirot. Harry had finished the lobster, used the finger bowl, and was reading the remainder of the menu with avid interest. Ian had stopped eating altogether and looked detached, as though he were engrossed in other more important matters.

Like the Financial Times Index, no doubt, Jeanne thought, disgusted with them all. Where was their imagination, their curiosity, their sense of adventure? Nonexistent. She dug into her lobster with grim resignation, feeling more alone than ever.

Alexis was so nervous that she had to brace herself from losing her usual cool façade. It was a major effort to keep her voice steady in talking to Sarah about crafty old Miss Marple, when all the time she was thinking of Harry's insanity in allowing his wife to wear that damned necklace tonight.

What in hell was wrong with him? Had he lost his mind? Didn't he realize the dreadful chance he was taking? Or hadn't he been able to stop Sarah from doing as she pleased? Probably the latter, but it made no difference in the long run. For now Ian would surely remember (his macabre jokes notwithstanding) that Harry had been in Paris the very week Paulette was murdered.

Ian had a good memory. Still there was no reason for him ever to associate Harry with Paulette's death, Alexis told herself, no reason in the world. A look-alike ruby necklace. A stolen ruby necklace. So what? Jewelry was stolen all the time and passed off to unsuspecting people. Ian would think it was one of those bizarre, twenty-million-to-one coincidences, as Jeanne had said. Or would he?

"Yes," Alexis said pleasantly to Sarah, "on the whole I would agree that Miss Marple's conclusions tend to be based on inductive thinking. Poirot leans more toward the deductive, doesn't he. . . ?"

Harry was silently cursing himself for having given the ruby necklace to Sarah to begin with. What a wild risk he had taken by doing so! What a young fool he'd been in those days! But who could have dreamed that the necklace he'd impetuously stolen in Paris would show up fifteen years later at a dinner table in St. Moritz and be recognized by the daughter of its rightful owner?

Ian Nicholson, that's who. *Maybe Mr. Maringo never bought the necklace at all.* Even though it was intended as a joke, Harry wasn't laughing. The joke was too close for comfort. Earlier that evening he had tried to dissuade Sarah from wearing the necklace by saying that he didn't think it went with her gown, a cream-colored silk.

"It's a bit too loud," he told her.

Sarah merely laughed. "Don't be an ass, darling. Pigeon blood rubies are too expensive to be loud."

Well, she was right about the expensive part. When Ian originally bought the necklace, the stone alone would have cost about two hundred thousand dollars. The price must have tripled since then—and that did not include the diamond chain. But Harry hesitated to say more on the subject for fear of arousing Sarah's suspicions. She would have wanted to know why he was so adamant about her not wearing her little treasure this festive evening. Sarah still naively believed that he had paid for the necklace out of his winnings at a Las Vegas roulette table, and it was best she continue to believe just that. Harry felt like strangling that little bitch Jeanne for being so astute, for putting dangerous thoughts into her father's mind. *Maybe Mr. Maringo never bought the necklace at all . . . maybe he murdered your mother and stole her jewelry.*

Harry realized that the older man was talking to him.

"Excuse me?"

"Insurance. I trust you've had that lovely necklace insured."

"Of course," Harry lied.

"Smart chap. It was only after the tragedy that I discovered the thief had stolen the one piece of jewelry Paulette owned that wasn't covered by insurance. Bloody stupid of me. I had asked Paulette to call our broker and make the necessary arrangements. Ordinarily I did that myself, but I was up to my neck in some business deal at the time." Ian shook his head, as though unable to believe his own foolhardiness. "Apparently Paulette forgot to make that call."

Harry looked properly sympathetic. "That was a tough break."

"Tough," Ian said, reflecting. "Yes."

Harry's mind was racing. A necklace originally purchased back in the early fifties. Uninsured. To Harry that meant virtually untraceable, identification exceptionally thin. Only one thing bothered him. If Ian had any suspicions at all, he might try to check with Van Cleef and Arpels in California to see if a pigeon blood ruby had been sold to one Harry Maringo fourteen years ago. Did jewelers keep sales records as long as fourteen years? Probably, but would they give out such information to a total stranger? Harry doubted it, still it made him uneasy. He went back to hide behind the menu. . . .

Ian hid behind his businessman's mask as he was used to doing at important meetings when he didn't want anyone present to know how he felt. Right now he felt infuriated with Jeanne for her blundering indiscretion. A fine diplomat's wife she would make, bringing up a subject that could only prove embarrassing to Sarah and Harry, distressing to himself, and distasteful to his second wife.

Before Jeanne had come down to the dining room, the four of them were having such a carefree, tipsy time. But she had managed to destroy that, separate them from each other somehow, and Ian was sure he knew why. Jeanne was vindictively paying him back for forbidding her to associate with that Scottish rock singer. He only had her best interests at heart, but she couldn't see that. She was blind to his true intentions of protecting her, as a father should. Instead she irrationally saw him as some sort of monster standing in the way of her happiness. Well, even though he didn't like it, he would rather she considered him a monster than a nice permissive father who let his beloved daughter go ahead and make a mess of her young life.

Never mind. Aside from Jeanne, the person he felt most concerned about at the moment was Sarah. She had been the most abused thanks to Jeanne's vulgar interrogation, but being a well-bred Englishwoman Lady Sarah Constance Ames-Maringo had taken it all in sporting good stride. Ian would not like to imagine what her true thoughts were. More, he couldn't blame her for them. She had a right to feel put out, even though she refrained from showing it.

As for Harry Maringo, he had borne up remarkably well considering the fact that he was an American of dubious background. Still Ian had to admit that in the last forty-eight hours he had come to admire Maringo's honesty, modesty, if not his enthusiasm about finding an occupation to call his own. He seemed utterly confused as to what to do with his life. "Lacking direction," would best sum it up, Ian surmised, remembering the zealous young man who had come to his office in Paris in 1959 trying to raise five million dollars. That man and this one were like two different people.

Possibly it was Maringo's devotion to his invalid wife that had prevented him, since then, from furthering himself in a business enterprise. Certainly Harry was devoted to Sarah, attendant to her every whim, and had been for a long time. It could not be an easy or satisfying existence, and not one for which Maringo was prepared when he got married. It made Ian wonder whether Maringo had married solely for money, and then after the accident decided to make the best of an unpalatable situation. Or perhaps he didn't find it as unpalatable as all that. It was cushy enough, no question of that.

In Ian Philip Nicholson's book, there was nothing the tiniest bit immoral about marrying a wealthy titled woman, but to simply glide along on that, making no effort to do anything on your own (it wasn't necessary that you succeed, it was making the effort that counted), well, it was highly suspect.

Ian spotted the waiter approaching with the roast goose plus accoutrements. To hell with all this intellectualizing about Harry Maringo. There would be time enough to find out if the man was genuine once they all returned to the sanity of England. Right now Ian was concentrating upon the goose, wondering what kind of stuffing it would have. Apple, prune, or chestnut, no doubt. His mouth was literally watering. . . .

Sarah felt like a horse, foaming. The exertion that it took to make pleasant chitchat with Alexis about Hercule Poirot was truly herculean, that's how distressed she felt. And all because of that little tease, Jeanne, who Harry found so attractive. He couldn't take his eyes off her, he hung on her every word about her murdered mother's ruby necklace. As though Harry cared! As though any of them cared about that morbid conversation. It was just Jeanne's way of drawing attention to herself, specifically Harry's attention.

Harry and Jeanne had made love the other night. Sarah knew it with the infallible instinct that every woman who is out of the running has. She could smell it on the two of them, and it made her sick with jealousy. She shifted in her chair, still agonizingly aware after all these years that she would never walk again, never lead a normal life, never be a real wife to Harry.

If she could walk, stand, move, she'd beat the two of them

to a pulp. It was what they deserved for sneaking around behind her back as though she were a fool and did not know
what was going on. Like that so-called painkiller shot Miss
Stark had given her two evenings ago, after she and Harry
returned from the Prince Regent's Club and she wanted to
make love.

Harry, apparently, did not want to. At least not with her,
or he wouldn't have instructed Miss Stark to give her a knock-
out shot instead. As a result she was dead to the world when
Harry returned from his late night date with Jeanne. Harry
had held Jeanne in his arms, undressed her, caressed her, and
been pleased with her firm young girl's body. No. More than
pleased. Thrilled. Excited. As he had not been with Sarah
for a long time now.

She wanted to weep. She had been so beautiful once, so
desirable. She still remembered the marvelous sex with Harry
before she became an invalid. It was a dream of hot, sensuous
colors, a dream she hadn't experienced in a long time. When
Harry made love to her now, it was like a duty he had to
fulfill, a sentence imposed upon him, rather than the consequence of his own desire. She repelled him and she knew it.
Of course he would be attracted to girls like Jeanne, girls
who were healthy, vibrant, bursting with life. It was natural.
It was intolerable.

Sarah was impatient for this holiday to be over so she and
Harry could return to their acres of retreat in the heartland
of Surrey. Just the two of them, alone. Perhaps she would
have her hair done differently, buy some seductive lounging
clothes, get a daily massage, tone up her flaccid muscles. She'd
been neglecting herself. Perhaps it still was not too late to
win back her appealing husband.

Sarah stroked the pigeon blood ruby, thinking how foolish
Harry had been earlier in asking her not to wear it tonight.
The ruby was her good luck piece, and she silently beseeched
it not to let her down now, *please. . . .*

The meal was finally nearing its seemingly interminable end,
Jeanne realized, as sweets and demitasse cups appeared. She
had eaten too much out of sheer boredom and felt stuffed. She
let the sweets pass and did not put sugar in her coffee. Sugar
was bad for your complexion, anyhow.

But that did not deter any of the others, including her stepmother, who had ordered her usual Hag decaffeinated coffee,
and was adding to it a large helping of sugar plus that white
sedative powder she took for insomnia. Jeanne noticed that

Harry Maringo seemed especially interested in the powder, and was asking Alexis about it.

"Oh, it's a special formula," Alexis said. "A chemist friend of Ian's prescribed it for me some time ago and I'm happy to say that it actually works."

"Isn't it a little early to be taking it now?" Harry asked. "Since you're planning on going to the Gala, I mean."

"No, that's one of the things I like about it. For some reason it doesn't take effect until about three hours later. Particularly if I've had a large meal like this evening."

"She's always suffered from insomnia," Ian said sympathetically. "Terrible thing, insomnia."

"Yes, it must be hell," Harry said.

As Alexis continued to stir the Hag, Harry continued to watch her, their dark eyes—it seemed to Jeanne—purposely avoiding each other. Dark eyes, straight dark hair, their imposing height, something about the cruel curve of their jawline. It had never occurred to Jeanne before how much alike Harry and Alexis were in physical appearance.

If anyone didn't know better, she thought, dreamily drinking her sugarless coffee, it would not be difficult to mistake the two of them for brother and sister.

31 &

The next week sped by without incident until the very last day.

We did all the usual things that wealthy people who come to St. Moritz normally do. We skied, we skated, we *langlaufed*, we swam in indoor pools, we sunbathed at terrace cafes, we went to the Cinema Scala, we played bridge, we ate well, we drank sparingly (except for Harry), we slept deeply, the mountain air a natural sedative for everyone other than me.

I still took my nightly sleeping powder, which I had become addicted to. I wanted to make certain I was totally knocked out so that no provocative thoughts could cross my mind and stir up my imagination. The thoughts I was trying to avoid had to do with my killing Sarah. How would I go about it when the time came? Would it be difficult? What if I slipped up at some strategic point and she survived? I couldn't help remembering Harry's reply when I warned him that I was a better skier than he:

"Yes, but are you a better murderer?"

The fact was that I did not like to think of myself as a potential murderer, it seemed such a crass label. Yet at the same time I was not really horrified or repelled by the prospect of taking Sarah's life. It was her life versus mine and Harry's, that was all I could focus on: being with Harry as soon as possible. I didn't even hate Sarah, she was merely an obstacle to my ultimate happiness.

Even so I felt relieved that during our last week in St. Moritz she was not around much. Except for the sedentary activities we engaged in, she mostly confined herself to the soothing and supposedly restorative mineral baths in the Engadine, while the rest of us were caught up in the impatient rhythm that always seems to mark the week between Christmas and New Year's.

I even gave in the other afternoon and tied Ian to the bed for two hours with leather thongs, during most of which time I tortured him by not torturing him. But his plaintive cries to be punished had to be met sooner or later. There was just no getting out of it.

"Please, Alexis," he all but wept. "I'm waiting."

In my executioner's leather hood mask, medieval-patterned leather apron, and studded cuffs (all bought in one of London's most exclusive discipline and corrective shops), I ordered him to control his lustful desires.

"I can't. Oh, I can't," he pleaded. "Just one fast lash."

"No."

It was no wonder that people generally considered me glacial. My sex face with Ian had permanently scarred my social face. Because in order to satisfy my husband's typically English whims, I had to harden myself into a kind of ice woman, devoid of compassion or pity, the last two emotions in the world that Ian desired from his beloved torturer.

The whip in my hand remained still as I thought about where to hit him first. He was lying spread-eagled on his stomach. Perhaps the best place for the whip to make its initial mark was his back. In order to frustrate him, naturally. Then on his ass, but not close to the anus or the testicles tucked beneath him. That would be offering too much pleasure too soon. Oh, it was a tricky business, particularly since Ian expected to be given his whippings as periodically as he expected to be served his favorite steak and kidney pie (not like kippers, thank God, his *daily* treat!).

Ian only needed to be flogged about twenty times in rapid succession to feel properly punished. But working up to it was the difficult part for me, all the tantalizing that had to be done, the threats, the verbal chastisements, the hints of pleasure-pain he would shortly receive providing he behaved and did as he was told, the total abasement I had to dole out.

How he loved the whisper of a command, how he loved to suffer in stoic silence while waiting for it! He enjoyed the waiting just as much if not more than the actual punishment. Everyone knows that the English upper classes of Ian's generation were all caned at school, which is where their sexual proclivities were formed. Also, their tendency toward strong food and drink seems to require equally strong sexual stimulant like flagellation. One balances the other. And it is considered an honorable heritage, one of which no Englishman I have ever met is ashamed to confess to. As though to prove my point, Ian had begun quoting from Lord Byron:

Oh ye, who teach the ingenuous youth of nations
Holland, France, England, Germany, and Spain
I pray ye flog them upon all occasions
It mends their morals, never mind their pain.

That quotation really turned him on, but wiggle as he might, he was too securely fastened to the bed to be actually able to move (not that he wanted to, you understand). Ian himself had taught me how to tie him up to make him as immobile as possible. It wasn't difficult, although at home in London we have two limb separators to do the bondage job more efficiently. One keeps the legs apart and the other does the same for the arms. They are both padded in foam rubber and covered in suede, very simple devices really. Ian had urged me to take them to St. Moritz, but I was nervous about customs inspections and told him I could still manage on my own, thank you very much.

"Silence!" I said.

He promptly stopped quoting Byron.

"I've told you that I never wanted to hear that poem again. You have purposely disobeyed me, haven't you?"

"Yes," he replied in a voice strangled with passion.

"Very well. Get ready for your punishment."

He lay there like a dead man with his eyes closed, but I knew how ready he was. I flicked the whip across his pale back. It made the stinging sound he savored. His body shivered with excitement, waiting for the next blow, which I had determined would fall across the back of his knees, a ticklish place. I would get around to his ass in about five more blows when he was practically ready to come. And I did. I thought he would go through the ceiling the first time the whip touched his ass, but in reality I knew better. He was controlling himself, stretching out his pleasure to the very last moment when I had completed the twenty strokes, and control was finally beyond him. Then he erupted in spasms of orgasmic delight, his white body clenching and unclenching itself, his suntanned face (eyes still tightly shut) turned away from me during his moment of euphoria. Whatever sounds came from his lips were lost forever in the bed linens, not that I cared to hear them anyway. . . .

So, between whipping and skiing, the week managed to pass.

Jeanne did not say another word about ruby necklaces, and neither did Ian. I wanted to ask him what he thought about Jeanne's robbery theory, but I was afraid to bring it up for fear of sounding too interested in the matter. Let it lie (as the English are fond of saying) was my reluctant conclusion. I never spent a minute alone with Harry during that week. We saw each other every evening at dinner and sometimes on the slopes, and managed to keep up the façade of being nothing more than vague childhood acquaintances. My desire to go to bed with Harry was overwhelming but impossible under the present circumstances. It would have to wait until we returned and could put our plans into operation.

At times I saw Ian studying Harry as he might one of the many business papers he brought home from work in London, but he had no comments to make.

Sarah and I occasionally spoke about Miss Marple and M. Poirot, but only because we had nothing else in common and wanted to appear sociable. Jeanne rarely spoke at all except when spoken to. Her feelings about Tom McKillup were not mentioned during that week, although I suspected that he still occupied much of her thoughts. I was no longer jealous of her and Harry. It seemed pretty apparent by now that her initial flirtation with him was either a form of acute desperation or a ploy to irritate her father. Noting that Harry did not respond to Jeanne's brash overtures, Ian was pleased with Harry and irritated by his daughter's show of bad manners.

"You're embarrassing Mr. and Mrs. Maringo," was his comment on the subject. "Kindly stop it."

The only person who continued to believe that Harry found Jeanne desirable was Sarah. And the only reason I knew it was because she went out of her way to be especially polite to Jeanne, a typically English put-down characteristic: the more you dislike someone, the more properly you behave. Otherwise known as killing the person with courtesy. Anyway, what did it matter? Jeanne hardly counted in the scheme of things, I thought, which only goes to show how unprepared I was for events that were to follow more swiftly and more dramatically than I could have imagined.

And then it was the last day in fairy-tale St. Moritz. Ian, Jeanne, and I were the first ones to be off. We were having breakfast downstairs in the dining room prior to our departure. Our luggage and ski equipment were in the lobby, bills had been paid, and we were warmly dressed in sweaters and tweeds and furs. The two weeks in St. Moritz were already beginning to fade into a dreamlike costume party, and now we were going back to our more sensible London selves.

"Happy New Year, folks. I hope you don't mind the intrusion." It was Harry, unexpectedly joining us for coffee. "Sarah's nurse is upstairs packing. I couldn't wait to escape the chaos."

He was wearing a thick, cable-stitched sweater and ski pants and looked as though he had a hell of a hangover. I thought of our father and his famous binges. I thought of our mother and how much they upset her. I thought of Pilgrim Lake. It would be just as frozen as the lake outside our dining room window, and people would be ice-skating there as they were here. Tears came to my eyes. Tears for the past and all its musty shadows and secret regrets. I suddenly missed Juliana for the first time in a long time. I missed my funny little home town. I missed that skinny twelve-year-old girl who had seduced her own brother. I missed myself.

We chatted about nothing until Ian had paid the breakfast bill and we were finally leaving. Harry walked with us into the lobby, which was even more active than usual with bellmen running about and clerks busily manning the desks. There were rapid cross-currents of conversation in English, German,

French, Italian, as money changed hands, instructions were given, farewells were said.

Ian and Harry shook hands. They had already exchanged telephone numbers and addresses in England. Harry told us to have a good trip and Ian said the same to Harry.

"We'll ring you and Sarah as soon as we're back to our normal routine," Ian said. "Perhaps you could come over for dinner some evening."

"I know we both would enjoy that," Harry replied. "And I'm sure that Sarah joins me in extending an invitation to visit us in Surrey. Possibly for a weekend if you can manage it."

Cars pulled up and departed. Jaguars, Mercedes, Porsches, Rolls-Royces.

"So this is good-bye," I said, turning to Harry.

"*Auf wiedersehen*, you mean."

We were both smiling now, the bond between us stronger and more intense than ever.

Before either of us could say another word, Ian motioned to me and Jeanne that our car was waiting to take us to the station. I started to walk away, then turned and waved good-bye to Harry. He stood there shivering and waving back. His lips mouthed the words "I love you," but I could not hear him. We were like two characters in a multimillion-dollar movie, with a sound track that had just broken down. But I knew it was going to be fixed soon. Very soon. It had to be fixed in time for the happy ending.

I love you too, I silently called to Harry.

Then I rushed through the cold, crowded lobby out into the fierce alpine sunlight. The happy ending was just beginning.

Part 4

London—1975

32 ❧

As usual I find London charming after having been away even for a short time.

I love the street we live on, with its quiet, self-satisfied shops and unobtrusive air of authority. It doesn't matter whether you're buying a Ming vase at the antiques place next door (which deigns to advertise its name in the window) or a cheese-and-tomato sandwich at Supersam, your purchase is given the same stamp of approval. Obviously you've made the right choice is the unspoken attitude, otherwise you wouldn't be there. And perhaps that is the quality I admire most about London, all of London: its gentle arrogance.

For the fact is that London doesn't care what you think. If St. Moritz is an excitable peacock with all its brilliant feathers flared, demanding to be noticed and petulant if it isn't, then London is a cool sleek thoroughbred stallion, so confident it will win first honors at Ascot that it shuns idle recognition.

"Mind you," Ian is saying before leaving for the City, "London is two thousand years old, whereas St. Moritz is a mere baby of one hundred and ten. That's what partially accounts for the difference in attitude. Age. . . . Mmmmm. St. Moritz. . . . Reminds me of that rather interesting Mr. Maringo."

He pauses while I feel as though my heart is going to jump out of my body.

"Why don't you invite him and his wife to dinner one evening next week? Wednesday, perhaps. Worst night for telly as far as I'm concerned."

"I'll call and see if they're free," I manage to say in a perfectly normal tone of voice.

"Right."

Then Ian kisses me on the cheek, advises me to have a nice day (without asking what I intend to do) and is off, leisurely, unhurriedly. My husband reflects the rhythm of the city we live in. And it is this very rhythm, this atmosphere of relaxation, that I need so badly right now because I have never felt less relaxed in my life.

When? Where? How?

Those are the questions that keep turning over in my mind as I go about my daily routine, waiting until it is decently late enough in the morning to make that telephone call. *When, where*, and *how* will I finally murder Sarah? I wonder as I bathe and dress, put on makeup, as I confer with Mrs. Cook (who, appropriately, is our cleaning woman and cook) about what we are going to have for dinner the next few days.

I feel certain that if I were plagued by the same questions, the same uncertainty, and were living in a volatile city like New York or Rome, my fears would show on my face, my hands might tremble. But after sixteen years, I too have become a Londoner of sorts and remain outwardly calm in times of tension and emergency.

It is ten o'clock and drizzling outside, a dark January drizzle. The light coming into the flat is bleak. At four-thirty it will turn dark again. I remember the blinding sunlight of St. Moritz, the baby-blue skies, the sharp mountain air, and it is hard to believe they still exist on the same planet, that other people are enjoying them this very minute. I would not be thinking of St. Moritz at all if it weren't for Harry and the renewed pact we made on the Salastrains ski slope about becoming the summer people.

I was still anxious as I took the telephone off its hook and dialed the Guildford number that Sarah had given me. It rang several times, then:

"Hello," said Harry.

For some reason I had been expecting to hear Sarah's voice and I was dumbstruck when I heard my brother's instead.

"Hello," I said. The intimacy seemed overwhelming. "This is Alexis Nicholson. How are you?"

"Fine. We're just fine. It's nice to hear from you."

So I knew that Sarah was in the immediate vicinity and he couldn't speak.

"I've called to invite you and Sarah to dinner next week. On Wednesday if that's all right."

"Just a moment, please." In a second he was back, apparently having conferred with Sarah. "Wednesday is perfect. We're delighted. What time?"

"Seven. Is that convenient for you?"

"Seven it is," Harry said. "I'm looking forward to it. Could we have your address again?"

As though it weren't engraved in his heart. But we went through the rituals because Sarah was listening, Sarah whom I soon would have to kill, and was now so politely inviting to dinner. Were killers born or made? I wondered as I told Harry that we too were looking forward to it. But before I could contemplate that question I had to say good-bye and jot down the invitation to the Maringos in my little red leather appointment book with an asterisk next to it to remind Ian to put it in his book as well. Oh, we were carefully organized all right.

I was distracted to see my own name, *Maringo*, written before me. I felt an acute sense of loss. Sarah had stolen my name by marrying Harry. Even worse, I had denied my own heritage by telling Ian that my maiden name was Storms. This entire business of names had never seemed very important before, now it struck me as extremely important, vital. By killing Sarah I was not only taking back Harry, who was rightfully mine to begin with, I was also reclaiming what was even more mine: my name.

"We're having guests for dinner next Wednesday," I said to Mrs. Cook when she returned with her marketing. "Could you manage something easy, something I can heat up?"

Knowing my aversion to kitchens and domesticity, she was surprised. "Of course, Madam. But are you sure you don't want me to stay and serve?"

"I don't think it will be necessary." I made a careless gesture. "They're people we met in St. Moritz. It's nothing elaborate."

"Whatever you say, Madam. Perhaps a nice lamb casserole will do." Mrs. Cook definitely had a taste for lamb. "With swedes, carrots, and potatoes. And prawn cocktail for starters."

I threw on my red fox, grabbed the nearest umbrella, and fled out the door. The minute I reached the street I realized I had no place to go, nothing to do for another two hours and considered returning upstairs. But suddenly that seemed even more unbearable—being imprisoned with nice Mrs. Cook—so I started to walk down Mount Street toward Park Lane. For consolation I told myself that I could use the exercise. For even more consolation I hugged the damp red fox around me as I walked, remembering that this was what I had been wearing when Harry saw me last.

When he saw me the following Wednesday I was wearing a

new black jersey jumpsuit and pearls that Ian had given me as a wedding present, and I was calm once more. On the surface anyway. Inside I was a wreck despite the two Libriums I had swallowed an hour before.

Hello, hello.

How nice to see you again.

Oh, isn't this a divine flat!

We've all lost our suntans, haven't we?

Please let me take your coats.

Won't you sit down?

What will you have to drink?

(Later it would appear to have gone very quickly, but at the time I felt there was no end to it.)

"Any trouble parking?" Ian asked Harry.

The difficulties of parking in central London were then discussed, as were the perils of drinking and driving.

"Anyone who drives to dinner or a business lunch is almost certain to be over the eighty milligram limit," Sarah said. "It's really a question of individual tolerance, and driving ability, isn't it?"

She then proceeded to admire the black and gold furniture of our drawing room, the overall colors of honey and beige, the fur rugs and leopard cushions, the walls of simulated tortoiseshell, the Flemish paintings.

"It's quite unusual," she said to me. "Did you do it yourself?"

"No, I had professional help."

"*Quite* unusual," she repeated.

Meaning unorthodox, which she would not care for, which most Englishwomen did not care for but were intrigued by.

She leaned back against the soft, golden sofa cushions (the same exact position she would be sitting in when she was fatally poisoned) and said: "Will your charming stepdaughter be dining with us this evening?"

"No, Jeanne is studying at the home of a school friend. They're going to gorge themselves on pizza, from one of those takeaway places."

Sarah made the appropriately horrified face, and I said, "That reminds me. Food."

I went into the kitchen on pretext of checking on the casserole, which needed no supervision. I loathed kitchens— they reminded me of my mother and her dreary life. Whenever I thought about my mother it was with a combination of resentment, rage, and regret. If only I had had a different mother, I often mused, a happier, more loving one, one who loved herself more . . . there, my futile wishes would come to a halt. The past could not be changed, only the present and the precious future.

When dinner was served, Sarah had to be put back inside her wheelchair for the short ride into the dining room and then lifted out by Harry and placed in one of the darkly stained bamboo chairs that flanked the rectangular table. The dining room was done in mahogany and bamboo with a chinoiserie motif, and again Sarah commented on the uniqueness of the furnishings. Only now her voice sounded different, thicker, and I realized she was slightly high.

She had drunk two rather stiff whiskeys and they seemed to have gone to her head. I never saw her the least bit intoxicated in St. Moritz. Suddenly she seemed quite vulnerable and pathetic, an unattractive invalid with more money than she knew what to do with and a husband who did not love her. But I caught myself just in time. The worst thing I could do was to start feeling sorry for Sarah Maringo, who was seated opposite me wearing an unbecoming mauve gown. I had to think of her as the enemy if I were to carry out my as yet unspecified plans.

When we got to salad and cheese, which I served after the entree, in the French tradition, I had almost given up hope that Harry was going to say or do anything significant tonight. Perhaps he intended to write to me or telephone when Sarah was not around. After all, what *could* he do under the present circumstances? Then I heard him say something to Ian about his tailor.

"I have an appointment with him next Monday," Harry said. "It's about a suit I've ordered. Although I must confess that lately I'm not too pleased with his work. Perhaps you know the firm."

Ian nodded as Harry mentioned the name of the tailor, who was located on Savile Row, not far from where we lived. It was the same tailor that Harry always used as an excuse in the past whenever he left Sarah at her father's in Surrey, to join me for one of our hotel reunions.

In his own special code, Harry was asking me to meet him on Monday. But at which hotel? At what time? Under what name? All I had to do was be patient and wait, I told myself, trying to contain my excitement, for surely Harry had worked out those details too. A tremendous sense of relief swept over me, reviving me.

Back in the living room Harry transferred Sarah to the sofa and arranged a long fur throw over her lap and legs. To watch him, he was surely the most devoted of husbands. Who would ever guess that he was secretly planning to get rid of the woman he so solicitously cared for? I put Beethoven's Ninth on the hi-fi and waited for Ian to return with the coffee tray, one of the few domestic chores he insisted on performing himself. Instead, Jeanne walked in, surprising us all.

"Good evening," she said, with a big smile. "Have I startled you? Didn't you hear me slam my way in? Or did Ludwig drown me out? Alexis is always complaining about how much noise I make."

She seemed in exceptionally good spirits and she looked exceptionally good too, in her lacy yellow sweater, matching beret, and tight blue jeans. Very French, I thought, remembering her Gallic heritage. Paulette would be proud of her daughter if she could see her now.

"You didn't make a sound," I said.

"That's terrible. I must be improving."

Then she properly greeted the Maringos, plopped down on one of the velvet-covered chairs, and said: "Where's Daddy? Hiding?"

"I'm right here, darling."

Ian stood poised in the doorway, holding a silver tray with coffee for four. Only my cup of Hag had been poured in advance. Also on the tray was a Waterford decanter which he must have refilled with his favorite cognac.

"No coffee for me?" Jeanne asked.

"We didn't expect you home so early." Ian glanced at the clock over the fireplace. It pointed to nine-thirty. "How are your studies coming along?"

"Quickly," Jeanne replied, with an uncharacteristic giggle.

"You're in a jolly mood," Ian said.

She shrugged. "Why shouldn't I be? I've had a very productive evening."

"You must be quite fond of your studies," Sarah said icily, reminding me of how much she had disliked Jeanne in St. Moritz, how jealous she had been of her. "What are you majoring in?"

"French, with Spanish as my subsidiary subject."

"I still think you should have chosen German instead of Spanish," Ian said as he proceeded to pour Sarah's coffee, which he placed before her on the low, glass-topped table. "But never mind."

"After four years in Gstaad, I've had enough German to last me a lifetime," Jeanne said.

"Touché," I said, adding two teaspoons of sugar to my coffee, as did Sarah. I could feel Harry's eyes upon me.

"I see that you've dispensed with your usual sedative powder," he said. "Does that mean you're sleeping better these nights?"

"Worse, if anything," I truthfully replied.

I was still thinking that Jeanne did not seem like her usual self. There was an exhilaration about her, an exuberance that I found hard to reconcile after an evening of study with a girlfriend. She had never had many friends of her own sex.

"Ian is afraid I'm becoming too dependent upon barbiturates," I said, "so he's appointed himself nursemaid here at home."

Ian cut in, somewhat sheepishly. "I prefer to dole out the medication myself."

"My husband is trying to reform me by lessening the dosage. Aren't you, darling?"

"Something like that."

I lifted the cup of Hag to my lips. Because of the sugar I could barely detect the sleeping powder, but I knew that even if Ian had tripled the normal amount I still would be unable to sleep tonight. I hadn't been this keyed up since that last morning in St. Moritz, when Harry and I shared a few memorable moments in the lobby of the Engadine.

"It's cold here, much too cold," he had said that morning. "Not our kind of climate at all. We're going to be the summer people. Never forget that, Alexis."

I hadn't forgotten. All I wanted to know was, *when* were we going to get started?

A few cognacs and one Beethoven vocal finale later, we seemed to be ending. Ian and I were saying goodnight to our guests. Jeanne had gone upstairs to bed. The evening was over. Then, as Harry thanked me for a lovely dinner and we shook hands, I felt him slip a tiny piece of paper into my palm. I smiled and quickly plunged both hands into the pockets of my jersey jumpsuit.

33 ⌒⌒

It took Harry seventy-five minutes to get from his stately home in Guildford to the rundown hotel in Victoria, where he had asked Alexis to meet him.

He had taken a train to Waterloo Station, then a taxi to the Adams Hotel. It was much quicker to come into London by train than by car, and much safer in terms of anonymity once you arrived. Not that he and Alexis were apt to run into anyone they knew around here. The flotsam and jetsam of Victoria, Harry thought, as he viewed the disagreeable area. He only wished that he and Alexis could meet in more attractive surroundings instead of this gray godforsaken hotel which seemed to cater to two types of people: (1) those who couldn't afford anything better and (2) those who could, but were driven into hiding for one reason or another.

After tipping the elderly clerk who had shown him upstairs, he lit a Players and sat down on the nondescript armchair to wait for Alexis. She was not long in arriving.

"I took the underground from Green Park," she said breathlessly. "I thought I was at a costume party. I didn't know what I was missing, going by taxi all these years."

Harry appreciated her effort to make a game out of the whole sordid business, but he knew from the expression in her eyes that she felt as regretful as he about the furtiveness of these meetings.

"Let me hang up your coat," he said.

She handed him the expensive but plain black coat she'd worn to avoid attracting attention, as she would have done with one of her spectacular furs. He put the coat on a warped metal hanger (the only kind there was) and shut the closet door.

"I'm sorry we have to meet like this." Harry stubbed out his cigarette. "But it won't be for much longer. Did you have any trouble getting away?"

"No, I didn't." Although her eyes still looked sad, she was smiling. "And why are we being so formal? Aren't you going to kiss me?"

"Oh, darling. . . ."

She walked into his arms as naturally as though she had

never left them. Harry was always amazed at how fast he and Alexis seemed to pick up the threads of their intimacy after having been separated for so long. In the past they would have gone to bed immediately, for fear of wasting precious time, but today there was a lot to talk about, plans to be outlined. Lovemaking would have to wait its turn, Harry decided.

Alexis seemed to have reached the same decision because instead of starting to remove her clothing, as she ordinarily would have done, she sat down at the edge of the chenille-covered bed and said:

"Okay. Shoot."

The American expression startled Harry, it sounded so incongruous here. From a dust-streaked window he looked down at the flow of traffic, which was dominated by the red double-decker buses that featured so prominently in color advertisements urging foreigners to visit historic London. For all he knew, the Adams had an honorable historic heritage of its own, but somehow he doubted it.

"It seems to me that poison is the most logical method," Harry said, plunging in. "What I suggest is that before very long you invite Sarah and me over for dinner again. After the meal, when Ian brings in the coffee tray, your cup will contain potassium cyanide, which Ian himself will have put into it, thinking it was your regular sedative powder. You will then proceed to get your cup switched with Sarah's so that dear Sarah winds up drinking the poisoned coffee and dies minutes later. Potassium cyanide works very quickly.

"At first the police will suspect me of murder, since I have the most likely motive: with Sarah dead, I inherit her fortune. Then when it's revealed that Ian, and not I, had access to the cyanide the police will think again. What possible reason would Ian have to kill Sarah? None. Ah, but he very well might have reason to kill *you*, which is what he tried to do—the police will conclude—only his plan backfired.

"The coffee cups got switched and my poor innocent wife drank your Hag by mistake. The fact that the cyanide is found in the only cup containing Hag, as opposed to regular coffee, clinches it. Ian goes to jail for life, I get Sarah's money, and you and I are free to be together at last."

Harry paused, pleased with his word-for-word memorization of the plan. "Well? What do you think?"

"That you're insane," was Alexis' prompt reply.

Harry frowned. "I was afraid you'd say something like that."

"What can you expect me to say?" Her voice had risen. She stood up and started to pace the room. "It's the most illogical, inconceivable, crazy idea I've ever heard. There are so many loopholes in it that I don't know where to begin."

"Begin anywhere and you'll find out that it's not so crazy as you think."

"Okay. The potassium cyanide. Now where am I supposed to get hold of that?"

"You're not. I have some, and it's virtually untraceable. I bought it in New York when I decided to become a reportage photographer, one of my many doomed careers. Anyhow, it's used professionally to reduce the density of negatives. Next question."

"Is it white?" she asked, somewhat disarmed by his blithe reply. "Like my sleeping powder?"

"Of course, or I wouldn't be suggesting it. However, cyanide is not a powder, it's crystalline. Each crystal is about the size of a grain of rice."

"That's no good. Ian would spot it as being different immediately."

"He would if you *substituted* the cyanide for the powder, not if you *mixed* it in with the powder."

"Why would Ian want to kill me? What would be his motive? We're supposed to be a very happy couple. It doesn't make sense."

Harry smiled. He had been waiting for that particular question. "Ian will want to kill you because he's insanely jealous that you've taken a lover."

"*A lover?*"

"Yes."

"But who? Do you mean for me to pretend to have a lover, or for me really to——?"

"Really to."

She slowly stood up, her long legs encased in laced leather burgundy boots. She was wearing a dark gray tweed skirt and vest, with a burgundy turtleneck sweater and silver jewelry. The silver tinkled and glittered in the shabby room. It had started to grow dark outside and looked like it was going to rain.

"The weather in London changes so abruptly," Harry said. "People don't. They tend to remain pretty much the same over the years. Like Ian. Don't forget that when Paulette and Rose were murdered, it was assumed to have been done by a man who knew one of the women intimately. Very possibly, Paulette."

"What does she have to do with it?"

"With Jeanne testifying to her father's jealous temperament, the police will now have to consider the possibility that the woman in the Paris case was Paulette, not Rose. That Paulette was playing around, and Ian could have found out and killed her. Or had her killed. It certainly will not work to his advantage to have the unsolved murder of his first wife hanging over his head on top of this. And you can be sure that the prosecuting attorney will bring it up."

"I don't understand your reference to Ian's so-called jealous temperament. Where did you ever get that idea?"

"Jeanne told me so. In St. Moritz. She went into quite a bit of detail, as a matter of fact. Called him a medieval maniac in his possessive attitude toward the women he loved. As his only daughter, I think her testimony will prove invaluable."

"But that's ridiculous. I've never know Ian to show signs of jealousy."

"Perhaps he hasn't had reason to in the past. However, I don't think he'll like it when he finds out that you and Tom are having an affair. No, he won't like it one tiny bit. And for that matter," Harry said, pausing to let the impact of his words sink in, "neither will Jeanne."

"Tom?" Alexis was genuinely puzzled. "Tom who? What are you talking about? Who's Tom?"

"Jeanne's Scottish rock singer. The one whose group was playing in St. Moritz. The one Jeanne is so hung up on. The Tom you're going to seduce."

This time Alexis did not sit down on the bed, as she had before. She seemed to sink into it, as though seeking oblivion from this madness. The expression on her face had changed from one of disturbed interest to outright fear, and despite the inadequate heating in the room she was starting to perspire. A thin line of wetness appeared above her upper lip.

"This is some sort of terrible joke, Harry. I know it is. And I don't think it's funny."

"It's no joke."

"But *Tom?* That little twit? Surely, you can't expect me to—"

"Make love to him? Why not?"

"No," she said flatly. "It's ridiculous. Out of the question. I won't do it."

Harry had been prepared for just such an emergency. He quickly stood up, went to the closet for his coat, and put it on.

"Where are you going?" Alexis asked in alarm.

"There doesn't seem to be anything more to say."

"But you can't just walk out like this."

"Under the circumstances I don't see much point in staying."

He was at the door when he heard her voice. It was subdued. "Harry, wait a minute."

He tentatively turned around.

"Please," she urged him. "Don't walk out on me like this. It's not fair."

"Fair? That's quaint, coming from you. You're the one who's not being fair. I've gone to a great deal of trouble to perfect this plan, to work out the most minute detail, and then you sit there like a cowardly child and tell me that all because of some personal distaste you refuse to go through with your end of it. Don't you realize this is the only chance we have to be together? Do you think I'm enjoying this? Do you imagine that I relish the prospect of your going to bed with another man? Don't you think *I* have feelings too? Good God, Alexis, use your damned brains!"

She had never seen Harry so angry in her life. It was a little frightening, but reassuring at the same time. His passionate outburst showed that he was not the heartless, calculating manipulator he appeared to be. He was suffering. Yet he was willing to suffer so that they could fulfill their childhood dream. Shouldn't she be willing, too?

"Why does it have to be Tom who I seduce?" she asked, realizing she had given in.

"Not only seduce, but leave clues for Ian to find. Clues that will make it plain you're being blatantly unfaithful to him, and with someone young enough to be your son."

Alexis blanched at this reference to her age. "I repeat, why Tom in particular?"

"There are several reasons. For one thing, Jeanne is crazy about him and she's bound to feel upset when she finds out—and she will—that he prefers you, her stepmother, to her. She'll become angry, vindictive. What better way to get back at you than to tell her father what's been going on behind his back? And that's precisely what we want her to do. Because Ian is then bound to explode with jealous rage."

"Ian is not the explosive type."

"Every man is the explosive type if given sufficient provocation." Harry had sat down again, but he kept his coat on. "Which brings me to the next reason why Tom is the most logical candidate for our purposes. Ian already dislikes him and everything he stands for. The whole hippie syndrome. So it figures that Ian will be even more incensed by the idea of your cheating on him with somebody like Tom, a man he openly can't stand, than with just any anonymous young man. And I emphasize the word *young*. How old is Ian? Sixty?"

"Fifty-nine."

"Even better. Men dread sixty. They're afraid of prostate troubles, impotence, high blood pressure, heart attacks, the irretrievable loss of youth. Particularly if they happen to be married to women much younger than themselves, as Ian is. Tom would pose a very real threat to Ian, a very ugly one."

"But you've never met Tom," Alexis protested. "What makes you think it would be so easy for me to seduce him? He might prefer girls his own age. He might not find me attractive."

"I'm sure you haven't lost your touch, Alexis. You're a very beautiful woman, very glamorous, very exciting. I should think our Tom would be flattered to have you pay attention to him."

Alexis looked up. "*Our* Tom? What do you mean?"

"Nothing. It's just a figure of speech."

"An unusual one considering the fact that you don't even know the man in question."

"But I do," Harry said quietly.

"What?"

"I said, I do know Tom. I know him quite well. I know that he was with Jeanne last Wednesday night, when Sarah and I were having dinner at your flat. When Jeanne pretended to have been studying at the home of a girlfriend."

"I don't understand. How could you know something like that, when even Ian and I—"

"Believed Jeanne's lie?"

"Yes."

"Simple. I met Tom in St. Moritz and then we renewed our friendship in London. He lives in Fulham. I've visited him several times."

"I had no idea."

"Of what? That he was with Jeanne last Wednesday or that I know him personally?"

"Both," Alexis said. "What was he doing with Jeanne?"

"Making love to her."

It had started to drizzle outside. A light patter of rain hit the solitary window in the room, blurring the sky.

"This is all a bit much for me." Alexis shook her head in confusion. "This sudden intrusion of Tom upon the scene. It rather complicates matters, doesn't it?"

"On the contrary. It simplifies them. Tom has already proved invaluable."

"How?"

"By setting the stage. By devirginating Jeanne, who is now more obsessed with him than ever." Harry laughed. "You look surprised, Alexis."

"Surprised? I'm stunned. Jeanne, a virgin? I can't believe it. Are you seriously saying that she went to bed with Tom last week? That he's the first man she's ever gone to bed with?"

"Yes."

"You're positive?"

"As positive as I can be without having been there in person. Remember how pleased with herself Jeanne looked when she came home last Wednesday, how giggly? How self-satisfied?"

"You mean that was the night?"

"Yes."

"I didn't think there were any virgins left in the world. But why would Tom tell you about it? That seems rather odd."

"He didn't tell me. I told him. To do it. I should say that I challenged him to seduce Jeanne, and you know how men's egos are. It probably wasn't much of a challenge anyway, considering Jeanne's interest in him. The point is that we need Jeanne to be crazy about Tom, which I assume she now is since she's been phoning him every day, and resentful toward you, which she soon will be, if our plan is going to succeed."

"What happens next?"

"You call up Tom tomorrow and say you want to speak to him privately. Say it's about Jeanne. He'll agree. He'll figure that you've found out about them and are angry. Instead, he discovers that you're jealous."

"Jealous?"

"Sure. You're attracted to him yourself. Perhaps it's his boyish charm. Perhaps you're driven on by competition with your own stepdaughter. It's a common enough situation. One way or the other you end up in the sack with him and prove so irresistible that he has no choice but to want to see you again, to continue the affair. You want to continue it, too."

"For how long?"

"It won't be forever. Just long enough for Jeanne and Ian to catch onto what's happening. As I said, you'll leave little clues strewn all over the place. Ian will have to be blind not to realize that you're cheating on him, and he'll be furious. Jeanne will be furious because Tom prefers you to her. But your affair with Tom also accomplishes another purpose, a very important one. It will stop the police from suspecting that you might have been responsible for Sarah's death."

"Me?"

"Since you have access to the cyanide too, the police will start poking around into your life as well as Ian's. At first they might think there's a romantic liaison between you and me, and you wanted to get rid of Sarah so we could be together. But they'll soon change their minds when they find out about you and Tom. Your affair with Tom will throw them off the track. If you're hung up on some randy rock and roll singer, what possible motive could you have for murdering Sarah?"

"None."

"That's right. But Ian who wanted to kill you, has the age-old motive of jealousy. And his jealousy will have been witnessed and documented by his own daughter, which makes it absolutely perfect."

"You're counting a lot on the police to deduce that the wrong woman was murdered, aren't you?"

"I have great faith in Scotland Yard," Harry said.

Alexis took out a cigarette. Harry lit it for her with the gold Dunhill lighter that Sarah had given him for his forty-second birthday. Although Harry admired the exquisite present, he had reached the point where he no longer wished to be reminded of his age. It seemed to him that he'd dribbled half his life away in meaningless pursuits and had grown stale as a result. He wanted to change that pattern. With Alexis' help, he could. It was Alexis he loved. Tom was only an accessory, he told himself. Tom could be dispensed with when the time came.

"There's one thing that bothers me," Alexis said.

"What's that?"

"If Tom had no intention of calling Jeanne to begin with, why did he change his mind? Why did he let you change it for him? That challenge to his male ego couldn't have been so irresistible. He must have girls flinging themselves at his feet wherever he goes. What did he need Jeanne for?"

Harry knew that sooner or later Alexis would ask that question, and he had debated whether to tell her the truth or to lie. In the end he decided to tell part of the truth, the part that would serve his purposes better.

"Tom and I became very friendly in St. Moritz," he began slowly. "We spent most of one night together. Sarah imagines that I was with Jeanne, but I was with Tom. And we've been together on several occasions in London since our return. I don't think it would be an exaggeration to say that Tom has grown fond of me. Quite fond. And when you're fond of someone, you want to help that person if you possibly can. Do you understand what I'm getting at?"

Alexis had turned white. Her hand, holding the cigarette, trembled. For a moment Harry was afraid she would faint, then he reassured himself that his sister was not the fainting type.

"I had no idea," she managed to say at last, tears in her eyes. "I never suspected. Oh, Harry, *why?*"

"Do you mean, why Tom? Or why the others?"

She buried her face in the folds of her gray tweed skirt. Her shoulders shook, but no sound came out of her mouth. The hand with the lit cigarette barely trailed the worn carpet. Harry went over and took her in his arms, realizing that the shock of his revelations had affected her far more severely than he had anticipated. Surely she was a sophisticated woman and knew that many people led bisexual lives. He had not expected her to take it this badly.

"Alexis, darling, it's not as terrible as you think." He stroked her long black hair. "Tom is just a convenience. He doesn't mean that much to me. Please try and believe that my feelings for Tom, as sincere as they are, in no way conflict with my feelings for you. They never could. Nobody could ever be as important to me as you are. Man or woman. Nobody. It's you I love, Alexis."

She raised her head and stared at him, the tears drying on her face. "I thought I knew everything about you, Harry. That's what hurts so much. I thought that despite our long separations, we shared everything, were honest with each other. Now I wonder what else there is that I don't know, what else you've left out."

"Nothing," he lied, "except the reason I've turned to men over the years."

She stopped him. "I don't want to hear."

"I think you should. It might be helpful if you knew. Besides, you just said that you wanted to know everything about me."

"Perhaps I was better off in my ignorance. I never liked to think of you making love to Sarah, still I assumed that you did—that you had to. I accepted it as part of the way in which you were trapped by marriage, just as I've been trapped. As repellent as it was, I could think of you and Sarah sexually. Even you and another woman from time to time, a faceless stranger you'd never see again. But I wasn't prepared for Tom. For men. I don't know why, but somehow that seems worse. I can't compete against a man. It's another dimension. It's something I can't cope with."

"You don't have to. That's the whole point. Tom is no threat to you, to us. Just the opposite. He's working *for* us. We're using Tom so that we can ultimately be together. Tom is only a pawn. Can't you see that, Alexis?"

"I'm trying to."

Harry glanced at his watch. "It's getting late. I have to be leaving soon."

"Oh God, we're doing it again! Separating. I can't stand it anymore, Harry. I can't stand these endless, horrible separations. I'm sick of being away from you. When I'm away from you, I feel as though I don't exist."

"So do I."

"I want us to be together for as long as we like . . . to be able to talk, make love, do whatever we wish, without this continual sense of pressure."

"There's only one way that can happen. But my plan doesn't appeal to you."

She walked back to the bed and started to unfasten her skirt.

"What are you doing?" Harry asked.

"Getting undressed. What does it look like?"

"We don't have time to make love, Alexis."

"Yes, we do." She smiled suddenly, impishly. "You can tell Sarah that you got detained at the tailor. Tell her you were run over by a truck. Frankly I don't give a damn what you tell her."

"But I have to catch a train!"

"There'll be other trains."

"What are you smiling at?"

"You and your ingenious plan. You didn't finish it."

She had removed her skirt, sweater, and vest, and was wearing only the laced burgundy boots and black tights.

"You still haven't explained how I'm supposed to switch coffee cups with Sarah and not leave any fingerprints."

Harry smiled and began to unloosen his tie. "I thought you'd never ask."

34 &

Tom McKillup was alone in his trendy house in Fulham, trying to finish a new song, when the telephone rang. His first impulse was to ignore it, but then he remembered Harry having told him several days ago to expect a call from Alexis Nicholson.

"It's all set," Harry jubilantly informed him. "She's agreed to get in touch with you about Jeanne. But remember, she has no idea you're in on the plan too. So play it cool when she tries to seduce you. Act hard to get at first."

"I don't understand why you want to keep her in the dark," Tom said, still mystified. "Wouldn't it be easier if you told her I had agreed to the seduction scheme? That way she wouldn't have to work so hard."

"Don't you worry about how hard she has to work to get you in the sack. Let her work her ass off. It will help convince her you're an innocent bystander as far as the money is concerned. We don't want her to know that the money is going to be split three ways or she might not go through with it. As it stands now, she thinks that she and I are the only ones who'll share the proceeds."

"You're one hell of a shrewd character," Tom said. "How did you ever get this lady to agree to such a far-out operation in the first place?"

"Same way I got you to agree. She needs the dough."

"She must need it real bad."

"Don't we all?" Harry said.

Tom liked Harry, admired him, identified with him. Like

himself, Harry had been a poor kid determined to break through the barriers of poverty and he'd succeeded. To a degree. Marrying money, as Harry had so adroitly pointed out, was not the same thing as *having* money. Which was why Harry had enlisted Tom's help in a little plan to extract some of Ian Nicholson's fortune from him. Twenty-five thousand tax-free pounds was what Harry had offered Tom, and all for taking the cherry from that kid, Jeanne, and then having a short-term affair with her stepmother!

Blackmail might be a dirty word to some people but it sounded great to Tom, particularly since Harry had promised that he would not have to get personally involved in the actual blackmail arrangements. Harry would handle those himself. Tom laughed and whistled as he walked across the cluttered room to pick up the phone. Something told him that his lucky days were just beginning.

"You don't know me," a female voice said on the other end, "but my name is Alexis Nicholson. I'm Jeanne's stepmother."

"Jeanne?" Tom managed to sound puzzled. "Jeanne who? I think you've got the wrong number."

"Isn't this Tom McKillup?" the imperious voice said.

"That's me."

"Then I have the right number, and there's no need to pretend. Jeanne has told me all about the two of you. I'm very upset, as you might imagine. I'd like to see you. When can we get together? The sooner the better."

Tom grinned into a mirror. He sure was a handsome bastard with those green eyes that knocked women cold, not to mention an occasional man like Harry.

"How about right now?"

"Now?" Her voice wavered. "I was thinking of—"

"Look, Mrs. Nicholson. I'm very busy. If you want to see me so badly, I suggest you get your bum over here fast."

"What's your address?"

Tom gave it to her. "It's just off Fulham Road. Although I doubt you're familiar with the neighborhood. It'd be a little too *nouveau riche* for you, wouldn't it?"

"I'm surprised you can even pronounce the words," Alexis said, hanging up.

Tom smiled to himself, then went back to his bass guitar and scribbled sheet music. The song he was working on needed a new hook, a catchy part. People responded to a good hook

and remembered it, sang and hummed it. A few good hooks
and you had a chance to get on the chart of *Melody Makers*
or *Sounds*, maybe even land a spot on BBC's coveted TV
show, "Top of the Pops."

Those were his hopes every time he began a new song, but
they had only materialized once, when "Wintertime Love"
became a best-selling single. He and the guys really got excited
then (that's when they bought the £35,000 house in swinging
Fulham), but that was two long years ago. Since then the
group had been sliding slowly downhill. They'd be falling
behind in their mortgage payments on the house pretty soon
if something didn't materialize, and the house represented a
great deal to Tom. It was a symbol of belonging to the new
affluent aristocracy in London that had sprung up in the
sixties, the glamour industries of films, fashion, and pop.

Tom wished that the other guys had hung around this
morning, as they usually did when he began to work on something new. He needed their exchange of ideas, the experimen-
tation with various instruments, he needed their moral support
to help him compose. But they all walked out, each with a
different excuse . . . a girl, a pub date, a visit to the West End.

Screw them, he thought. Maybe it was just as well they
had left, what with Alexis Nicholson due to arrive shortly.
He couldn't very well have his four mates hanging around,
watching him pretend to resist her seductive ploys. Aside
from the monetary promise Harry had made involving Mrs.
Nicholson, Tom was glad she'd be there soon, that *someone*
would be there.

Tom did not like to be alone. He wasn't used to it. He'd
grown up in a council tenement in the lower-class Gorgie
district of Edinburgh, the oldest of five children. The snob
section of Murrayfield was not far away and it was there that
Tom had his first enticing view of wealth, one that was to
stay with him for a long time to come.

It made Tom determined to improve his station in life.
He'd be damned if he would end up running a crummy pub
like his father, he told his family, who had nicknamed him
"the millionaire" as a joke. To Tom it wasn't funny. Music
was one of the few opportunities open to somebody like him
and he grabbed it, thinking that if the Beatles could make
it so could he.

Now, after eight years of exhausting road tours and dis-
appointing recording dates, Tom had begun to wonder whether
the effort was worth it. Maybe he just didn't have what it

took to get to the top. And complicating things even more was the problem of his age.

Although he looked considerably younger than his twenty-five years (the kilts, argyle socks, and clean-shaven appearance when performing helped there) the professionals he had to deal with all knew how old he was. And in the teeny-bopper world of pop, twenty-five was practically ancient. Only Mick Jagger and Paul McCartney seemed to have successfully overcome the age hurdle, but they were in a class by themselves.

The doorbell rang.

"Hello," the woman in the luxurious black and white fur coat said. "I'm Alexis Nicholson."

Even with the hood of the coat partially concealing her face, it was obvious she was a beauty. Tom could not believe his own good fortune and he decided that Harry must have been kidding about her age. Either that or she had a special formula for youth. She could easily have passed for late twenties.

"Please come in," he said, suddenly aware of his own appearance.

Which was more than she seemed to be. Most women would have been favorably impressed by his Italian knit sweater and designer trousers, but she brushed past him as though he were nonexistent, her perfume filling the air.

So this was Jeanne's middle-aged stepmother! Harry had warned him to play it cool, but he should also have warned him how difficult it would be. Tom could feel himself getting excited already as he watched her move aside a mandolin, a copy of that day's *Express*, and a pair of someone's socks, in order to sit down on the modern chrome and leather sofa.

"You'll have to excuse the mess," he said. "Five blokes on their own. Well, what can you expect?"

"Where are the others?"

In one corner of the room was a replica of a bandstand where the group rehearsed. Now it appeared dismal and forlorn, with nobody seated behind the drums or electric piano. Only the photographs on the wall, huge blowups of the group at work, seemed to bring life to the deserted area.

"They've all gone out," Tom said. "Appointments and things. They won't be back for a while, if that's what you're worried about."

"I'm not worried about anything," she said in the same imperious voice she had used on the telephone.

"Glad to hear it." He'd be damned if he was going to let her intimidate him. "Would you like a cup of tea, Mrs. Nicholson? Or coffee? You're American, aren't you?"

Overlooking his last question, she said, "Do you happen to have any Hag?"

"Hag? What's that?" He felt very provincial. "It sounds like haggis—Scotland's recipe for instant indigestion."

His joke made no impact on her. "Never mind. Coffee will do just fine, thank you."

"I'll be back in a tick."

Tom located some Nescafé and put the kettle on. Then it occurred to him that he should have offered his visitor a drink or a smoke, something to relax her. Despite her self-confident façade she must be on edge too, having come here under false pretenses. Tom wondered how she managed to look so sure of herself, so aggressively superior, when she was as mixed up in Harry's blackmail scheme as he. Perhaps the amount of money she expected to get out of it accounted for her lofty behavior. Her share might be a lot larger than his.

Tom hadn't considered that possibility before. And now that he did, he realized how little he knew about the entire operation. All he had was Harry's word on what they were going to ask Ian Nicholson for (seventy-five thousand pounds) to hush up the fact that both his wife and daughter were screwing the same unsavory character.

"Here we are," he said, giving her his bandstand smile when he returned with the coffee. "I see you've made friends with Winter."

She was stroking the ginger cat that had wandered in from the garden. "I wondered what he was called."

"We named him after our first big hit, 'Wintertime Love,'" he said, discreetly omitting that it was their only hit. "He's a real beauty, isn't he?"

"Yes. I like cats."

"So do I."

"Well, now that the amenities are over, let's get down to business." She drank her coffee black, with two sugars. "You know why I'm here of course."

"I assume it's because of Jeanne."

"How interesting." Her sardonic tone seemed to cut into him. "I thought you didn't know anyone by that name. At least that's what you said on the telephone."

"I was just having you on, Mrs. Nicholson. What about Jeanne?"

"I want you to stop seeing her immediately."

"Is that an order?"

"Call it anything you like. Just let her alone."

"Why should I?"

"Because I'm telling you to."

Not even *asking*. Telling! "Listen, lady—"

"Don't lady me," she warned in an ice-cold voice. "Jeanne might find your lack of manners exotic, but I don't."

"Well, excuse me," he said, standing up and bowing with mock sincerity. "I didn't realize I was in the presence of royalty. Maybe I should kiss your hand or something."

"You can kiss my ass for all I care. Just stop seeing my stepdaughter. That's all I have to say."

If Tom didn't know better, he would have believed she was on the level, that this was all she'd come here for. She certainly had a neat act, there was no denying it. Infuriating. Strange. But neat.

"And if I refuse?" he asked.

"You'd be a very foolish young man to do that. Jeanne's father doesn't know yet that you and she have become friends, to put a polite label on it. But I assure you that you'll have more trouble than you can handle if he does find out. As you might remember from your brief meeting with him in St. Moritz, he doesn't care for you and your type."

Tom could feel the anger rising within him. "What type is that?"

"Predatory."

Tom walked across the room to where his guitar was lying, picked it up and strummed a few chords of the new song he was writing. He had to calm down.

"I'm just a simple Scottish lad, Mrs. Nicholson. I don't even know what that word means."

"It means a creep who uses other people for purposes of exploitation, profit."

"You know, Mrs. Nicholson," he said, grappling with his rage, "you should be more careful how you speak to people. I have feelings too."

"I doubt that very much. If you did, you might have thought twice before seducing an innocent girl like Jeanne. A virgin, to be exact."

"Innocent?" Despite his anger, he broke into incredulous laughter. "That's a panic. You don't know your own stepdaughter, Mrs. Nicholson. It was all I could do to keep my clothes on my back."

"But Jeanne *was* a virgin until last Wednesday. Or do you deny that?"

"Hell, no. I don't deny it. Why should I? I'm not ashamed of what happened. I certainly didn't force Jeanne to do anything against her will. But I didn't have to. Your stepdaughter is the most agressive virgin I've ever run across. To put it in plain words, she practically dragged me into bed."

Alexis set aside her coffee cup, her long coral fingernails shimmering in the pale January light. "She claims that you raped her."

"What?"

"You heard me."

"I don't believe you. That's ridiculous. You're lying. Jeanne would never say a thing like that."

Alexis stood up, walked over to him, and to his amazement slapped him across the face. "How dare you call me a liar? Who do you think you are? You're nothing but a cheap, conniving musician. I've never been so insulted in my life."

The bitch was crazy, Tom thought, laying down his guitar. What kind of way was this to seduce a man? Then, to his own amazement, he felt a familiar bulge in his expensive Italian trousers. He was so used to women throwing themselves at him that he hadn't realized until now how bored he'd become by their eager availability. In contrast, Alexis Nicholson's insolent rejection proved to be having a startling, stimulating effect.

"Cheap and conniving, am I?" His anger and desire had meshed into one burning sensation. "So that's your opinion of me, is it?"

"Exactly."

"You asked for it," he said under his breath.

Then he grabbed her by the collar and ripped open the front of her coral shirt in one fast, jagged motion. Buttons flew to the floor. The cat ran out of the room. A clock chimed two. Otherwise nothing happened. To Tom's surprise she made no attempt to cover her bare breasts or protect herself in any way. She merely stood there, her long black hair flowing over her shoulders, her eyes steely and contemptuous as they met his. The barest hint of a smile threatened her lips.

"What do you plan to do now?" she asked.

"Fuck you, Mrs. Nicholson. Do what I didn't do to Jeanne if I have to. Rape you." Devour you, he thought to himself. "And you're going to love it."

"We'll see," she said as he grabbed her.

35 ~

Jeanne returned home from university feeling even more deranged than when she'd left. She had spent most of the day translating Pascal's pithy *Pensées* into English and dreaming about Tom McKillup in the weird, wordless language of love. Even the omniscient Pascal seemed stumped when it came to love. He had to borrow from Corneille.

"The cause [of love] is a certain something, as Corneille says, and the effects are dreadful."

Jeanne didn't need either of the 17th century geniuses to tell her that. Tom had not telephoned since last Wednesday when he relieved her of her hated virginity, and she was rapidly going crazy as a result. Five days of silence. Today didn't count. Not yet, she thought, as she threw her raincoat on a chair and raced into the kitchen where Mrs. Cook was polishing the silver with zealous determination.

"Are there any messages for me? Did anyone call?"

"Someone called, Miss, but not for you. For your step-mother."

"Oh." *Six* days of silence. "Where is my stepmother?"

"Out shopping."

Jeanne didn't know why she even bothered to ask. Alexis was always out shopping. It seemed to be her main interest in life, and she devoted herself to it religiously, fervently, compulsively. Shopping was Alexis' main outlet for boredom and frustration.

Now that Jeanne was living at home again, she realized how empty Alexis' existence was, how unfulfilled, how devoid of love. It was sad. When Jeanne lived at home before, she was too young to understand the situation. Now that she did, she resolved never to become like her stepmother.

The downstairs doorbell rang.

"I wonder who that could be," Mrs. Cook said.

It was Alexis, her arms empty for a change. Usually they were overflowing with that afternoon's purchases, and her lips would be drawn into a tight line of weariness. Now she appeared radiant, glowing.

"I left my keys home." Alexis laughed, her coral lips the

same shade as the pants that peeped out from beneath her long lynx coat. "Stupid of me, really."

"I thought you were shopping," Jeanne said.

"I was, darling. I had everything sent."

"What did you buy?"

"Let's see." Alexis' eyes glittered with enthusiasm. "A shirt, scarf, and belt at Hermes. And a yellow porcelain rose at Algernon Asprey. I decided that's what this kitchen needs. I also bought a porcelain pussy willow to go with it."

"My goodness," Mrs. Cook murmured. "That does seem extravagant, Madam."

"Nonsense. Every kitchen in London should come equipped with a porcelain rose and pussy willow."

"Whatever for?" Mrs. Cook said to herself.

Jeanne scrutinized her stepmother. Aside from the fact that she was not the sort of person to forget her keys, her manner was decidedly strange, giddy.

"You don't look as though you've been shopping," Jeanne said.

"Really?" Alexis laughed again. "What makes you say that?"

"Because you seem so happy and relaxed. When you've been shopping your face gets very tense."

"I didn't realize you were so observant."

"Also, I can smell your perfume." Her stepmother still wore the same scent, Les Fleurs, manufactured by Thérèse. "Ordinarily it would have worn off by now."

Alexis turned to Mrs. Cook. "I think this young lady is wasting her time studying languages. She should be going to detective school. But never mind. I'm certain that Scotland Yard will muddle through without her services. And now if everyone will excuse me, I'm going upstairs to bathe." She nodded to Jeanne. "Aching feet. A sure sign of the weary shopper."

The next day after a Spanish class, Jeanne telephoned Algernon Asprey on Bruton Street, pretending to be Mrs. Ian Nicholson. Affecting an American accent, she said she wanted to make certain that the porcelain rose and pussy willow she had ordered would arrive in time for a dinner party she was planning at the end of the week. After several minutes the sales assistant said there was no record of a Mrs. Nicholson having ordered anything recently.

Her hunch had been right.

Alexis had found a lover. Alexis was having an affair. Jeanne wondered who the man was. She wondered if her father suspected anything. She would have to keep an eye on her stepmother in the future. She sighed and decided to go for a walk along the river. The Thames looked muddy today, and the four large ships moored off the Embankment seemed to emphasize the leaden atmosphere. Her father told her that one of them, H.M.S. *Chrysanthemum*, had been used during the Second World War for training men of the Merchant Navy in antiaircraft gunnery, a fact which he obviously hoped would impress her by its historic significance. He seemed to forget that she was born in 1956, and the last war could not possibly have the same kind of nostalgia for her as it did for people of his generation, who were forever going on about Dunkirk, Montgomery, and the daring exploits of the RAF.

Jeanne knew that "the generation gap" was an overused phrase, but that was because it so accurately described the maddening situation. How could she expect her father to appreciate Tom and his music, when Ian was still humming outmoded tunes? As Tom had so rightly said last Wednesday:

"The Beatles changed more than just the world of music, they changed the *world*. It will never be the same again, thank God. Kids are people nowadays, not merely appendages of their parents. We've got buying power, we set the styles, we make the headlines. Kids are big business."

Even her father should be able to understand that, but unfortunately he clung to the traditional English upper-class values, which had not progressed an inch for over a hundred years. Ian was still living in the dusty past, still concerned about belonging to the right club and marrying his only daughter off to a suitable diplomat. Was he ever in for a big surprise!

Like most girls she'd always wondered what her first lover would be like, what the experience itself would be like. She had heard so many stories from other girls that she didn't know what to believe. Would it be wonderful or terrible? Or something even worse: mediocre, meaningless? One girl she knew in Gstaad said that she didn't even realize the much-heralded event had taken place until afterward when the boy rolled over on his side and said: "That was terrific, wasn't it?"

In retrospect, Jeanne couldn't understand anything like that happening, but she had no reason to doubt the girl's word. She was merely grateful it hadn't happened to her. Tom was everything she ever dreamed of. Gentle but passionate, tender in his actions yet fierce in his desire, considerately taking care not to frighten or rush her, adjusting himself to her slower pace until she had caught up with him, and then he let all barriers down and made love to her with the untamed ardor of a savage.

To her surprise she reacted in kind.

She never suspected the depths of her sensual hunger, nor the sheer carnal appetites she had hidden from everyone (including herself) all these years. In fact, the greatest revelation about Jeanne's first sexual experience had been her own wild enjoyment of it. The pain was secondary. Although even that, in its way, added to the overall pleasure and triumph she felt. There was something primeval about the sight of her blood on the bedsheets that thrilled her beyond expectation.

She had thought in advance that she might be ashamed of the mess or embarrassed by it, instead she was proud. Not because she'd been a virgin, but because with the wondrous rite completed, she was now a woman. It was a little like leaving behind a restricted area of existence and graduating into a world of higher, more thrilling achievement, a world which she would belong to forever.

What a romantic fool she was, she thought, as she turned into the Strand entrance to King's College. A week had gone by without so much as a word from Tom. Her considerate lover indeed! He didn't even care enough to telephone and say hello, if nothing else. Who was she kidding? She didn't want a mere hello from Tom, she wanted him to ask to see her again, to *want* to see her as badly as she wanted to see him.

It occurred to Jeanne that while the experience had been a momentous one on her part, for Tom it might have been a routine roll in the hay. Rock musicians were notorious for going to bed with a lot of girls, those tenacious groupies forever hanging around. Jeanne had heard all the stories about their supposedly promiscuous behavior, but did not know how much of it to believe.

Besides, even if it were generally true, there were always exceptions and she preferred to blame Tom's silence on something other than sheer indifference. Like what? she asked herself. That was the problem. Jeanne couldn't think of another explanation for his insulting, inexcusable conduct.

As she took the elevator to the top floor for her French class, she debated whether to call Tom or to wait. Either way there were drawbacks. On the one hand, the prospect of humiliating rejection. On the other, more sleepless, anxiety-filled nights. Insomnia was new to Jeanne and she did not know how to cope with it. She felt tired all the time now. Maybe she should ask Alexis for some of her sedative powder, but then she would have to answer questions. Her father would become alarmed and probably send her to the family GP, who would ask even more questions. No. That was out.

The most logical thing to do was call Tom and take her chances. What was the worst thing he could say? she thought, as she got off the elevator and marched into a telephone booth.

"I never want to see you again."

He had said it! Jeanne was shaking as she listened to the dreaded words of rebuff.

"I don't understand," she said. "Why? What did I do?"

"Oh, not much. You merely told your stepmother that I raped you."

In the background she heard a woman gasp, "No-o-o!" The voice sounded oddly familiar.

"I did *what?*" Jeanne said.

"You said I raped you! What the hell ever made you say a crazy, lunatic thing like that? Are you out of your mind?"

"But I didn't say it. There's been some terrible mistake."

"I'll bet."

The Beatles were singing "I Want to Hold Your Hand" in German. Tom had played the same record (a collector's item) last Wednesday when they made love. He hadn't wasted much time finding someone else to play it for.

"Tom, listen to me. I never even mentioned you to Alexis. You. Or us. Or what happened on Wednesday. I never told a soul. And I certainly never said that you raped me. You've got to believe me. Please, Tom."

"If you never told a soul, how come Alexis knew we were at my place last Wednesday night?"

"I don't know. I have no idea."

"Maybe your stepmother reads tea leaves in her spare time. Maybe that's how she found out."

"I'm sure there's a logical answer, Tom. There has to be."

"When you figure out what it is, do me a favor. Keep it to yourself. I never want to see you again."

"Tom!"

He had hung up, leaving her shattered and stunned. She contemplated throwing herself in the river, walking in front of a bus, buying a gun and blowing her brains out. But she didn't have the courage to commit suicide, it was too final an act. Besides, if she killed herself now, she would never discover how Alexis knew she and Tom had made love last Wednesday or why Alexis had gone to him with such a filthy, outrageous, damaging accusation as rape. There was only one thing to do. Confront Alexis with her own duplicity. Jeanne ran out of the school and hailed a cab on the Strand.

"Mount Street and South Audley," she said to the driver, who was looking at her strangely.

She realized why a moment later. Tears were rolling down her cheeks. She knew Alexis had never liked her, but she didn't think her stepmother hated her enough to ruin the most important relationship of her life.

36 &

To my immense surprise, Tom turned out to be a real sexual delight.

It had been so long since I'd gone to bed with anyone except Ian, whom I couldn't stand, or Harry, whom I desperately loved, that I'd nearly forgotten how much sheer plain *fun* sex could be. Ian's lovemaking revolted me by its sordidness and Harry's mesmerized me by its seriousness. In contrast, Tom's brand of lovemaking was lighthearted and whimsical, despite his dark threats of raping me yesterday.

We had had such a good time that he suggested I come back today, and I agreed. I felt guilty about enjoying myself, because I knew I wasn't supposed to. This was strictly a business deal and perhaps that only made me enjoy myself even more. You can always count on guilt for a good time.

What I hadn't counted on was the telephone call from Jeanne a few minutes ago, while I was getting dressed. I knew that sooner or later she would phone Tom to find out why he hadn't gotten in touch with her, but somehow I thought she would wait awhile if for no other reason than sheer pride. I should have remembered how hard it was to be proud when you were in love, how difficult it was to wait, how impatience finally won the day.

Tom's bedroom was a happy mess, something else that

added to my enjoyment after the careful order of my Mount Street maisonette.

The pungent smell of pot brought back my old youthful, carefree life before I met and married Ian, when I had screwed my way around the world in a variety of languages. It was something I never regretted and often missed: the lack of commitment, not knowing where I'd be the next minute or with whom. Earlier I asked Tom if he and Jeanne had smoked last week.

"No, I don't dig being a recruiter," he said. "It was bad enough finding out she was a virgin."

"That must have come as quite a surprise."

"Surprise? It was a shock, a nasty one. Who the hell needs virgins?"

"Why did you go to bed with her to start with?" I asked, playing dumb. "Do you find her attractive? You must."

He couldn't very well say he had done it because Harry asked him to. As far as Tom knew, Harry and I were recent acquaintances who met for the first time on holiday in St. Moritz. I could just imagine the expression on Tom McKillup's innocent face if he ever found out that I was Harry's sister and knew all about him and Harry, sexually. I wondered if there wasn't an extra kick in making love to Tom, being aware of the fact that he had also made love to Harry.

At first I was afraid the knowledge would revolt me and put me off, instead it had the exact opposite effect. There was something oddly thrilling about the whole three-sided business. Four, if Jeanne were included. Even though I hadn't enticed Tom in order to spite Jeanne, I could not rule out my strong sense of competition with my stepdaughter.

"I went to bed with Jeanne because I had hot pants," Tom lied, pretending to answer my question. "But it wasn't much fun, it wasn't anything like this."

"*In deinen Armen bin ich glücklich*," the Beatles chanted, at which point the telephone rang and Tom wearily picked it up. When I realized it was Jeanne, I was sorry I had ever told Tom that she said he raped her. I hadn't planned to say anything of the sort when I came to visit him yesterday. It was one of those spur-of-the-moment remarks prompted by my desperation to anger and arouse him, get him to take the sexual initiative rather than vice versa. Well, he'd taken it all right. To prove it, I still had the black-and-blue marks on my arm where he grabbed me.

But after we made love I admitted that I'd lied, that Jeanne had never said a word about rape. I told him I merely used it as a ploy to get him steamed up and seduce him, which wasn't very far from the truth. My motive for doing so, of course, was quite different from what Tom imagined. Like any other man in a similar situation, he assumed that I found him physically irresistible and was flattered, little realizing how Harry and I were planning to use him in our murder scheme.

And I never gave the rape matter another thought. I never dreamed he would toss it back at Jeanne as a reason for not wanting to see her again. In fact I was so startled to hear him mention rape on the telephone that I literally gasped. Now I would have an infuriated Jeanne on my hands when I went home. I could cheerfully have strangled Tom.

"You started it," he said, grinning, after he had hung up on Jeanne. "You gave me the perfect alibi."

"And you put me in the perfect hole, you rat."

I threw a pillow at him, he threw one back, and pretty soon he had undressed me and we were making love for the third time that day . . . another thing I'd forgotten was the fantastic virility of a twenty-five-year-old. Sexual manuals are forever saying it's quality not quantity that counts, and they're right to a degree. But I can tell you that there's nothing quite the same as fast recuperative powers and instant, rock-like erection to make a woman feel wanted.

"You sure have a great body for an older woman, Mrs. Nicholson," Tom said teasingly when I climbed out of bed minutes later. "Not a wrinkle on your ass. How do you manage it?"

"Shut up and help me find my tights. God, what time is it? I have to stop off somewhere on my way home."

Ignoring my remarks, he said, "When am I going to see you again?"

"I don't know. I'll call you. Whatever you do, don't call me." My tights were rolled up in a ball under the bed, along with my shoes and skirt. I must have taken them all off together. "I'm married to an extremely jealous man."

"If I were your husband I'd be jealous too. You give great head, Mrs. Nicholson."

I actually felt myself blushing. The last man to say the same thing in the same words was that bisexual American actor I had met in Morocco years ago. It seemed to be an unknown expression except among Americans and musicians, I thought, still looking for my sweater. I finally found it beneath one of the pillows.

"And I really dig your being so tall." Tom was perched at the edge of the bed. "I don't know what it is about your height that turns me on so much."

"Maybe I appeal to your filial instincts."

"My *what?*"

"Maybe I seem maternal to you."

He laughed. "Maternal? That's a giggle. With those breasts?"

I stopped, the sweater halfway over my head. "And what's wrong with my breasts?"

"Nothing. I like small ones, but they hardly remind me of Mum."

I kissed him on the lips. "I'm glad to hear that, son."

He got up and went to the door. "Methinks I hear human voices from below. My mates are back."

His bantering tone had turned serious. "I feel very possessive toward you, I suddenly realize."

"I'll wear a veil in the future. Now put your clothes on and let's go downstairs together so you can introduce me. I guess it's inevitable. Use a false name."

"How about Carmen?"

"Perfect. I'll speak with a thick Spanish accent."

Spanish. Spain. The summer people. All the lightness evaporated as I remembered what I was doing here in the first place. Somewhere, something had gone wrong. I was having too much fun without Harry and it frightened me. This was not the way it was supposed to be.

"What's wrong?" Tom asked.

"Nothing."

"You've turned pale."

"I said, *nothing!*"

It came out more sharply than I intended, and he looked at me for a moment before getting into his clothes. I hated him for seeing me with my careful defenses down. A naked body was nowhere near as intimate as a naked face, and I resolved not to let my allegiance to Harry stray again. Harry was all that mattered, I thought, wondering if after all these years of atheism Harry had become my religion.

I took a taxi to Algernon Asprey and ordered the yellow porcelain rose and pussy willow that I was supposed to have ordered yesterday. The saleslady seemed to be staring at me.

Could she tell that I had just come from a stranger's bed, and if so, how? Then I caught a glimpse of myself in a mirror, and I looked the same as always. Elegant, cool, unruffled. It was my guilty conscience playing tricks on me, I decided, realizing that I did not feel the least bit guilty cheating on Ian, only on Harry. Yet it was Harry who talked me into seducing Tom, it wasn't my idea. I had nothing to feel guilty about. Still the uncomfortable sensation lingered, like a dream you cannot shake off.

As I came around the square, I saw the doorman of the Connaught out in the middle of Carlos Place aggressively blowing his whistle for a taxi. Several of the hotel's guests stood huddled beneath the canopy, waiting. It had started to rain again. I'd left my Hardy Amies umbrella at Tom's flat, I suddenly realized, and I was going to get soaked.

What a stupid thing to have done! Aside from the fact that the papers predicted showers for today, I invariably carried an umbrella, the weather in London being so erratic. I wondered what my excuse to Jeanne and Mrs. Cook would be.

"Jeanne, did you walk off with my Hardy Amies umbrella this morning?" I said sternly, coming into the drawing room. "Because if you did, I'm going to be very cross indeed. Look at me. I'm drenched!"

Mrs. Cook had left for the day. It was later than I thought.

"No," Jeanne said, "I didn't take your umbrella."

"You didn't?" I looked puzzled. "I can't imagine what happened to it. I saw it in the stand just last evening. You know, the one with the bamboo handle."

"I said, I did not take your damned bloody umbrella!"

"What's the matter with you?"

"You, Alexis."

I shook off my chinchilla coat, feeling like a drowned cat. "I beg your pardon."

"You accused Tom of raping me!" She jumped up from the sofa, her eyes dark against the golden colors of the room. "You said I told you that he had raped me. Why? Why, Alexis? Why did you tell such a filthy, deplorable lie?"

One of the greatest benefits of having been a model was the haughty demeanor you never forgot. "First, I'm going to light the fire if you don't mind. It's freezing in here. Then I'm going to pour myself a brandy. And then I'll answer your question. Providing you think you have the patience to wait."

She sat down again and stared morosely at the tortoiseshell walls. I took my time. That was another thing I learned working for Madame Thérèse: never appear ruffled or agitated, particularly if you were.

"I guessed you had been with Tom last Wednesday when you came home looking so smug and self-satisfied," I said, standing next to the fireplace, calmly warming myself. "I didn't believe you were studying with a girlfriend at all. So I went to see Tom. Knowing how much your father disapproves of him, I thought it would be best to nip this ill-advised affair of yours in the bud before too much damage was done."

"You bitch."

"Tom freely admitted that you and he had gone to bed last Wednesday, as I suspected. In fact, the little bastard seemed quite pleased with himself. Which brings me to my main point. I knew Tom didn't rape you. He didn't have to. I merely *pretended* you said he had. I wanted to scare him off, keep him away from you in the future. And judging from the tearful expression on your face, my scheme appears to have worked. He doesn't want to see you again, I gather."

"No, he doesn't. Thanks to you."

"I find that very interesting. It only proves your father was right about him to begin with. If Tom cared for you even one iota he'd never allow himself to be so easily intimidated. He would have fought back. But you don't mean anything to him, you were a quick roll in the hay, that's all. And that's why I'm not sorry about having gone to him with that fake rape story. Your father didn't send you to the best schools in the world only to have you throw yourself away on a cheap, gutless musician."

Jeanne's skin had become mottled, as though my words were causing it to break out in angry blotches of red. She looked hideous in her fury.

"You're the worst hypocrite I've ever met, Alexis. Who do you think you're kidding with that noble explanation of yours? Not me, I can assure you of that. I'm not so dumb that I don't see through you and your miserable, conniving lies."

She was on her feet now, moving toward me.

"I'll tell you what really happened. You went to see Tom not to protect me, as you claim, but to seduce him yourself. You never ordered anything from Algernon Asprey yesterday. I called them and checked out your ridiculous porcelain rose and pussy willow story. They had no record of it. I knew you were being unfaithful to my father, but it didn't occur to me until just now that it was with Tom. In fact, you were with him this afternoon. You were the woman I heard gasping on the telephone when I called him. If you want your lousy umbrella so badly, why don't you ring up Fulham? *Because I'll bet my last pound that that's were it is!*"

Then, to my astonishment, she raised her hand and smacked me across the face just as the door opened and in walked Ian, home from a hard day's work.

"Good Lord," he said, looking from Jeanne to me. "What on earth is going on here?"

The timing could not have been more perfect than if I had arranged it myself.

The unexpected sight of his daughter striking his wife was not Ian Nicholson's idea of a pleasant homecoming, particularly after a fruitful and exhilarating day in the City. Sometimes the most insidious prejudices on the part of others turned into financial bonuses for one's own company. And to Ian's wry amusement, that was exactly what happened this afternoon.

A large supermarket chain which had retained the services of another merchant bank decided today to switch over to Nicholson's because of anti-Semitism. The other bank was Jewish-owned, and an Arab consortium had stated that no Jewish money could be involved in contributing to a certain issue of shares that the supermarket wanted to float. Since the Jewish bank did wish to provide part of the funds, the supermarket executives had to rule them out of the picture in order to placate their new Arab backers.

While Ian did not approve of anti-Semitism any more than he approved of any other form of racism, he had long ago learned to put aside his personal beliefs when it came to business. As a result, his firm now stood to earn a substantial amount of money.

He and his associates still had to determine whether to

charge a flat fee for arranging the issue transaction or to gamble on a percentage of the funds raised. He himself was in favor of the latter procedure because he suspected the profits would be greater that way, but first he had to convince the other managing directors of his company, who were more conservative in their outlook.

Tomorrow promised to be a very busy day, which was one of the main reasons he had been looking forward to a quiet evening at home tonight. A man's pipe and his slippers summed it up very well indeed, he thought. Instead he found himself confronted by a clearly hysterical daughter and an understandably outraged wife, both of whom seemed to turn to stone upon his arrival.

No one spoke for a moment. The two women stood next to the fireplace, mute anger outlined on their differing profiles. Alexis was all in black except for an occasional flash of her emerald and diamond ring. Jeanne, so much smaller and frailer, faced her stepmother in a tan corduroy pants suit that was too severely tailored for her slight figure (it seemed only yesterday that she had been wearing knee-length white socks). They made an unlikely pair of adversaries.

Ian sighed. Ever since he decided to send Jeanne to university in London, he'd been afraid of a clash of temperaments between the two women. They had never liked each other, but now that Jeanne was grown up the tension between them had worsened. He'd seen that in St. Moritz and knew it was just a matter of time before a full-blown explosion occurred. Well, this seemed to be the day.

"It's a personal matter," Alexis said, breaking the silence.

"No, it isn't," Jeanne said.

Ian poured himself a whiskey from the sideboard.

"Whatever it is, Jeanne, it can't possibly condone your physically assaulting your stepmother. I want you to apologize at once."

"I didn't assault her. I slapped her and she deserved it. I don't know why you always take her side against mine."

"I'm not aware of having taken anyone's side about anything. How can I? I don't even know what the issues are. It's just that I abhor violence and will not have it in my own home. Jeanne? I'm waiting."

"I'm sorry," Jeanne said without conviction to Alexis.

"Let's forget it," Alexis replied. "I detest quarrels."

"That's the most sensible thing I've heard since I walked in," Ian said.

"Not to me it isn't," Jeanne declared vehemently. "The only reason Alexis wants to forget it is because she's afraid I'll tell you what we were quarreling about. Isn't that true, Alexis?"

"Why should I be afraid? I have nothing to hide. But I think you might have some consideration for your father. He looks tired. Wouldn't you say this is hardly the time to burden him with our problems?"

"I would not!" Jeanne seemed to spit out the words in heated defiance. "I would say this is the perfect time. Why wait? The sooner Daddy hears the bad news, the better off he'll be."

"Bad news?" Ian said.

They had followed his example and sat down. How pleasant it was here, he thought, with the open fireplace and the whiskey warming his insides. He wished that he'd returned home when the quarrel between the two women was over. But since he hadn't, he could not shirk his responsibilities. He owed it to his daughter to let her speak her mind, particularly since he had neglected her so much in the past.

Poor little Jeanne. As an only child, with a mother and nanny murdered when she was still so young, her life had been a lonely one in spite of their wealth.

"Very well, Jeanne." He was resigned to a barrage of tedious details on a subject that would hold little interest for him. "Go ahead if you must."

Jeanne took a deep breath. "Alexis is being unfaithful to you."

Total silence descended upon the room except for the ticking of the old clock above the fireplace and the occasional crackling of flames. A soundless rain beat against the windows, and trees shook in the wind. But those could not be heard in here. They were outside and unimportant. The only important things were in this room. The clock ticking. The flames crackling. Alexis' impassive face. Jeanne's words suspended in midair by their own weight. The smell of something delicious coming from the kitchen. He wondered what Mrs. Cook had prepared for dinner this evening. He wondered why he could not get angry at Jeanne.

Perhaps because he secretly knew she was telling the truth, although he would never admit it. He could not get angry at Alexis either. He had neglected and abused her, too. The only thing he found surprising was that she had not been unfaithful to him before this. Maybe she had, but covered her tracks very cleverly. With Jeanne living at home now, her cleverness hadn't worked. For some reason that he did not comprehend, he felt sorry for the two women. The only person he did not feel sorry for was himself, the alleged victim in the case.

"Didn't you hear me, Daddy?" Jeanne asked. "Aren't you going to say anything? Aren't you going to ask me who the other man is?"

"No."

"Why not? Don't you care that you're being made a fool of? Or is it that you don't believe me? You think I'm lying, making it all up. That's it, isn't it? Well, I'm not!"

Ian wished he was back at his office, dealing with clear-cut issues like stock market prices and anti-Semitic Arabs. They were so much less complicated than the treacherous world of emotions.

"What I think," he said quietly, "is that you've blundered into areas of behavior that are none of your business. Alexis' fidelity to me, or lack of it, has nothing to do with you. Nothing at all. You should have realized that before you put your foot in your mouth. And therefore as far as I'm concerned, this entire conversation has never taken place."

Jeanne seemed to shrink into her chair as though she'd been struck by him. The expression in her eyes spelled betrayal. In that moment he'd lost her, he realized. Their relationship would never be the same after this. He had chosen his wife over his daughter, and Jeanne would never trust him again. Possibly she would grow to hate him, but he doubted it would last very long. Only until she fell in love and got married. Then she would forgive him and they'd be friends once more.

He smiled sadly to himself. *Friends.* What a weak and dismal substitute for the precious love link that existed between father and daughter. In years to come they would each remember that this was the moment he had irretrievably broken that link.

"Well, then, that ends that," Alexis said. "Who's getting hungry?"

Nobody was.

In the weeks that followed, Ian found himself being kinder and more considerate to Alexis than usual without quite knowing why. It was almost as though he were trying to condone her infidelity, assure her that he did not find her guilty of betraying him, tell her (without words) that it was not her fault she favored another man. Occasionally he would wonder who the man was, how Jeanne happened to know his identity. But he never asked.

These moments of curiosity always occurred at inopportune times. He would be at an important business meeting or dictating a letter to his secretary when the image of Alexis and a faceless stranger making love would swim across his mind, causing him to lose track of what he was listening to or even worse, saying.

One of the oddest things about the entire business was that Alexis did not seem the least bit embarrassed or humiliated herself. Perhaps she was innocent after all. Perhaps Jeanne had made a mistake or was lying. They never discussed the matter again after that first awkward evening, and Ian never privately questioned Alexis about it.

Another woman would have protested her innocence even without being questioned, but not Alexis. Cool and reserved as always, she said nothing in her own defense. Ian corrected himself. She said nothing, period. It was as though Jeanne's accusation of infidelity had never been leveled against her.

Didn't she care what he thought? Or was she so sure of him that she knew he would not blame her for her digressions? How many times had he digressed himself? More than he cared to remember. At least his wife had the good sense to keep her mouth shut and not tell him about it, as he so sadistically used to. He was younger then, more foolish. He wanted to hurt her, and he had no doubt that he succeeded with his explicit details of every one of his sexual encounters.

He'd spared her nothing. She was not sparing him either. Her silence was far worse than any outpourings of confession. She was letting him imagine what he liked, such as the faceless stranger caressing her in unknown ways, whispering secret words, promising endless thrills.

A few nights later Alexis came into his room. He was reading in bed before going to sleep. The book, which was partially devoted to banking in Britain, listed all the major merchant banks, the date of their founding, senior partners, and total assets in 1970. He was pleased to see his own firm's name listed between Hambros and Samuel Montague.

1850 . . . E. H. Nicholson . . . I. P. Nicholson . . . 225 (£ millions).

Thank God for Edward Henry Nicholson, his great-grandfather, for having the brains to form such a productive and challenging institution, Ian thought, as he put the book down and looked at his wife. She was lovely in her dressing gown, her face devoid of makeup. The familiar scent of Les Fleurs filled the room.

"I just wanted you to know that it's not true. What Jeanne said about me being unfaithful to you."

Weeks had passed since the incident. "I know it isn't."

"You never asked me about it. I thought you might have doubts."

He smiled at her concern. "No doubts."

"Good. I can't imagine why Jeanne would say a thing like that."

"Neither can I, and I'm sorry that she did." He tried to sound comforting. " I had hoped that the two of you would get along better, now that Jeanne is grown up. I wanted you to become friends. But I imagine that will work itself out in due time."

"I'm sure it will. Well, good night, Ian."

"Good night, darling. Sleep well."

"You, too."

She kissed him on the cheek and left the room. He was sorry she had come in with that false story of denial. It only confirmed what he knew all along: that the faceless man existed, that Jeanne had been right.

"Not to worry," he told himself.

Tomorrow he would go to his favorite pleasure haunt in Mayfair. There was a very alluring Swedish girl there named Ulla, who advertised "stocks and bonds for rent," which tickled Ian in more ways than one. She had a riding crop with gold mountings that drew blood when she cracked it across his naked ass as he lay helplessly bound from head to toe.

Ulla claimed that the crop came from the same establishment that was whipmaker to the Queen, and in view of this she charged thirty pounds for the regal chastisement. Ian was only too happy to pay that amount. If anyone should be able to recognize good value for money, it certainly was a merchant banker.

He picked up his book again and began to read about the Barings, one of the oldest and most prestigious banking families in Great Britain. They were descendents of a deaf clothing manufacturer, Sir Francis Baring, who died in 1810, leaving millions of pounds to his heirs. Ian regretted not having a son to leave the business to. Perhaps Jeanne would surprise him and marry an enterprising young banker. Perhaps the faceless man would soon win disfavor with Alexis.

He continued to read until he could keep his eyes open no longer, then he fell into a deep dreamless sleep.

38 &

Patty Hearst and the remnants of the Symbionese Liberation Army were still at large in America, John Dean had announced his intentions to write a book about his part in the Watergate coverup, and the Arab oil-producing nations were continuing to pour billions of dollars into the sagging British economy.

Harry knew all this because he had just read that week's issue of *Time*, on the train into London to see Alexis. Instead of their usual sleazy hotel rendezvous, Alexis had asked him to meet her at Harrods. He thought she was kidding at first, but she turned out to be serious and adamant.

"The china department, at two tomorrow," she said, hanging up before he could get another word in.

He put the receiver down, cursing his sister, himself, and their delayed plans. Why the hell was everything taking so long? It had been two months now since Alexis first went to bed with Tom the Twit (Harry's new nickname for him) and her reports so far were negative, negative. Ian, apparently, was turning the other cheek, pretending not to notice his wife's adulterous activities.

Harry had been looking forward to an exciting afternoon with Alexis until this letdown of a telephone call. He wondered why she did not want to be alone with him, but the answer seemed so obvious that he pushed it away.

Tom was a very talented liar. He had been pretending that his affair with Alexis was one big gigantic pain in the ass, not realizing that Harry was even more talented than he when it came to spotting liars. Harry could see right through Tom's seemingly reasonable complaints ("Man, she's too *old!*") to the truth of the matter: Tom was turned on like crazy.

What about Alexis? Was she equally excited? She claimed she wasn't, that she was only doing her job, but that was the problem with Alexis. Harry could never tell when she was lying. The possibility that the two of them were having a fabulous roll in the hay while he was out in the cold only put an extra edge on his already rotten mood. Nothing seemed to be going as planned. He began to doubt the wisdom of having included McKillup in on the deal, but it was too late to do anything about that now.

Harrods was jammed.

He spotted Alexis immediately in the china and glass department. She stood out above everyone else partly because of her sheer height, but mostly because of her startling arrogant beauty. Seeing her at a distance gave Harry a fresh perspective. If he didn't know better he would have taken her for just another rich, spoiled, married woman out for an afternoon of conspicuous consumption. A moment later he realized that that was what she was.

No, she was that only in part. That was the façade. Beneath the layers of pretense she was still the same smalltown girl he had grown up with, the mischievous sister he had always loved. No amount of money or gold-coating could ever dim Harry's earliest memories of their life in Pilgrim Lake where they had gone skinny-dipping in the summer and ice skating in the winter. Either way, naked or bundled up to her ears, she was always the headstrong, fresh-mouthed, irresistible Alexis, the despair of their mother, the object of their father's affections.

Harry remembered how devastated Alexis had been when their father died, and how relieved he felt. No longer would he have to put up with those taunting remarks from the other kids at school about his father's drinking. Even now, more than thirty years later, he could still recall the humiliation he suffered as a result of their adolescent jokes.

Q. Why does Harry's father think he's a fish?
A. Because he's always tanked to the gills, ha ha ha.

A. Knock, knock.
Q. Who's there?
A. Mark.
Q. Mark who?
A. Mark my place at the bar while I go take a piss, ha ha ha.

Q. What's fifty percent Injun, fifty percent Dutch, and
   one hundred percent Canadian Club?
A. Mark Maringo, ha ha ha.

Harry popped a peppermint into his mouth. He had gotten
drunk last night at dinner and when he woke up this morning
with a giant-sized hangover he knocked off three of his
whiskey sour specials before Sarah even came down to
breakfast. Now he had a dry unpleasant taste in his mouth
and considerably more sympathy for the father he had never
loved. He could understand how an unhappy, unfulfilled
marriage had driven his father to the bottle. Some men would
have lost themselves in their work, taken a mistress, found
an absorbing hobby.

Harry envied such men. Their emotional needs were simple,
they could live quite happily without the deep commitment of
love. Mark Maringo had not been able to, and neither could
Harry.

The possibility that that was why Alexis loved him had
occurred to him before. In many ways he had a lot to thank
the old man for. Like that first time with Alexis, when she
was twelve and he was thirteen.

It was amazing how vividly he still remembered the colors
of that day: the red and gold treetops, the brown and white
bearskin rug, the radiant blue Spanish sky in the book Alexis
stole from the library, Alexis' pink rabbit pajamas. . . .

Harry suspected that a lot of guys all over the world had
made it with their sisters at one time in their lives, and then
gone on to establish perfectly normal relationships with other
women. Why not him? He'd like to see a psychiatrist answer
that one.

He walked over to the china counter, where Alexis was
conferring with a dark-suited salesman about a Minton dinner
service for twelve.

"The set contains one hundred and seventeen pieces,
Madam," the salesman said. "And the price is—"

He named a figure of over ten thousand pounds, which
averaged out to a little less than one hundred pounds per
plate. "It's a real bargain," Harry said, coming up behind
Alexis. "Grab it while the supply lasts."

She turned around, her gold ear clips twinkling at him.
"Don't be cheeky."

It was funny, Harry thought, how fast you got used to

spending large sums of money and watching it being spent, particularly when the money was not your own.

"Where to now?" he asked after she had signed the sales slip.

"The next department. Towels and linens. They also sell terry cloth robes. I want to buy one for Jeanne. She has a birthday coming up."

"Alexis, don't you think it's pretty risky for us to be seen together?"

"In *Harrods?*" She laughed. "What could be more innocent?"

"Nothing, I suppose."

Her spirits were so high that he didn't want to dampen them with his own depressing mood. Besides, she might have something to tell him which would change that mood, bring their plans for Sarah's demise into more immediate focus. He was so tired of waiting for Ian to come to his senses and acknowledge his wife's flagrant behavior, create a jealous scene, *do* something.

"Ian simply will not acknowledge my affair with Tom," she said, stopping before a rack of Yves St. Laurent toweling robes. "It's as though he's become deaf, dumb, and blind these last couple of months. Frankly, I'm getting desperate."

Harry pressed his hand over his mouth for fear that if he didn't he would shout obscenities at the top of his lungs.

"Shit, fuck, screw," he mumbled under his breath as an elderly lady wearing a large black velvet hat walked by, looking at him suspiciously.

"Did you say something, darling?" Alexis asked.

"Yes. I think we're planning to kill the wrong person."

Alexis held up a cocoa-brown Empire robe with batwing sleeves. "What do you mean? The wrong person?"

"I mean, I think we should murder Ian on grounds of sheer stupidity."

The elderly lady had stopped a few feet away from them and was supporting herself on her cane. The curiosity was apparent in her face and she made no attempt to conceal it.

"She's listening to us," Harry hissed. "She heard me say 'murder.' "

Alexis put the brown robe back and picked out an orange one. "Who did?"

"Stop talking so loud, damn it! That old woman with the fucking cane."

"Don't be paranoid, darling. You're in Harrods. There are no spies here."

Harry turned partially around so that the elderly lady could not see his lips move. "Let's get out of here. This place gives me the creeps."

"You know, Harry, you've turned into a total hysteric. Who would ever think that you once strangled two innocent women, single-handed?"

"I didn't strangle them." He glanced anxiously over his shoulder. "I broke both their necks."

"Oh, that's right. It's been so long, I've forgotten. You certainly weren't worried about little old ladies in those days, that's for sure. I think I'll take the brown robe."

"I'm glad that's settled. Now we can leave."

Both Alexis and the elderly lady looked at him askance.

"Leave?" Alexis said. "We're not leaving. I still have to go to shoes on the first floor and buttons on the ground. We can talk while I shop."

Harry approached the elderly lady. "We'll be in the shoe department in case you're interested."

"Thank you." She smiled brightly at him. "So kind."

When they got downstairs to the elegant shoe salon, Alexis headed straight for the Rayne section, which was displaying lovely strappy evening sandals at stylish prices.

"How are things going with Tom?" Harry asked.

Alexis had removed her own shoes and was wiggling her toes. "As well as can be expected."

"What does that mean?"

"It means I'm bored to death with this cooked-up romance. It's no fun making love to a kid who's young enough to be my own son. I want to put an end to it, but it hasn't paid dividends so far. Harry, I'm stuck. I honestly don't know what to do next. Ian just goes on pretending that nothing unusual is taking place, that I'm still the same devoted faithful wife I've always been. *Why?* I've left enough clues around for a fool to find, and Ian is no fool. He's driving me crazy."

"I'd like to know why, too." Harry thought it fascinating that both Alexis and Tom had denied interest in each other on the basis of the age difference between them. "Maybe you've been too subtle up until now. Maybe you're not being obvious enough, Alexis."

"Obvious? I've done everything except screw the kid in my own bed."

"Well?"

"You've got to be joking."

"Why?"

"I couldn't do it," she said.

"Yes, you could."

"It's too vulgar."

"What we're planning to do to Sarah and Ian wouldn't exactly be considered the height of good manners."

He made a quick subject change. "Why did you suggest Harrods, of all places? Why not one of our hotels? I get the distinct feeling that you want to avoid making love to me."

To his surprise she said: "You're right. I can't explain it, but I would rather wait until . . ."

She swallowed and Harry realized that beneath today's flippant façade she was as nervous and apprehensive as he.

"I would rather wait until matters are completed. I can't bear the thought of another dingy hotel room. That part of our life belongs to the past. Let it stay there. Do you understand what I'm trying to tell you?"

He pressed her hand. "Yes, I do."

"You're not jealous about Tom, are you, Harry?"

"Let's say that I've been uncertain."

"You have no reason to be. Tom means nothing to me. Please believe that."

"I want to."

"Then do. Because it's the truth."

"Okay," he said, feeling better than he had all day.

The salesman returned with Alexis' black patent t-straps, which he slipped on her feet.

"Would you please have them sent?" Alexis said to the salesman as she sat down again. "It's on account."

Harry waited until the salesman had left, then he kept his voice significantly low. "Invite Tom to lunch as soon as possible and get him into bed. It's our only hope."

"Surely you don't mean to have Ian find us there when he comes home from work, do you? That would be asking too much, Harry."

"Nothing as melodramatic as that. Tom will be long since gone by the time Ian gets home, but there must be some clue, some piece of damaging evidence which Ian cannot overlook that a man has been in his bed earlier that day. And it should be obvious that the man was Tom McKillup."

"Maybe I can arrange for him to leave one of his kilts on Ian's pillow."

"I'm not amused."

"Neither am I. It's easy enough for you to issue orders, bu
I have to carry them out." Alexis sighed in resignation. "Okay
I'll invite McKillup for Thursday. It's Mrs. Cook's half da
off. I hope he can make it."

"So do I. Don't forget that an Englishman's home is hi
castle, and while Ian might have been willing to ignore you
indiscretions elsewhere, he won't be so good-natured when i
comes to his own domain. Believe me. You can expect a
explosion."

"But what good will it do if nobody is there to hear him?"

"Jeanne will be home from school, won't she? She's th
ideal witness."

"Oh, she'll probably be home, but I doubt if Ian would
blow up in front of her no matter how provoked he is. He'
got too much control for that. He'll speak to me privately
And then we're right back where we started."

"Not necessarily." Harry grinned, and a lock of dark hai
fell across his forehead. "Leave that part of it to me."

39 ᴄᴇ

While Harry was busily engaged at Harrods, Sarah was busily
engaged trying to figure out why none of her attempts to
improve her appearance were having any noticeable effect
upon her husband. God knows she had gone to enough
trouble and expense.

In addition to a shorter, fluffier, more youthful hairdo, she
had brightened her somewhat conservative wardrobe with a
variety of exotic outfits, as well as toning up her flaccid
muscles by means of daily massage. A large, capable, Finnish
woman had been coming to the house every morning since
Sarah's return from St. Moritz for that very purpose.

And yet, in spite of the new enticing self she now presented,
Harry did not seem any more sexually interested in her than

he was before she began her campaign. As humiliating as it was, the only way Sarah could get him to make love to her these days was to initiate the process herself. Aggressively. Was she so repellent to him? She must be. Either that or there was another woman in the picture.

On impulse she dialed Tom McKillup's house in Fulham. Harry had mentioned he was going to listen to Tom's new song. Nobody answered. Maybe they had gone out to a pub. Half an hour later she rang the number again. This time Tom picked up the phone. When she asked if she could speak to Harry, Tom sounded surprised.

"He's not here."

"Oh? How odd. Did he stop by earlier?"

"No. Was he supposed to?"

"I must have gotten my signals crossed." Sarah laughed lightly. "I'm sorry, Tom. My mistake."

"Is there anything I can do for you, Mrs. Maringo?"

"Thank you, I'm afraid not. I wanted to ask Harry to buy some flowers on his way home, but it's not terribly important."

"Well," Tom said, uneasily. "Nice to talk to you."

"Yes. Good-bye for now."

" 'Bye."

Sarah was shaking when she put the receiver back on its hook. So her suspicions were right. It had to be another woman. Why else would Harry lie about where he was going? And Sarah suspected she knew who that "woman" was. "Girl" would be more like it.

She still remembered how Jeanne Nicholson had gobbled Harry up with her eyes the first day they all met in St. Moritz. She remembered the intimate way Harry danced with Jeanne at the Prince Regent's Club that same night, and how later he went out ostensibly for a breath of fresh air and did not return to the hotel before dawn.

Sarah remembered how careful Harry had been to avoid Jeanne's gaze when they dined at the Nicholsons' flat several months ago. Since then, Harry's periodic trips to his tailor in London had failed to produce one new stitch of clothing. And now he was using Tom McKillup as an alibi. It all added up. How could she have been so stupid, so trusting?

Tears of defiance came to Sarah's eyes as she wheeled into her study and took a sheet of rose-colored stationery out of the top desk drawer. Slowly, she began to write:

MY DEAR IAN:

This letter will be as awkward and painful for me to write, as I know it will be for you to read. But I am certain that I can count on you to deal with the contents as discreetly as possible.

I have reason to believe that my husband and your daughter are having an affair. . . .

40 ~

Tom was in love with Alexis and it hurt.

All those painful love songs he had written over the years now came black to haunt him with the uncanny truthfulness of their emotions. Anxiety, jealousy, misery, fear. He had experienced the lot during the brief two months of his affair with Alexis.

So this was love, he thought as he swung his bright blue Jaguar into Mount Street and looked for a parking space. Miraculously he found one just across from the Nicholsons' well-kept but unpretentious building. Tom understood the difference between this neighborhood and his own all too well. It was the difference between old money and new, and in Great Britain age was revered. But not in America. Which was one of the reasons he had hoped to tour there with his group, Castle Rock.

The booking for the proposed concert tour, with all its great financial promise, had fallen through. His agent had called that morning to tell him that the group's records were not selling well enough in the States to warrant a tour. It was too risky a chance to take at the moment.

"Maybe next year," his agent said. "Right now the market is saturated there. I could never get you the kind of exposure you'd need to insure a profitable return on investment. Sorry, lad."

The other guys had gone out to get pissed when he told them the bad news, and if it weren't for Alexis' luncheon invitation he would have joined them. Happily. He would be twenty-six next month, and his life seemed to be going nowhere both personally and professionally. Being in love with an older married woman who was not in love with him was nearly as bad as having the American tour canceled. Both were miserable experiences he had not foreseen, and now that they were realities Tom felt more dependent than ever upon the £25,000 Harry promised him for his part in the plan to blackmail Ian Nicholson.

Since Alexis still had no idea that he was going to be cut in on one third of the £75,000 extracted from her husband, Tom found himself in an uncomfortable position. His reasons for going to bed with Alexis had changed considerably, but how could he tell her that without admitting that his original motive had only been money? It seemed so crass. Yet money had been her motive too, and as far as he knew still was.

Perhaps if he told her that he was not just the wide-eyed enamoured young man she imagined, but a shrewdly enterprising young man as well (as enterprising as she and Harry), she would respect him more. And with women, respect was the first stepping-stone to love. But Harry had specifically warned him not to let Alexis know that he was part of the blackmail scheme. As Tom got out of the Jaguar and locked the door, he remembered Harry's words on the subject.

"We don't want her to know that the money is going to be split three ways or she might not go through with it. As it now stands, she thinks that she and I are the only ones who'll share the proceeds."

A sudden sense of elation soared through Tom as he realized how outdated Harry's warning was. It applied to the situation *before* he let Alexis "seduce" him, not now. Now that she had gone through with it, what difference could it make if she found out that he was as entangled in the blackmail plan as he?

It could only work to his personal advantage, make her see him in a far more daring and favorable light, bring them closer together. He smiled to himself as the old expression came to mind: *partners in crime*. Well, that's what he and Alexis were, whether she knew it or not.

The fact that Harry was a partner too only mattered in the financial sense. Once the money was divided up, there would be no further dealings between Alexis and Harry, whose relationship was flimsy to say the least. They barely knew each other. Although every once in a while Tom got a creepy feeling that there was something more going on between those two than the casual picture they each presented to him. But he knew it was just displaced jealousy talking, the nagging notion of Alexis making love to another man that loomed before him now and then.

It was pointless to worry about old Harry in that department. Despite his heterosexual appearance and manner, Harry was too much of a pouf to be interested in women except for their money. Like his rich, tightfisted wife. Tom still wondered why Sarah had telephoned him the other day, expecting Harry to be there. He made a mental note to ask Harry about that the next time he spoke to him.

Now Tom shivered as he walked across Mount Street and rang the bell of the Nicholsons' maisonette. The words of his only hit song came back to him as he stood there in the blustery March weather waiting for his beloved to buzz him in.

> Will you still be my wintertime love
> When summertime rolls around?

It was a damned appropriate question.

Just as the buzzer sounded, the door swung open and a middle-aged woman came through, a shopping bag in each hand. She glanced at Tom, her blue eyes clear and disapproving before going on her way.

"Was that your Mrs. Cook?" he asked Alexis when he got off the elevator. "She looked at me as though I were carrying the plague."

Alexis laughed. "It was Mrs. Cook, all right. She's an eternal pessimist, always suspecting the worst."

"That sounds jolly."

"It's not so bad. If the worst does happen, Mrs. Cook can say that she predicted it. And if it doesn't, then she has one less catastrophe to deal with that day."

"Am I today's catastrophe?"

"In Mrs. Cook's eyes, probably."

"What does she think I'm doing here?"

'Oh, she thinks you've come to make mad, passionate, illicit love to me," Alexis teased him. "Outwardly, she disapproves. Secretly, she's jealous. Why all the questions?"

Tom grabbed her and kissed her. She yielded promptly, mechanically.

"I'm nervous, I guess," he said.

"Why?"

"I'm not sure."

Alexis took him into the drawing room, where champagne was cooling in a silver ice bucket. Next to it sat a tray of thinly sliced smoked salmon, garnished with watercress and lemon wedges.

"Is it Ian?" Alexis asked. "He's at work. He won't be back until this evening."

"What about Jeanne?"

"You *are* nervous. Jeanne's at university, and she never comes home until around five. We have four lovely hours to ourselves. Now do you feel better?"

"Much."

But he didn't feel better. He was being set up. Some tangible evidence was needed to convince Ian that his wife had taken a lover, and he was to be that evidence. Hence the luncheon invitation. Two months ago Tom would not have objected to being used like this, but now that his feelings for Alexis had grown so intense, he did object. He did not want to make love to her on assignment anymore. He wanted to make love to her, period.

And seeing her in her own home surroundings for the first time only increased his desire. She fit in here amidst the exquisite furnishings and fine oil paintings, the touches of velvet and fur, the huge gilt-framed mirror above the fireplace that reflected the room's splendor. Gracious living suited her.

At his insistence Alexis showed him the rest of the duplex, and he was agreeably impressed by the combination of elegance and comfort. The fact that both Alexis and Ian had their own bedrooms struck Tom as the height of luxury, the epitome of sophistication. It was a notion he'd never entertained before, but he could tell that she found nothing unusual about the arrangement.

This was her natural habitat, he thought enviously, remembering his own shabby origins and the house he had grown up in, where his parents still lived. What lingered most was the lack of space (he had to share a bed with his younger brother until he left home at the age of seventeen). That, and the inadequate plumbing, the drab uninspired furniture, the worn carpets, his mother's hands red from too much work.

"Why did you invite me here?" he asked Alexis when they were downstairs again, drinking champagne.

She smiled charmingly. "I thought it would make a nice

change. I'm always coming to your place. I thought you'd like to see where I lived."

In addition to her other accomplishments, she was a terrific liar as well. If he didn't know better, he would have believed her. She looked so innocent sitting there against her leopard cushions, wearing a simple black jersey ankle-length dress, her only jewelry a heavy white and gold chain draped around her waist. Although Tom hardly considered himself an expert on fashion, he was willing to bet that the cost of the two items was more than his father would ever earn in a lifetime of hard, honest work.

Was that why he had leaped at Harry's blackmail offer? Because he knew the futility of hard honest work, in the long run? How it got you nowhere except six feet under, way before your time? Perhaps. Tom did not regret his decision to make some easy money. The only thing he hadn't counted on was falling in love with the lady whose husband they planned to blackmail. Unfortunately that complicated matters.

After the business part was over, he would want to go on seeing Alexis. The thought of having to give her up was too painful to contemplate. He even considered asking her to divorce Ian and marry him, despite the difference in their ages. But what about *her?* What did *she* want?

"I like where you live," Tom said, figuring that two could play the same game, at least he could try. "It suits you very much. Was your family wealthy?"

"Fairly wealthy."

It was the first time they had ever referred to her background. "That's what I thought."

"What do you mean?"

"It shows. I was a slum kid myself."

"Well, it doesn't show." She flashed another engaging smile at him. "Would you like some smoked salmon?"

"Sure. Thanks. It comes from the same part of the world that I do. Not that we could ever afford it."

His main memory of food when he was growing up was porridge for breakfast, peas and tatties for lunch, and smelly fried herring for dinner.

"You're spoiling me, you realize."

"That is exactly my intention," Alexis said.

She placed a plate of smoked salmon before him and re-filled his wineglass. Tom was not accustomed to drinking, particularly during the day, and he could feel a pleasurable self-confident glow from the champagne. This was the life all right, he thought giddily. The guys back home on Dalry Road should see him now! They'd fall flat on their astonished faces.

"Don't you ever wonder why I continue to go on with our affair?" he asked Alexis, feeling bolder now.

He could see the spark of surprise in her eyes, but it was quickly wiped out by a conciliatory, coquettish manner.

"I assume it's because you like me," she said.

"I do like you."

"Well then, what's the mystery?" But she seemed on edge, about to pounce. "I don't understand."

He finished his second glass of champagne. "Let's put it this way. Maybe I like you, but I also have another reason for making love to you. A more practical one."

She watched him carefully as she refilled his glass. Her own glass was untouched, he noticed. "Another reason? Like what, darling?"

She had called him darling before, but there was an almost ominous overtone to it now. "You should know," he said. "It's the same reason you're in on this, too."

"In on *what*? What are you talking about?"

"Knock it off, Alexis. You don't have to play dumb with me. I know everything. You might say we're partners."

Her eyes had grown huge and dark with fear, but her voice dropped to a whisper. "Partners?"

"In crime."

She attempted an unsuccessful laugh. "Really, Tom, you've had too much champagne. I don't have the vaguest idea what you're babbling about."

"Why don't you ask Harry, then?"

At the mention of Harry's name, she froze. "What does Harry have to do with it?"

"It was all his idea, wouldn't you agree? The whole setup. He masterminded it. But I guess he failed to inform you that he was cutting me in on one third of the action."

"One third of the action?" she repeated dumbly.

"Why are you so surprised? I deserve it. I played my part very well."

"What part?"

"I pretended to let you seduce me, didn't I?"

"You mean—"

"Yes, I knew you were going to try. Harry alerted me. Although I must say you went about it very subtly. You didn't throw yourself at me, just the opposite. You got me to do all the work, didn't you? It was an impressive performance."

She was staring at him in astonishment.

"So you see I'm not quite the gullible, love-smitten little lad you took me for. There's more to me than you imagine. Much more." To his chagrin, he hiccupped. "Understand, partner?"

"You've known all along," she said at last.

"That's right." He finally had the upper hand and he was enjoying every sweet second of it. "I've been in on it right from the beginning."

"St. Moritz . . ." She seemed to be talking to herself. Her façade had totally crumbled. "Harry told you in St. Moritz."

"But he didn't tell you. About *me*, I mean."

"No."

She looked as though she were in shock. Tom knew she would be surprised, but he didn't expect her to take it this hard. She must be more upset about having to split the £75,000 three ways than he had imagined. Suddenly he felt sorry for her. Maybe it wasn't so great to grow up with money. When you lost it, you did not adjust as well as someone who never had it to begin with. Poor Alexis. But she still had him. He loved her. If they pooled their resources they would end up with £50,000 between them, and that wasn't exactly oatmeal.

"You've known about the murder all along," she said, dazed.

He was certain he had heard wrong. "Murder?"

"Harry told you everything. *Why?*" She started to sob uncontrollably. "*Why did he do it?*"

Tom took her in his arms and tried to comfort her, but she was like a stick of wood. Inert. Lifeless. He could not understand her strange outburst.

"I don't know anything about murder," he said.

She dried her tears with the back of her hand like a child and seemed to collect herself. "You don't have to lie anymore, Tom. I realize that you know about Sarah. It's all perfectly clear."

"Not to me, it isn't. What's this about Sarah?"

But she seemed lost in her own world of sadness. "Harry must care for you more than I thought."

Tom was on guard instantly. "How much do you know about Harry and me?"

"Everything."

He could feel a ghastly sensation in his stomach. "What's everything?"

"You and Harry were lovers," she said expressionlessly. "Maybe you still are. I'm no longer sure what to believe."

Tom moved away from her as though Harry had driven a wedge between them, which in a sense he had. Harry had tricked them both.

Tom was sorry now that he ever let himself be seduced by Harry that night in St. Moritz, after the Alpina discotheque closed. After St. Moritz Tom had gone to bed with Harry only once, and that was before starting the affair with Alexis. Since then he had no interest in men at all. It was one of the reasons why he felt so convinced that he loved her. More, why he needed her to return at least a portion of that love. By doing so, she would be ensuring against any further lapses of his into the netherworld of homosexuality.

But Harry had betrayed him by telling Alexis about the two of them. Why? It seemed such an unnecessary and unlikely thing for him to do under the circumstances. What did Harry have to gain by it? Tom felt confused, angry. Harry had really screwed him up with Alexis but good, goddamn it.

"Harry doesn't mean anything to me," he anxiously tried to reassure her. "We were both drunk that night in St. Moritz or it never would have happened. And it hasn't happened since." Well that was almost true; intention was what counted. "You've got to believe me, Alexis. It's you I'm in love with."

It was the first time he had actually put it into so many words, and he waited expectantly for her reaction. But she just sat there staring off into space, as though he hadn't opened his mouth. Did she think he was lying? Probably. After what he had said earlier about "playing his part" in letting her seduce him, how could she believe him now? He never should have boasted so much. He had overdone it. He hated Harry's guts.

"I know what you're thinking," he said, "and I don't blame you, but you're wrong. I really am in love with you."

All of a sudden she began to laugh. Harshly. Stridently.

"What is it?" he asked. "What the hell is so funny?"

"You are."

He could feel himself turn red. "Perhaps you'd like to explain that."

"You and Harry, both. You're a pair of jokers, aren't you? With your claims to be in love with me. *We're just wild about Alexis*," she said in a horrible, mocking voice. "Is that what you and Harry say when you're in bed together? How much you each love me?"

"*Each?* What do you mean? I'm certainly in love with you. I've already said·so. But how did Harry get into the act? I thought you barely knew one another."

The clock chimed two.

"Harry is my brother."

Then she told him everything.

41

Jeanne was in such a rush to get home that she did not bother catching her regular Number 9 bus from King's College to Piccadilly. Going by bus could take anywhere from thirty minutes to a full hour, depending on how long she had to wait and how heavy traffic was. She simply could not spare the time, not if she wanted to arrive at Mount Street before three P.M.

And according to the mysterious note that had arrived in yesterday's mail, that was what she had to do. The note looked like the kind blackmailers supposedly sent to the families of their victim when demanding ransom. Its large block letters were cut out from a newspaper and pasted on a sheet of white paper, to form the following message:

IF YOU WANT TO KNOW WHAT YOUR STEPMOTHER
REALLY DOES IN THE AFTERNOON, GO HOME BEFORE
3 PM ON THURSDAY!

There was no signature and the envelope was postmarked West Central London. Jeanne didn't have the vaguest idea who had sent it or what it meant. Supposedly she would not know until she reached her destination, and judging by the way her taxi was expertly slipping in and out of traffic, that would be pretty soon now.

Providing the note was not some stupid practical joke compelling her to go on a wild-goose chase. But its contents seemed to imply that the sender knew what he (or she) was talking about. The possibility that Mrs. Cook might be behind it had occurred to Jeanne although she wasn't quite sure why. Maybe Mrs. Cook knew something that she did not. Still, it seemed odd.

The taxi had to let her off across the street from her building, and the first thing Jeanne noticed when she paid the fare was a bright blue Jaguar that looked suspiciously like the one Tom McKillup owned. It was parked several spaces in front of her cab, and stood out brashly from the rest of the sedate gray and black cars that lined the block.

Jeanne's hands were shaking as she tipped the driver and put the change in her shoulderbag. Part of her was tempted to tell him that she had forgotten something and to take her back to King's as fast as possible. She could just pretend that she had never received the anonymous note and knew nothing of its dire contents. But her curiosity was too great.

She glanced at her watch. It was only two-twenty. If she popped into the pub for a fast tomato juice, she would still be home before the three o'clock deadline proposed by the anonymous note. Also, it would give her a chance to calm down a bit and collect herself. Since receiving the note late yesterday afternoon when she came home from university, she had been a nervous wreck. She barely slept at all the previous night. And as three o'clock approached, her anxiety only seemed to worsen.

Feeling like a total coward, she walked into the popular pub, which had been remodeled several years ago. It now resembled a kind of smoky, gilt and velvet, late-Victorian movie set. Several people were seated in the cozy window sections, talking, and a few men stood at the bar, looking superior. At the last minute Jeanne ordered a Bloody Mary with ice and debated whether to have one of the delicious meat and cheese platters, but her stomach was too fluttery for food. No. The best thing to do was sit down, slowly drink the Bloody Mary, and smoke a cigarette.

She found an empty table in the corner, glad of an excuse —any excuse—to prolong what she was now certain would be an ugly confrontation. Seeing the blue Jaguar parked outside had accelerated her worst fears. If Tom were with Alexis, as seemed most likely, then it was also possible he had sent her the strange note. But why? She didn't need additional evidence that her stepmother and Tom were having an affair; she was more than convinced of that unpleasant fact by now despite her father's ostrichlike attitude.

Jeanne lit a Player's and remembered the disdainful and insulting way her father had stifled her efforts the first time she tried to tell him that Alexis was being unfaithful to him. He said that she'd blundered into areas of behavior that were none of her business. That's where he was dead wrong of course. If Tom McKillup was anybody's business, he was hers. But she couldn't admit that to Ian without also admitting the reason for her possessiveness.

"Daddy, Tom was my first lover."

Her father would have flipped out if he ever heard that one. So she reluctantly kept her mouth shut. But the next morning before going to King's, she took the underground to Tom's house in Fulham. It was very early. The drummer, whom she'd met ice skating in St. Moritz, came to the door in an old robe, rubbing his eyes.

"Good God! What are you doing here? What time is it?"

"Almost nine. Is Tom home?"

"He's asleep."

"Can I come in for a few minutes? I won't stay long."

The drummer was so punchy that he automatically opened the door wider. "What's the matter?"

"Nothing. I wanted to see Tom, but if he's sleeping I suppose it will have to wait. Could I have a cup of coffee?"

"Why not? Come on in."

She did. And sure enough there it was in the hallway stand: Alexis' bamboo-handled, Hardy Amies umbrella, with the designer's initials on the handle. It was unquestionably the very same umbrella that Alexis accused Jeanne of walking off with by mistake yesterday, and it only proved to Jeanne that her hunch was right after all. Alexis *had* been with Tom the previous afternoon, forgotten her umbrella at his house, and deliberately lied about it.

When Jeanne returned home that evening the umbrella was back in its original place, and in the kitchen were the yellow porcelain rose and pussy willow from Algernon Asprey, both in a slender silver vase next to the window. All Jeanne could say on her stepmother's behalf was that she sure knew how to cover up her guilty tracks fast. When Jeanne asked her where she found the missing umbrella, Alexis did not bat an eyelash. She said that she left it at Algernon Asprey the previous day.

Neat, Jeanne thought, *very neat.*

From then on Jeanne was certain that Alexis' visits to Tom continued on a regular basis, despite insistence on the part of both Alexis and Mrs. Cook that her stepmother was always out shopping in the afternoon. Today, however, the routine seemed to have changed. Tom was the one doing the visiting.

Jeanne wondered why. She also wondered what Mrs. Cook must think of Tom's unexpected presence. A distinct sense of excitement, mixed with dread, shot through Jeanne as she imagined the scene being played out this very minute in the Nicholsons' maisonette.

Where were they?

In Alexis' fragrant green and white bedroom, no doubt, making love. Jeanne felt like a cheap voyeur as several graphically sensuous images floated across her mind. The one of Tom and Alexis locked in a passionate embrace lingered longest, cut deepest, hurt the most. Not too long ago *she* had been the woman in Tom's arms; now he would not even talk to her. She had been forced to stop calling him out of sheer humiliation. Her handful of telephone attempts were invariably greeted by the same grim response:

"I don't want to see you again. Please let me alone."

Jeanne rattled the ice cubes in the bottom of her glass and gulped down the rest of the watery drink. As she stood up to leave, she realized that it was Mrs. Cook's half day off. Of course! How could she have forgotten? With Mrs. Cook conveniently out of the way, Alexis and Tom were free to do whatever they liked, wherever they liked. The ghastly possibility of finding them making love on the drawing room floor had to be faced, Jeanne decided. There was no way around it. Her heart was pounding with determination when she finally walked out of the pub and crossed Mount Street, the keys to the flat jingling in her hand.

When Jeanne got off the elevator, she debated briefly whether she should ring the doorbell. But that would defeat her very purpose, wouldn't it? It would give the two of them a chance to pull themselves together, put on their respectable faces, and she would learn nothing. Besides, it was her own home. She always used her key.

Quietly, stealthily, like a thief, she opened the door and tiptoed in. The hallway was thickly carpeted and seemed to absorb her footsteps. But she did not dare move more than a few feet for fear of being overheard. From the drawing room up ahead came a muffled, unfamiliar sound. She listened intently. It was a man, crying. Tom!

Jeanne realized that she had never seen or heard a man cry before except in a movie or on television. Even when her mother was so savagely murdered, she could not recall seeing her father in tears. Englishmen did not cry, he once told her, it was a sign of weakness. They bore their grief and disappointments with the stoic nobility that the world had come to expect of them.

"The Latin races cry," he had said. "But they're an unduly emotional lot. Not to be relied upon in times of duress. The Irish are known to cry, too. I suspect it's their diet."

Jeanne speculated upon the reason her father would give for Scottish tears, but unfortunately he had never spoken of them. What had Alexis said or done to make Tom so unhappy? she wondered. If only she had not stopped off at the pub, she might know. Well, it was too late to think about that now. She stood perfectly still and waited. The door to the drawing room was open, and the long connecting hallway acted like a funnel through which sounds were readily conducted.

Tom blew his nose and said: "Speak of being naive and unsuspecting! I win first prize. I feel like an absolute idiot."

"There's no way you could have known," Alexis said.

"I guess not. It's all too far-fetched."

"Of course, it is."

"But still . . ." He hesitated. "Do you realize that I was going to ask you to marry me?"

The sound of Alexis' tinkling laughter drifted down the hallway. "*Marry* you?" There was incredulity in her voice, and condescension as well. "What a perfectly bizarre idea."

"Not if you look at it from my point of view."

"Which is?"

"Well, as I said, I'm in love with you. And I suppose that beneath this modern rock and roll façade, I'm an old-fashioned guy at heart. Where I come from, marriage usually follows on the heels of love."

It was even more horrible and hideous than Jeanne had anticipated. To have found Tom in bed with Alexis was nowhere near as bad as finding him in love with her. Jeanne felt dizzy from the shock. She sat down on one of the two straight-backed chairs that flanked the long refectory table they used as a dumping place for things like mail, messages, and keys.

It was on this very table that she had picked up the anonymous note yesterday afternoon, and having overheard what she just did she wished now that she'd thrown it away, unopened and unread. She would have saved herself a great deal of heartache. The nagging question returned: *who could have written it?*

She realized that it could not have been Mrs. Cook, and nobody else made any sense. Tom would have no reason for getting her home from school earlier than usual, and neither would Alexis. It seemed pretty obvious from the personal nature of their conversation that the last thing in the world they were expecting was an interloper. The only possibility then was somebody who knew that Alexis and Tom were having an affair and wanted to make certain that she knew too. But who could that be? Jeanne shook her head in confusion.

"There are two things you're overlooking," Alexis was saying. "I'm not in love with you and I'm already married."

The cynicism in Tom's voice was unmistakable. "Some marriage."

"There's no need to be nasty about it. I may not love my husband, but he is still my husband. For better or worse, as they say."

"It sounds more like worse to me."

Jeanne could hear Alexis' sharp inhalation of breath.

"It's getting late, Tom. I think you should leave. I'm tired."

"What's the rush?"

"I'd like to be alone."

"We haven't even had lunch yet. Just hors d'oeuvres. You did invite me for lunch, didn't you?"

"Yes, and I apologize. But I don't feel well."

"I'm sorry to hear that." He did not sound sorry. "Maybe a glass of champagne would help. I was just going to have one. Can I pour one for you, too?"

"No, thank you. I've had enough champagne. And frankly, so have you."

"That's no way for a hostess to act. My, my, aren't we forgetting our wonderful manners? I'm surprised at you, Mrs. Nicholson."

"Stop it! I'm not in the mood for your little jokes. They're not very entertaining."

"You used to think they were."

"I'm glad you used the past tense."

"In that case I'll try better next time."

"There's not going to be a next time," Alexis said flatly.

A momentary silence followed. When Tom spoke again, his voice was different. A note of fear had crept into it.

"What is that supposed to mean?"

"Quite simply, it means I don't think we should see each other again."

"Are you crazy?"

"No, the party's over."

"Not for me, it isn't. I'm in love with you, Alexis. You can't put an end to it just like that."

"But I am. That's precisely what I'm doing. Putting an end to it."

"*Jesus Christ, woman, don't you have any feelings for me at all?*"

"The feeling I have at the moment is that I would like you to stop shouting and go home. Okay?"

"No, it's not okay. Because I'm not going. I came here today to make love to you and that's what I intend to do."

Alexis switched tactics. She began to purr.

"Tom, please don't be difficult. We've had a lovely time these last few months, it was fun, I enjoyed it. But now it's finished. I don't want to quarrel. I like you too much. So why don't you be a nice boy and leave gracefully?"

"That's one of the advantages of growing up poor, like I did." Tom chuckled. "You never learn good manners. You don't learn how to leave a place gracefully, not when there's something there that you still want. And I want something. Alexis. You. Now. And you don't have too much to say about it either. Not anymore. You shouldn't have told me what you did. That was stupid of you."

No, Jeanne thought, Alexis never should have told him that she didn't love her husband. It *was* a stupid mistake.

"Are you threatening me?" Alexis asked.

"Yes, and I mean it. Either you come upstairs with me now, or—what the hell are you grinning at?"

"Your stupid notion of going upstairs."

"What's so stupid about it?"

"Do you prefer 'lower class'?"

"You'd better watch it, Alexis."

"But it's so funny. On the one hand you're all anger and lust. Yet it's got to be consummated in the traditional domain of the bedroom. Typical."

"Typical of what?"

"A jerk like you."

"We'll see who's the jerk around here."

Jeanne heard something rip, then she heard Alexis' cry of surprise. "What do you think you're doing? You've torn my dress!"

"Why don't you call the police?" Tom laughed.

"Stay away from me."

"Try and make me."

There was the sound of scuffling footsteps, something overturned, a glass crashed to the floor. Tom had grabbed Alexis.

"*Let me go!*" she shouted, hitting him, struggling to get free.

"Here. I'll make it easier for you."

Rip. Tear. It sounded as though he had torn the dress right off her back. Jeanne was transfixed.

"You barbarian!" Alexis screamed.

The end of her cry was cut short by what Jeanne could only imagine was a persistent and unwelcome kiss. For a few seconds afterward all she heard were muted sounds of the aggressor and his victim each struggling to take command. Breaths were coming fast. Alexis gasped. Tom cried out in pain. Something hit the floor with a heavy thud.

Jeanne could bear it no longer. Picking herself up off the chair, she marched boldly into the drawing room. They did not see her at first, they were too engrossed in their lovemaking. Tom lay on top of an unclothed Alexis, his mouth on her right breast, his hands under her ass. Alexis' long black hair was spread out on the carpet like a fan. Her eyes were closed, all signs of struggle totally gone. She looked ecstatic.

"If only my father could see you now," Jeanne said, gazing down at the two people she hated most in the world.

42 ❧

Tom had left, I was dressed once more (in a lounging robe, since my black Jean Muir was ripped beyond repair), and Jeanne and I were uncomfortably alone.

I was shaking so badly as a result of what had just happened that I lit a cigarette despite the fact that I hardly smoke at all these days. When I worked as a model for Thérèse, all we girls used to smoke incessantly to try to kill our hunger pangs and stay skinny. Those long-ago days had been on my mind a lot lately. I wasn't quite sure why. Maybe because life seemed so much less complicated then and the future held so many shining promises.

When you're young you can joke away an awful lot of daily deprivation and discomfort, you're so convinced that a wonderful world of fulfillment is just around the corner. But how many people ever see their most poignant dreams come true? As you get older, you tend to do one of two things. Either you compromise and make the best of your situation, whatever it might be, or else you stubbornly cling to those early youthful hopes.

I was still clinging, but by a thread now. I was afraid that once Harry and I were finally together we might not find the contentment we'd been counting on. And then what? We had invested everything in each other. The horrible possibility that our emotional investment would not pay dividends had been causing me a lot of sleepless nights lately. I would toss and turn, thinking: what if it's too late for Harry and me? What if we've waited too long to seize the happiness we always prayed for?

Right now I managed to comfort and console myself with the thought that I was having a case of last-minute jitters. Since Jeanne had witnessed my flagrant behavior with Tom, she was sure to tell Ian, whose outrage and fury were inevitable. He had been cuckolded and made a fool of in his own home, by the wife he trusted. Men were known to kill for less provocation than that. Yes, Sarah's "accidental" murder was very imminent now. No wonder I was shaking.

I realized that Jeanne was staring at me, waiting for me to try to defend myself. Contempt and revulsion were written plainly on her pale face. We had not exchanged a word since Tom walked out, infuriated with Jeanne for barging in like that, infuriated with me for not returning his love.

I couldn't blame him for being hurt and resentful, nobody likes to be rejected. But the fact was that once the novelty of the sexual fun and games had worn off, I realized how little Tom and I had to say to each other. Outside of bed he bored me. And as soon as that happened, he began to bore me in bed as well. I could not help comparing him to Harry in every way (hadn't I compared all men?), and he was sorely lacking. The last few times we made love I tried to pretend it was Harry holding and touching me, but even that didn't work.

Why did I have to be born Harry's sister?

"Look, Jeanne," I began, "there is obviously nothing I can say that will undo the unfortunate scene you've just witnessed. I'm at a loss for words."

"I'm glad to hear that you're at a loss for *words*," she said in a stony voice, "because you sure as hell aren't at a loss for anything else. Like good taste or decency. The least you could have done was to keep Tom away from here, but even that simple consideration didn't seem to cross your deranged mind."

I decided to overlook her insults for the time being.

"There's one thing that bothers me, Jeanne."

"Not your conscience, surely."

My desire to slap her face was overcome by my curiosity.

"What bothers me is your arriving home from school so early today. How come? Usually you don't get here until around five."

"This is how come."

She handed me a sheet of white paper. I recognized Harry's handiwork immediately.

IF YOU WANT TO KNOW WHAT YOUR STEPMOTHER
REALLY DOES IN THE AFTERNOON, GO HOME BEFORE
3 PM ON THURSDAY!

"That's very interesting," I said.

"I think so, too. Look at all the fascinating information I would have missed had I left school at my regular time. I never would have learned that you didn't love Daddy, for instance, or that Tom did love you."

"Eavesdroppers get what they deserve," I said with a self-confidence I did not feel. "Is that all you heard?"

She looked at me in astonishment. "Isn't that *enough*? I thought I was at a summit conference of confessions. Don't tell me there's more."

"No, Jeanne, I guess you arrived in time for the main events." Obviously, she had not been present when I told Tom about the plot to murder Sarah. What a relief!

"I suppose you're going to tell your father everything you saw and heard here today."

"What do *you* think?" Her eyes were sparkling with anger, revenge, her long-time hatred of me. "That I'm going to keep my mouth shut?"

"I wish you would." Oh, what a liar I was! "It will only hurt him, you know."

"You should have thought of that before you invited your

boyfriend over for lunch. Maybe when Daddy hears what I have to say, he'll finally come to his senses."

"Meaning what?"

"He'll divorce you."

I smiled. "You'd like that, wouldn't you?"

"I wouldn't like it. I'd *love* it."

"Too bad," I said. "Because it's not going to happen."

"How can you be so sure?"

"Because I know things that you don't."

She was wavering now. "Such as what?"

"Such as the fact that your father has had quite a few affairs himself over the years. And he didn't spare me any of the details either. He threw them all in my face. How do you think *I* felt?"

"I don't believe you. You're saying that to justify your own inexcusable behavior."

"Think whatever you like," I said, knowing that she would. "But at least I've tried to be discreet. And up until today, I've succeeded. If it hadn't been for that strange note you received, Tom would have long since been gone by the time you came home from King's, and you wouldn't be any the wiser. Can't we leave it that way?"

"*Are you kidding?*"

"It will never happen again. I promise." Playing the repentant stepmother was so boring, it made me sick. "As I'm sure you overheard, I told Tom that I didn't want to see him anymore. And I meant it. It's over between us. Finished."

"Finished?" she sneered. "Is that why you looked so blissful when I walked in here a few minutes ago? I didn't get the impression that anything was finished or over. Far from it. It struck me as though a new sick chapter in your relationship with Mr. McKillup was just beginning. Who knows? The two of you might be next found having it off in the middle of Hyde Park on a Sunday afternoon. I wouldn't be surprised. Not after what I've seen today."

"I realize how squalid it must have appeared," I said, practically choking on my own hypocrisy, "but I did try to fight Tom off. We had quite a tussle. I was no match for him."

"Please spare me the virtuous married lady speech. You have the morals of an alley cat, Alexis, and you know it. At this point there's nothing I'd put past you. And as for Tom, he's as contemptible as you are. I can't understand what I ever saw in him. The two of you deserve each other. God knows you certainly don't deserve my father. He should have

left you where he found you, working for that lesbian
Thérèse."

My good nature was rapidly deteriorating. "For your information, Thérèse does not happen to be a lesbian. She's
just a desperately lonely woman who revolutionized the
fashion industry single-handed. Her talent is extraordinary
and so is her courage."

Jeanne hesitated. "I guess you haven't heard, then."

"Heard what?"

"Thérèse is dead."

I suddenly felt weak. "Oh, no."

"She died late last night in Paris. It was after she showed her
new collection to the press. Apparently she decided to take
a nap in her office and never woke up. One of the girls at
school told me this morning."

I shook my head, unable to speak.

"You're really upset, aren't you?" Jeanne asked in surprise.

"Yes." I was being truthful at last. "Yes, I am."

Jeanne's voice became disdainful and sneering again.

"You're more upset about the death of some old dyke you
haven't seen in years than you are about my finding you and
Tom starkers on the living room floor!"

In a burst of fury I slapped her across the face as hard
as I could. Before she was able to recover from the blow, I
slapped her again. She looked paralyzed with fear. Then I
grabbed her by the collar of her blue denim shirt, lifted her
out of the chair, and hurled her across the room. Being so
much taller than Jeanne, it was not a particularly difficult
thing to do, just a highly satisfying one. She landed next to
the fireplace, dazed and shaken, but unharmed.

"You smug, stupid, self-righteous little brat," I said. "Who
do you think you are to sit in judgment on me? You may have
gone to a lot of expensive schools, but all you've learned is
how to be a spectacular pain in the ass. Tom thought so too,
considering all those telephone calls you've been bombarding
him with. I understand you even went over to his house at
some ungodly hour in the morning last week, uninvited and
unasked for."

She turned red. "Who told you that?"

"Who do you think? A little birdie? You're still in love
with Tom, aren't you?"

"No," she said unconvincingly.

"Oh, yes you are! That's the real reason you're so upset.
Not just because you found me cheating on your father, but

because I was doing it with the man who won't even give you the time of day. What's killing you is that Tom prefers a grown woman to a little girl."

"A grown barracuda would be more like it."

"In fact, something suddenly occurs to me. I wouldn't be surprised if it was Tom who sent you that anonymous note about my afternoon activities. I don't know why I didn't think of it before."

Jeanne picked herself up from the floor, tucked her shirt back into her blue jeans, and snapped: "That's ridiculous. Why would he do a stupid thing like that?"

"Probably to stop you from annoying him for once and all. He might have thought that if you saw him with me, you'd come to your senses and realize what he's been trying to tell you all along."

"And what is that, stepmother darling?"

"That he wants you to get the hell out of his life."

"Oh, I'm out all right. After what I saw today, I wouldn't even *speak* to Tom McKillup, much less let him touch me."

"There's not much danger of that. He said you were the lousiest lay he's ever had the misfortune to encounter." If that didn't make her spill her guts out to Ian, nothing would. "I thought you might like to know."

Jeanne was rapidly turning purple. "You'll regret those words, Alexis. You'll see." Jeanne gave me a look of the purest hatred I have ever seen, then she ran upstairs to her bedroom.

It felt good to hit and insult Jeanne after all the rotten things she had said to me. Our hatred for each other was out in the open at last, and I was glad. Now nothing could prevent my poor, mistreated stepdaughter from telling Daddy all about Tom and me. Thank goodness Harry had sent Jeanne that note!

I poured myself a brandy and sat down again on the golden silk sofa. A thin afternoon sunlight was streaming into the room. Before long the daffodils would be in bloom, and spring would be here. My thoughts returned to Thérèse. She once said that the older she became the more that spring, with its promise of birth and rejuvenation, frightened her.

"Spring is for the young," she said. "They don't know what it is yet to fear old age."

I suppose I shouldn't have been surprised that her death had affected me so strongly. She was a vain, eccentric, stubborn despot, but in my own way I loved her. She was so terrified of growing old. Now she had nothing to fear anymore, she was at peace. But by dying she had wiped out a part of my past that I clung to with a kind of sacred nostalgia. Life seemed so innocent in those days. Before Harry killed Paulette and Rose.

I thought of my roommate, Eva, who was always rouging her nipples different colors whenever she was planning to meet her boyfriend. I wondered what had happened to her. I knew that she had returned to Alicante and married Eduardo, but that was the last postcard I received from her. And that was a long time ago. She probably had at least three children by now, was happily plump and ate all the french-fried potatoes she liked.

Alicante.

Maybe when Harry and I went there we would run into them. It was not going to be long now before we found ourselves the summer people. But what would Harry say when he discovered that I had told Tom about our plan to kill Sarah? He would be furious no doubt. No more furious than I was with myself for being so damned stupid. On the other hand, how could I have known that Harry had made up some crazy blackmail story for Tom to swallow? Harry should have been more honest with me.

And as for giving Tom £25,000 . . . well, I was still trying, unsuccessfully, to digest that one. Tom was too closely involved with our plans and I didn't like it. How much did he really mean to Harry? Obviously more than I had imagined. The thought made me shudder.

I had a terrible premonition that Tom McKillup was going to be a part of our lives for a long time to come.

43 ∾

When Ian came home from work, Alexis was upstairs resting.

"She has a headache," Jeanne said, smiling maliciously.

"What are you trying to tell me this time?"

"You will never believe what happened today, Daddy. Right here. Under this very roof."

Ian sighed and poured himself a stiff whiskey.

"All right. What happened?"

Half an hour later he was sorry he had asked. Jeanne went into the entire episode, detail by detail, drawing a lurid picture of Alexis and Tom sprawled out on the floor, naked, blissful, making love. When Jeanne had finished, she looked at her father triumphantly.

"I told you she was cheating on you! What do you have to say now, Daddy?"

"I'd like to know who the hell sent that damned note."

Jeanne was crestfallen. She had expected a fierce response from her father, and all that interested him was the identity of the person who had blown the whistle on his wife. To Jeanne's amazement, he showed not a sign of anger against Alexis, not a smidgen of jealousy, disgust, outrage, only curiosity about the note that had brought Jeanne home from school earlier than usual.

"What's the difference who sent it?" Jeanne tried to reason with him. "It's what I saw that counts. Not how I happened to see it."

"Maybe." Ian looked pensive. "Maybe. But it's all most odd."

"Daddy, is that all you have to say?"

"At the moment, yes."

Jeanne shook her head. "I don't understand you at all. I mean, aren't you even *jealous?* How can you sit there so calmly?"

"What would you like me to do? Grab a telephone and call my solicitor about a divorce?"

"Frankly, yes."

"That's a very easy decision for you to make, but you haven't been married to Alexis for a long time. And this is the first affair she's had that I've known of. Everyone is entitled to make a mistake now and then. God knows I've made enough of my own. Well, Tom McKillup was Alexis' mistake, but if what you tell me is true, she's putting an end to it. So to all intents and purposes it's over. Finished. Therefore, I don't see what the panic is all about."

"Finished? Over?" Jeanne was stunned. "That's what Alexis said when I accused her of being unfaithful. But how can you forgive her so easily? Don't you have any pride, Daddy?"

"Pride can be a very expensive emotion, a very dangerous one. I don't intend to throw away sixteen years of marriage because of one foolish indiscretion. As far as I'm concerned, Alexis is my wife and will remain so."

"But she doesn't love you. I heard her say so to Tom. She made no bones about it. Why do you want to stay married to a woman who doesn't love you, who doesn't have any respect for you, who makes a fool of you in your own home?"

"I think the real question is, why are you so anxious for me to divorce her?"

"Because she's hurting you," Jeanne said lamely.

But Ian knew his daughter better than that. He remembered how much she had cared for Tom McKillup in St. Moritz.

"No, Jeanne, she's hurting *you*."

When Harry received Alexis' telephone call the next day, he was feeling pretty good. He had just played nine holes of golf and his game was rapidly improving. He'd gone around in forty and was optimistically hoping for scratch next time.

"It's no damned use," Alexis said, dimming his high spirits. "Ian was his usual genial self last evening. No scenes, no outbursts, no jealous ultimatums. He acted as though nothing out of the ordinary had happened. It's hopeless, I tell you."

She then went on to explain exactly what had taken place with Tom the preceding day, the confrontation with Jeanne, and Jeanne's repeated threats to reveal all to Daddy, which Alexis was certain Jeanne had done.

"I even invented a headache to give the two of them a chance to be alone," Alexis said, "before I came down to dinner."

"Maybe Jeanne backed out at the last minute. Changed her mind for some reason or lost her nerve."

"Not a chance. She was much too angry at me, too vindictive to let me off the hook that easily. I'm positive she didn't spare Ian any of the details either, including Tom and me having it off on the drawing room floor."

"I can't understand it," Harry said. "Ian's lack of response, that is."

"Neither can I. But I've done everything I can, and he seems stubbornly determined to ignore my most blatant indiscretions. I'm stumped. Where do we go from here?"

"Invite Sarah and me over for dinner. As soon as possible."

Alexis caught her breath. "You mean, this is it?"

"Yes. There's no point in putting it off any longer."

"Harry, I'm scared."

"Don't be. It will work."

"When do I get the stuff?"

"Meet me tomorrow at the Regent's Park Zoo. In front of the panda cage. I'll give it to you then."

The weather was clear, bright, and cold the next day.

Harry had arrived before me. I spotted him immediately, standing in front of the cage containing the two giant pandas who, to my disappointment, were tan and black, not snowy-white and black, as their many photographs showed. One of the pandas was sound asleep and the other was cavorting around for a limited number of spectators. I noticed that Harry was carrying a dark leather attaché case.

"Greetings," I said. "This is a hell of a place to meet."

"I was trying to get even with you for Harrods."

"Well, you're even." I shivered. "Is there anywhere we can talk?"

"Why don't we just walk around a bit?"

"Okay."

I was wearing a large, roomy shoulderbag slung over my chinchilla. When we got to the flamingo pond, Harry opened his attaché case and handed me one of Harrods' small green shopping bags, securely stapled at the top. I could see the outline of a jar inside. I put it in my purse.

"Mix it in with your sleeping powder the morning of the dinner party," Harry said. "Ian will never know the difference. Particularly if he's had enough to drink by the time coffee is served. He still *is* serving coffee himself, isn't he?"

"Oh, yes. Ian's habits don't change very readily."

"We can be thankful for that."

The pink flamingos were making spluttering noises as they used their bills to retrieve something from the water. They were so elegant, so beautiful, so innocent. I thought of what Harry and I were planning to do. And of Tom knowing about it. I had been all set to tell Harry today that Tom knew of our plot to murder Sarah, but now I decided not to say anything.

I was afraid of my brother's angry reaction. And besides, I asked myself, what would be the advantage in telling him? The damage was done. True, he might suggest that we postpone the murder until we were positive that Tom was going to keep his mouth shut. Or else he would call me an idiot and we would become sidetracked in argument, insults, recriminations. This was not the time for any of that. Harry and I needed to be in accord, in harmony with each other, if we were to carry out the tricky murder scheme as planned.

As for Tom going to the police afterward, I didn't think there was much chance of that happening. What would he have to gain by it? True, he could put Harry and me in jail for life, but he would also lose the £25,000 Harry had promised him. No. I was sure that Tom would keep his mouth shut as far as the police were concerned. He had an outlaw mentality or he never would have agreed to Harry's make-believe blackmail scheme to start with. Our problems with Mr. McKillup would not involve the law, I feared, they would merely involve our future happiness.

Harry and I walked around the zoo some more. The two California sea lions jumping in and out of icy water made me feel even colder. Their yowls were almost humanoid, as though they were having a domestic squabble. I would have suggested going to the cafeteria for a cup of coffee, or tea, something to warm us up, but suddenly I wanted to go home.

I looked at Harry's weak, proud, delicious, familiar profile, and felt like crying. I loved him so much. We had been through so much together. It was why I had to get away right now. The physical closeness was too overwhelming, it frightened me. I was afraid that if I stayed a moment longer, I would suggest that we check into one of our sleazy hotel rooms and it wasn't a good idea.

Like professional athletes before the big game, we had to conserve our energies, keep our priorities in order. Anyhow, we had accomplished what we set out to do this afternoon and there was nothing more to say. Each of us knew our role backward and forward.

"I'd like to find a taxi," I said.

"They should be lined up outside."

And they were, four of them. Harry and I formally shook hands, as though we were casual acquaintances saying so long after a pleasant outing with the animals. He opened the door of the first taxi for me.

"Don't forget to wear gloves when you add the crystals," he whispered in my ear, as I stepped into the cab.

"Yes, it has been great fun," I said cheerfully. "We must do it again when the weather gets warmer."

Then I gave the driver my Mount Street address and did not look back.

Sarah Maringo was in her study reading the latest issue of *Forum* when the butler entered with the afternoon mail on a silver tray. There were two letters. One was from her solicitor, and the other, postmarked London, bore no return address.

When Sarah first started to subscribe to *Forum*, the magazine that dealt with sexual problems of the most unusual and often perverse natures, she thought that perhaps she might learn how to reinstill some of Harry's physical interest in her. But after a few issues she realized that the difficulties she was experiencing were child's play compared to those of the majority of people who sought *Forum*'s advice.

Here was a desperate plea from a man who wanted his wife to defecate on him. It was the only way he could reach orgasm, he said. But his wife flatly refused to do it and as a result the poor man had to turn to masturbation, which he did not find satisfactory. He wanted the editors of *Forum* to tell him how to convince his wife that his request was not as disgusting or depraved as she seemed to think. Or was it? he asked as an afterthought.

Before Sarah could read *Forum*'s reply, she decided to open the London letter. It was from Ian Nicholson in response to the one she had written him about Harry and Jeanne having an affair. The letter said:

My dear Sarah:

I appreciate your writing to me, as you did several days ago. I read your letter with a great deal of interest, and I might add, surprise.

If it is of any consolation to you, I am of the firm opinion that my daughter and your husband are not having—and never did have—an affair.

I do recall Jeanne flirting with Harry in St. Moritz, but I am certain I know the reason for her foolish (albeit innocent) actions.

She was then, and still is, attracted to a young man to whom I violently object and will not permit her to associate with.

Knowing my daughter as I do, I suspect she was trying to irritate me by drumming up a false flirtation with your husband. When Jeanne cannot have her own way, she often resorts to childish, outlandish behavior, and I regret to say that that was what she was doing in St. Moritz.

Since our return to London, Jeanne not only has been busily immersed in her studies at King's College, but is still pining away for the same objectionable fellow. Being as single-minded as she is, I strongly doubt that your husband (or any other man, for that matter) would hold much appeal for her.

I also doubt that Harry, who strikes me as quite levelheaded, would involve himself in the kind of sexual situation you describe.

I apologize for any anguish or embarrassment my daughter might have caused you, but please try to take my word that she is not amorously involved with your husband.

Needless to say, this entire matter will be kept in the strictest confidence. I have not mentioned it to my wife, nor do I intend to do so.

It was signed "With fondest regards."

Sarah put the letter down, wondering whether Ian knew what he was talking about. She respected his judgment, but there was the distinct possibility that he would be prejudiced on the side of his daughter, perhaps even covering up for her. Or merely unwilling to face the fact that Jeanne was capable of seducing another woman's husband. Even a basically intelligent and sensible man like Ian Nicholson could be blindly deceived when it came to the sexual indiscretions of his own flesh and blood. It happened all the time.

"Hello, darling. Did you have a good day?"

Sarah had been so immersed in Ian's letter that she did not hear the door to her study open. Harry stood before her looking ruddy and healthy as though he had just come from a long, invigorating walk in the countryside. But he had gone into London that afternoon to see Tom McKillup, he said.

"I had a fine day," Sarah said. "Quiet but pleasant."

"Any interesting mail?"

"No. Just a note from my solicitor and another charity request." She casually but methodically began to tear Ian Nicholson's letter into tiny shreds. "It's becoming quite a bore actually, being asked to sponsor so many worthy causes."

Even as she spoke, she wondered where Harry had really been that afternoon. She wondered again whether Ian Nicholson's denial of the affair between Harry and Jeanne was accurate. The only thing she did not wonder about was whether Ian Nicholson saved letters. He did. He had saved Sarah's. But how could she have guessed how important that seemingly insignificant fact would become after she was murdered?

44

People who have come close to death often say that they saw their entire life flash before their eyes just as disaster was about to strike. I now know what they mean. That's how I felt a few minutes ago as I smilingly welcomed Sarah and Harry to our home for a quiet evening of murder.

Even though it was Sarah who was in danger, not I, I suddenly remembered things I hadn't thought about in years, like the hamburger and milkshake lunches that Harry and I used to gobble down every schoolday at Charlie's ice cream parlor when we were kids.

I remembered our grandmother, Juliana, cleaning other people's houses for a living and telling funny stories about her late husband making gin in the bathtub during Prohibition. I didn't even know if Juliana were still alive, what had happened to polite Charlie, to thrifty Dennis who ultimately bought our store, to that rich little girl whose parents drive up to Pilgrim Lake in a long black Cadillac, the summer I was twelve. . . .

Sarah was wearing a washed-out, teal-blue floral print that clung in all the wrong bony places. Maybe if she had known it was to be her funeral dress, she might have chosen something a bit more flattering.

I was wearing a long, emerald-green gown tonight. Sleeveless. With panels floating back from narrow straps. And my square emerald ring and ear clips, tarty high silver heels which made me even taller and more willowy than usual. I looked forbidding and that was exactly how I felt, now that I was about to break out of my prisoner's cage at long last.

Maybe murder was in my blood. Harry had kissed my virginal blood off the bearskin rug right after we made love, and before my mother came rushing home to find us naked on the floor. As Jeanne had found Tom and me. Why was it my fate to be found naked on living room floors, making love with men who were taboo? It was an amusing image. *There she is, fucking on the floor again.* I could not help laughing.

Jeanne, Sarah, Harry, and Ian looked at me for explanation. They had been discussing the possible thirty percent pay rise that Britain's engineers were going to receive, thanks to the efforts of union chief Hugh Scanlon, and what a mockery such an increase would make of the Social Contract.

Not that those few domestic items weren't ridiculous enough all by themselves, in these days of England's grimmest hour since the Second Warld War, except that I was the only one laughing.

"I fail to see the humor in a lamentable situation such as this," Ian said, reproaching me in his best merchant banker voice.

I felt like telling him to stuff it, that he'd be in prison soon enough and could spend the rest of his life trying to figure out what I was really laughing at. I suddenly realized that in a lot of ways, Ian reminded me of my mother. They both had the same humorless personality, they both were so damned respectable, so above reproach, so conventional, they tried to be so proper. Even Ian's whorehouse outings were considered proper for an Englishman of his class. Well, look where it had gotten my mother, and where it was about to get Ian. So much for being above reproach.

There was an uncomfortable pause and then Mrs. Cook came in.

"Dinner is served," she said stiffly, saving us all from another round of embarrassment.

It was Harry's idea for me to have Mrs. Cook present to-night, at least for the duration of the meal. He said that the police might find it suspicious if I gave her the evening off when we were having guests over. I told Mrs. Cook that she could leave after dessert was served. Mrs. Cook knew of my husband's quaint domestic habit of doing the coffee-and-cognac bit himself, and was only too happy to go home as early as possible.

She seemed tense and nervous right now, as though she were terrified of making a mistake in carrying out her formidable duties, an error such as serving from the left, heavens forbid, or some equally horrible faux pas. Mrs. Cook would sooner stick her head in the oven than breach etiquette.

"What have we here?" Jeanne asked as Mrs. Cook placed a steaming bowl of soup in front of her.

"Lobster bisque," I said.

"I *adore* lobster bisque," Sarah said.

It seemed appropriate that she was wearing her ruby pendant tonight.

"I'm glad you do," I said.

I meant it. It would be the last dish of lobster bisque she

ever ate, and it happened to be one of Mrs. Cook's culinary masterpieces. Boiling live lobsters and crushing the tails afterward appealed to Mrs. Cook's stifled primeval instincts, even though she denied it. But I had watched her at work and it was obvious how much secret pleasure she derived from killing a living thing and then cooking and serving it to a tableful of civilized diners.

"To be followed by a simple roast beef and Yorkshire pudding" I added, thinking that the occasion waranted a typically English main course. "I assume there are no vegetarians present."

"I don't know," Jeanne said. "I might become one. I've been thinking about it a lot lately. It sounds much healthier to me than all this"—she made a gesture at the beautifully laid-out table—"rich food."

"Where did you get that brilliant idea?" Ian asked.

"No doubt from Tom McKillup," I said before Jeanne could reply.

Everyone looked at me as if I had said "Adolf Hitler," including Sarah, which surprised me. Why was she rattled by the mention of Tom's name? I could not imagine.

"Tom McKillup," Sarah mused. "That's your songwriter friend, isn't it, Harry?"

"Acquaintance, really."

"I didn't know that you had met Tom," Jeanne said excitedly. "When did this happen?"

"In St. Moritz," Harry said. "You told me what a fantastic musician he was. Remember? So I went over to the Alpina to see him perform. You were right. He's very good."

"Harry loves music," Sarah said.

"So does Jeanne," I cut in. "Particularly when it's performed by Scottish guitar players. She absolutely *dotes* upon it then."

"I see," Sarah said after a minute.

She and Ian exchanged glances which I did not understand. Something was going on that I did not know about. Harry looked at me with a glance I understood perfectly. Here was my opportunity to goad Jeanne into a public declaration of my affair with Tom, thereby humiliating Ian and turning him into the jealous, betrayed husband with a premeditated motive for murder.

"Yes," I went on. "I find Mr. McKillup's whereabouts very interesting. He and his group were playing in St. Moritz when we were there, and now that we're all back in England so is he. If we should decide to go to Monte Carlo tomorrow, I wonder what Mr. McKillup's travel plans would be."

"Tom didn't *follow* us, you know," Jeanne said. "I mean, he does live in London."

"I don't understand what it is that you find so attractive about a vulgarian like Tom McKillup," I said.

"I suggest we change the subject," Ian interceded.

"Yes," Sarah murmured uncomfortably. "It would seem like a good idea."

But Jeanne was fuming. She had put her soup spoon down and was glaring at me with unconcealed hatred. "If Tom is vulgar, what does that make *you*, Alexis?"

"I don't know what you're talking about."

"Yes, you do!"

"Jeanne, control yourself," Ian warned her.

"Why should I?"

"Because I'm your father and I'm asking you to."

"It's Alexis whom you should be asking to control herself, not me."

"Why?" I said. "What have I done?"

"Nothing," Ian replied.

Sarah and Harry maintained a discreet silence, although for different reasons. Sarah was genuinely embarrassed. Harry was delighted, praying that Jeanne would be incited into making more damning statements, exactly my intention.

"Yes, she has," Jeanne contradicted her father. "Alexis has done something, all right, even though you refuse to acknowledge it for reasons best known to yourself."

"And what is it that I've supposed to have done?" I asked sweetly.

There was a moment's silence. Then Jeanne said:

"Had an affair with Tom McKillup."

Sarah looked stricken, Harry was trying not to look pleased, Ian was overcome with humiliation, and I was plain delighted. Jeanne had walked right into my trap.

"That's a disgusting lie!" I said to my stepdaughter. "How dare you make such a filthy accusation? What gives you the right?"

"Because I saw the two of you with my own eyes. Right here. Last week. Remember? Naked on the drawing room floor. Surely your memory can't be that bad, Alexis."

I turned helplessly to Ian. "Why don't you say something?

Stop her. This is inexcusable. I always knew she disliked me, but this is going too far. I've never been so insulted in my life."

Ian looked haggard, as though the internal struggle he was waging had grown too much for him. Ordinarily he never would have tolerated such an outburst from Jeanne, but I suspected that she had aroused all his latent resentment toward me and he felt powerless to stop her. Perhaps in a way he was even vicariously enjoying her denouncement of me. As though sensing this, Jeanne went on.

"Besides, it was Alexis who mentioned Tom's name to begin with. There was no reason for her to drag it into the conversation, merely because I said I might become a vegetarian. What does Tom have to do with that? Nothing. She mentioned him in order to disgrace you, Daddy. I'm not the only person with bad manners around here."

Jeanne then turned to Sarah and Harry in an attempt to exonerate herself. "I realize how awkward this must be for both of you, and I apologize. Not because I was lying about my stepmother. I wasn't. But because I embarrassed you. I'm sorry."

I could feel Sarah's well-bred eyes sneaking a curious glance my way as we politely sliced our roast beef and ate our hearty Yorkshire pudding with little appetite or zest. Ian, I noticed, was drinking more than his usual amount of the excellent 1970 claret he had decanted earlier, and his face was flushed. The combination of wine, anger, bile, resentment, humiliation and self-disgust showed on him all too clearly.

For a moment I pitied him, but then I remembered all the anguish he had caused me over the years, all the unhappiness, and I pitied myself even more. I was frightened, I realized, as the roast beef plates were taken away and a quivering mound of a trifle was brought in by Mrs. Cook. Of course I was frightened, I reassured myself, it was only natural considering what I had to do shortly.

In a few minutes Ian would bring the customary coffee tray to us in the drawing room and then it was up to me to make sure that Sarah unwittingly drank my cup of Hag containing the potassium cyanide.

Harry had made a very good point that afternoon we met at the Adams Hotel in Victoria when he suggested how this could best be done.

"Instead of switching cups, switch people," he said. "Sarah sits down by mistake in the seat intended for you. Your fingerprints never touch the poisoned cup, but Ian's do of course."

"Great. There's only one minor problem. How do I switch people?"

Harry grinned at me as I had grinned at him years ago in Paris before he set off to murder Paulette. He had asked me then what he should do to gain entrance to the Nicholson flat if Paulette merely accepted the yellow roses at the door, gave him a tip, and said goodnight.

My answer was:

"That, my darling brother, is for you to figure out."

Precisely Harry's answer to me at the Adams. I was still thinking about it now as I took Mrs. Cook aside and reminded her that she was free to leave as soon as we had finished dessert.

"Thank you, Madam," she said.

"And please don't forget to put the kettle on for coffee."

"No, Madam."

I marveled at my own composure. My legs were strong again, my palms dry, my Indian will intact.

I tried my best not to think about Tom McKillup.

45

Ian was trying not to think about Tom McKillup either.

In fact, he was trying not to think at all. The ordeal he had just survived during dinner was worse than any business battle he had ever encountered. Far worse, because there were no logical guidelines to go on. Ian was used to living by a set of fixed rules, and when his own carefully brought-up daughter broke those rules, with no apparent eye to the consequences, he felt at a total loss.

He knew he had behaved badly himself, and that bothered him more than anything. He had not managed to silence Jeanne, nor instruct her to go upstairs to her room and stay there. That's what he should have done. Why hadn't he?

His train of thought was interrupted by Mrs. Cook, who came into the kitchen, where he was measuring out the coffee, to say good night. She was wearing her street clothes now, and he almost didn't recognize her.

"Thank you for a lovely meal, Mrs. Cook. Everyone enjoyed it."

"They didn't eat very much," she said, looking at him for explanation.

He wondered how much of Jeanne's outburst she had overheard, how much she knew of Alexis' behavior. Shameful business when even the servants could not be spared the personal problems of their employers.

"You did your best, Mrs. Cook. And that's all anyone can ask."

"Yes, Sir. Good night, Sir."

"Good night, Mrs. Cook."

He went back to his coffee measurements and his miserable thoughts.

Ordinarily he savored his little coffee-making ritual, his few peaceful moments alone in the kitchen after a satisfying and companionable meal. But now he was in a hurry to get back to the others, for fear of another explosion from Jeanne. His nerves were jagged, his movements clumsy. He was in such a rush that he spilled some of the boiling water on his wrist by mistake, winced, cursed, and continued pouring into the French drip pot until the kettle was almost but not quite empty.

Mrs. Cook had arranged five cups and saucers on the silver tray. In one of those cups Ian now put a heaping teaspoon of Alexis' decaffeinated Hag, another heaping teaspoon of her white sedative powder, and then filled the cup to the top with the water remaining in the kettle. In order to distinguish which cup was Alexis', he placed it on the saucer that had a slight chip on the edge. That way there would be no error afterward.

He put a sugar bowl and a cream pitcher on the tray. Napkins and spoons were already there. And by now the water should have dripped through. Ian peeked inside. Yes. He filled the four other cups with fragrant, freshly roasted coffee, sat the French pot on a heat-resistant pad over the pilot light on the stove, and picked up the tray to take it into the living room where the others were waiting for him.

". . . and what's more, young lady, I think you owe me an explanation," he heard Alexis say as he walked in.

Her voice was cold, hostile, and she was talking to Jeanne, who sat diagonally across from her. Alexis looked tired, but instead of leaning back against one of the sofa's cushions, her body was poised forward as though for imminent attack.

"I don't owe you anything," Jeanne said. "All I did was tell the truth about you and Tom."

"Not the whole truth, certainly."

"I thought this conversation was finished," Ian said, looking from his wife to his daughter, both of whom ignored him. "I thought that we'd all heard the last of this wretched subject."

Harry stood at the mahogany sideboard, pouring cognac for everyone, pretending not to hear what was going on. And Sarah was still in her wheelchair. Unlike her poker-faced husband, she seemed to reflect the tension in the room as her hands gripped the metal arms of the chair, making her knuckles white, her mouth taut.

"I'm afraid I don't know what you mean by 'the whole truth,'" Jeanne said to Alexis.

Ian wondered why Harry had not helped Sarah out of the wheelchair into a more comfortable seat. Probably because in the heated controversy between the two women nobody was behaving very rationally. Jeanne had disrupted the rhythm of what otherwise would have been an extremely pleasant dinner party. Ian would never forgive her. Under the circumstances, he could hardly blame Alexis for demanding an apology, although he had hoped that she would let the matter rest. Was there no end to it?

"The whole truth includes *your* relationship with Tom, as well as mine," Alexis said, as Ian began to serve the coffee.

Even though it was impolite, he served Alexis first because it was easier to get the slightly chipped saucer out of the way. He placed his wife's Hag on the end table, to her right. Then it didn't matter who got which cup, since the rest were all the same. When everyone was served, he left the tray in the center of the glass-topped table so that they could help themselves to cream and sugar if they wished.

"Well, well," Jeanne was chuckling, "so at last you admit that you did have a relationship with Tom. That's progress."

"A relationship," Alexis replied "doesn't imply a sexual or love relationship, as you seem to assume. It simply means that I know the man. And as your stepmother, I daresay I should."

Hearing a new danger signal, Ian spoke up. "What are you getting at, Alexis?"

Harry stepped forward with glasses of cognac which he set down in their appropriate places, holding his own in his hand. Ian sipped the smooth drink, letting it warm him. Despite the fact that there was a crackling fire in the hearth, he felt cold because of all the anger in the air.

"What I'm getting at," Alexis said, "is that my acquaintance with Tom McKillup came about as a result of my desire to safeguard Jeanne's best interests."

"That's a lie!" Jeanne protested.

"Best interests?" Ian said. "What do you mean?"

"When the Maringos were here for dinner several months ago, Jeanne was supposed to have been studying at the home of a school friend. Remember? She came in when we were having coffee?"

Ian nodded.

"She wasn't with a school friend," Alexis said. "She was in bed with Tom McKillup."

"How dare you?" Jeanne exploded, leaping up from her chair.

Alexis instinctively stood up. Ian watched the two of them as though he were a spectator at a play nearing its climax.

"You were a virgin when that bastard seduced you," Alexis said. "Don't bother to deny it. I suspected as much and that's why I went to see Tom. He admitted everything."

"You're lying," Jeanne said. "You went to see Tom to seduce him yourself. You don't give a damn about me, you never have. And you don't love my father. You only married him for his money. Who do you think you're kidding, Alexis? You're nothing but a whore."

Alexis moved so swiftly that it was a blur to Ian. The next thing he knew she had smashed Jeanne across the face. Jeanne tried to hit her back, but Alexis grasped both her hands in her own and held them together. Both women stood in the center of the room, shaking with rage.

They drew the three others to them like a magnet. Even Sarah in her wheelchair moved toward the action, although she was powerless to do anything. Harry tried to step between Jeanne and Alexis, but seemed to sense that he lacked the proper authority to intercede.

It was Ian who took Alexis by the arm, urged her to release Jeanne, handed her his cognac to settle her nerves. He was astonished by this latest revelation: that his daughter was no longer a virgin and that she had Tom McKillup to thank for her dubious new status.

Alexis slumped against Ian, as though worn out by her stepdaughter's barrage of accusations and insults. For a moment Ian was afraid she would faint. She looked so pale and shaky. He guided her to the nearest chair and held her arm as she gratefully eased herself into it. The expression on her face said: *I can't take much more of this.*

"Are you all right?" Ian asked her.

She nodded weakly.

"Why don't you ask me if *I'm* all right?" Jeanne said.

She had sat down at one end of the sofa, as Harry lifted Sarah out of her wheelchair and settled her into the seat at the other end. Sarah looked confused, embarrassed, bewildered at having witnessed this personal family drama. Ian felt truly sorry for her. She deserved better, poor woman. So did Harry, for that matter. Tonight's exhibition had been inexcusable. He addressed himself to the Maringos.

"I hardly know what to say except that I'm deeply sorry for this show of bad manners on the part of my daughter. I'm just beginning to realize how upset she is, still that does not excuse what has happened here this evening. When Alexis and I invited you to dinner, we had no idea that anything of this sort would occur. Please accept our apologies."

"Perhaps we should leave," Sarah said. "Under the circumstances—"

"I know how you must feel," Ian cut in, "but can I implore you to stay? You would be doing me a great favor if you would stay."

Jeanne shot him a look of sheer hatred, betrayal written plainly in her eyes. As sorry as he felt for her, he could not condone her atrocious remarks, her attack upon Alexis, which was in effect an attack upon him.

"I trust no one will object to a little music," he said, getting up.

"Not at all" Sarah replied, sounding grateful for the distraction.

Ian went over to the hi-fi set and put on Beethoven's Ninth. If anything could deter Jeanne from a further verbal outburst, it was appropriately enough Beethoven's choral first movement. The dramatic power of the recorded voice would surely drown out his daughter's voice if she were foolish or insensitive enough to raise it again.

As the majestic music filled the room, Ian was pleased to see that its most vociferous occupant was silenced at last. Jeanne drank her coffee and cognac like the others, and remained quiet, listening to the overwhelmingly imaginative symphony which was capable of evoking either exultation or despair in the hearts of its audience. It lifted Ian out of his gloom, out of himself, and he was only too happy to escape that self and soar into the realm of an infinite universe, as he was sure the composer had soared in creating this, surely his most complex, his most heroic piece of work.

Minutes later, while engrossed in the vast crescendo, Ian heard a strange sound. Looking up, he was stunned to see Sarah desperately gasping for breath and clutching her stomach. Her face had turned a strange bluish color, her eyes were filled with terror. Before he could move, she had slumped over, her head on one side, her eyes closed, one arm still languidly extended toward the coffee cup on the end table to her right.

"I can't get a pulse," Ian said seconds afterward. "It seems as though she's dead."

"But that's impossible!" Harry cried.

The two women looked mutely at Sarah's lifeless form. Ian's words appeared to be meaningless to them, too. In desperation Harry started to shake his wife, talk to her, try to arouse her.

"She's only fainted," he said. "That's all it is."

Ian laid a hand on his shoulder. "I don't think so."

"But how—? Why—? What—?" Harry was too distraught to complete his thoughts. "There was nothing the matter with her. She can't be dead!"

"I had better call the doctor."

Alexis and Jeanne remained in their seats, as though frozen. Harry mechanically poured himself a stiff cognac and downed it in one gulp. Beethoven played on. As Ian dialed the family GP, he suddenly realized that Sarah had been drinking Alexis' coffee just before she died. She had been sitting in Alexis' original seat, the chipped saucer at her side. Even as he reached the doctor's emergency answering service, a horrible thought crossed his mind.

What if Sarah had been poisoned by mistake?

Someone could have put poison in the cup of Hag intended for Alexis, not being able to anticipate that the seating arrangements would become mixed up. But who would want to kill Alexis?

"Yes, could you please have Dr. Williams come over here immediately?" Ian said into the receiver. "A woman has just died."

No, he thought swiftly, been murdered. He looked at his daughter as he put the receiver back on its hook. Jeanne looked back at him, her young face clouded with despair. She had killed the wrong woman. For the first time in his life, Ian Philip Nicholson was totally at a loss for words.

He let Beethoven play on.

46 ⤸

When the doctor arrived minutes later, he examined the body and confirmed that Sarah Maringo was dead.

"I had better call the police," Dr. Williams said, dialing 999.

When he got them on the line, he asked for C.I.D. We all looked at him in astonishment. That was the Criminal Investigation Department. Dr. Williams proceeded to identify himself and give the address he was calling from. Then he said:

"I have just found a body dead under suspicious circumstances. Could you please send some of your men over immediately? Thank you."

"What do you mean by 'suspicious circumstances'?" Harry asked after Dr. Williams hung up.

"It would appear that your wife did not die of natural causes," Dr. Wililams said. "But of course we will have to wait to have that confirmed by a coroner's report. At any rate, the police will be here soon and they'll get the matter sorted out."

We all looked at each other.

"The police?" Jeanne said. "Do you mean that she's been murdered?"

"I never said that."

"But that's what you're implying."

Dr. Williams tapped his fingers on the glass-topped coffee table. "I suggest that we all remain calm and not touch anything until the police arrive."

When the police came, they were very polite, as I had imagined they would be. In English movies the police were always polite, and that's what I felt I was living through: an English detective movie in which I had a featured role. Oddly enough, I did not feel the least bit frightened or nervous as I watched the police enter our drawing room. For reasons I did not completely understand myself, I felt as cool as the proverbial cucumber.

There was the detective-inspector and a younger man, a sergeant. They both wore hats and raincoats and were not in uniform. One of the first things the detective-inspector did after conferring privately with Dr. Williams and examining the body was ask the sergeant to call for an ambulance and have Sarah taken to the mortuary at Horseferry Road.

"An autopsy will be performed there to determine the cause of death," the inspector said to us. "Meanwhile I want to get on with the circumstances surrounding the death of Mrs. Maringo. What she ate and drank tonight. In fact, I will need to know what each of you ate and drank."

"Do you mean that she might have died of food poisoning?" Jeanne asked.

"It's possible," the inspector said. "I would like to officially question everyone present and then ask each of you to fill out a written statement form, if you will."

"Question everyone about *what?*" Jeanne said. "We all had the same dinner."

"A woman is dead," the inspector reminded her. "And she died very suddenly. In such a case it is my business to find out where each of you were when the mishap occurred, your relationship to the deceased, the chronological events of the evening, and so on. It's quite routine. The sergeant will take your statement first, Dr. Williams, and then you'll be free to leave. If you would step into the study, please."

"I don't see why I should answer any questions without a solicitor present," Jeanne said.

The inspector smiled. "That's your privilege, Miss Nicholson, but if you do decline you must realize that your refusal will be looked upon with extreme suspicion."

"I didn't kill her!" Jeanne said.

"Of course my daughter will answer questions," Ian hastily assured the inspector. "She's just upset by this dreadful accident. We're all upset, for that matter. Ghastly thing to have happen in one's own home."

"Quite," the inspector said, turning to Harry. "You are the next of kin, Mr. Maringo, are you not?"

"Yes, I'm her husband. *Was* her husband, I suppose I

should say." His eyes were moist. "I still can't believe that Sarah is gone. It was so sudden."

"It's a nasty shock," the inspector said. "But I trust that you feel up to being questioned as soon as the sergeant is finished with Dr. Wililams. We do need your statement."

"Of course."

The inspector glanced at our coffee cups and cognac glasses. "In the meantime may I remind everyone not to touch anything. Please leave it all exactly as is. And that applies to the dishes and pots and pans in the kitchen, Mrs. Nicholson. No washing up, no putting away any of the foodstuffs or condiments. Had a little dinner party here tonight, did you?"

"Yes, Inspector," I said.

"I see. A dinner party for five, was it?"

"Yes."

"Good. Then everyone is present and accounted for."

"Yes."

"Fine." The inspector picked up the telephone. "I'm going to call my office and ask a few of my men to come over. We'll have to go through your kitchen and drawing room, Mrs. Nicholson, and remove every item that's been in use this evening. Not to worry. It will all be returned to you intact, after examination."

"I'm not worried," I said, "but I *am* confused."

"What are you confused about, Mrs. Nicholson?"

"Why Sarah died."

The inspector smiled again. It seemed to be his standard reaction to foolish remarks. "We'd like to know the answer, too. And we will, Mrs. Nicholson. We will. All in good time."

After Dr. Williams had given his statement and left, Inspector Langdale began to question each of us in turn, and then we were asked to write out our statements on the printed Metropolitan Police Station form. We were instructed to precede our remarks by writing: "I make this statement of my own free will. I have been told that I need not say anything unless I wish to do so, and everything I say may be given in evidence. . . ."

Jeanne was heard to mutter something about "damned hypocrites," and I noticed Ian glancing at her nervously. Inspector Langdale noticed it, too. In fact, Ian had seemed very concerned about Jeanne's behavior ever since the police arrived, and I could not figure out why. True, she had made a couple of brash remarks to the inspector, but they were harmless little outbursts, nothing to get worried about.

And Ian was worried. I knew the signs. He appeared to be afraid for his daughter. Surely he didn't imagine that *Jeanne* had killed Sarah! Yet that was how he looked. I wondered if Inspector Langdale thought so as well.

I began to understand Ian's apprehension when it was my turn to be questioned right after Harry.

"Mrs. Nicholson, who in the household had access to the food and drink served here this evening?" the inspector asked me.

"I did, of course. Also my cook, whose name is Mrs. Cook. She'll be here in the morning. And my husband and step-daughter."

But as yet Inspector Langdale had no notion that the "wrong woman" had been murdered. He wouldn't find that out until the contents of our coffee cups were analyzed in the police laboratory. Once it was established that the poison was in the decaffeinated Hag, and that I (not the deceased) was the only person present who ever drank Hag, then the inspector would realize Sarah had been poisoned by mistake.

I would give anything to see the expression on the good inspector's face when that delicious piece of news reached his ears. He would undoubtedly have to question all of us again, but from a different point of view this time. He would have to stop trying to find out who might have wanted to kill Sarah, as he was now doing, and start trying to find out who might have wanted to kill me.

Meanwhile I was still a suspect and Inspector Langdale plodded on. After asking me about the preparations for the dinner itself, and how it was served, he got to the post-prandial part.

"And you say, Mrs. Nicholson, that it is customary practice for your husband to serve coffee and cognac after dinner? And that he did so tonight?"

"Yes, Inspector. He enjoys doing it."

"I see. Did Mr. Nicholson pour the coffee beforehand?"

"Yes. In the kitchen, as he normally does."

"And where were you at the time?"

"In here. With my guests and stepdaughter."

I decided not to bring up the fierce argument that had taken place between Jeanne and me. I thought it would look better if someone else mentioned Jeanne's accusations against me, her insults, her vindictiveness. So far Tom McKillup's name had not come into the conversation.

"Then Mr. Nicholson brought in five cups of black coffee.

Is that correct?" The inspector pointed to the creamer and sugar bowl, which were still on the tray, on the glass-topped table. "With cream and sugar on the side?"

"He brought in five cups of black coffee, Inspector, but mine was different from the others."

The sergeant, who had been taking notes, looked up from his pad. The inspector regarded me with quiet interest.

"Different, Mrs. Nicholson? How?"

"I don't drink regular coffee, Inspector. I can't tolerate the caffeine. I only drink Hag. I have trouble sleeping."

"Are you then saying that one of the cups your husband placed on this tray contained decaffeinated Hag and the other four ordinary coffees?"

"That's right."

"And you drank the cup with the Hag in it?"

"Well, I drank some of it. As you can see"—I indicated my cup—"half is still full. I probably put it down when Sarah, Mrs. Maringo, collapsed."

"About how long after coffee was served did Mrs. Maringo collapse?"

"I'm not sure. It happened very suddenly."

"Approximately, Mrs. Nicholson."

"About seven or eight minutes, I would say. We were listening to Beethoven's Ninth, and the first movement hadn't ended yet. I remember that."

"I see. I notice that your coffee is black, Mrs. Nicholson. You don't take cream, then?"

"No."

"Sugar?"

"Yes. Two teaspoons."

Harry had previously said that Sarah drank her coffee black, with two sugars. He and I had gone over these details very carefully in planning the murder. According to my brother, the taste of the sugar would override the taste of the cyanide so that Sarah would not suspect anything.

"And did you add the sugar yourself, Mrs. Nicholson?" Inspector Langdale asked. "Or did your husband put it in your cup when he prepared the Hag?"

"No, he only put in my sleeping sedative. Not the sugar."

Inspector Langdale's eyes brightened. "What's this about a sleeping sedative?"

"I suffer from insomnia, as I've already explained. So I take a sleeping sedative every evening. It's mixed in with the Hag."

"And you say that Mr. Nicholson does the mixing?"

"Yes."

The sergeant was scribbling frantically, his face flushed. Inspector Langdale seemed very interested in this latest piece of information, and who could blame him?

"Where is this sleeping sedative kept?" the inspector asked me.

"In the kitchen. In a jar."

"Not in the medicine cabinet upstairs in the bathroom, as would be usual?"

I thought of my mother's bare medicine chest in Pilgrim Lake. Come to think of it, ours was pretty bare too. I had never realized the similarity before.

"No, Inspector, we keep it in the kitchen because it's more convenient that way."

"More convenient for mixing with your Hag, you mean?"

"Yes."

"There's something here I don't understand. If you drank even half a cup of Hag containing a sleeping sedative, why is it, Mrs. Nicholson, that you're still wide awake?"

"Oh," I laughed. "That's easy to explain. You see, this is a special formula that a chemist friend of my husband has devised, and it works very slowly. It doesn't take effect until about three hours after consumption. Which makes it quite practical really. I can still enjoy the evening and know that I'll sleep later."

"A chemist friend of your husband's . . ." Inspector Langdale glanced at Ian. "The chap must be brilliant. I've never heard of a sleeping potion taking three hours to work. What you're describing is most unusual."

"It is?"

"Yes, Mrs. Nicholson. I'll go one step further. It's virtually unheard of."

I had a feeling that it was going to be a very long evening, what with Ian and Jeanne still to be questioned. But since I'd been drinking regular coffee with all that hyperenergizing caffeine, I didn't think I was going to have too much trouble staying awake. In fact, I had never felt so alert or keyed up in my life. Still, what happened next took me totally by surprise.

"If I may interrupt for a second, Inspector?"

It was Ian, looking agitated.

"Yes, Mr. Nicholson. You have something to say?"

"It's about the sleeping powder. I've lied about that, I'm afraid. It's merely a harmless placebo."

"*What?*" I gasped in astonishment.

"Please, Mrs. Nicholson," the inspector said. "Let your husband continue."

Ian had turned pale and he spoke slowly. "The truth is, Inspector, I've been pretending to my wife that this potion would induce sleep, in the hope that her powers of suggestion would take over from there. And most of the time they have. You see, I'm very much opposed to drugs of any kind."

I was stunned. Not only had the bastard been lying to me for years, but he was even more like my mother (the anti-medication freak of Pilgrim Lake) than I had ever imagined.

"A placebo," the inspector mused. "Well, I certainly will want to know more about this chemist friend of yours, Mr. Nicholson. I assume you do know a chemist who prepared this placebo for you."

Ian was not pale now, he was white. "Yes, Inspector, I do."

"I'm not surprised. You seem to have a decided interest in drugs, Mr. Nicholson. Considering your distaste for them."

Things were going even better than Harry and I had hoped. If Ian could successfully practice deception using a placebo, why couldn't he be just as successful using poison? I was sure that Inspector Langdale was asking himself the very same question, and it was all I could do to keep from grinning triumphantly at my darling brother.

47

The police were back the next day, as I had anticipated.

Inspector Langdale said that he wished to question Mrs. Cook, whom I had told beforehand about Sarah's death.

"Are you aware that Mrs. Nicholson takes a sleeping sedative in her Hag?"

Mrs. Cook looked at me in embarrassment. "What Madam takes is none of my business. But yes, I've seen the jar it's kept in, if that's what you want to know."

"I believe the jar is usually right here in the kitchen," the inspector said.

"On the second shelf of the cupboard."

"Meaning out in the open so that anyone could get at it," Inspector Langdale suggested.

"Anyone who was so inclined," Mrs. Cook said tartly.

"Thank you, Mrs. Cook."

Ian had gone to work, Jeanne was at school, Harry had returned to Surrey. Inspector Langdale, the sergeant, and I escaped to the drawing room where I learned that the chemical reports had come back from the police laboratory.

"There was cyanide in Mrs. Maringo's coffee," the inspector said to me. "Even though we don't have a statement from the coroner yet, it appears that Mrs. Maringo was murdered."

I tried to look appropriately shocked.

"But who would want to do such a horrible thing?" I managed to say after a moment.

"It's a bit more complicated than that, Mrs. Nicholson. You see, the potassium cyanide was found in the cup containing the Hag."

I allowed myself to remain speechless as the intent of Inspector Langdale's words seeped into my incredulous brain.

"You mean—"

"Yes, Mrs. Nicholson. Apparently the poison was intended for you. The laboratory reports indicate that the cyanide had been mixed into your sleeping powder-placebo. That's why we were questioning Mrs. Cook about who had access to the jar. From what she said, four people did: Mrs. Cook, your husband, your stepdaughter, and yourself. Unless during the course of dinner last night either Mr. or Mrs. Maringo went into the kitchen at any point. Did they?"

"No. I'm virtually certain that neither of them left the table."

"Not even to go to the toilet?"

"Not that I recall."

"Mrs. Nicholson, do you know anyone who would want to kill you?"

"No, I don't." I buried my face in my hands. "This is all too terrible."

Inspector Langdale seemed quite concerned. "Yes, it is. Because, as you must realize, the killer is free to try again."

"What should I do?"

"I think that for starters you should tell us a little more

about the argument you had last evening with your step-daughter. A Mr. McKillup seems to have been the crux of it. From what Jeanne has told us already the argument created a vast amount of confusion . . . people moving around the room, much excitement. . . ."

"Yes, I suppose they were excited. It was a very nasty argument."

Inspector Langdale was obviously getting at the confusion that resulted in all of us sitting down in different places from where we had originally been seated. Hence Sarah picking up my cup of Hag. After I had finished telling the inspector my side of the argument, he said: "Given enough impetus, the most mild-mannered person is capable of murder. Your husband is so obviously the murderer that it almost rules him out. Do you understand?"

"You mean, why would he lay such an apparent trap for himself?"

"Exactly. He adds cyanide to your sleeping powder, he stirs the concoction into your Hag, he serves the coffee. He has the perfect opportunity to kill you and, I might add, the perfect motive. Jealousy. Revenge. You've been found cheating on him with a younger man, you've humiliated him. His own daughter knows about it. It's classic. There's only one thing wrong with Mr. Nicholson being the murderer."

"What's that?"

"It's too neat. Your husband is almost asking to be caught. Now why would such an intelligent man do something so stupid?"

I thought about it. "Maybe because he figured that by being so obvious, or as you say, so stupid, you would do precisely what you're doing: eliminating him as a suspect."

Inspector Langdale smiled. "We've considered that, Mrs. Nicholson. It's a possibility. The obvious murderer very often *is* the real murderer. But there's another possibility."

I held my breath. "Yes?"

"The other possibility is that the murderer, or murderers, wanted us to think that a mistake had been made."

For the first time since I had put poison into my sleeping powder-placebo yesterday morning, I was frightened.

"Are you saying that the poison was actually *intended* for Mrs. Maringo?"

"It's a thought."

"If that's true, then I'm not in danger."

"I didn't say that. You very well might be. Or the killer

might have accomplished his purpose already. We're not certain. We haven't reached any conclusions yet. This is a most tricky business."

My heart was beating so loudly that I felt certain the inspector could hear it. To my surprise, he said:

"What do you know about an affair between your stepdaughter and Mr. Maringo?"

"Jeanne and Harry? But that's impossible! She's in love with Tom, Mr. McKillup. You heard her say so yourself. That's what our argument was all about. That's why she resents me so much."

Inspector Langdale eyed me shrewdly. "Or pretends to."

"Pretends?"

"She could be pretending to be in love with this McKillup fellow to cover up the object of her true affections."

I could barely speak. "You mean Mr. Maringo?"

"She had quite a flirtation with him in St. Moritz, didn't she?"

"How did you find out about that?"

"The sergeant and I have just come from your husband's office. He told us that Jeanne was very taken with Mr. Maringo when you were all in St. Moritz. And what's even more interesting is that the deceased thought so too."

"Sarah?"

"Yes. In fact, it bothered her so much that she wrote to your husband about it only a few weeks ago."

"That's strange. Ian never mentioned it to me."

"Possibly he didn't consider the subject worth discussing. Your husband felt that it was a harmless holiday flirtation, with no lingering aftereffects. But Mrs. Maringo didn't agree with him. She seemed certain that the affair was still going on, that it was quite serious indeed. Naturally she was very upset."

"I see."

"Your husband has given us permission to go through his personal files. Where would we find them? Assuming you have no objection, Mrs. Nicholson?"

"Of course not. They're in his study, Inspector. The second door to your left as you go out."

"Thank you. We'll do that right now. I'm anxious to get a look at that letter."

So was I, but I didn't think it prudent to show too much interest in it. My head was swimming. I was starting to see what the inspector was leading up to. If he believed that

Sarah had been killed *intentionally*, then her letter could be of vital importance.

I put myself in Inspector Langdale's shoes. Jeanne and Harry working together could have poisoned Sarah and tried to make it appear as though Ian had tried to poison me! It was a terrifying thought. They might both be convicted on circumstantial evidence and Harry sent to jail while Ian went free!

Then a more horrible possibility occurred to me. What if Inspector Langdale were playing a cat and mouse game? What if he had the same exact plot and motive in mind, but instead of Jeanne being Harry's mistress he secretly suspected that I was? What if he were on to Harry and me?

I felt paralyzed with fear. All the inspector had to do was poke around in my background to find out that Harry and I were brother and sister and the jig would be up.

I sat there on my beautiful golden sofa, trying to think what I could do to stall the inspector from taking that dangerous step. Suspicion had to be diverted from Harry and me. Then I remembered something. Ian's anxiety about Jeanne. I remembered the way he had looked at Jeanne last night after Sarah had died. He was afraid for her. His fear was confirmed later on, when we were going upstairs getting ready for bed.

"What do you make of it all, Alexis?" he had asked me.

"I don't know. It can't have been food poisoning, because the rest of us feel all right."

"I wasn't thinking of food poisoning. I was thinking of . . . poisoning."

"What do you mean?"

"The cup that contained your Hag was on a chipped saucer. I put it there. Did you notice it?"

"No. I was far too busy trying to protect myself from Jeanne's insults and accusations to pay much attention to saucers. Chipped or otherwise."

"I think Jeanne noticed it."

"What if she did?"

He looked deeply troubled. "It was the cup that Sarah was drinking from when she died. She picked up your cup of Hag by mistake. I only realized it after she had collapsed."

"So what? The Hag certainly didn't kill her."

"No, of course not. But what if the sleeping sedative in it had been tampered with before I put it in?"

"Tampered with? What do you mean?"

"Mixed with poison."

"Ian! What are you suggesting?"

"Jeanne *did* resent you."

"Surely, you don't imagine—"

There were tears in his eyes. "I'm afraid I do. Jeanne had every reason in the world to want to see you dead. You know that as well as I."

"Yes, but—"

He interrupted me. His voice was fierce. "I'll do anything to keep my daughter from going to jail. She's suffered so much already. *Anything.*"

Would he go so far as to confess to the murder himself? Yes, now that I thought of it, I was pretty sure he would. My only hope of saving both my neck and Harry's was to subtly persuade Ian that the police were after Jeanne, and at the moment it seemed as though they were. Inspector Langdale was a help there. If he were trying to trap me, he might be unwittingly aiding me by using Jeanne as bait. Ian would fall for the bait. He had no reason in the world to think that I had killed Sarah.

Meanwhile I wondered what Sarah's letter had revealed. I also wondered how much significance the police would attach to the business of the chipped saucer. Plenty, I imagined. The fact that Ian had not told them about it did not look good. Not for him and not for Jeanne.

I picked up the telephone and dialed my husband's office.

I had a strong hunch that things were going to work out just as Harry and I had planned. A strong, Indian hunch. It was the best kind.

48 &

At the inquest which Ian attended in the company of his wife and daughter it was stated that Sarah Maringo had died of cyanide poisoning as a result of drinking a cup of coffee which had been tampered with "by an unknown person or persons."

The coroner's report further stated that in view of the

evidence presented, it appeared as though the cup of poisoned coffee had not been intended for Mrs. Maringo at all, but for Mrs. Nicholson.

Ian glanced at Jeanne as this was read. She had been looking very pale and withdrawn since the murder two days ago, and he was extremely worried about her. Yesterday the police had questioned her again, after reading the letter Sarah sent him about Jeanne's purported affair with Harry Maringo. Jeanne vehemently denied ever being involved with Harry. Ian believed her, but he was afraid that Inspector Langdale did not.

His fears were confirmed when they were walking out of the coroner's court. Harry had just left to make arrangements for the funeral, and Jeanne was going to take a bus to King's College when Inspector Langdale stopped her.

"We'd like you to come down to the station for further questioning, Miss Nicholson."

Jeanne looked helplessly at her father.

"You had better go along," Ian said. This was what he'd been dreading. "We'll see you at home later."

"I wonder if we will," Alexis said as the two of them headed for Mount Street.

"So do I. If they keep her longer than a few hours, it will be very bad indeed. I wish I had never saved that damned letter of Sarah's. It sounds so convincing."

Ian knew that Inspector Langdale would not give up until he had found the murderer, he was that kind of man. Ian had met his counterpart in banking: quiet but determined, and *thorough*. Ian shuddered for his daughter's life.

"Why don't we have lunch at the pub across the street?" Alexis suggested, taking his arm.

"That's a good idea."

They had two Bloody Marys apiece and a cold meat and salad platter. The pub was jammed, noisy, smoky, everything that Ian normally detested but now felt grateful for. The atmosphere made real conversation virtually impossible, and since he had nothing to say but plenty to think about, it was perfect. By the time he paid the bill, he had decided what he was going to do if Jeanne was still being detained at the police station when they got upstairs.

She was.

"I'm afraid we can't release your daughter just yet," Inspector Langdale said apologetically but firmly. "We're still making certain inquiries."

Which was a polite way of saying that Jeanne was under deep suspicion. Ian did not want to ask how much longer they were planning to keep her. It was too long already for it to be anything but serious. He drank a large brandy and rang his solicitor next. Alexis was upstairs, taking a nap.

"Look here," Ian said. "I don't quite know how to put this, but the fact is I've killed a woman by mistake. I want to go to the police and confess."

His solicitor was stunned when he heard the details of the crime. He was even more stunned when he heard his client say that he wished to make "generous financial provision" for the wife he had tried to poison only a couple of days ago. The two men were old friends, and the solicitor tried to reason with him.

"Do you know what you're saying, Ian? Do you know what you're doing? Are you sure you're not doing this just to save Jeanne's neck?"

"Only insofar as I fail to see why she should be sent to prison when I'm the guilty party."

"But are you *really?*"

"Yes. Yes, I am."

"I can't believe it."

"It's true, nonetheless. I was obsessed with jealousy, revenge. I know it sounds ridiculous, but I was out of my mind."

Ian then proceeded to outline the amount of money he wanted to deposit in Alexis' account and in Jeanne's after he was sent to prison.

"I suspect that my wife will wish to leave the U.K. once I'm convicted," he added. "Whatever you can do to facilitate the transfer of her funds would be most appreciated."

"Why do you imagine that she'll want to leave?" his solicitor asked. "There's always the possibility that you'll be paroled after a few years for good behavior. Then the two of you could be together once more, providing you can forgive each other. I've seen it happen before."

Ian could hardly say that Alexis would want to leave the country because she'd be afraid that Jeanne would try to kill her again. In his own mind he was firmly convinced that Jeanne had somehow obtained the potassium cyanide and doctored her stepmother's jar of placebo powder, with murder in her heart.

It seemed to Ian that the next month sped by like an express train rushing toward its final destination. Even though he was the central figure in the dramas that unfolded, he felt curiously detached from the somber goings-on. For the first time in a long while he was at peace with himself.

Oddly enough, he slept and ate well during the five weeks he spent in his cell in Brixton. He even gained a few unflattering pounds and laughingly told Alexis when she came to see him that it was a good thing he would soon be forced to wear a prison uniform.

"If I continue at this rate," he said, "my own clothes won't fit me before long."

She was crying. "I don't know how you can make such a joke out of it."

"My dear," he said, "what else is one to do?"

"You're so English," she said mysteriously.

Her concern for him was touching. Although she now seemed to accept the fact that he was guilty, and not merely covering up for Jeanne, she never questioned his base actions, she never sat in judgment on him. Perhaps she knew that as guilty as he was, she was equally guilty.

He had never loved her as much as he did during the five weeks he spent in Brixton Prison. Even Jeanne, who visited him regularly (but on her own), could not dispel the deepening love he felt for Alexis. Jeanne refused to believe that her father was guilty and continued to protest her own innocence.

"That only leaves Harry and Alexis herself," Jeanne said to Ian one day. "They're the only ones who could have done it. Either of them. Or both of them together."

"But, darling, *I* did it," Ian had to gently remind her.

Unlike Alexis, Jeanne did not cry. Her most prominent emotion seemed to be an iron determination to clear her father's name one day.

"And I will," she told him. "I will, Daddy. You'll see!"

Even Harry came to see him. It was awkward and embarrassing for them both, and Ian was glad when the younger man finally left. He struck Ian as a lost soul now that his wife had been so cruelly and unjustly taken from him. What could Ian say to compensate for that kind of tragic loss? Nothing. He did not even try. It would have been a mockery.

The trial was held in the famous Number One Court at the Old Bailey. Since Ian had pleaded guilty to murder (the prosecution refused to accept a manslaughter plea), there was no jury present. Only a grave-faced judge, other court officials, the witnesses, relatives of both the deceased and the accused, the press, and the ever-curious public, who had been following the case in the papers.

The trial lasted one hour and twelve minutes.

At the end of it Ian was given the sentence he had expected: life.

He was told that he would first go to the prison at Wormwood Scrubs, and there await final allocation.

The last thing Ian saw as he was being led out of the packed courtroom was Alexis' tear-stained face, somewhat overshadowed by the unwavering expression in Jeanne's eyes. He had come to recognize that expression only too well in the preceding weeks.

It was one of frozen, steel-like revenge.

Part 5

Spain—1975

49 ⟫

The Rabasa airport in Alicante was rapidly emptying out as I passed through Customs. My plane from London had been less than half full.

It was mid-October, six months after Ian had been sentenced to life imprisonment for the murder of Sarah Maringo, and the tourist season on the Costa Blanca was over. Instead of the brilliant Mediterranean skies I had hoped to see, the weather was cloudy, gray, overcast.

For a moment I panicked as I realized that this was precisely what I had left behind in England. But even before I went through the glass doors, out into the street lined with palm trees, I could feel the distinct difference in atmosphere. As a result of my long-ago traveling days, I still considered myself somewhat of an airport specialist. After all, airports had once been part of my métier.

At Heathrow, in spite of its labyrinthine corridors, there were no great mysteries. Everything was clearly marked, voices were low-keyed, colors were understated. Here there was an air of charged-up, trumpetlike vitality, mustachioed masculinity, strong cigarette smoke, and the smell of conflicted happiness.

England was neat, polite, detached, resigned; Spain was tumultuous.

My fears had nothing to do with Ian, who was being left behind, but rather with Harry, who had gone on ahead. Harry had taken off for Alicante shortly after Ian was tried. The plan was that I would wait six months and then join my brother in Spain. The plan was Harry's, and although it did not appeal to my impatient nature I finally saw its clear, practical virtues.

"It'll look suspicious if you leave England too soon," Harry had explained. "It will arouse speculation. You're supposed to be a grieving wife. What are you going to tell Jeanne and Mrs. Cook, for instance?"

"That I'm too nervous to remain in a flat where a murder has taken place. That's natural enough."

"What are you going to tell Ian? He'll be counting on your visits."

"Ian will understand. He thinks I'm afraid that Jeanne is going to try to kill me again. He'll understand my desire to get away somewhere safe. That's why he's made such generous financial provisions for me."

"And Jeanne. What does *she* believe?"

"Well, she knows that she certainly didn't kill Sarah. And she doesn't think her father did, either."

Harry looked at me triumphantly. "That only leaves you or me."

"Or you *and* me." I was remembering Jeanne's expression of vengeance throughout the trial. "Maybe you're right. Jeanne is a potential troublemaker."

"Exactly. Which is why I want you to cool it for six months. Go about your daily routine. Have lunch with your friends. Go to Harrods. Visit Ian at Dartmoor. (He had been transferred from Scrubs.) Play the role of the bereaved wife. Try to help Jeanne over this difficult period in her life. Maybe drink a little too much from time to time, to drown your misery. And for Christ's sake, be convincing!"

I stared at him silently, angrily. What he was saying was very reasonable. The trouble was that I felt impatient to be away from England, from London, from Jeanne and Mrs. Cook, from my plushy but sorrowful life as Mrs. Ian Philip Nicholson.

"Then when everything is calmed down," Harry said, "you tell Jeanne and Mrs. Cook some careful story (that they can't check up on) and take a plane to Alicante. I'll have rented a house near there. I'll be waiting for you. Six months isn't such a long time."

"What about Tom?"

Harry looked away. "We're going to have to take him along. He knows too much. It'll just be for a little while."

"You mean, *you're* going to have to take him along."

Ignoring my implications, Harry said: "Tom will follow me in about a month's time. I don't think that should look suspicious. His group is disbanding, anyway, and musicians are always moving around. It's you and I together that we want to avoid at first. We can't be too careful, you know."

"So it will be you and Tom together."

Harry seemed tired. "It won't be like that."

"Won't it?"

"No. I promise."

"I don't believe you."

"Please, Alexis, let's not quarrel, not now. Now that it's all over and we've gotten what we wanted. Please not now."

"I wonder if we have."

"Have what?"

"Gotten what we wanted."

"The summer people." Harry flashed one of his old sweet grins. "That's what we're going to be."

The six months that had just gone by felt more like six years, so slowly and laboriously had they passed. And now that I was here at last, going through the glass doors of the Alicante airport out into the surprisingly warm Spanish day, there wasn't a sign of my brother in sight.

A row of taxis stood in front of the arrivals building. They were painted black with either a red or a green stripe on the side, and their drivers were looking for fares. The porter who was wheeling my bags on a luggage rack glanced at me curiously. I had told him that someone would be meeting me. Now he wanted to know if I saw my friend. I was just about to say "No" when I heard a familiar voice.

"Hi, Alexis. Sorry I'm late. I was held up in traffic."

A pair of green eyes peered out of a freckled, suntanned face. The good-looking young man was wearing faded jeans, a rough shirt open at the neck, and thonged sandals. He said something quickly in Spanish to the porter, who began to take my bags to a nearby parked car.

"Don't I even rate a kiss after all this time?"

To my amazement I realized that I was staring at Tom McKillup.

"I haven't changed that much, have I?" he said, laughing as I continued to stare at him.

"My God, Tom, I really didn't recognize you. How are you? You look *wonderful*. Yes, you have changed. I can't believe it's you."

We kissed each other on the cheek.

"It's me, all right," he said with a crooked smile.

He did look wonderful, different, much more adult and sophisticated in spite of his boyish clothes.

And then I saw what it was.

He looked more relaxed and self-confident. His hair was bleached from the sun and had grown in a bit. No longer was it clipped very short in the teen-age style that his entire rock group affected after they had left Switzerland, and the extra length suited his lean face. To my dismay I realized that I found him maddeningly attractive.

There were lines of dissipation under his green eyes, which the suntan partially concealed. I could see them now as he moved into a clearer light, but they only seemed to add to his sexy new good looks. I wondered where and how he had been spending his nights since we last met at the Old Bailey, during Ian's wretched trial.

Tom helped me into the car, tipped the porter, and said something to him in rapid Spanish. I had been studying Spanish at Berlitz for the past six months, yet I could not understand Tom. He was too fast for me, too fluent. Now I wished I had studied harder, worked more diligently. But having to keep my studies a secret from Jeanne and Mrs. Cook hindered my efforts.

"Where does Jeanne think you are?"

"In Paris. I told her that's where I was going. But Jeanne seems to have beaten me to the punch in the travel department."

"What do you mean?"

"She's disappeared from home."

"*Disappeared?*"

"Yes. Vanished. Run away."

"But where? How? What happened?"

"Well, it was several days ago. I'd just come back from paying my monthly visit to Ian at Dartmoor, and she was gone. It was Thursday, Mrs. Cook's half day off, so neither of us actually saw her go. But from what we could figure out, Jeanne took two suitcases of clothing with her and didn't leave a damned clue behind."

"You mean, no farewell note? Nothing?"

"Nothing."

"That's pretty weird," Tom said, "Jeanne disappearing so mysteriously. Did you inform the police?"

"No. Although I pretended to Mrs. Cook that I had."

"Aren't you worried?"

I'm plenty worried, but not about Jeanne. About Harry and me."

Tom looked perplexed. Who could blame him?

"What did you tell Ian?" he asked.

"As far as Ian knows, Jeanne is still going to college, still pursuing her studies, still cursing your guts. I didn't want to upset him. Besides, she might have returned home by now."

Tom laughed and switched on the radio. "Maybe she's moved in with some other randy guitar player."

Even before I saw the Mediterranean, I smelled the change in air. The music sounded wetter, louder, noisier. I couldn't wait to get out of my city clothes and into something more casual, less restricting. I felt so pale beside Tom and many of the people we were passing, who looked as though their skin had been permanently browned from the summer sun. I couldn't wait to see my brother and the house he had rented for us.

"We're about twenty minutes away from home," Tom said, as though reading my mind. "Harry thought it would be better to live outside of town. We're near a small village called Campello."

"I know. That's where Harry's letters to me were postmarked."

"Yes, well, Harry thought that we'd be less conspicuous there than smack in the center of Alicante."

"Is it nice? The house we've rented? Harry's description wasn't very explicit."

"Oh, very nice. It has a tennis court, swimming pool, all mod cons. It even has a name: Los Amantes. It means The Lovers."

"I know what it means. I've been studying Spanish." I tried not to think of the sinister possibilities of the name. "Where's Harry?"

"He's sleeping off a bad hangover."

"Oh . . ."

"Harry has been boozing a lot lately."

"I'm sorry to hear that."

"It gets worse as the days go by."

"Can't you do anything to stop him?"

"I've done my best, Alexis. He won't listen. Maybe you'll have better luck."

I tried to tell myself that Harry's drinking was due to the fact that he missed me, was miserable without me, was drowning his sorrows until I could join him. On the surface it sounded like a logical enough explanation. But something about it bothered me. I had not come here to be Harry's nurse. Then I remembered that Sarah had been an invalid who needed a nurse. Was Harry now taking over Sarah's old

role of the helpless but tyrannical victim? Not likely, I thought.
I was merely being foolish, melodramatic. I had been alone
too long. Still, the eerie possibility made me shudder.

"The beautiful harbor of Alicante welcomes you," Tom
said.

I looked up. First there were the boat masts spiraled into
a suddenly brilliant sky. The sun had just come out. And then
I saw the sea.

50 &

Harry's head was pounding and it felt painful to open his
eyes. He cursed Tom for not having drawn the drapes before
he went to meet Alexis at the airport. Tom knew that Harry's
eyes were especially sensitive to sunshine nowadays. The least
Tom could have done was to leave a pair of dark glasses next
to the bed.

Perhaps Tom just didn't give a damn, Harry thought, remembering the blissful protection of the wrap-around goggles
he had worn when he and Sarah spent Christmas in St. Moritz
last year. Of course his hangovers weren't nearly so bad then.
The sharp, exhilarating mountain air had seen to that. But
it wasn't only the air. His drinking in St. Moritz (or England,
for that matter) had not yet reached the dangerous proportions it seemed to be taking on in Spain.

For one thing he had had to gauge himself much more
cautiously while Sarah was still alive or he would never have
heard the end of her carping and bitching. At the time he
bitterly resented her intrusion upon his freedom to do just
as he wished, yet within the last six months he had begun to
see that without her controlling influence he had been rapidly
going to hell. In fact, if it weren't for Tom, he'd probably
be there by now.

Next to the bed stood an almost empty bottle of Pernod,
one glass still half-full, a second glass containing the dregs of
last evening's little party. They had set out to celebrate
Alexis' arrival today, but caught in the treacherous maze of

alcohol and ambivalent emotions, the celebration disintegrated into hostile argument.

"You can't wait for her to get here, can you?" Harry taunted Tom. "You've still got the hots for her. It sticks out all over you, so don't bother to deny it."

"You're the one who can't wait," Tom replied. "You've been marking the days on that dumb flamenco calendar ever since we arrived. Do you think I'm blind?"

"Maybe I've been marking the days *unhappily*. Has that ever occurred to you? Maybe I'm not exactly thrilled by the prospect of sharing Los Amantes with my beloved sister."

Tom was sucking on a cigarette. "Why not? What's changed?"

It was a damned good question. The problem was that Harry didn't know the answer. He had been trying to figure out why the longer he was separated from Alexis, the less he desired her, the less she seemed to mean to him, the more of a burden she became.

He had thought that he would be anxiously, eagerly awaiting her arrival. Instead, he found that he was dreading it. He'd been dreading it for months now, and the change in his feelings was too painful for him to bear without the anesthetic effect of alcohol. Every time Harry thought of his sister and the promise they made to each other to become the summer people, he choked down another drink. The stronger the better.

"I'll be relieved when your supply of kif runs out," Harry said, thinking what a risk Tom had been taking, smoking this drug in front of the maid. "It can't be soon enough for me."

"There are local dealers," Tom said casually.

Harry looked at him, appalled. Dealers, dealing, pushing. If Tom got involved in that end of it, the authorities might send him to jail for life. It was known to happen, the drug penalties here being as severe as they were. Of course, the police had to know about you first. It was an interesting lever, Harry thought, something to definitely bear in mind in case Tom ever got out of hand. He raised his glass of Pernod in a toast.

"To our last night of freedom," he said, noting the frown on Tom's tanned face. "I see that doesn't appeal to you. What's the matter?"

"Nothing. I just hope you're sober enough to make it to the airport tomorrow."

"What time does her plane get in?"

"At three. And her room is all fixed up. I think she'll like it."

"Your eagerness is showing," Harry said.

"Yours certainly isn't."

Harry did not bother to answer him, he was too busy trying to account for the changes he had undergone since leaving England. The biggest change was the switch in his affections from Alexis to Tom. What if it were merely a matter of proximity, plain and simple? he thought. Tom was here and Alexis was not. Still, if that were the case, then he would be doubly impatient for Alexis to join him so that he could finally shake off the unhealthy liaison with Tom.

But he *wasn't* impatient. He was terrified, he realized, reaching for his drink. Alexis would expect so much of him, now that after all these years of plotting and scheming they were free to be together at last.

"You're still in love with her!" he accused Tom.

"What if I am?" Tom admitted. "It's more natural than . . . this. Alexis is a very beautiful woman."

Harry eyed Tom shrewdly. "You're quite the little opportunist, aren't you? Keeping me happy until Alexis could get here. Now you're all set to switch roles and do your best to keep her happy."

"I'm in love with Alexis."

As though that explained everything, solved everything, simplified everything. Harry felt himself in the grip of an uncontrollable rage. But giving into it would serve no worthwhile purpose, he realized, it would only make Tom more smug and self-confident to see the usually suave Harry unnerved.

"You may be in love with Alexis," Harry said calmly. "But there's one important fact you're overlooking."

"What's that?"

"Alexis is in love with me."

"Maybe."

Harry felt like strangling the younger man, but he kept his voice steady. "Alexis has always been in love with me, ever since we were children. And she always will be. What do you think about that, you arrogant bastard?"

"I'm not so sure you're right. After all, if you can change in your feelings, why can't she?"

Tom's blithe reply caught Harry unprepared. It was the one possibility he hadn't counted on, but what if it turned out to be true? What if during the last six months Alexis had stopped loving him, just as mysteriously and inexplicably as he had stopped loving her?

"That's ridiculous," he snapped. "You obviously don't know Alexis as well as you think."

"Do you?"

"Yes," Harry said uncertainly. "I should. I have a head start on you, you see. About forty-three years' worth, to be exact."

It was almost four.

He had taken a refreshing shower and was nearly finished shaving when he heard the Seat in the driveway. To his annoyance he nicked his cheek in the rush to get through and hastily dabbed some talcum powder over the spot of blood, then covered it with a Band-Aid. A splash of Dior's Eau Savage aftershave, a gargle of minty mouthwash, and Harry felt almost human again. Thanks to his suntan (evened out with the help of a men's bronzer), the ravages of months of drinking were mercifully concealed.

Harry removed the towel that was wrapped around his waist and put on a tan and white toweling robe that bore the Lanvin logo, another of Sarah's many gifts to him. Then he appraised himself in the bedroom's long oval mirror and was gratified to see that his eyes were less bloodshot and more sparkling than a few minutes ago. All in all he looked pretty damned good, he decided. He opened the windows wide to try to get rid of the foul-smelling air, just as he heard the door to the house slam and Tom say cheerfully:

"Here we are. Home at last!"

"What a lovely house," Alexis replied. "It's name suits it."

The sound of her voice, soft but with that underlying tremor of determination, made Harry shiver. He put his hands in the robe's deep pockets. In the past he had never been able to fool Alexis, she invariably saw right through him as though he were made of glass. He wondered whether today would be any different.

"Darling!" he said, striding into the hallway, where Alexis stood waiting for Tom to bring in her bags. "It's so good to see you!"

"It's so good to be here." She walked slowly, almost hypnotically, into his arms and nestled there. "I feel safe at last."

Harry felt just the opposite. Now that she had actually arrived at Los Amantes, his fears turned into concrete reality.

He could not imagine making love to this tall, dark-eyed, dark-haired woman. He had grown used to the smaller frame of Tom McKillup, with his green eyes, freckled skin, and sandy-blond hair. Making love to Alexis would be like making love to himself.

Tom took Alexis' luggage into the bedroom that he and Harry had decided would be hers. It was decorated in peach and melon colors, with a huge canopied four-poster bed. Over the dressing table was a lovely mirror rimmed in sea shells. A bamboo chaise covered in peach chintz sat in one corner. Next to it was a small, round, bamboo table that had a vase of fresh wildflowers on it. Tom must have gathered the flowers, Harry thought, annoyed.

"What a charming room," Alexis said, obviously pleased.

"We hoped you'd like it," Harry said as Tom piled suitcases everywhere.

"I think I'm going to be very happy here," Alexis said. "It's so peaceful."

When Harry and Tom first moved into the sprawling white stucco house, there had been five bedrooms. Now there were only three. The other two had been converted into bathrooms, so that with the one bathroom the house originally boasted, each of the occupants had a complete suite of his or her own. It was the kind of luxurious privacy that Alexis and Harry had previously achieved only through marriage and Tom through hard work. Now, as Tom had rather maliciously pointed out, it was all of theirs through murder.

Alexis' room faced the Mediterranean, as did Harry's. Tom had chosen the bedroom that looked out on the garden, saying the sound of the sea kept him awake. Harry had been amazed to discover that not only had Tom never learned how to swim, but he was absolutely terrified of the water. The only use he ever made of the sparkling blue pool was to hesitatingly wade in up to his waist, hold his nose while he dunked himself, and then quickly come out. Harry had nicknamed him *el gato* because of his catlike aversion to water.

"You've certainly made a remarkable recovery," Tom said as they stretched out on the patio's wicker chairs. "I don't know how the hell you do it. When I left here earlier, you looked like death."

"I have a fabulous constitution. I take after my father." Never before had Harry felt so close to the man he'd despised as a child.

51 ∽

I had followed Harry's advice: gotten out of my traveling clothes, taken a shower, and was now wearing hot pink culottes, a purple cashmere sweater, a printed scarf around my neck, large gold hoop earrings, and flat gold sandals that laced up the legs.

It was quite chilly, quite beautiful outside. I pulled up the slatted wooden blinds and looked at the Mediterranean shimmering in the cool moonlit night air. A few men were fishing down the beach, their poles remotely still. The air smelled marvelous after the traffic-polluted congestion of London, and the sense of peace was overwhelming. Off in the distance I heard guitars and a lone voice singing.

I had only partially unpacked, I would do the rest tomorrow. I was too excited right now for practical tasks like putting away clothes, sorting things out. After all, this was my first evening in Spain! From the way my heart was beating, you would think I had never traveled anywhere before this, that was how thrilled I felt . . . like a virgin about to have her first affair. A travel virgin.

"Alexis, what's happened to you?" Harry called from the patio.

"I'll be there in a second."

But there was something I wanted to do first, *had* to do. Treading softly on the beautifully tiled floor, I slipped out of my room and went down the corridor in search of Harry's. By sheer luck I came upon it right away. As soon as I turned on the light, I spotted the flamenco calendar that Tom had mentioned earlier.

It was crookedly thumbtacked over his bureau, with the days until today crossed off in a heavy red pencil. I remembered telling Harry when we were children that I always thought of Cortes as a flamenco dancer in tight red pants. But what had amused me then no longer struck me as funny. No. Just the opposite.

It was the room. Even with the windows opened, it reeked of licorice-flavored alcohol. I saw the empty bottle of Pernod next to the bed and the two glasses alongside it. Both pillows on the bed appeared crumpled, used. Someone had obviously been drinking with Harry prior to my arrival. But who? A girl he'd picked up in Alicante? Or Tom?

Feeling like a fourth-rate detective, I searched both glasses for lipstick stains but there were none. Which proved absolutely nothing. After making love, a woman's mouth is usually wiped clean of all cosmetics. And if it had been a woman who shared Harry's bed last night (and possibly this morning), why did I automatically assume that she was a casual pickup? What if my brother had gotten seriously involved with someone these last six months, while I was being stupidly faithful to his memory?

The thought made me sick. I dimmed the lights and tiptoed out, sorry I had ever come in. I tried to tell myself not to worry, not to jump to conclusions, but the combination of Harry's absence at the airport, the awkward way he had greeted me earlier, and now the suggestive condition of his room hardly indicated that he welcomed my arrival. For some reason I remembered our mother's last hurtful estimation of Harry and me just before she died:

"A bum for a son and a tramp for a daughter."

Even in death she had done her best to separate us, and I wondered what she would think if she could see Harry and me now. Would she be bitterly disappointed that her efforts had failed? Or would she realize that, even though we were together at last, she had grotesquely succeeded in her vindictive mission?

I did not want our mother to succeed. Harry and I were going to be happy, I promised myself fiercely as I stifled all thoughts of Tom's lean good looks and sun-bleached hair, Harry's attempts to mask his haggard hangover, my own desires suddenly divided between the two of them. . . .

"Here she is at last," Harry said, applauding lightly as I appeared on the patio. "A vision in pink and purple."

I kissed him on the cheek, pretending not to notice his licorice breath. "Well, isn't this pleasant!"

The patio was lit by a string of multicolored lanterns and there were flourishing green plants everywhere. On a table sat a large platter of toasted sandwiches neatly cut into triangles, surrounded by plump green olives and juicy red peppers. Tom was just opening a smoky black bottle of something as I seated myself between him and Harry.

"I didn't realize how hungry I was," I said, taking one of the toasted triangles. "I haven't eaten since lunch on the plane."

"These are just *tapas*," Harry explained. "We'll go out to dinner later on. Nobody in Spain has dinner before ten."

"That's a long time off," I said. "I hope I'm still awake by then."

"You'll get used to it eventually," Tom chimed in. "Spaniards are the original night people. Nothing really happens here until Franco goes to sleep."

The Mediterranean lay in front of us, illuminated by a thin sliver of a moon. Now I could see farther down the beach than from my room, and there were rows of lighted places broken up by patches of total darkness. I suspected that during the season everything would be lit, festive, colorful. I was sorry that I would have to wait until next year to see all of that. The cork of the smoky black bottle popped, and a little champagne overflowed before Tom caught it in a goblet.

"We've found the best local sparkling wine" he said, filling our glasses. "Cordon Noir. Here's a toast to Alexis. To your very good health, love."

We drank to my very good health and I tried to make conversation, but it was awkward. Harry smoked and drank incessantly and ate nothing. Between us, Tom and I managed to finish off the toasted *tapas*, which turned out to contain shrimp and spicy ham flavored with garlic mayonnaise.

"How is Ian?" Harry asked me suddenly.

"As well as can be expected. He works in the library at Dartmoor and keeps a canary in his cell."

Tom laughed and Harry solemnly said: "It's not funny!"

Tom and I looked at each other. Was Harry now feeling sorry for the man that he and I had framed? Then, with an ugly smile on his face, Harry retorted:

"It's *hilarious*. What the hell is he doing with a canary?"

"I suppose it's some sort of company. Ian isn't used to being alone. He feeds the canary, looks after it."

"And the canary sings," Harry said in a mocking voice.

"I believe they're known to."

"What's the bird's name?"

"Rudolph."

"Why Rudolph? Who's Rudolph, for Christ's sake?"

"I wouldn't know," I said, getting angry.

Tom broke in, trying to ward off an unpleasant clash between me and my brother.

"I have an idea. Why don't we take Alexis to a few of the waterfront places in Campello before we drive into Alicante for dinner?"

"It's a better idea than talking about goddamned canaries named Rudolph," Harry agreed. "Wait a minute while I get out of this robe."

Campello was the local village, which up until a few years ago, Tom informed me, didn't even have paved streets.

As we got out of the Seat, people turned to stare at us, especially at me.

"They can't decide if you're with Harry or me" Tom said. "They've never seen either of us with a woman before."

"They figure you're married to one of us," Harry said. "Or engaged. But they're not sure which."

"Why do I have to be married or engaged to anyone? Why can't I just be on my own?"

"Spaniards don't think that way," Tom said. "A beautiful woman like you is never on her own, not unless she's a *tortillera*."

"What's that?"

"A lesbian."

"They didn't teach me that at Berlitz."

I wondered what it would be like to live and die in this obscure part of Spain, and never see anything of the rest of the world. Peaceful, perhaps. Uncomplicated, certainly. Dull as dishwater.

Yet as a tourist, I found it enchanting. The first *cantina* we went into was rowdy and boisterous. Music was blaring, Spaniards love noise. There were many different appetizers under glass along the bar, and I was surprised to see women (with babies) drinking Coca-Cola or orangeade and eating some of the unidentifiable appetizers as their children slept peacefully, oblivious to the racket. Everyone seemed familiar with everyone else. There was a lot of smiling and laughter, a lot of touching.

Tom and Harry knew the proprietors, a fat middle-aged couple. I was introduced to them as Harry's wife, and that brought forth even more smiles. The proprietor's wife asked me if we had any *niños*, and I said no, but we were thinking about it.

"*A los niños*," they toasted us. "*A los niños de los Maringos*."

The wine turned to vinegar as the unintended irony of the toast registered upon me. I glanced at Harry, but he appeared unperturbed by the fact that because of our brother and sister relationship we could never risk having children. Besides,

I was too old for that now, which made the wine taste even more like vinegar than before.

"Shouldn't we be leaving soon?" I asked Tom.

"In a minute. We don't want to abuse their hospitality."

I had a hunch that a very long evening stretched ahead, and although I was starting to feel tired I was determined to see it through to the end. But how much nicer it would have been, I thought wistfully, if Harry had set this evening aside just for the two of us, instead of expecting me to share it with Tom.

I tried to pretend that it would be rude and impolite to leave Tom out of the celebrations, but I knew that politeness had nothing to do with it. Tom was here because Harry did not want to be alone with me. It was as simple and mystifying and insulting as that. And what would Harry do later tonight when we returned home to Los Amantes and went to our bedrooms? Would I be alone with Harry then, or alone with myself? The possibility of being with Tom had not yet occurred to me.

"Don't look so sad, Alexis," Harry teased me. "This is your first evening in Spain. Smile! Be happy!"

I choked down another glass of the proprietor's musty red wine, tears threatening my eyes, and did my best not to think of how the evening would end. There were many hours before that . . . Alicante was still to be seen, dinner to be savored, other glasses of wine to be drunk. Maybe by the time we got back to Los Amantes Harry would have started treating me more like the wife I was supposed to be, instead of the sister I really was.

52 ⌒

As Tom swung the Seat into the circular driveway of Los Amantes hours later, he could only thank God that Spain's traffic laws were infinitely more lax than England's. Otherwise he would have been arrested for drunk driving by now. According to the car's clock, it was nearly three in the morning. Alexis nodded sleepily beside him, and in the back seat Harry was snoring. Tom turned off the ignition.

"All right, you two," he said. "Time for bed."

Alexis straightened up immediately and looked around her. "I must have dozed off. What an evening! I'm thoroughly exhausted."

"But you did enjoy yourself, didn't you?"

She laughed in the cool darkness. "I think so. Right now I'm too tired to remember. I'll sort it all out in the morning." She turned around. "Wake up Harry! It's time to go to sleep."

Between her and Tom they managed to get Harry into the house, undressed, and into bed. There they left him, still snoring, his mouth opened, his arms limp at his sides.

"He'll be okay by tomorrow," Tom said.

"It *is* tomorrow," Alexis replied, frowning.

Tom could guess what she was thinking, feeling, how much she must resent Harry's abandonment of her on this, her first day in Spain. For hours now, Tom had wondered how this evening was going to end, how Harry would handle himself, whether he had been serious yesterday when he said:

"Maybe I'm not exactly thrilled by the prospect of sharing Los Amantes with my beloved sister. Has that ever occurred to you?"

No. Yesterday Tom hadn't believed him. But judging from Harry's actions during the last frenetic hours, it would seem that he was telling the truth about *unhappily* marking the days off until Alexis' arrival. Because now that she was here, Harry had treated her like a chance acquaintance who just happened to tag along with them on their giddy joyride . . . from the waterfront *cantinas* of Campello, to the lively sidewalk cafes, elegant rooftop restaurant, and frenzied nightclubs of Alicante.

And, feeling no further obligation or responsibility toward her once the festivities were over, Harry proceeded to quietly, drunkenly pass out, and have to be put to bed alone. Yes, Tom believed him now. And he was both delighted and dismayed by this turn of events.

Delighted because it meant he was free to try to win Alexis' love once more.

Dismayed because he was afraid Harry would expect him to continue the homosexual affair that Tom found so shameful, so degrading.

"Would you like a cup of hot chocolate?" he asked Alexis.

"It's not a bad remedy after an evening like this, helps you sleep."

Why had he said that? Sleep was the last thing on his mind. After months of a man-to-man, *maricón* relationship, he was dying to make love to a woman, to Alexis, dying to re-assure himself that he still knew how. Fortunately she was not as dense as he.

"No hot chocolate, thank you, Tom. I can sleep without it."

But she didn't look as though she could sleep, tired as she appeared to be. She looked fearful, confused, and who could blame her? For one mad moment, Tom considered dreaming up some palatable excuse for Harry's bad manners and lack of consideration tonight, then he came to his senses—he would be cutting his own throat by doing so. Let his Highness fend for himself.

"How lovely it is," Alexis said. "How quiet. Except for the waves."

They had wandered out onto the patio and stood facing the sea, two people in a strange land. Yet once they had been close, intimate. Once in a moment of unguarded bliss she had whispered, "I adore you, Tom." Did she remember too?

"Well," Alexis said, rubbing her eyes and inadvertently smearing her mauve eyeshadow, "I guess I'll say goodnight."

She reminded him of a child at that moment, a child who had fallen down while playing some raucous game and given herself a black eye. Vulnerable, wounded, defenseless. That was the picture she presented. How different from that first one when she commandingly strode into his trendy house in Fulham, pretending to protect her stepdaughter's honor. What an admirable act she had put on then! What a change from that upper-class bitch to this wan little-girl lost!

Tom grabbed her by the shoulders and wrapped his arms tightly around her, kissed her as he had not kissed a woman for a very long time. His hunger must have shown, for she did not resist or try to stop him. Instead she seemed to melt into him, to dissolve in his embrace, as though it had been a long time for her, too (a possibility that he had not con-sidered). He could feel her breasts through her sweater, they pressed against his chest. He could taste the sweetness of her lipstick, smell her familiar perfume, touch the soft yet firm texture of her skin. He was starting to remember how nice it was to make love to a woman, how heavenly. How could he have ever forgotten?

She suddenly grinned at him. "Your room or mine?"

He laughed. It was all so simple. "Mine."

"Okay."

In her flat gold sandals they were the same height. He took her hand and guided her inside toward his room, which stood at the end of the long dark corridor. It was separated from her room and Harry's by the kitchen and dining area. As soon as they entered it, the salty smell of the sea was replaced by the sweet fragrance of summer's last flowers.

They undressed by the light of the moon and fell upon the bed with the abandon of ardent savages intent upon devouring each other's flesh. Quickly, quickly, slowly. They rushed and they took their time, knowing all the time that when morning came they would blink their eyes in the sun and have to account for these brash erotic actions. To themselves. To each other. To Harry. Silently they prayed that morning would never come.

Tom was the first to awaken.

He rubbed the stubble on his cheek and looked at his watch before remembering the naked figure huddled beside him, her face buried in a pillow. It was ten past eight. He had been asleep less than four hours, yet he felt wonderful, fabulous. He kissed Alexis softly on the back of her neck, careful not to disturb her. She moaned and gurgled something, flung an arm around the pillow, then suddenly, alarmingly, sat upright in bed.

"Good God! What time is it? Where am I? I've been having the strangest dreams. Lakes. I've been ice skating on a frozen lake." She shook her head. "No. *We* have. Harry and I, when we were children. I was dreaming about Pilgrim Lake!"

Then, as memory of last night returned, she smiled.

"Oh, Tom, I'm so glad it's you. I just wish I didn't feel so disoriented, so guilty."

He kissed her on the lips. "Good morning. You're not awake enough to feel guilty. Besides, there's nothing to feel guilty about."

"Isn't there?"

She looked even more childish and defenseless than ever, with all her makeup gone and her hair disheveled. It was somehow reassuring to know that the impression of last night had not been some maudlin whim of his, etched in alcohol. She really *was* a different person from the Alexis he had known in London. Without the trappings of luxury, without her husband's powerful presence always hovering over her, without the stern stepmother guise, she was a beautiful, desirable, adorable, woman.

He wanted to make love to her again and he wanted to take a shower. The two disparate urges struck him funny as he considered combining them into one and thereby solving the dilemma.

"What are you grinning at?" she asked.

"Making love to you in the shower."

"What's so funny about it?"

"You're too tall," he said, trying to visualize it. "I don't think it would work."

"Actually, I'm not tall enough. I could always put on heels." She seemed quite serious. "Then it would work."

"Is that what you do with Harry?"

The minute he said it he could have shot himself. Her face clouded over and her voice changed.

"I haven't done *anything* with Harry for a very long time. Need I remind you?"

He was instantly, sincerely apologetic. "Alexis, I'm sorry. I don't know why I made such a moronic remark. It was inexcusable. Forgive me."

"Sure."

"No, I mean *really* forgive me."

She smiled remorsefully. "I do. You're as rattled as I am. We have a lot of talking to do."

"I know."

And all of it revolved around Harry.

"Look, Tom"—she was nervously braiding her hair—"I came to Spain to be with Harry. That was the whole idea, the whole plan. It's been the plan for a very very long time, even before Sarah, before Paulette. That's why I'm here. As for last night, I don't understand what happened, why Harry treated me so coldly, indifferently. But there must be a logical explanation."

She looked at Tom as though waiting for him to provide that explanation. In order to avoid doing so, he said:

"Who's Paulette?"

"Oh, she was Ian's first wife. Jeanne's mother. I don't know why I mentioned her, it must be this hangover. I'm jittery. But to get back to the main point. Harry. Well, I suppose my feelings were hurt when he ignored me last night, more hurt than I fully realized at the time."

"Are you trying to tell me that the only reason you're in this bed is because Harry didn't invite you into his?"

She reddened at the accuracy of his thrust. "Don't make it sound so callous. It wasn't like that."

He felt like shaking her, slapping her. "Really, Alexis? What *was* it like? You tell me. Go ahead."

"I care about you very much. You were very loving last night. It was very nice."

"It sounds very boring."

"Please, Tom." She put a hand on his shoulder. "Don't hate me. I'm only trying to be honest. I don't want to lie to you."

"I'd rather you lied."

"No, you wouldn't."

He backed down. "Maybe not."

"I'd rather you didn't lie either," she said. "If you know something about Harry, I wish you'd tell me."

He was starting to feel that old sinking sensation in his stomach. "I've got nothing to tell."

"Well, I do."

"Yeah?" He tried to sound casual. "What?"

"I sneaked into Harry's room, earlier last night. Before we went out to dinner. I saw the empty bottle of Pernod, the two glasses, the two crumpled pillows. What's going on, Tom? Does Harry have a girlfriend? Is that it?"

Tom began doing situps in bed. "You have a hell of a lot to learn about drunks, that's all I can say."

She seemed genuinely interested. "Such as what?"

"They've got funny habits," he said, in between breaths. "Like ending up with more than one glass of booze at a time. You see, they forget where they put the first, so they go and get a second. A third. An eighth. Sometimes Harry's room looks as though there'd been a party for twenty people the night before. Does that answer your question?"

"Partially."

Tom stopped halfway through a situp. "You don't mean the mystery of the two glasses, for Christ's sake! Do you? You're not still harping on that."

"They'd both been used," she said lamely.

"Harry does not have a girlfriend. He's just a guy who drinks out of two glasses, sleeps on two pillows, and probably has two heads this morning. Period!"

"You don't have to get so angry."

But he was angry. At himself. Angry, confused, conflicted. He wanted to tell Alexis that Harry had lost interest in her, had been dreading her arrival, that—in plain unvarnished words—her precious Harry no longer loved her. Ordinarily he would not have hesitated for a second, but there was one problem.

Tom was afraid that Harry would retaliate by telling Alexis about the two men having been lovers these last lonely months (which was how they now struck Tom), and he did not want Alexis to know that. In fact, he was terrified of her finding out, humiliated at the prospect. Her estimation of him would sink to zero. If she found out, he would lose her before he even had her.

Unless he had a reason to justify his homosexual behavior, a way to prove to Alexis that his actions had been based on solid, practical motivation. Unless he had a plan that would not only exonerate him, but make him a hero in her eyes. Then Harry could tell her anything he liked and it wouldn't matter. But what kind of plan? It would have to be a damned good one. Ingenious. Brilliant.

"Tom, what's the matter?" Alexis asked. "You look so strange."

"I've been thinking."

"About what?"

"You and me."

"Go on."

He couldn't. No matter which way he turned, all roads led back to Harry. Tom remembered a piece of their conversation, the night before Alexis arrived. Harry had seductively said:

"We haven't been having such a bad time, just the two of us. Have we?"

Yes, they'd been having a terrible time, Tom now realized. At least from his point of view. But apparently Harry didn't feel that way, he wanted to continue their relationship. He had said as much. Yet even as he said it, he admitted that he was not willing to give Alexis up. It was as though Harry felt bound somehow by that old pledge of theirs to become the summer people, that old childhood dream. Otherwise why did Harry claim that Alexis was still in love with him, insist that he had a head start on Tom because of her love?

"About forty-three years' worth, to be exact," were Harry's triumphant words on the subject.

Tom shook his head in confusion now.

Harry wanted a head start on Tom with Alexis. But at the same time, he seemed to also want a head start on Alexis with Tom! What the hell was Harry trying to do? It didn't make sense. It was ridiculous. Then a terrible thought occurred to him.

Harry wanted them both.

"What's wrong?" Alexis asked. "You've turned white."

"I'm afraid."

But the panic subsided quickly and he could feel the color rush back to his face, could hear his heart thumping wildly, could relish the smile that curved his lips.

"Afraid of what?" Alexis asked.

Tom wanted to answer, but his mind was racing too fast for him to speak coherently. He was trying to sort it all out first. Then he would tell Alexis about the money, Harry's money, and how he had let himself be physically used by Harry because he had a plan (yes, that was it, good, right!). In order to execute the plan they both might have to go along with Harry's bizarre sexual wishes for a while. Afterward— Tom chuckled to himself—afterward there would *be* no Harry.

"I'm afraid we might have to let Harry succeed—" he started to say.

Before he could explain what he meant, there was a light knock on the door. Then the door opened and Harry himself walked in. As he surveyed the intimate little scene, a slow smile spread over his face.

"Succeed?" Harry rubbed his bloodshot eyes. "The only thing I seem to have succeeded at is waking up with the world's worst hangover. If you can call that success. What are you two talking about?"

"Nothing," Tom said angrily.

He was outraged by Harry's brashness. Eavesdropping on them, barging in like that without being invited! What a presumptuous bastard he was! Tom felt himself shaking with rage.

"You know," Harry was saying to Alexis, "you look very Indian with your hair in a braid. *Muy india, muy bonita.* I haven't seen it combed that way in years. It becomes you."

Instead of objecting to her brother's rude intrusion, instead of telling him to get the hell out, she said:

"I was dreaming about us last night. We were kids again, ice skating on Pilgrim Lake. Remember how cold it used to get in the winter?"

Harry sat down at the edge of the bed, on Alexis' side, totally ignoring Tom. "Of course I remember. Our noses used to freeze. Those were the innocent days, all right."

Tom felt as though he had ceased to exist. They were unaware of him. They were together in their own private world of flesh and blood, just the two of them: brother and sister, childhood allies, grown-up lovers, killers.

Tom wanted to kill Harry.

He hadn't realized how badly he wanted to kill him until just now. And not only so that he could then have Alexis to himself, although that was part of it, a significant part. But just as significant was the money that he and Alexis would inherit if Harry were to die. He and Alexis were Harry's sole beneficiaries. Harry told him so, shortly after Tom arrived in Spain.

The disclosure came about when Harry paid Tom the twenty-five thousand pounds he had originally promised him for his help in that phony "blackmail" plan. In view of what subsequently happened, twenty-five thousand pounds seemed to Tom like a drop in the bucket. Particularly when he considered how much money Harry had come into as a result of Sarah's convenient death. Wasn't Harry underestimating the important role Tom had played in the murder scheme?

"No, I don't think so," Harry had said.

"Can I point out a few strategic facts that you seem to have overlooked?" Tom asked.

"Be my guest."

"Okay," Tom said. "Without my help, you and Alexis might never have gotten away with murder. Without my help, the police might not have arrested Jeanne for the crime. Without my help, Ian might not be rotting in prison this very minute. Without my help, you might not be such a damned wealthy man today. I made love to Jeanne and Alexis. I provided plenty of motives, alibis, excuses. You couldn't have done it all without me. I was instrumental in the whole damned thing. Now what do you think about that?"

Harry had only laughed. "We made a deal for twenty-five thousand pounds and I'm not budging. Take it or leave it."

"Your good nature continues to astound me."

Harry was halfway through a bottle of Pernod at the time. "As a matter of fact, I'm a much nicer guy than you think. I've put you and Alexis in my will, fifty-fifty."

"I'll bet."

"It's the God's honest truth."

"I believe it about Alexis," Tom said. "But *me?*"

"Sure. You and my sister. Who the hell else would I leave the dough to?"

Tom did finally believe him, not because Harry was drunk and showing off, but because Harry was so arrogant he thought he would never die. As though reading Tom's mind, Harry had said:

"Naturally, I intend to outlive the two of you."

Tom now wondered whether Alexis knew the terms of her brother's will, whether she was aware that *millions* of pounds were involved (Sarah had been richer than even Harry imagined). Tom would have to tell her, spell it all out. Later. Right now she and Harry were immersed in their own special brand of nostalgia.

"I was thinking of Juliana the other day," Harry mused. "She was a great old lady, wasn't she?"

"I always remember those stories of hers about our grandfather, Frank, making gin in the bathtub during Prohibition."

"Those stories really used to infuriate Mom."

"What didn't infuriate her?"

"Making a fast buck."

Alexis nodded. "I wonder if Juliana is still alive."

There was a faraway expression on both their faces. Had they bothered to look, they would have seen the same expression on Tom's face.

If Harry were to die.

Of course he would need Alexis' help. . . .

53 ❧

Jeanne had finally tracked down Juliana Maringo.

The old woman, well over ninety, was still alive, nearly blind, and living in Pilgrim Lake's gleaming new chrome and glass retirement home when Jeanne arrived for her first visit.

The search had been a long and at times bewildering one. Fortunately Jeanne possessed a good memory or she never would have remembered the name of Alexis and Harry's birthplace. And without that she would have had nowhere to start. But luck had been on her side.

Now she stood at the reception desk of the retirement

home, identifying herself to the brisk nurse-in-charge. Her appointment with Juliana was for two-thirty, and she was slightly early.

"Would you wait in our visitors' lounge?" the nurse asked. "Mrs. Maringo is having her medication at the moment. She'll be able to see you shortly."

"Thank you," Jeanne said, heading for the lounge.

"Don't forget," the nurse called after her. "She's an old lady. She tires easily."

"I won't forget."

Jeanne went into the lounge and sat down. It seemed to her that the last few months, since her father's cruel and unjust punishment, had been one long sequence of not forgetting, of forcing herself to remember everything she could about Alexis and Harry. She had relentlessly plumbed her mind for any bit of stray information she could dredge up, conversations that seemed meaningless at the time, idle facts that might turn out to be important.

She had sifted and sorted, balanced and weighed, subtracted and divided, nearly gone crazy in the process of trying to find the key that would unlock what she felt certain was more than a casual friendship between the two of them. *Much more.*

So far she had not succeeded in her task, but she had not given up. If anything her determination only became stronger, fiercer. One day, she promised herself, one day she would have them where she wanted them.

Jeanne knew that her father had not killed Sarah, and she knew that *she* certainly hadn't. Therefore, only Alexis and Harry remained. That they were the murderers was as clear to Jeanne as the large clock on the wall, quietly ticking away, but to prove her suspicions and have the case reopened was another matter entirely.

Juliana would be a beginning, however slight. Hopefully the old woman would have something revealing to say about Harry's early relationship with his friend Alexis (née Storms). It was another miracle that Jeanne had recalled Alexis' maiden name. She could have asked Ian, of course, but she did not want to upset him with her own anxieties, her own raging quest. He was upset enough as it was.

The first time Jeanne had been to Dartmoor, she could see why. From the outside it was a gray dungeon of a place with a front gate that dated back to the Napoleonic Wars and a group of dismal cell blocks looming out of the mist. Ian said that nobody had ever successfully escaped from there, which was pretty simple to understand. The surrounding area was one vast, black, wet moor that would provide little refuge or comfort for a man on the run.

Everything about Dartmoor struck Jeanne as gray, including most of the clothes the prisoners wore. Gray trousers, gray tie, gray jacket, only Ian's shirt was as blue as his eyes. Jeanne felt thankful that her father was color blind and unable to see his own gray face. He had aged ten years within the few weeks since his arrest for Sarah Maringo's murder. Still, he tried to act cheerful, optimistic, not to let Jeanne know how dreadful he felt, but his haggard gray appearance gave him away.

"Is there anything I can bring you?" Jeanne asked her father when she was leaving. "Anything you need?"

"There is something." He hesitated and smiled. "I wouldn't exactly call it a necessity, but I'd appreciate it just the same."

"Yes, Daddy? What is it?"

"A canary."

For a moment she was certain she had heard wrong. She stared at him. "Did you say a canary?"

He was grinning now, in almost childish delight.

"We're allowed to keep a small bird in our cell if we wish. Providing we feed it and clean the cage, of course."

Maybe he had cracked up under the strain of imprisonment.

"I see," she said.

"I know it sounds balmy, but you have no idea how lonely it can get here. Particularly late at night when the lights have gone out. A canary is a living, breathing thing, it's . . . company."

Jeanne kissed her father on the cheek, trying to suppress her tears. "I'll bring you one next month. I promise."

"I think I'll call him Rudolph."

"Who's Rudolph?"

"A chap I used to know in Zurich. He chirped a lot but never said anything."

On the train returning to London, Jeanne wrote the word canary in her notebook, then rested her head against the high, upholstered seat and let her mind drift.

It drifted back to her first meeting with Sarah and Harry Maringo in St. Moritz last Christmas, when Ian had taken Alexis and her to the Chesa Veglia on that clear, cold, après-ski afternoon. They all ordered hot drinks to warm themselves up. Jeanne could still smell the tart aroma of her steaming *citron pressé*, could still see Alexis choking on her mulled claret when Jeanne asked Harry where in America he was from.

Why had Alexis been so disconcerted by the question?

Jeanne recalled her stepmother's acute embarrassment and wondered whether it had anything to do with Alexis' admission that she came from the same remote place as Harry: Pilgrim Lake. To Jeanne, the name sounded romantic and she said so. But perhaps Alexis found nothing romantic about growing up in what Harry described as a very small, very provincial, very insignificant little town in upstate New York.

"I doubt that you could even find it on a map," he had said.

Was Alexis ashamed of her humble origins? Jeanne wondered as the train carried her back to London. Yet according to Harry's reminiscences that day, Alexis' family sounded prosperous, well regarded in Pilgrim Lake, her father a successful lawyer and wartime hero, her mother a lovely lady who died young and sent her daughter to a fashionable boarding school in Switzerland. What the hell was there to be ashamed about?

Jeanne was still pondering that question when she got out at Paddington and took the underground train home. During the change at Oxford Circus one possibility occurred to her: what if, for some reason, Alexis were lying about her background? But it seemed too unlikely, too implausible, and besides that would mean Harry had been lying too. *Why? What did they have to hide?* Jeanne didn't have the faintest idea, but the puzzle intrigued her and she decided then and there to find the answers.

That had been five months ago.

Since then all of her efforts to trace Alexis' family, Storms, had proven fruitless. There seemed to be no record of them in Pilgrim Lake's official documents office, no indication of their existence. Perhaps Alexis had been born elsewhere and moved to Pilgrim Lake at an early age, Jeanne thought. In that case, the local schools would surely be able to attest to her attendance, but they couldn't. Another blank. No Alexis Storms. No Storms at all in the town's archives, as it turned out.

This omission intrigued Jeanne, and she shifted her energies to tracing down Harry's family, the Maringos. There she had better luck. Yes, there had once been a Maringo General Store, Pilgrim Lake's chamber of commerce informed her, but that was quite a long time ago. The site now housed a large, modern supermarket. As for any surviving Maringos, the only one still left was Mrs. Juliana, who had gone into the old folks' home recently.

Jeanne's attempts to communicate with Juliana Maringo by mail were unsuccessful. The medical authorities wrote back saying that Mrs. Maringo was ninety-three, arthritic, and semisenile; under the circumstances she could not possibly be expected to answer letters. Could she receive visitors? Yes, providing the person did not stay too long or unduly excite the patient, who needed her rest.

It was then that Jeanne decided what she had to do. She booked a BOAC flight to New York, packed a few bags, and slipped out of Mount Street while both Alexis and Mrs. Cook were gone. She debated leaving a note for Alexis, giving a false destination, but that would have been almost too good-hearted. Let Alexis worry and wonder as to her mysterious whereabouts. That is, if she were capable of worrying about anything or anyone except her own greedy, selfish, murderous self.

It was Jeanne's first time in America. She spent a busy weekend in Manhattan, seeing all the strange sights, then she took a long busride upstate and here she was:

PILGRIM LAKE'S PARADISE HOME

The large clock on the wall now pointed to half past two, the exact time of her appointment with Juliana Maringo. Jeanne stood up and walked down the cheerfully decorated corridor, her heart thudding in anticipation. It was silly to get so excited over what promised to be a difficult and probably unrewarding visit, but she could not help it. Something told her that after months of idle digging and searching she had at last come to the right place, the right person.

As Jeanne knocked on the door to Juliana Maringo's room, it occurred to her that she did not even know what the relationship was between the old woman and Harry. Juliana might very well be a distant cousin by marriage who barely remembered Harry. A surprisingly strong voice called out:

"What are you going to do? Stand there all day?"

Jeanne took a deep breath, pushed open the door, and walked in.

"The big bad wolf," Harry said, walking in.

I continued to busy myself with unpacking. "What do you want?"

He leaned against the doorway, holding a glass of milky Pernod in his hand. He had changed into tan cotton drills, a red t-shirt, and he needed a shave.

"I want to talk to you," he said sternly.

"What about?"

"You. Me. Us. Tom."

"What about Tom?"

"I don't want you to go to bed with him again."

His dictatorial tone startled me. "Really? Why not? Don't tell me that you're jealous, Harry."

"Would that be so unbelievable?"

"After your vanishing act last night, yes. Yes, it would be."

"I was plastered last night. I couldn't help it. It was one of those unfortunate things."

I glanced at his glass of Pernod. "And I suppose you can't help it now, either."

"This is different. This is just a hair of the old dog," he said, dismissing the lethal-looking drink. "Yesterday I was overly eager. I'd been looking forward to your arrival for so long. I began celebrating too soon. I never intended to get so smashed. That's the truth, Alexis."

I suspected that my brother wouldn't know the truth these days if it came up and socked him in the solar plexus.

"Tom says that you've been drinking a lot lately."

"Tom's a damned liar. Why do you listen to him? He'd say anything to discredit me."

"Why should he want to do that? I thought the two of you were the best of friends."

"Friends!" Harry jeered. "I thought so too, but your arrival put matters into their proper perspective. Apparently Tom's never gotten over you. You must have made quite an impression on him back in London town. He was so anxious to get to the airport yesterday to meet you that he dashed out of here without even waiting for me."

"That's not what Tom said. He said you were sleeping off a bad hangover."

Harry nodded knowingly. "He would."

"I saw your room," I confessed. "From the way it looked, Tom would appear to be right. How long has this binge of yours been going on?"

"What binge? I'm not on any goddamned binge. Tom's

trying to poison your mind against me. Can't you see that, Alexis? The jerk is in love with you. He's trying to make me look lousy in your eyes."

I felt like saying that Tom didn't have to try, Harry was doing a swell job all by himself. "Maybe I'm in love with him, too," I replied.

Wham! Bang! The thrust hit home even harder than I had expected. Harry glared at me.

"You don't mean that, Alexis. You can't mean it. Not after what we've been through together. Not after all these years of waiting. You couldn't care about a kid like Tom."

"But I do," I persisted. "I do care. Very much."

"I don't believe it. I *refuse* to believe it. It's a filthy lie!" Harry was shouting now; he looked quite deranged, quite drunk. "You belong to me, Alexis! You always have. Nothing can change that. Nothing. Certainly not a snot-nosed kid like McKillup. Okay, I was drunk and you spent the night with him, that's natural enough considering the circumstances. And I forgive you."

"*You* forgive *me?*" I laughed shrilly. "That's hilarious. That's a riot. You're in no position to forgive anyone. You're the one who needs forgiveness."

"For what?" the maniac asked.

I was so close to exploding that I don't know how I managed to control my temper. "For not meeting me at the airport yesterday. For treating me like a casual acquaintance when I got here. For ignoring me wherever we went last evening. For getting drunk and passing out, my first night in Spain. For abandoning me to Tom. That's for what."

"I thought you were in love with him," Harry said cagily.

I stared at him, forcing myself to confront the reality of what had happened to Harry. Alcohol had warped his brain. It had transformed him from a charming, rational man into a devious cunning monster who could twist and turn any remark to his own crazy advantage. I wanted to laugh. I wanted to weep. What had become of the beautiful brother I had always loved? Was this whom I had waited and prayed and killed for? This hideous caricature of a man? This implausible drunk? It was hard to believe Harry had changed so much. It was even harder to deny that he hadn't.

For a moment we just stood there looking at each other, like resentful sparring partners who'd been separated by a zealous referee. I half-expected to hear the go-ahead signal in another second, and then we would be back in the ring, throwing verbal punches, saying hurtful things, trying to maim, wound, destroy.

But all we were doing was destroying ourselves. As though sensing the futility of our battle, Harry placed his glass of Pernod on the bamboo table next to the vase of withered flowers and moved toward me.

"I love you, Alexis." He took me in his arms. "I love you very much."

His breath reeked of Pernod, and there was a weariness to his body that I had never felt before. His muscles seemed to have turned to jelly. It did not feel like the body I once knew, desired, ached for. It was the body of a stranger, as alien as the drunken personality to whom it belonged. I didn't know what to do or say. I could tell that Harry was getting ready to make love to me, and it was the last thing in the world I wanted. Even kissing him was distasteful because of the alcohol fumes coming out of his mouth.

"Harry, please, not now." I pulled myself away, trying to think of a graceful excuse. "I'm very tired. I'd like to take a nap first, wash up. . . ."

His eyes hardened. "Wash off the smell of Tom McKillup, is that it?"

"Please, Harry. Don't."

"Don't what? Don't mention a few home truths?" All signs of tenderness were gone, he was back to his previous sneering self. "Don't remind you who you were fucking last night? What's the matter, Alexis? Tom is the man you love. You shouldn't be ashamed of him, although he's literally young enough to be your own son. Well, what's a little incest these days? Nothing to get excited about, not after all the practice you've had with me."

My hand crashed across his face and his nose began to bleed. I looked at his weak features and shaky countenance, and realized that because of his drinking he no longer seemed like a man to me. I had old-fashioned ideas about men, maybe it was all those Clark Gable and Humphrey Bogart movies I used to sneak into when I was growing up. Whatever it was, I expected Harry to be noble, tender, tough, not a petty backbiting fool. But the Harry I knew had died, and in his place stood another person I did not recognize, an unappealing stranger who insisted upon making love to me.

I could have refused, screamed, hurled abuse at him, thrown him out, called for Tom. But I didn't. Instead, I calmly gave in and lent myself to a hideous act of collaboration with a ghost. It was like making love in a coffin, one of the bodies still warm. His. Mine was as frozen as the ice on Pilgrim Lake in February.

I thought again of Harry and me (the old Harry) skating over that smooth glistening surface, hand in mittened hand. I thought of the long, laced white boots I used to wear, the same kind that Sonja Henie wore in her extravagant musicals. I even thought of Clark Gable, always so gallant to the dance-hall whores. I thought of everything except the fact that my body was being invaded by someone I did not know or like, someone who frankly repelled me.

"What's the matter?" he asked.

I leaped out of bed the second he stopped and ran into the adjoining bathroom, my hand over my mouth. It was the first time I'd ever vomited after sex. But then, it was the first time I'd ever been fucked by a corpse.

The rest of the day passed in a jumble of high-strung nerves and interesting developments. I joined Tom and Harry for lunch at a nearby beach restaurant.

"Where does everybody in London think you are?" Harry asked me, his eyes nervously darting around. "What story did you tell Jeanne and Ian?"

He was in no condition to hear about Jeanne's disappearance, I decided. I could discuss that with him some other time when he was less wound up.

"I said I was going to Paris."

"Paris. Oh." Harry's voice wandered off in distraction, then drifted back. "Funny choice."

"I once was happy there."

"Never much cared for Paris, myself. Damned depressing city."

Tom looked at Harry in surprise. "I didn't know that you'd spent any time in Paris."

"There's a lot about me you don't know."

I thought of the Yellow Rose Murders and was just about to change the dangerous subject when the food started to arrive.

I knew that Spaniards ate their largest meal in the middle of the day, but I was still unprepared for the size of each course. Compared to the sensible, moderate portions of England, these were enormous. Someone in the kitchen was playing music very loudly, an unthinkable intrusion in London, yet here—as with the bountiful portions—it seemed appropriate somehow.

The restaurant was half full. We were the only foreigners, and I noticed with what apparent relish the Spaniards ate and drank. I suspected that they killed and made love with the same unabashed gusto. They were a sensuous race, but with a much darker side to their souls than the more lighthearted Italians to whom they were often unfairly compared. Spain's violent, blood-soaked history was proof of that. So were its pastimes.

I was thinking of the matador's ritualistic flirtation with death in the bullring I had yet to see, and the deep underlying grief that characterized the flamenco dancers I had seen in Alicante. I was unconsciously dreaming about the next murder I· would commit in this country of nighttime people when I realized that Tom was speaking to me.

"What would you like for dessert, Alexis?"

"Melon, please."

It was a good choice. Its flesh was firm, succulent, yielding.

The meal ended in happy spirits. Harry seemed quite drunk as we walked to our car, but it was a cheerful drunk, all signs of irascibility gone. He had mellowed. In addition to the morning's Pernod and the generous amount of wine he'd consumed during lunch, he had also thrown down three glasses of fiery Fundador brandy for dessert.

I was just beginning to understand the gravity of my brother's drinking problem, but at that moment I felt grateful for it. He would be too immobilized when we got home to entertain any amorous thoughts. I needn't have worried, though. As soon as we reached Los Amantes, Harry headed for his room with a fresh bottle of Pernod, telling us he was going to have a little siesta-fiesta all by himself.

"Just me and my friend," he said, waving the bottle in the air.

Neither Tom nor I were especially sad to see him go, and as it turned out, he would not reappear until the following morning. I spent the rest of the afternoon finishing my unpacking, while Tom read the *Herald Trib* and a Spanish paper out on the patio. The house felt peaceful but I knew it was a false peace, the treacherous lull before the inevitable storm. There were too many unresolved conflicts floating around in the air.

By the time evening came, it was raining. Not the soft, mild, comforting drizzle of London but a heavy howling downpour that slashed against the windowpanes, making visibility almost impossible.

"We had better stay in tonight," Tom said. "This won't let up for hours. It's too dangerous to drive."

Originally he had promised to take me to a small seafood restaurant in Albufera that he thought I would enjoy. Instead we ended up in the kitchen, eating scrambled eggs and bacon (the only thing either of us could cook), and drinking flat champagne left over from yesterday.

A pleasant spirit of camaraderie drew us together, each acutely aware that only a few feet down the corridor Harry was passed out cold and probably snoring, oblivious to us. I didn't see much point in telling Tom about the sexual experience with my brother that morning and how it had revolted me. Yet I was more resolved than ever to keep Harry away from me in the future. Just the memory of his odious breath and flaccid body, his altered personality, made me shudder with disgust.

After Tom and I finished eating we went into the living room. He lit a fire and we danced to Spanish radio music. Like every other musician I had met throughout the world, he was a lousy dancer. But it didn't matter. We were only dancing to hold each other close. I had arrived in Alicante a little more than twenty-four hours ago, yet so much had happened within that short space of time, so many dreams had been shattered.

Too many, perhaps, for the heart to absorb.

I felt tired and confused, dead on my feet, as Tom and I moved around the room. I should be dancing with Harry tonight, I thought. Not the drunken Harry who was passed out on his bed, but that other Harry who was my sole reason for having come to Spain. I had to remind myself that that other Harry no longer existed, he'd died and taken with him all my dazzling hopes for the future.

"What are you thinking about?" Tom asked.

"Harry."

"He's a mess isn't he?"

"Yes."

"What are you going to do?"

"I don't know."

Suddenly Spain struck me as a dead end street. What was I doing here, anyway? Yet if I left, where would I go?

To return to my dull life in London and continue playing the role of the patient, faithful, long-suffering wife (while Ian languished in Dartmoor) was an unappetizing alternative. Then where? And with whom? I was no longer the young adventurous girl of my traveling days, ready to run off for a fast weekend in Monte Carlo with some enterprising stranger. That part of my life belonged to the past.

I wanted something else, something more permanent than a chance encounter, yet something that contained the same element of excitement. I thought of independence in the form of a high-powered, lucrative career. But what could I do? The only jobs I'd ever been trained for were courtesan, model, and wife. I was now too old for the first two, and too disgusted and fed up for the last one. Considering all circumstances, I undoubtedly wanted the impossible. As always, I ruefully amended.

"Are you still thinking about Harry?" Tom asked.

"No."

"Good."

"I'm thinking about you."

"That's even better."

I was conscious of his tanned face close to mine, his sun-bleached hair highlighted against the dark downpour of rain, his lean hard body caressing my own. Just as Harry had changed, so had Tom. But in this case, it was a distinct change for the better. Gone was the awkward, insecure guitar player I remembered from London. Tom had matured into a self-confident and attractive man, a man who desired me.

Last night I resisted his lovemaking because I felt guilty about cheating on Harry. I had held back, kept part of me in reserve. A surge of excitement shot through me now as Tom softly repeated last night's question.

"Your room or mine?"

"Mine."

As I said it, I knew that I'd be holding back nothing from now on.

55 ∽

After spending the second night with Alexis, Tom expected to have a lot of trouble with Harry the next morning and he was ready for it. But to his surprise Harry acted as though nothing unusual had happened when they joined him for coffee on the patio.

Harry merely glanced at the two of them bundled up in sweaters, Tom with his arm protectively around Alexis' waist, and said:

"Looks like it's going to be a nice day."

They all gazed out across the sea at the bluish-white sky, at the sun trying to break through, at the small red sailboat coming close to shore.

"I hope it gets warmer," Alexis sighed. "I'm dying to go swimming."

"Why don't you take *el gato* with you?" Harry said. "Maybe he's overcome his fear of the water by now."

Alexis turned to Tom for an explanation, but he decided to ignore this familiar taunt of Harry's. If that was the extent of Harry's jealousy, it was a small price to pay: to be ridiculed because he had never learned how to swim.

"It would have to get a hell of a lot warmer than it is right now," Tom said to Alexis, "or you'd freeze your ass off."

She smiled into his eyes. "It's *my* ass."

"Not anymore, it isn't."

"Since when?"

"You know."

"Bastard."

Harry could hear them quite clearly, but he evinced no further interest in them, no sign of jealousy. He started to read a newspaper, oblivious to their intimate remarks. And he remained oblivious in the weeks that followed. There were no nasty scenes, no drunken outbursts, no shows of competition on his part.

He seemed to have relinquished Alexis without a second thought, turning his back on her and Tom as though whatever they were doing was not worth a second of his valuable time. Since Alexis' arrival, Harry had begun to devote more and more of that time to drinking, and he often spent a large part of the day in his room, alone.

Tom slept with Alexis every night and made love to her with an insatiable ferocity. He had assumed he knew all about sex because of the active amorous life he previously enjoyed, but now he saw that compared to her he was a rank novice. Their relatively brief affair in London had not prepared him for the dynamic explosions of sensuality she guided him toward with a frank and voluptuous abandon.

He did things he had never dreamed of doing. And he loved

every lascivious second of it. Just when he feared they had exhausted all possibilities, she would cunningly teach him a new approach that drove him even crazier than he already was. There were moments when he felt as though his head was going to go clear through the roof of Los Amantes.

The house might have been named in their honor, Tom thought one night as Alexis lay sleeping beside him. She looked so peaceful, so innocent, so guileless, proving how deceitful appearances could be. She'd fooled him in London, all right. There she had revealed only a fraction of her erotic nature, but since then she must have decided to pull out all stops and dazzle him with her versatility.

Tom could not imagine how he had gotten along without her. His life up until now struck him as bland and meaningless. Alexis had given it substance. She was not merely the most exciting woman he'd ever met, she was as addictive as the hardest drug he had never gotten hooked on. And she would be as difficult, if not as impossible, to kick.

But he had no intention of ever having to face that horrifying dilemma. He needed Alexis and he knew how to ensure that his need was well safeguarded: *by getting rid of Harry.*

The plan that Tom began to formulate, even before he became so heavily dependent upon this strange and compelling woman, was now worked out in his mind, detail by detail. The first thing he had to do was tell it to Alexis.

Perhaps she still cared about Harry, Tom thought as he lay in the double bed in Alexis' room, facing the sea. Normally he would have found the sound of the waves disturbing, unsettling, because of his inability to swim, his morbid fear of drowning. But now the waves were a friendly, reassuring reminder to him of his plan to kill Harry.

Could he count on Alexis' help? That was the crucial question. He could not do it by himself, it was an operation that required both their efforts. But Alexis spoke about her brother so rarely these days that Tom was uncertain what her true feelings were toward him. He had tried asking her only recently.

"Harry?" she said, as though the name barely registered. "He's a drunk. What more is there to add?"

"That's exactly my point."

"What is?"

"That drunks like Harry are pretty depressing to be around all the time. I don't know how you feel, but I can't stand the sloppy sight of him any longer."

"What do you propose we do?"

"Get away from here. Far away. It's a big world. We could go anywhere you like."

She glanced at him sharply. "Such as?"

"You're the experienced traveler, not me. I leave our destination in your hands."

"I'll have to think about it."

She never mentioned the subject again. Tom did not know what to conclude, so he began to watch the way she treated Harry . . . indifferently, sometimes disdainfully, often contemptuously. But did Harry mean as little to her as she pretended? Or did she still harbor nostalgic vestiges of the love she once felt for him? Tom couldn't answer those questions with any degree of certainty. Alexis was an enigma.

And just as he was unsure about her feelings for Harry, so was he unsure about her feelings for him. Her passion didn't prove that she loved him. Perhaps she was incapable of real love. He had read about women like that. But of one thing he was positive. She sure as hell wasn't incapable of hate. She must hate Jeanne plenty to have been ready to let her go to prison for Sarah's murder. She must equally hate Ian to let him spend the rest of his life in Dartmoor for a crime of which he was innocent. Tom could only hope that in her quiet and noncommittal way Alexis had come to hate Harry.

Suddenly he realized that she was awake and staring at him.

"You look so absorbed and distant," she said in the silvery blackness of the night. "What's on your mind?"

"Harry."

"You mean, what you were suggesting the other day? About getting away from here?"

"No, I think I have a better idea."

She turned on her side, propping herself up on one elbow. "What is it?"

"Maybe Harry should go away."

"I don't understand. Where would he go?"

"To his death."

She did not flinch. She just kept looking at Tom, waiting for him to continue. Her total lack of dismay or horror gave him the impetus he needed to tell her the rest. She listened intently as he outlined his plan to drown Harry in the Mediterranean.

"It would have to be done late at night," Tom said. "After

he's eaten a large meal and had plenty to drink. That way we can make it look as though he drowned accidentally."

"I always imagined it would be very hard to drown someone unless he were previously drugged."

"No drugs!" Tom said emphatically. "That's out. I've even thrown away my grass. Drugs lead to too many police investigations, which we want to avoid. My plan is much more simple. The most important thing is that Harry eats a lot beforehand."

"Why is that?"

He marveled at her cool composure. "Because that way when we hold his face down, his windpipe will be full of food. He'll inhale the sea water and choke to death on his own vomit."

She seemed fascinated by these morbid details. "How do you know so much about drowning?"

"Because I can't swim, and when I was a kid I nearly drowned myself. I had just eaten a large lunch and some of my mates were fooling around with me at the public swimming pool. They tried dunking me as a joke. Some joke! I could feel this awful sensation, like the food was going to fly through my nose. And I learned later I was right. That's what happens if you drown after a large meal. Whatever you've eaten comes squirting up through your nose. It's supposed to be pretty disgusting"—he paused for breath—"but effective. And this is the perfect time of year to do it. The beach is totally deserted at night."

"So nobody will see us."

"Right."

"It would take both of us to carry it off," she said, as though she didn't want to be left out. "Harry is quite strong in spite of all his dissipation."

"Yes, I know. That's why I said, 'when *we* hold his face down.' It will definitely have to be a joint effort. Everything fifty-fifty, right down the line. Including the money of course."

He had recently told Alexis how much money Harry inherited from Sarah's estate. As he expected, she'd been startled by the enormous sum.

"It's a bloody fortune," she said at the time. "I had no idea."

"And we're the sole beneficiaries."

She seemed to be remembering that now. Her eyes grew even darker and her voice was curiously flat, toneless.

"If it weren't for us," she said, "Harry would never have come into all that money, would he?"

"He sure as hell wouldn't. And what have we received for our efforts?"

"You got twenty-five thousand pounds, which is more than I did," she said coldly.

"But that's porridge compared to what we could get."

"I suppose so."

"Well?" He looked at her. "What do you think?"

"It's a pretty neat plan."

"And the beauty of it is that we can do it in shallow water." Tom was really warming to his subject now. "After the cops make their tests, they'll find a high concentration of alcohol in Harry's bloodstream. They'll figure that here's a guy who got smashed and decided to go for a midnight swim. What happens? He stumbles on the rocks, passes out cold from too much booze, and drowns facedown in eighteen inches of water! It's foolproof, I tell you."

"What about marks on him? Where we've been holding him? Wouldn't the police find bruises on his arms or shoulders?"

Tom grinned. "I thought about that. And I figured out the solution. *We hold him by the hair.*"

"The hair?" she said incredulously.

"That's right. When we're ready, we grab his hair. His arms will be free, but don't forget that there are two of us. And we'll be sober. The only marks Harry will have on him will be from those sharp, slimy slippery rocks in the sea. Otherwise, nothing. Not a thumbprint."

She thought for a long time. Tom wondered whether she was thinking of the plan's ability to succeed without their getting caught or whether she was thinking of her own ability to kill Harry without remorse. Whichever it was, she appeared to be doubtful about something, fearful.

"What happens afterward?" she asked.

"When the smoke clears, we can decide what we want to do. We could stay on here, maybe rent another house nearby. Better yet, buy one. Or we could go anywhere you like. As I said the other day, you're the world traveler. You must have some place in mind where you want to live."

"The only place I ever wanted to live was Spain."

"You mean, with Harry?"

She looked away. "Yes."

"That doesn't seem to have worked out as you hoped," he said gently.

"No, not by a long shot."

The suspense was killing Tom. Would she agree to do it or not?

"Something occurs to me," she said suddenly. "What if Harry doesn't want to go for a midnight swim with us? I gather that that's what you're going to suggest when the time comes. I mean, what if he flatly refuses? We can't very well drag him into the Mediterranean. What do we do then?"

It was a damned good question. "You know Harry better than I do. What do you think would work?"

"I'm not sure. He can be pretty stubborn when he makes up his mind. Also, don't you imagine he'd find it a little peculiar that we should want to go swimming in November? When it's miserable and cold out there? At night? It would strike *me* as peculiar, if I were in his shoes."

"Yes, unless . . ." Tom was thinking fast. "Unless it's some sort of dare. Harry always struck me as the kind of guy who'd never pass up a dare, particularly if he were drunk and in one of his John Wayne moods. We could challenge him to go into the water, we could say he didn't have the guts to do it or that he was too plastered. Something like that."

For what seemed like an eternity, Alexis did not speak. Then a slow smile started to form on her lips.

"I know a better way," she said. "Instead of challenging Harry to go into the water, I'll get Harry to challenge you."

"*Me?*"

"Sure. He'd love that. He was ribbing you only recently about being afraid of the water. What was that he called you?"

"*El gato*," Tom said, embarrassed. "The cat."

"The cat who's scared of the water. It's perfect."

"I don't understand."

"Look, once Harry challenges you to go in, he has to go in with you to make sure that you don't chicken out. And then I'll decide to come along as well. For the fun of it. That's how Harry would see it: as a great big practical joke."

"Except the joke would end up being on him," Tom said, tickled by the ingenious turnabout. "And he'd be totally unprepared for his fate, totally relaxed. It's easier to drown someone when he's relaxed, you know."

"I'm sure it is."

Tom felt really elated now. Alexis had put the finishing touch on his handiwork and it was an exquisite piece of irony. The more Tom thought about it, the more he liked it. After all these months of being subjected to Harry's ridicule because he couldn't swim, drowning would be the most appropriate death imaginable for his cruel tormentor.

"When should we do it?" he asked, his heart pounding with excitement. She had agreed! "As far as I'm concerned, the sooner the better. I don't see any point in waiting, do you?"

"Only one."

"What's that?"

"I want to look at Harry's will, personally. All we have right now is his word that we're his sole beneficiaries. That's not good enough for me. What if he's lying? What if he's left the money to someone else?"

"Like who?"

Alexis grinned. "A home for cats?"

They laughed. They made love again. He loved her even more than before, now that they were collaborators. They would kill Harry and live happily ever after, just like in the story books. Everything was settled, everything was perfect, the future looked great. Yet despite all this, Tom could not fall asleep.

He felt a slight gnawing discomfort that he was unable to account for. Alexis' idea to check out the will was certainly sound. In fact, he should have thought of that himself. Harry was a sneaky bastard. It would be foolish to kill him and then discover that they weren't going to get the money after all.

Okay, they would look at the will. Alexis said she could get Harry to show it to her. Tom wondered how. He hadn't thought to ask. After all, he trusted Alexis, didn't he? Yes, of course he did. Then what was bothering him? He didn't know. He turned over on his side, wishing he hadn't thrown out all his grass. Three puffs and he'd be off to dreamland like a shot.

Something was not quite right.

56 ✒

Harry's days started and ended with the Pernod bottle now, and he spent most of his time in a hazy dreamlike stupor, barely aware of what was going on around him.

He drank himself into unawareness to avoid thinking about Alexis and Tom. He felt guilty because he'd abandoned Alexis and guilty because he still desired Tom. The fact that they had turned to each other for sexual gratification made Harry so angry that at moments he fantasized killing Alexis, as he had killed Paulette and Rose. One quick chop of the hand and it would be al lover. Then he and Tom could take up where they'd left off, as though nothing had happened, nothing had changed.

But when Harry sobered up long enough to remember his murderous thoughts, he felt even more guilty and remorseful than before. That was where Pernod came in.

It proved to be a fabulous painkiller and he gratefully welcomed the relief it brought. Only after he'd been at it awhile did he realize how addictive the stuff was. The first couple of drinks tasted so mild, so innocent (because of the licorice flavor, reminiscent of childhood), that he was unprepared for the sneaky way they crept up on him, immobilizing him. By then he knew he was dealing with dynamite, but it was too late to do anything about it. Except wait for the effects to wear off.

Before Harry went to bed at night he would solemnly promise himself that tomorrow he was going to quit. But tomorrow never seemed to come. He would often wake up a few hours later, shaking and sweating. Then he would reach down for a slug straight from the bottle, which he carefully kept next to the bed for just such emergencies. The strong alcohol would sear through him, quieting his jangled nerves and making it possible to escape into sleep a little while longer.

Sometimes he slept until late afternoon, sometimes he was wide awake at dawn. Either way, a large shot of Pernod in his black coffee set him up temporarily, brought him back to life, made him feel almost human again. But an hour or so later he would have dispensed with coffee and was splashing the lethal stuff over ice, watching it turn milky (this had become his favorite pastime), sensing himself sink into that dreamy state of passivity where nothing mattered except his own disoriented but pleasurable thoughts.

Occasionally he made a feeble attempt to ration his intake, but it never proved successful. His craving for what he'd begun to refer to as "my medicine" increased so gradually and stealthily that he was knocking off two bottles a day by the time Alexis had been in Spain a little more than a month.

When Harry realized it was November, his mouth dropped open in surprise. What happened to October? Where the hell had it gone? Sitting up in bed, he felt an acute sense of loss, as though a dear friend had quietly passed away.

The only reason he knew it was November was because he'd brought a copy of Sunday's *London Times* into his room at some vague point yesterday. And there was the date, dimly printed at the top of the paper: November 16, 1975. Harry started to leaf through it, hoping that the exercise would improve his blurred vision, when somebody knocked on the door.

He did not want anyone to see him like this. Only recently, in a burst of alcoholic fury, he told Alexis and Tom to let him the hell alone when he was "resting," and they had followed his wishes. Neither of them had disturbed him for weeks now. Perhaps it was an emergency of some kind, Harry thought, glancing nervously at his watch.

It pointed to ten to nine. But was it ten to nine in the morning or ten to nine at night? Total panic gripped him as he tried to figure out the crucial answer. The dark sky outside was no help at all. It could easily be dark at that hour in the morning if it was going to be a sunless overcast day this time of year. Between having an unexpected and undesired visitor and not knowing if it was morning or night, Harry felt a familiar, compelling urge. He grabbed the Pernod bottle and swilled down a fast one.

"Who is it?" he barked.

"*Por favor, Señor,*" came a hesitant female voice. "*¿Me permite limpiar la habitación?*"

Oh shit, he thought. They've hired a maid.

"*Momento,*" he replied. "*Momento, Señora.*"

The fact that he was naked did not bother Harry. Spanish maids were used to naked men. It was the bottle that he wanted to hide before he let her come in. He screwed the cap on tight and buried the bottle and his empty glass in a bureau drawer, underneath an untidy pile of personal papers.

Among the papers were bank statements from London, New York, and Alicante; his passport; an insurance policy; his marriage certificate; Sarah's death certificate; stockholders' reports; and a photocopy of his last will and testament (the original having been left for safekeeping with his solicitor in Guildford).

Something about the will stirred Harry's lapsed memory. Then he remembered Alexis asking him about it only recently. He was suffering from a hangover when she brought up the subject, and his head was pounding. That was why he recalled hearing Tom drive noisily off to Campello to get the car's muffler fixed.

"How come you're so interested in my will all of a sudden?" Harry asked his sister, who was painting her toenails a bright ruby red.

"I'm not the one who's interested. It's Tom. He's curious whether you really made him a beneficiary."

"I told him that I did. What's the matter? Doesn't he believe me?"

"He was afraid you might have been kidding him. He said you were a great one for kidding people."

"If he's so doubtful, why didn't he come to me himself?"

"He's too embarrassed to ask you about it. He's afraid you'll think he's being pushy."

"So Momma is asking."

Alexis flushed. "Forget that I ever mentioned it. Frankly, I don't give a damn if you've included him in your will or not."

"Sure. Why should you? As my next of kin, you'd like it better if I left him out altogether, wouldn't you?"

"I don't care what you do, Harry." Some of the red polish landed on her toe instead of the nail, and she angrily blotted it off. "I don't think you even know what you're doing these days. Look at you. You're so hung over you can barely see straight."

"I may be hungover, but my faculties are still intact, thank you very much."

"Not for long," she snapped.

His drunken fantasies of killing her with a karate chop loomed up again. "You had better watch it, Alexis, or you won't be in the will either."

"*Either?* What do you mean?"

"I mean that I wasn't lying to Tom. He gets as much money as you do. And if you want a piece of advice, sister of mine, stop being so damned greedy or I'll—" He nearly said, "Or I'll kill you." Instead he muttered, "Or I'll cut you off without a bloody cent. Is that clear?"

"Quite clear," Alexis said, hiding a smile as she sprayed her toenails with Revlon's Quick-Dry. . . .

Now that the Pernod was safely stashed away, Harry got back into bed and pulled the covers over the bottom half of his body. What the hell. There was no point in forcing his nudity upon some poor old crone of a maid.

"*Venga,*" he said.

A beautiful young blonde girl entered, a broom and dust-pan in her hands. She sniffed the air in the room and made a face.

"*¡Que olor fuerte!*"

Then, seeing Harry's expression of astonishment, she murmured her apologies and asked if it was all right to straighten up. He assured her that it was and she began by opening the windows wide. A cool breeze drifted in from the Mediterranean. That seemed to please her, she said it would be beneficial for the air.

Her English was stilted, formal, as though she had learned it from some antiquated grammar book. She told him that her name was Marguerita, and she came from a small inland town called Munera.

"Marguerita from Munera," Harry repeated. "It sounds like a popular song."

She laughed and went about her work, leaving him to marvel at her untouched good looks. She was slender, small-waisted, with large brown eyes and hair that fell over her shoulders in soft, golden waves. He could not imagine Alexis hiring Marguerita (from Munera), who looked too much like Sally-Anne (from Pilgrim Lake) for comfort. Perhaps Tom had done the hiring while Alexis was out. That would make much more sense.

Whoever was responsible was unwittingly responsible for Harry's sudden erection. To his amazement he could feel it bulging up from under the covers, the first erection he'd had in a long time that was prompted by the presence of an attractive woman. Odd how Pernod killed his craving for women, how he never thought about them when he went through the motions of routine masturbation.

Instead he thought about Tom McKillup . . . and drank even more to blot him out . . . and wondered whether a member of the opposite sex would ever excite him again . . . and feared that she wouldn't. . . .

This young blonde maid, who couldn't be more than eighteen, had very definitely quelled his fears. Harry watched her graceful movements, intrigued. As she bent over to plump up the pillows on a chair, her short blue skirt hiked up even higher, and he could see her breasts sway forward beneath the thin blouse she was wearing.

His penis throbbed. If he had the guts he would grab the girl right then and there, lock the door, and give the two of them a whacking good time. It was all he could do to control himself from leaping out of bed and lunging at her.

"Where do you live?" he heard himself ask.

"You are acquainted with the post office in Campello?"

"Very acquainted."

"My home is a few meters from the post office."

She lived right in the center of the neighboring village. A ten-minute car ride away, Harry thought, dazzled by how close she was.

"Are you married?"

She giggled. "No, but I have a *novio*. We will marry each other next year."

Harry had not made love to a virgin in so long that the idea was positively enticing. He'd forgotten there were still eighteen-year-old virgins left in this decadent world, beautiful ones at that. But he knew that in staunchly Catholic Spain, men did not have intercourse with their sweethearts; they went to whores for sex.

Yes, Marguerita was among the last of a dying species, and she was bound to be horrified if he dared to approach her. That was all he needed, a scared and trembling girl on his hands. There was no telling what she would do. Yet the prospect of being her first lover, of teaching her the ropes, appealed to him tremendously. She was so innocent, so pure, so unjaded, so unlike him and Alexis.

He tried to think about the other side of it, the less attractive side . . . the blood, the mess, her eyes wide with fear, the fact that she probably had an older brother who would beat the shit out of him, if not kill him. But all the drawbacks and dangers only made him want Marguerita more. He had never needed a drink worse than he did at that very moment.

"Your wife," Marguerita said, sweeping the floor, "she is very beautiful, yes?"

It took Harry a second to realize that she was referring to Alexis.

"Yes, she is very beautiful," Harry agreed. "Where is my wife? Is she at home?"

"She eats breakfast in the dining room." Marguerita smiled proudly, shyly. "I cook the breakfast."

"And our friend, Señor McKillup? Is he eating breakfast too?"

"Señor McKillup?" She seemed mystified. "I do not see another person. I clean your wife's bedroom, but the third bedroom door is closed, locked. Perhaps Señor McKillup is in there, yes?"

"Perhaps."

Harry knew damned well that Alexis and Tom had been spending their nights in the same bed, and he wondered whether they decided to put on a front for this new maid and sleep separately. It did not sound like something that either of them would do, they were too unconventional for such a charade. Maybe they had an argument, a falling out. That could explain why they had slept in their own rooms last night.

"When did my wife hire you?" Harry asked.

"Ah, the Señora did not hire *me*. It was my mother she hired, last week. But my mother had a most unfortunate accident yesterday. She fell and broke her leg."

Well, that cleared up the hiring puzzle.

"Good morning, darling, did you sleep well?"

A fondly smiling Alexis stood framed in the open doorway. She wore pale green jeans, a green cashmere sweater, and a lot of gold jewelry. The scent of her familiar perfume, Les Fleurs, reached his nostrils as she kissed him on the cheek, affecting a marital intimacy that was not lost on Marguerita.

"How is your head?" Alexis cooed. "Do you have another hangover, poor sweetheart?"

Harry stared at her dumbly. Keeping up a front for the servants was one thing, but going to these theatrical lengths was ridiculous.

"Yes," he said. "Poor sweetheart has another hangover. How did you guess?"

He held out an unsteady hand for Alexis' inspection. "I've got to have a shot, I tell you!"

Alexis glanced at Marguerita in despair, quietly shaking

her head as though unable to do anything about her husband's self-destructive demands.

"Where's the bottle?" she asked, her voice filled with resignation.

"Bottom bureau drawer."

She fished out the bottle and glass from underneath the pile of papers and poured him a large shot. The undiluted Pernod was the same filmy color as Alexis' sweater and jeans, Harry thought as he choked it down and motioned for another. Marguerita averted her eyes, clearly embarrassed by this delicate marital scene.

"Knock, knock. Is anybody home?"

It was Tom, looking bright-eyed and cheerful. He entered the room just in time to see Alexis give Harry his second drink. Tom's face clouded over.

"Trouble?" he said to Alexis.

"Just the usual," she replied as Harry knocked off the Pernod and wiped his lips with the back of his hand.

"What the hell do *you* want?" he asked Tom.

"I came to see how you were feeling, *amigo*."

"Okay, you've seen how. Now fuck off."

Tom gazed sympathetically at Alexis. "I don't know how you put up with it."

"I'm his wife."

"His wife, his nurse, and his whipping boy."

"Oh, it's not as bad as all that."

"You're a wonderful sport." Tom made an obvious effort to brighten up. "I think I'll have some breakfast. Can I bring you a cup of coffee, Harry?"

"I told you what you can go and do."

"You must excuse my friend," Tom said, introducing himself to Marguerita. "He's not well this morning."

She stared diplomatically at the floor.

"I was sorry to hear about your mother's accident," Tom said. "Please give her my best wishes."

"Thank you, Señor McKillup." Marguerita timidly raised her eyes. "You are very kind."

"*De nada.*"

"What the hell is going on around here?" Harry shouted. "What's all this super-Spanish politeness, this apologizing for my behavior, this crummy playacting?"

"Harry, please," Alexis whispered. "Control yourself darling."

He had started to shout again, his mouth curled downward

in scornful contempt. Grabbing the bottle from Alexis, he tipped his head back and drank in long thirsty gulps until the bottle was empty. Then he yelled:

"Okay, everybody out! Get lost! Scram! Adios! Hasta la vista!!!"

Alexis beckoned to Marguerita, who followed her and Tom out of the room. Alexis softly shut the door behind them. A lone tear dribbled down her cheek.

"Please do not cry, Señora," Marguerita urged her.

"It's so awful," Alexis sobbed. "I feel so helpless."

"Every family has its sadness." Marguerita picked up her broom and dustpan. "I go now and clean your room, Señor. And tonight I say a prayer for Señor Maringo."

The minute she walked off, Tom turned hopefully to a dry-eyed Alexis. "Well? What do you think?"

"She'll make a very effective character witness at the inquest."

"That's what I think."

"I just wish she weren't so damned attractive."

Tom grinned. "Jealous?"

"Don't be silly," Alexis snapped. "What do I have to be jealous about? Harry's not interested in women any longer."

"He sure seemed interested in Marguerita."

"Don't be silly," Alexis repeated.

Her voice had softened, but the scowl on her face was harder. Unlike her crocodile tears, there was no mistaking its authenticity, Tom thought, looking forward to Harry's death more than ever.

57 ∽

On the 20th of November, four weeks and two days after Jeanne left London for New York, she checked into the JFK airport ready to board BOAC's morning flight back home.

She was surprised at how long she'd been away. It seemed quite incredible. She had not anticipated this lengthy a trip, but due to a series of unforeseen circumstances she'd been forced to remain in Pilgrim Lake for more than a month. Her stay there had paid off handsomely, in fact it exceeded her wildest most optimistic expectations.

But now she was impatient to return to England. She had a lot of things to do. One of them was to see if Tom McKillup was still in the country. Something told her that he wasn't, that he hadn't been in England for quite awhile, that he'd run away with Alexis and Harry. And if she were right, it could be very important. Very important indeed.

So as not to be disturbed, she'd chosen a window seat, told the stewardess that she didn't want anything to eat or drink, covered herself with a blanket, and put on a pair of dark glasses. The seat next to her was empty, and the one on the aisle was occupied by an English businessman who seemed to be catching up on his reading matter. Good. She would be left in peace.

As soon as the plane was safely in the air, Jeanne pushed her seat into the reclining position, closed her eyes, and let her thoughts drift back to the first conversation she'd had with Juliana Maringo at the retirement home.

"So, young lady, you just happened to be passing through Pilgrim Lake," Juliana mused, looking intently at Jeanne from her propped-up position in bed. "And you stopped off to bring me regards from Harry. Is that what you're saying?"

"Yes. That's right, Mrs. Maringo." Jeanne prayed that her flimsy story sounded convincing. "Harry made a special point of asking to be remembered to you."

"He did? The rascal! Where is he living these days? And how is that blonde hussy of an actress he married? Or are they divorced by now? Everybody seems to be getting divorced lately. It's plain *disgusting*, that's what it is. Immoral. When I was young, only loose women and millionaires got divorced. Now the whole world's doing it."

Jeanne could see that it would be difficult to keep Juliana from digressing, but it certainly wasn't going to be difficult to get her to talk. She was obviously a compulsive chatterer. And the fact that she turned out to be Harry's grandmother, rather than a distant cousin by marriage (as Jeanne had feared), was a stroke of sheer good luck.

"I'm afraid that Sarah—Harry's wife—passed away recently," Jeanne said. "She had pneumonia and complications set in."

"Oh, dear. I'm sorry to hear that, even though I never approved of her. Movie actresses! They're not cut out to be

homemakers, you know. Still, I shouldn't talk badly of the
dead, God rest her soul. The last I heard from Harry they
were living in England. Is that where my grandson is now?
England?"

"Yes." It was Jeanne's second lie since the conversation
began. "Sarah left him the house and he decided not to sell it.
I guess he likes England."

"His mother was of English stock. Louise. Maybe that
accounts for it. But his father's side was half Dutch and half
Indian. I'm the Dutch half. I'm Harry's paternal grandmother, you see."

"You look a little bit alike."   *

"Nonsense!" the old woman scoffed. "Harry is the spitting
image of his grandfather, my late husband, who was fifty
percent Nemsi Injun. And not a finer class of people in the
world, even though Louise didn't quite see it that way. Terrible
snob she was, Harry and Alexis' mother, always putting on
airs just because her ancestors settled in Pilgrim Lake first.
Back in the eighteenth century it was, when the English came
over here. Still, that doesn't give people the right to feel
superior. A good woman, Louise, but not one to ever let you
forget her precious English heritage. She died young, too."

Jeanne was certain she had heard wrong. "Did you say,
Harry *and* Alexis' mother?"

"Yes, of course I did. Louise. Louise Smith was her maiden
name, before she married my son, Mark. He was killed in the
war, shot down by the Japs."

"And Mark was Harry *and* Alexis' father?"

"What's the matter? Why do you look so startled? Do you
think I'm lying?" Juliana's voice had risen to a shrill, frightened pitch. "I'm not lying, I'm only telling what happened!
It's not my fault that Kay died in childbirth. It's not my fault
that Wilfred deserted her. What else could we do? We had
no choice. These things happen in the best of families. Ask
anybody if you don't believe me."

"Mrs. Maringo, I don't know what you're talking about—"
Jeanne started to say, but a nurse was at her side.

"I'm afraid you'll have to leave, dear. As you can see, the
patient has become very agitated. You've upset her." The
nurse lowered her voice. "If you do come back again, please
try to avoid any unpleasant subjects. The patient's blood
pressure is high. It isn't good for her to get so agitated."

"I'm sorry," Jeanne said. "I didn't realize."

She tried to say good-bye to Juliana, but the old woman

seemed to have forgotten about her. She had clasped her blue-veined hands tightly together and was murmuring:

"Its not my fault, it's not my fault there've been so many deaths in the family, it's not my fault. . . ."

Jeanne walked out of the retirement home in a state of shock.

Harry and Alexis were brother and sister.

That was what Juliana had clearly and unequivocally said. Could she have been mistaken? Yes it was possible, Jeanne had to admit. The old woman's memory might easily be blurred. And there was the way she had lapsed into incoherence at the end.

Yet if it were true . . . *brother and sister* . . . Jeanne felt dizzy just thinking about it. All these months that Alexis and Harry were pretending to be nothing more than casual acquaintances who had accidentally met for the first time in St. Moritz, after not seeing each other since childhood, they were really *brother and sister*.

They had the same mother, the same father, the same last name. No wonder Pilgrim Lake's records showed no trace of a family called Storms! No such family ever existed. Alexis had made up her maiden name. It was really Alexis Maringo. Alexis and Harry Maringo. They even looked alike, the same dark eyes, the same straight dark hair, the same imposing height.

But why?

Jeanne was still thinking about that when she headed back toward the center of town. Before going to visit Juliana, she had taken her two suitcases and checked into the Windsor for a few days. It was the oldest and most prestigious hotel in Pilgrim Lake, the taxi driver assured her, and she would be well looked after there. Right now all she wanted to do was bathe and lie down. She doubted if she could sleep, not with her mind racing about all over the place, but at least she could rest awhile before dinner, have a martini sent to her room.

After being treated as a naive schoolgirl for so many years, Jeanne relished this new worldly image of herself. She would wear her revealing, fire-engine red maxi to dinner tonight, the one her father had disapproved of so vehemently when she wore it to the Prince Regent's Club last December. Yes, nearly a year had gone by since their chance meeting with Sarah and Harry Maringo that afternoon in St. Moritz. And now Sarah was dead, murdered, and Ian was serving a life sentence in Dartmoor.

Jeanne nearly tripped on the pavement outside the Windsor Hotel as she realized that the meeting with the Maringos had not been by chance at all. On the contrary. Knowing what she now did about the brother-sister relationship between Alexis and Harry, it seemed obvious that the two of them had planned the meeting well in advance, and then made it appear accidental.

But why?

As Jeanne took her room key from the hall porter's desk, only one answer made sense: even then they were planning to murder Sarah!

The next morning was sunny, cold, and brisk. After a light breakfast in her room, Jeanne got dressed and went downstairs to see the head porter. Mr. Adams was a thin, white-haired man whose proprietary behavior led Jeanne to believe that he'd worked at the Windsor for many years, and knew a lot about Pilgrim Lake and its inhabitants.

She was right. Mr. Adams was not only a prolific source of information, but happy to find someone so interested in the town's history.

"Most of our guests don't give a tinker's damn," he said. "So I just direct them to the nearest drive-in movie and take-out pizza parlor, which is all they want anyway. But now that you mention it, yes, there most certainly did used to be a general store in these parts. Owned by a family named Maringo—oh, that was a long time ago. Then Mrs. Maringo, she died right after her husband was shot down by the Japs, left the store to her son, Harry, and he sold it eventually to their clerk, Dennis. It's a supermarket now, all modern and glass and gleaming, with everything wrapped in plastic so as you can't see what you're getting."

Mr. Adams would have rambled on forever if Jeanne hadn't asked: "What is Dennis' surname?"

"Reilly. Dennis Reilly."

"And you say he owns the supermarket now."

"Owns it outright, if I'm not mistaken. Yes, ma'am, Mr. Dennis Reilly has made himself a nice pile of money, but you can't begrudge a man that, not when he's earned it by years of hard work. And Dennis worked hard all his life. Honest man, proud. Even named the supermarket after himself. You can't miss it. It's the biggest store in the shopping center."

Jeanne's head was whirling as she set out for the shopping center. So far everything seemed to be falling into place like pieces in a jigsaw puzzle, and she prayed that Dennis Reilly was the talkative type. If he was, he might be even more informative than Mr. Adams. After all, he'd worked for the Maringos, he probably knew them as well (if not better) than anyone else in Pilgrim Lake.

The supermarket was exactly as Mr. Adams had described it. Large, modern, and gleaming. Boldly lettered, red and white signs hung in all the windows.

MONDAY-TUESDAY SPECIAL SALE! ! ! ! ! !
APPLE FESTIVAL
HALF-PRICE!
Bushels of fresh-picked apples
and
Gallons of delicious apple cider
HALF-PRICE!

A tall, bald man in his mid-sixties was carefully rearranging one of the many apple displays when Jeanne walked in. Assisting him was a young clerk. They both wore identical white jackets over their shirts and ties, and seemed to reflect the crisp, clean atmosphere of the supermarket. Jeanne waited until the bald man had finished rearranging the display to his satisfaction before learning that he was Dennis Reilly.

"Why don't you come into my office?" he suggested. "We can talk in there."

She followed him down a long aisle, to the back of the store.

"So you're interested in the Maringo family," he said when they were seated in his small but meticulously neat office. "How come?"

The bluntness of his question startled her. Getting Mr. Adams to talk had been no trouble at all, he didn't seem to care what it was that prompted her interest. But Jeanne could see that the inquisitive Dennis Reilly would be a different proposition altogether. She decided to be just as blunt as he.

"Alexis Maringo is my stepmother."

His pale eyebrows lifted for the barest of seconds.

"Indeed?"

"Yes, my father married her when I was only three. My own mother had just died, and I suppose I never gave Alexis a fair chance. I resented her for many years for trying to take my mother's place. It's only recently that I realized how unkind I've been, and I thought that perhaps if I came to her home town, saw where she grew up, spoke to people who knew her—"

"—that you might get to like her better," Dennis Reilly concluded.

"Yes. Something like that."

"I see." His clear eyes rested on her face. "So Alexis married a Limey, did she?"

"My father is her second husband. She was married to a Swiss first."

"A Swiss and a Limey. Well, well," Dennis drawled. "I guess that's what happens when you send a twelve-year-old girl to a fancy finishing school in Europe. She goes and marries foreigners. No offense intended, Miss Nicholson. I'm sure your father is a fine man. It's just that when you like people, you want to see them marry their own kind. It's only natural, if you get my meaning."

"Then you *did* like Alexis?"

"Couldn't help it. She had plenty of spirit, that girl, just like her brother. Come to think of it, he married a Limey too. I suppose Mrs. Louise would be pleased, having been of English blood herself."

Jeanne thought it odd that Dennis didn't mention Sarah's murder or piece together the fact that the man convicted of it was Jeanne's own father. She had not expected Juliana to know anything about it, but surely Dennis would have read reports of the sensational trial in one of the newspapers or national magazines. On the other hand, he was an old-timer, provincial and insulated against the rest of the world. Maybe his reading matter was limited to the *Pilgrim Lake Banner*, the town's weekly gossip sheet.

"We were all shook up when Alexis was sent away from Pilgrim Lake," Dennis said, looking out the window at the sunny autumnal sky. "But that's what her mother wanted. It was in her will, nothing anybody could do about it. Saddest part was how much Harry missed his sister. It really hit him hard, even though he wouldn't let on. But you could see it in his face, plain as day."

"Then they were very close," Jeanne prompted.

"Close as twins, the two of them. Only a year apart in age, you know. It was cruel of Mrs. Louise to separate them like that, but she was a mighty strange woman. Mysterious. I worked for her right up to the day of her death and I never understood her.

"I don't know how it affected Alexis, her being in a foreign country and all, but if you ask me Harry never got over it."

"I see."

"Yes, ma'am. Harry loved Alexis very much." Dennis went on as though Jeanne were not there. "And she returned that love. Why, Alexis never looked at another boy long as I knew her. You might say she was stuck on her brother, and it troubled Mrs. Louise, their being so close. 'Unhealthy, that's what it is,' she once snapped. 'Not normal, their carrying on like that.' "

"Carrying on? What do you mean?"

Dennis reddened. "Now don't get me wrong—I'm not saying anything sexual took place between Alexis and Harry. It was just the way they acted when they were around each other. Real intimate. Had fanciful ideas for kids their age, and nothing Mrs. Louise could do about it."

"Except separate them by sending Alexis off to Switzerland," Jeanne prompted.

"The funny thing is, the two of them were always planning to run away to some foreign country when they were grown up. That's what I meant by fanciful ideas. I can't say they were thinking of Switzerland specifically, but they sure wanted to get out of Pilgrim Lake. I'd hear them talking about it. And it was kind of unusual then, to plan on living in a foreign country. Jet travel was unknown in those days."

"Which foreign country did they have in mind?"

"That I wouldn't know. I doubt if they took anyone into their confidence." Dennis laughed. "Didn't trust any of us hicks, I guess."

Jeanne knew that Harry had left England because she tried to phone him at Guildford sometime ago. He had sold the house and the new owners did not have a forwarding address for him. They thought he was somewhere on the Continent.

"You've been very helpful, Mr. Reilly. I only have one more question. Do you recall two people named Kay and Wilfred? They might have been related to the Maringo family in some way."

Dennis scratched his head. "Kay and Wilfred, you say? Mr. Mark did have a sister named Kay, but she got married and moved to the Midwest a long time ago. I don't rightly remember her husband's name, but it could have been Wilfred."

"Mark's sister. Then Kay was Juliana's daughter."

"Why, yes." Dennis seemed surprised that Jeanne had not known this.

"What happened to Kay?"

Dennis shrugged. "Still living somewhere in the Midwest, I reckon. . . ."

After Jeanne left the supermarket, she walked around the lake until it was time for lunch. Then she went into an Italian restaurant and gorged herself on a gigantic concoction called a hero sandwich. Dennis' last words about Kay kept playing over and over in her mind.

Still living somewhere in the Midwest, I reckon. . . .

But Juliana had said that Kay died in childbirth. In a town this small and gossipy, it struck Jeanne as very odd that Dennis wasn't aware of a simple fact like that, that it wasn't common knowledge. Very odd indeed. She mentally filed away the mysterious, unfinished business of Kay Maringo and thought of the early relationship between Alexis and Harry. There was certainly nothing mysterious about that, according to Dennis. Alexis and Harry loved each other.

Yes, it was all starting to make sense. The love that Alexis and Harry felt for each other as children had lingered and festered throughout the years, due to their enforced separation, exploding finally into an incestuous love as adults. Perhaps they tried to fight it at first, married other people, then realized they could only love each other.

Jeanne stopped, stumped. Why didn't they simply get divorced? What made them resort to murder?

Jeanne had grown up with money, she'd never had to worry about it. It took her a moment to realize that Alexis and Harry didn't have money of their own. In order to be together, they needed the financial security they had come to rely upon. So they killed Sarah and managed to get Ian convicted of the crime. It was probably the only way they could see.

For a second, Jeanne nearly felt sorry for them and the hell they'd been through. Then she remembered her father in gray and dismal Dartmoor, with a canary for companionship.

She left the Italian restaurant, planning to go back and see Juliana again now that she knew Kay was Juliana's daughter. But when she called the retirement home, they told her that Juliana could not have visitors for a while. It seemed that the old lady had come down with a viral infection overnight and was being given antibiotics. Jeanne sent flowers and a get-well note, saying she hoped to come visit when Juliana was better.

Then she walked slowly back to the Windsor, wondering why she didn't return to New York City and from there to London. Why was she hanging around Pilgrim Lake? What more did she hope to unearth? What more did she want? Didn't she have enough information for Scotland Yard to reopen the case of Sarah Maringo's murder? The very fact that two of the key witnesses had lied about their relationship, perjured themselves at Ian's trial, was probably sufficient.

Still, the mysterious fate of Kay Maringo intrigued Jeanne. She went up to her hotel room and stared at the telephone. She was starting to feel guilty about having left London without telling anyone where she had gone. Alexis might tell Ian that she'd disappeared, and she didn't want her father to worry. Jeanne debated calling home now. Then she realized that Alexis wouldn't be in London, she'd made her own travel plans. Paris.

"To try and forget," Alexis had said.

"What about poor Daddy? He'll be heartbroken to miss your faithful monthly visits," Jeanne said.

"Save the sarcasm for someone else. As it happens, your father will not have to miss my visits. There's a regular ferry from LeHavre to Southampton, so I'll be able to hop over every month. It's very convenient."

"You have it all worked out, don't you?"

"Yes," Alexis said, smiling. "I do."

Jeanne now wondered whether Alexis had postponed her trip to Paris, whether she had alerted the police about her missing stepdaughter. Jeanne doubted it. But even if she reached Alexis in London, how could she tell her that she had gone to Pilgrim Lake? It would give the whole show away. She could lie, of course, pretend she was in Chicago or Texas or someplace equally crazy, just to let everyone know she was safe.

Mrs. Cook would be relieved. Alexis wouldn't care if she were safe or not.

No. Alexis had probably checked into the Ritz in Paris, and was sitting at the Vendome Bar this very minute, sipping an aperitif and smiling at Harry.

Jeanne was still staring at the telephone, trying to decide whether to call Mrs. Cook in London, Ian in Dartmoor, or Alexis in Paris (just to torment her) when to her surprise the telephone started to ring. It was Dennis Reilly.

"I hope I'm not disturbing you, Miss Nicholson, but I just

remembered someone who used to know Alexis and Harry very well. Yes, indeed. That's young Charlie, next door."

"Young Charlie?"

"Young Charlie Ehlig. He must be fifty by now, but I still think of him as young Charlie. Alexis and Harry used to eat lunch at his drugstore every schoolday afternoon. That was back in the days when young Charlie still had luncheonette facilities. Of course now his place is a streamlined pharmacy."

"I can't tell you how much I appreciate your help, Mr. Reilly."

"There's only one problem with seeing young Charlie," Dennis drawled.

"What's that?"

"He's on vacation in Canada. Doesn't return until the beginning of November."

58 &

Two things happened last week. Franco died and Harry fell in love with Marguerita.

Tom claims that Harry isn't actually in love, that it's more of a middle-aged man's infatuation with a young girl. I was horrified to hear Harry described as middle aged, because that meant I was too, a concept that had about as much appeal to me as waking up ugly and penniless. So I decided that when it came to age, Tom didn't know what he was talking about. He was too young, his ideas on the subject were too distorted.

But maybe he was right in saying that Harry was only infatuated with Marguerita, and I tried to think of it that way . . . as a temporary craziness on my brother's part, a fleeting loss of reason, a mild form of insanity. But it didn't help very much. Actually, it didn't help at all. For the point was that Harry wanted Marguerita, and as a result I wanted Harry again.

Or had I never stopped wanting him?

Naturally, I didn't say a word to Tom about my change of heart, but I began to pray that Harry would soon tire of the virginal Marguerita. To do her justice, I must admit that she didn't appear to return his feelings. In fact, she seemed oblivious of them. Unfortunately, that only made Harry work harder to win her over. It was a sad and pitiful situation, for me as much as anyone.

I remembered the way he watched her that first morning as she tried to tidy his room, and I pretended to try to keep him away from the Pernod bottle.

After that he flirted with her openly, included her in conversations that a maid would normally take no part in, began to brush up on his Spanish since her English was so limited, and most amazing of all stopped drinking!

"If we fire her now," Tom said, "it's going to look damned suspicious after we knock off Harry. The police will think we were afraid to have any servants around who might have seen something, who might have been on to us."

It was a sunny afternoon, and Tom and I were exploring the castle of Santa Barbara on the outskirts of Alicante. The castle, situated at the top of Mount Benacantil, was the very same one that Harry and I had fantasized over when we were kids in Pilgrim Lake. I still remembered the two of us looking at the colorful, enticing photographs in that book on Spain.

We were climbing to the top of the highest ruin now, from which we stood and admired a dazzling view of the Mediterranean. According to the pamphlet, the Santa Barbara castle had been built as a fortress by the Carthaginians back in 230 B.C. Its multileveled height ranged from between three hundred to six hundred feet.

None of that interested me as much as the fact that instead of being here with Harry, as we had always planned, I was with Tom. It didn't seem right, it didn't seem fair. ("Whoever said that life was supposed to be fair?" I recalled Ian asking me at Dartmoor.)

"I thought you were going to get a look at Harry's will," Tom said. "To make sure that I'm really included in it. What's happening?"

"I can't find it," I lied. "I was positive that Harry would have a copy in his room, but it's not there. I've gone through everything."

Tom's green eyes glinted suspiciously in the fading sunlight. "When did you do that?"

"Yesterday morning, when he was at the post office."

"He's been going to the post office a lot this past week. What for?"

"How should I know?" I said impatiently. "To get stamps, I suppose."

"That's what I need. A stamp."

He waved the handful of postcards we had bought at the souvenir desk at me. As far as I was concerned, the postcards (like the pamphlet about the castle) were simply memento of our visit, nothing more. Much as I would like to, I could hardly send one to Mrs. Cook or Ian, both of whom thought I was safely ensconced at the Ritz in Paris.

"You're not planning on *mailing* one of those cards to somebody, are you?" I asked.

"Sure. Why not? I promised the drummer I'd drop him a line from exotic, faraway places. And so far I haven't written him a word."

"The drummer?" I said in astonishment.

"The guy in my group who played the drums."

"I know what a drummer is, you fool! I'm talking about advertising our whereabouts. Do you want everyone in London to know exactly where we are? What's the matter with you?"

"Calm down." Tom seemed amused. "You shouldn't get angry. It makes you look too beautiful."

"Never mind the compliments. I don't want you to send that card. Do you understand?"

He had chosen one that showed the castle of Santa Barbara illuminated at night. It was quite beautiful in an eerie way.

"There's nothing to worry about, Alexis. First of all, nobody in London realizes we're together. It would never occur to them to connect us. Second of all, the guys in my group think I'm traveling around. That's what I told them—that I was going on a worldwide jaunt. Third of all, the drummer himself isn't in London. He's moved to L.A., to escape Inland Revenue. Fourth of all, this lovely card won't have a return address. And fifth of all, just to make you happy, I won't ever sign it. Now, will you stop worrying?"

He was smiling at me and suddenly I felt foolish.

"I'm sorry, Tom. I'm a bit on edge today."

"It's understandable, considering what we're planning to do shortly."

"That's the problem." I looked down at the deserted Postiguel Beach, at the mountains jutting up in the distance. "I think we should put it off for a while."

"Put it off?" He had stopped smiling. "Why?"

"I told you. I couldn't find a copy of Harry's will. Oh, I

located his papers all right. There was his marriage certificate, Sarah's death certificate, and his passport. But no will."

"Where do you suppose it is?"

I leaned back against a bastion and lit a Bisonte.

"Probably with his solicitor in England. Which is no help to us at all."

"It sure as hell isn't." Tom was frowning now. "I don't like this, Alexis. I don't like it in the least."

"Do you think I do? But I'm not a magician. I can't conjure up a will, if it's not there."

He took a drag on my Bisonte, a habit he'd gotten into which infuriated me. If he wanted a cigarette, why didn't he light one of his own? A lot of Tom's habits had begun to irritate me lately, I realized. Even his lovemaking was getting dull, since it was always I who had to initiate anything new. Either he was too unimaginative or too timid to take the first step. I couldn't be sure which it was, and frankly I didn't care.

I sensed a repeat of what happened in London: my own rapid loss of interest. It was odd how love situations had a way of duplicating themselves, whether for better or worse. A person who had once magnetized you would somehow continue to magnetize you even after a separation of many years. And conversely, one who bored you before would bore you again.

Was it really as simple as that? I wondered.

Perhaps I had to become bored with Tom, fall out of love with him, and ultimately leave him because I knew (in my heart of hearts) that I could never ever kill Harry.

"*Una peseta para los pensamientos,*" Tom said.

"They're not worth a peseta. I was wondering how to get Harry to tell me the truth about his damned will. But so far, no success."

"Funny. I've been thinking about that too. And I have a hunch that he has been telling the truth, that I really am a fifty-fifty beneficiary."

"What makes you so certain all of a sudden?"

"Because I just am," he said petulantly. "And besides, I'm sick of all this hanging around, waiting. Let's do it as soon as possible. Will or no will."

"I'm not so sure that's a brilliant idea." I crushed out the Bisonte. "There's no point in killing Harry and then ending up with nothing."

"*Nothing?* We'd still have each other, wouldn't we?"

I looked at him curiously. He wasn't kidding. He meant it. I shivered in spite of my chinchilla coat and woolen trousers.

"Why don't we head for home?" I suggested. "It's starting to get cold."

"Okay. We can talk in the car."

I wondered how much longer I could go on stalling Tom. Patience was hardly one of his major virtues. From what he'd just said, he was anxious to go ahead with the plan despite lack of proof that he'd been included in the will. Apparently, he didn't care about the money anymore, just so long as he had me.

This turnabout of Tom's put a new light on things, and I began to be afraid . . . that if I stalled too long, he would try to drown Harry without my help.

"Today's Thursday," he said. "Let's set a date. How about Monday?"

He might have been talking about going to the movies.

"Why Monday in particular?"

"Maybe because it's the first of December, a new month, a new beginning for us. What do you think?"

My only hope of saving Harry's life was to pretend to go along with Tom. "If Monday suits you, darling, then Monday it will be."

We were driving through a pine grove now, and the fresh clean smell reminded me of Pilgrim Lake. The first time Harry and I made love, I told him that he smelled of pine. And here I was seated next to a man who planned to kill Harry on Monday. No, not just a man. My lover, my collaborator.

"Then it's all settled," he said happily.

"Yes. Of course."

"Great!" He put an arm around me. "It will be a relief to get the whole business over with. And Harry won't suffer more than a minute or two. Death comes very fast."

"I'm glad to hear that."

"Just don't forget what I told you. About our signal. When I whisper, 'Now,' that's when we grab him by the hair."

"I won't forget."

"You know, you're an exceptional woman, Alexis. You're brave, beautiful, sexy, smart—"

"Don't leave out sweet-tempered."

"I'm not kidding around." His voice had become harsh, menacing. "You're all of those things and more. I adore you. You have no idea how much you mean to me. I don't think you can possibly imagine. I've never met anyone like you before. If you ever left me . . ."

I looked at his fierce wild profile in the rapidly descending twilight and realized I had a maniac on my hands. There was only one solution: tell Harry the whole sordid story.

59

The champagne sat in an ice bucket next to the bed.

Tom lay in bed, naked, and looked out at the dark and forlorn garden as he waited for Alexis to join him. She had been talking to Harry for nearly twenty minutes, and Tom felt himself growing impatient. She was trying to find out once more about the will. Although he realized that she was discussing business, important money business, he could not contain his uneasiness, his jealousy. He wanted her with him *now*, goddamn it!

Tom was only too keenly aware of how possessive he'd become toward Alexis, how much his need for her had grown, how much he loved her. And how badly he wanted to spend the rest of his life with her. Their being together was all that mattered. The money that he had been so concerned about at first no longer seemed so important. The money was secondary.

That was why he didn't care about Harry's will anymore. Alexis could walk in this very minute and tell him that he hadn't been in it and he wouldn't care. But he cared very much about seeing his rival dead. Because that was how he thought of Harry now (despite the man's infatuation with Marguerita), how he would always think of him. So long as Harry was alive, there was the grim possibility that Harry and Alexis might get back together again. They had had so many years together, many more than he and Alexis did.

He smelled her perfume before he heard her footsteps.

"I'm sorry it took so long." She looked radiant, beaming. "You *are* in the will, Tom! Just as Harry promised!"

She was wearing the black lace nightie that came to her ankles, but it had a long slit up the front which revealed the curve of her beautiful legs, her luscious thighs.

"Come here," he said.

She walked into his arms and they kissed for a long passionate moment. Someday she would be old and he would tire of her, he thought, but he didn't believe it. Just holding her like this, feeling her body pressed against his own, was worth all the anxiety she caused him, all the hours of despair when he found himself alone in bed, waiting for morning.

"How about some champagne?" he asked.

"Lovely."

He filled two glasses. "You see? I told you I was in the will. I was right, after all. Now are you happy?"

She was smiling like a little girl at Christmas. "Yes. And I'm in it, too."

"You never doubted that part, did you?"

"I have a suspicious nature, Tom. You must realize that by now."

It was amazing how quickly she could switch roles, he thought. In a second, she'd shed her little girl image and was once more the self-assured sophisticate. Their glasses clinked together.

"To crime," Alexis said.

"To crime," he repeated solemnly.

"Shouldn't we be making plans?" Alexis asked, as though reading his mind.

"I thought we'd make love first."

"No." She shook her head adamantly. "Plans first."

"You *are* a practical bitch."

He sighed. "Still, I suppose you're right. Let's see now. Should we tell Harry in advance that we're planning a little dinner party on Monday? Or should we leave it until the last minute so he doesn't get suspicious?"

"I think we'll have to let him know in advance. Otherwise he's liable to take himself off to Alicante for dinner. The way he did last night."

"True."

"We could say that we decided to celebrate Harry's return to sobriety," Alexis said. "But then he wouldn't drink, and it would defeat our purpose."

"True again."

"Oh, my God!" Alexis suddenly sat upright in bed, spilling some champagne on the sheets. "How could I have forgotten?"

"What is it?"

"*Monday is Harry's birthday!*"

"You're kidding."

"No, I swear it."

"It's too good to be true."

"But it *is* true! He was born on the first of December. He's a Sagittarius. He'll be forty-four on Monday. I totally, but totally forgot all about it. I was so wrapped up worrying about his will."

"What a birthday present," Tom mused. "A trip to the bottom of the sea."

"Let's go to Alicante tomorrow and buy Harry some birthday gifts." Alexis was bursting with enthusiasm. "We'll have them wrapped up so they look very gay and festive."

"Isn't that a bit gruesome?"

"I don't think so. We can give them to him just before he dares you to go into the water."

"How do we get him to do that?" Tom asked dubiously.

Alexis thought for a moment. "I have an idea. My gift to Harry will be a pair of swimming trunks. That's bound to make him start to tease you about not being able to swim. . . ."

Tom and Alexis spent the weekend quietly.

They had hidden away Harry's birthday gifts, and Alexis seemed especially pleased with their selections. From her, a pair of sea-green Massana bathing trunks, tight and sexy. From Tom, a box of Alvaro Brevas, one of Spain's finest cigars, the clerk at the tobacconist assured them.

Alexis persuaded Marguerita to bake a whipped cream cake at her own home, then bring it over to Los Amantes on Monday morning, covered, so Harry would be sure not to see it. For dinner, Marguerita was going to cook Harry's favorite local dish: paella. And Tom had already purchased a case of pink champagne in a bodega in Alicante.

Everything was set.

Tom could not help noticing how Harry hung around the kitchen Monday morning as Marguerita started to lay out the long list of ingredients needed for paella. Poor Harry. He sure was stuck on the pretty blonde maid, Tom thought, unable to help sympathizing with his victim. Still, it was nice that Harry could have a little flirtation on this, his last day on earth. It was like watching a convicted criminal enjoy one final wish before he went to his death.

Marguerita left for home at her customary time of six

o'clock, telling Alexis that all she had to do was turn the oven on high in order to heat the paella. The salad was getting crisp in the refrigerator, and four bottles of pink champagne were getting chilled.

"I can't thank you enough," Alexis said to her. "You've been very helpful, very kind."

"It is my pleasure Señora. I hope that the Señor will have a good time at his party. *Buenas tardes*."

"*Buenas tardes*," Alexis said. "I'll see you tomorrow."

Tom turned anxiously to Alexis as soon as Marguerita was out of sight. "I wonder how she'll react tomorrow when she hears the tragic news."

"Surprised. Saddened."

"Very surprised, I should imagine. Won't she consider it pretty peculiar that Harry chose to go for a midnight swim in December? It's not as though he's the athletic type."

"We're foreigners, don't forget. The Spaniards think all foreigners are crazy. They don't judge us by their own standards."

"I just hope Marguerita isn't suspicious."

"About what?"

"You and me," Tom said.

"We've been very careful, very discreet. I'm certain she doesn't suspect a thing. Also, Harry's miraculous recovery from Pernod addiction has made me a happy wife." Alexis smiled mischievously. "I told Marguerita only yesterday that the Señor and I were going off on a second honeymoon in a little while."

Tom gazed at her, admiration mixed with revulsion.

"You think of everything, don't you?"

"Let's say that I try to. Which reminds me. Harry is taking a nap. Why don't we get the birthday candles and put them on the cake while he's asleep?"

"You didn't actually buy *candles?*" he said, appalled.

"Why shouldn't I have?"

"It's gory, Alexis. That's why."

She glanced at him in disapproval. "If you're that squeamish, you should never have suggested what we're about to do. Either you have the stomach for it or you don't."

"It's not the actual act that bothers me so much. It's all these"—he shivered—"all these grotesque and macabre little touches of yours. The cake, the candles, the gifts, the champagne. Couldn't we have done without them?"

"No, we certainly could not! They're props. To lend authenticity to the occasion. Now let's get to work on the candles."

"I suppose you even bought an extra one, for good luck."

"I sure did, honey-bunch." Alexis was in marvelous spirits again. "We don't want Harry to think he's not going to live another year, do we?"

Several hours later, Alexis, Tom, and Harry were finishing the remains of a superb paella dinner, washed down with plenty of champagne.

The pink variety was a delightful improvement over the ordinary kind, Tom thought as he went to put two more bottles in the fridge. It tasted fruitier, smoother, less acid. To his surprise, he realized that he and Harry had drunk almost four bottles between them. Alexis' consumption was so minimal that it could hardly be counted. Harry teased her about it earlier.

"My feelings will be shattered if you don't celebrate my birthday with the proper enthusiasm."

"You know I've never had any capacity for alcohol." She swallowed a few sips. "I'm doing the best I can."

"You take after our mother. I, unfortunately, have inherited father's bad habits."

"You seem to be holding it very well."

"Come off it, Alexis. I'm sloshed up to my eyeballs, for God's sake."

"Oh? Are you?" She looked so innocent. "Honestly, Harry, I'd swear you were sober."

"I don't feel the least bit sober, I'm happy to say, I feel wonderful, super. This has been a great meal."

"It's not finished yet. There's still dessert to come."

"You know I'm not keen on desserts."

"You'll be keen on this one. Marguerita made it especially for the occasion."

The maid's name brought a look of expectation to Harry's face. "Really? What is it?"

"It's a surprise."

Tom returned now to the dining room. The cozy round table has been set for three, as usual, and he could not help but visualize the two place settings there would be after tonight. One for him and one for Alexis. He glanced nervously at his watch. It was almost eleven. H-hour was coming up. His hands were clammy and his throat felt dry, constricted.

He hoped that his apprehension was not noticeable to Alexis, who seemed as cool and nonchalant as always. Her composure was remarkable, Tom thought.

Again, his mind went back to that other dinner party in London, the one at which he had been absent in body (but present in spirit), and he wondered if Alexis had conducted herself with the same degree of equanimity that evening. He could only surmise that she had. If anything, she might have been even more composed when killing Sarah, a comparative stranger, than Harry, her own flesh and blood.

Also, in that case, the poison had been administered (albeit unwittingly) by another person, not by Alexis herself. It was totally different from the brute force they were about to employ. She should be shaking in her proverbial pants. Instead she smiled and glowed in the new ruby red gown she'd purchased in Alicante the day they were buying Harry's birthday gifts. Around her neck she wore what looked to Tom like a real ruby necklace. If it was, it was probably a present from Ian and worth a minor fortune.

"I'll clear away these dishes and bring in the dessert," Alexis said, getting up. "You both just sit there and enjoy your wine. I won't be a minute."

Tom poured another glass of champagne for Harry and himself. Thank God Harry was swilling the stuff down. What a relief! Was Alexis relieved, too? She certainly didn't show it. But then she didn't show any emotions other than the socially accepted ones. How could she talk and act and move as though nothing out of the ordinary were happening tonight?

The only answer Tom was able to come up with was that perhaps by now murder did not strike her as such an unusual occurrence. *Perhaps she'd grown to like it.* Considering the fact that this was the woman he loved, the woman he hoped to spend the rest of his life with, it was a hideous but undeniable possibility.

"What a beautiful cake!" Harry said when Alexis returned carrying Marguerita's whipped-cream masterpiece. "This is one hell of a birthday party. I really don't deserve it."

"That's true enough," Alexis said dryly.

"Please. No flattery."

Tom took out his cigarette lighter and began to light the forty-five candles. He forced himself to sound casual, even though his hands were shaking.

"You old bugger," he laughed.

"Okay, Harry, now you have to make a wish," Alexis said. "Close your eyes like a good boy."

Tom had an instant image of the two of them having gone through this very same ceremony countless times before, when they were children. It only reinforced his incredulity that Alexis could behave in such a heartless, cold-blooded way. Tom's main reason for wanting to kill Harry was jealousy, at least it was emotional. But Alexis was mercenary, she was doing it solely for the money. It was amazing how much money meant to her. Unless she had another motive, Tom thought, a dark brooding secret that he did not know about. Would he ever truly understand this curious and unflappable creature?

"And now for the presents," Alexis said after Harry had blown out the candles. "Would you please get them, Tom?"

"Sure."

Tom was glad to be alone, even for a few seconds. He went straight into the bathroom, washed his hands, and threw cold water on his face. His face was burning, but his hands felt like pieces of ice. Then he looked at himself in the mirror. A stranger with freckles and green eyes looked back. He could not imagine what it was that made him seem so different, so alien. A moment later he saw the answer. Fear. It stuck out all over him. He didn't know why, but he brushed his teeth, gargled with a mint-flavored mouthwash, and wiped his lips on a towel. Then he went to get Harry's gifts, which he and Alexis had hidden in a closet.

"Here we are," Tom said, placing both ribbon-adorned packages on the round dining table.

Harry picked up the smaller package first. It was the box of Alvaro Brevas that Tom had bought him.

"Hey, thanks, *amigo!* I've begun to develop a taste for these foul-smelling things lately." Harry held one of the skinny cigars under his nose. "*Fantástico.* Now let's see what my darling sister has chosen for me."

Tom was positive they could hear his heart racing. He felt as though it was going to choke him. To try to abate his nervousness he downed another glass of champagne.

"Well, well." Harry was grinning. "Sexy swimming trunks. Thank you, Alexis. I always knew you were a lady who planned ahead, but aren't you rushing the weather a bit? It won't be warm enough to go swimming for a long time yet."

"Probably. But I didn't know how you were fixed for swimsuits." She began to slice the tiered cake. "I thought you might be able to use an extra one."

"The weather is supposed to be pretty changeable around these parts," Tom added. "Somebody told me just the other day that it was warm enough last Christmas to go swimming."

"No kidding," Harry said.

"That's what the guy at the newspaper shop claims."

"Would you believe that?" Harry looked at Alexis. "*El gato* can hardly wait for it to get hot so he can run into the old Med for a refreshing swim."

"Cut it out, Harry," Alexis said, handing him the first slice of cake.

"Cut *what* out? I was just making a perfectly innocent remark about *el gato*'s sudden urge to take to the sea. What's wrong in that?"

"You know what I mean," she said. "You know that Tom doesn't appreciate your referring to him by that silly childish name."

"What silly childish name? Oh, you mean *el gato?*" Harry chuckled. "Tom doesn't mind. He knows it's only a harmless little joke. Don't you, Tommy?"

The only other times Harry ever called him Tommy was before Alexis arrived, when the two of them had been lovers. The memory of those shameful hours, combined with Harry's snide insinuations about swimming, made Tom's face feel hotter. He told himself that everything was working out exactly as he and Alexis had planned, that Harry was falling into their trap, that his goading of Tom was exactly what they'd counted on, what they needed for their scheme to work. Still, he resented Harry's cruel teasing.

They were both cruel, Tom thought, both Harry and Alexis. Maybe it ran in their family like a strain of bad blood. Would there be any blood when Harry's head hit the slimy rocks in the sea? No. Tom doubted it. And even if there were, it would be quickly washed away by the water. They would only hear a dull thud, then they'd leave Harry there, face-down, to drown.

"I'm used to Harry's teasing by now," Tom managed to say in a steady voice. "It doesn't bother me."

"Doesn't it?" Harry asked.

"No."

"I find that very interesting. I should have thought it would infuriate you. But maybe you've mellowed since you fell in love with my sister."

Tom held his hands behind his back so they could not see his fidgety fingers. "That must be it."

"Well, they say that love is supposed to bring out the best in people," Harry tenaciously went on. "I've never been sure of that, myself. I'm in love with Marguerita and I can't see that I've changed very much."

"Yes, you have," Alexis said. "You've stopped drinking."

Harry raised his glass of champagne. "Does this look like I've stopped?"

"I meant that filthy Pernod."

"I'm trying to impress my beloved," Harry said. "But somehow I don't think she's very impressed. She's still going to marry that clerk who works in the Campello post office, despite the fact that I keep asking her to break off her engagement and marry me instead of that jerk."

Was that why Harry had been making so many trips to the post office lately? Tom wondered? To check out Marguerita's fiancé?

A second later, Tom realized that his conjectures were based on the foolish assumption that Harry would be around after tonight. What did it matter if Marguerita broke off her engagement or not? What was the matter with him? He had to keep his mind on the main objective, not get sidetracked.

"How about a little brandy to finish off a splendid meal?" Harry asked.

"I'll get the Fundador," Tom said.

The brandy tasted good, it warmed Tom's hands, helped blur his conscience. He noticed that the box containing the swimming trunks still lay open on the table, the tissue paper spilling over.

Harry touched the smooth fabric. "I must be a cynic," he said. "I don't think people change so readily, no matter what they say. I'm still potentially addicted to Pernod, even though I haven't had a drop for two weeks. And Tom is still potentially scared stiff of the sea, and hates to be teased about it. Even though he pretends otherwise."

This was Tom's big moment. "I am not scared stiff, as you so charmingly put it, Harry. I just don't know why you continue to harp on the same subject."

"It only *seems* like the same subject to you because it's such an unpleasant one. Actually, we've been talking about a lot of different things. But all you remember is your swimming hangup."

"It is not all I remember!" Tom forced his voice to rise. "And it's not the gigantic hangup you make it out to be!"

Harry flicked the tip of his cigar in an ashtray.

"Isn't it?"

"No, goddamn it, it isn't. Now can we change the subject?"

"That's a good idea," Alexis started to say, but Harry cut in.

"Just a second. If there's one thing I can't stand, it's a liar. I don't see anything wrong with being afraid of drowning. Most people are afraid of it. I wouldn't be surprised if Jacques Cousteau himself were afraid. It's a natural enough fear. So why all the fuss?"

"*Because I am not afraid of drowning, I tell you.*" Tom stood up from the table and squared his shoulders. "I've taken all the insults and all the patronizing remarks from you that I intend to take, Harry. And if you think I'm kidding, I'll prove I'm not."

Harry seemed amused. "Really? And how do you propose to do that?"

Minutes later the three of them were on the dark beach, walking toward the shoreline. Only a sliver of a moon shone in the sky, and very far out at sea the lights of fishing boats flashed intermittently. Harry and Tom had put on heavy sweaters over their bathing suits, and Alexis was wrapped up in a warm Spanish shawl. On their feet they all wore the white plastic sandals that were sold everywhere in Campello, and were worn by everyone who ventured into the slippery, rocky waters.

"It's chillier than I thought it would be," Alexis said.

"Nonsense," Harry laughed. "Look at *el gato*. He doesn't mind the cold. Heroes are immune to the elements. Didn't you know that?"

"Oh, shut up," she said.

At the shore they took off their outer garments and laid them down on the beach, with rocks on top to secure them from the wind. It was blowing quite a bit.

"Which one of us lunatics is going first?" Harry asked.

Tom felt glad that Harry was still in a jocular mood. At least he would die happy.

"Me," Tom said.

Holding out his arms for better balance, he started in, followed by Harry and then Alexis. The water was freezing, Tom thought as he slowly waded into the Mediterranean, shivering and shaking. Pretty soon Alexis and Harry were alongside him. They had goosebumps on their skin, just as he did. It made Tom feel better to know that he was not the only susceptible one, that even Harry, for all his bluff and bluster, was sensitive to the inclement weather.

"I never thought I'd end up celebrating my birthday like this," Harry said.

"You only have yourself to blame," Alexis said.

This might not be how Harry expected to celebrate his birthday, Tom thought, but it was what he deserved for trying to frighten *El gato* to death. What an ironic twist! Then suddenly Tom realized that he was in between the two of them, which was not how he and Alexis had planned it. The idea was that Harry should be in the middle, so that when the time came it would be easy for them to reach out and grab his hair.

As it was, Tom had Alexis on his left and Harry on his right. The most logical move would be for him to get over on the other side of Harry, thus putting Harry in the middle. Unfortunately it was not as simple as it sounded. He tried hanging back a moment, letting them go on ahead so that when he caught up with them he could ease his way into the desired position. But Harry stopped as soon as Tom did.

"What's the matter? Scared?"

"I had a cramp in my foot. It's nothing."

Perhaps it would be less noticeable if he could get Alexis to maneuver her way around onto the other side of Harry. Tom tried catching her eye, but she was looking downward to make sure she didn't slip on the rocks. Maybe she was aware of the problem and would initiate the move herself once they got a little farther out. At the moment, the water only reached their calves.

"You were right about it being shallow around here," Alexis said.

Harry said nothing. He just plodded on, a skeptical and amused shadow on Tom's right. Soon Harry would cease to exist. Soon it would be just he and Alexis. Soon. Tom's feet felt slimy in spite of the protective sandals, and he wished it were over, he wished that he and Alexis were heading back to shore right now. It was a damned good thing he'd drunk the Fundador, it was probably keeping him from freezing to death. He never imagined anything could be as cold as the way he felt now.

Now.

That was the password he and Alexis were going to use just

before they drowned Harry. But their positions were still not right, and the water was getting higher. He took Alexis' hand and pressed it tight, hoping to get her to look at him. But either she thought he was just being friendly, or that he was trying to help her keep her balance. It seemed impossible to attract her attention, with her eyes stubbornly cast downward. And they didn't have much more time. They had to get Harry in between them. The water was nearly up to their thighs now. *Now!*

To Tom's astonishment he suddenly heard the word being spoken. Alexis had said it. He turned toward her, confused, bewildered. The next thing he knew, the two of them had grabbed him by the hair and were throwing him down on the rocks, pushing his face in the sea.

"No!" he screamed. "No!"

He struggled, but they were too strong for him. They were holding his face down in the water. Tom's worst fears were coming true. He was drowning. But it was supposed to be Harry who drowned. Something had gone terribly wrong, and he fought to extricate himself from their grasp, he flailed out trying to escape their fierce hold. At one point he managed somehow to come up for air, for the briefest of seconds, before he went completely under. The last thing he saw was their faces, glazed and grinning in the pale moonlight. Then he saw nothing. Nothing at all.

They left him lying there on the rocks, the water washing over his inert body. Then they walked back to the shore, dried themselves with Tom's sweater, picked up the other sweater and shawl, and headed up the beach toward Los Amantes.

"And it's not even your birthday," Alexis said.

Two weeks had passed since Tom's death, and Harry could hardly believe that the police investigation and coroner's inquest went off as smoothly as they did. He expected a much tougher ordeal.

Although both he and Alexis had to answer a lot of questions about the events leading up to the fatal accident, never at any time did the authorities seem to suspect foul play. The police officer in charge took a philosophical attitude toward Tom's drowning, which in his opinion was caused by the basic peculiarity of the English.

"They are strange people, the English," he said to Alexis and Harry. "They like the risk, the adventure, the conquest. They do not want to give us back Gibraltar."

"But Señor McKillup wasn't English," Harry said. "He was Scottish."

"*Es la misma cosa.*"

It was as Alexis had said to Tom, that the Spaniards thought all foreigners were crazy and did not judge them by their own standards.

Marguerita's interrogation was mostly confined to the meal she had prepared. She was close to tears as she told the court about the large *cazuela* of paella, the elaborate whipped-cream cake, and the case of pink champagne that had been ordered for the occasion. When asked about Tom's character, she replied that Señor McKillup was a very *simpático* person who played the guitar. No, she could not imagine him committing suicide. He was too cheerful to kill himself, she said.

"*Un accidente alcohólico y desafortunado,*" was the official verdict of *la necroscopia*.

Now that the case was closed and Alexis and Harry could relax, an anticlimactic lethargy seemed to take possession of them. Los Amantes felt empty without Tom and the friction that his presence had created between the two of them. Secretly they both missed him, but to admit it would be tantamount to admitting they might have made a mistake in killing him. Since they couldn't do that, they told themselves that Tom had come between them, turned them against each other, destroyed their love, and therefore they had to destroy him. Without remorse.

"After all," Alexis pointed out, "he was all set to murder *you.*"

Harry's interest in Marguerita came to an abrupt halt right after Tom's death. Her attraction for him simply evaporated overnight, and he wondered what it was that he ever saw in the milk-faced blonde.

"It was probably convenient for you to fall in love with someone as long as I was busy with Tom," Alexis said.

"That must be the reason. I really don't understand any of it. Do you know that I used to hang around her house in Campello, hoping to get a glimpse of how she and her family lived? That I used to go to the post office and try to figure out why she was planning to marry that chinless clerk?" Harry shook his head in bewilderment. "I must have been crazy."

"You had a disease. Like I did. Yours was Marguerita. Mine was Tom. Now we're cured. Neither of them are of any consequence. They never really were, they just filled in the spaces. Our relationship is the only thing that matters."

Yet now that they were alone with each other, as they always dreamed they would be, they were unable to relax or unwind. They were still keyed up from the role they had played in Tom's death, and their testimony at his inquest. They were still searching for the happiness they had hoped to find as the summer people. They had everything they once thought they wanted: money, freedom, each other. But a sense of restlessness pursued them, kept them feeling unfulfilled.

Even the old sexual attraction which had sustained them for so long was gone. Why? It had endured so many years, so many obstacles, so many murders. Why should it disappear now, when they could finally indulge themselves in all the eroticism they wanted? Harry wondered.

They tried making love, but it was a quiet disaster. Harry was impotent and Alexis was dry.

"Go into the bathroom," Alexis said, "and run some hot water over a hand towel. Until it's soaked through, and really hot. Then wring it out and bring it back here."

Curious, Harry did as she suggested. When he returned she told him to lay the towel over her breasts, her public hair.

"Where did you learn this?" he asked.

"Singapore."

"I didn't know you'd ever been to Singapore."

"Oh, yes. Many years ago, when it was still owned by the English."

Harry felt a bit like a doctor as he applied the hot towel to the different parts of Alexis' body. "What were you doing there?"

"This, mostly. A government official taught it to me. He said that aside from me, the best thing about Singapore was having a large curry lunch on Sunday at the Tanglin, then going home and lying down on top of his wife while the

eiling fan blew air up his ass. Nothing was air conditioned
n those days."

But even the wet towel trick, which was supposed to make
he woman moist and desirous, didn't work. They stared at
ach other in the dim candlelight of Harry's bedroom, unable
o conceal their disappointment.

"I wonder what's happened," Alexis said.

"So do I."

"Maybe we feel too guilty about Tom to be able to enjoy
urselves."

"Maybe," Harry said.

But he knew that wasn't it. They had strayed too far apart
ver the years, even though they tried to delude themselves
therwise. Time had taken its inevitable toll. They were no
onger the innocents they would have liked to be.

Peace and solitude weighed heavily upon them, and day
fter day they found their conversation persistently returning
o the murders they had committed. They sat for hours re-
ashing details of their crimes. When it came to practical
ousehold matters, their memories had begun to slide, and if
t hadn't been for the conscientious Marguerita their needs
night have gone unattended to. But when it came to their
nurders, they had perfect recall.

Harry could still remember the name of the florist in Paris
where he bought the bouquet of yellow roses before killing
Paulette and Rose (Les Fleurs Majestueuses), and Alexis
could remember the exact color and design of Sarah's gown
the night she died (a teal blue, floral print), the way the ruby
pendant flashed against her withered and shrunken breasts.

"That pendant sure has been around," Harry mused. "Ian
bought it for his first wife. My wife owned it for a while.
And now it's passed on to Ian's second wife."

"Thank you for giving it to me. I've always wanted it. I
remember many years ago, while Paulette was still alive, seeing
a photo of her and Ian in French *Vogue*. They were attend-
ing some charity ball, and Paulette had the pendant around
her neck. She looked so elegant, so *soignée*."

"She was a hell of a good-looking woman, even tousled. I
hated to kill her."

Alexis and Harry had decided to go to lunch at the Carlton
Hotel in Alicante. They were now walking along the marble
esplanade, a swirling mosaic work of cream, red, and black
tiles, flanked on each side by rows of palm trees.

"Did you, Harry?"

"Did I what?"

"Hate to kill her?"

He hesitated for a moment. "It's strange you should ask that question. I've told myself many times that what I did was repugnant and unforgivable. I've tried to convince myself that although it was for a good cause, I found it quite hateful to murder two perfectly innocent women. But you know something?"

"You really found it quite exciting."

"How did you know?"

"How do you think? Because I found it exciting, too. To watch Sarah unwittingly lift that cup of Hag to her lips, to see her face turn blue. Still, she was poisoned by someone else. It was done secondhand. It wasn't anywhere near as exciting as what happened with Tom. I actually felt a kind of exaltation when we held his face down in the water."

"Now you sound morbid."

"But that's the point." Alexis stopped on the colorful tiles. "I didn't *feel* morbid when we were out there in the Mediterranean. I felt a kind of sexual high. I don't know how else to describe it. But it was thrilling."

Harry admired his sister. She was more honest than he could ever be. Alexis might have been describing his own deepest, darkest emotions, which he was too ashamed to own up to. She was not. But then Alexis always seemed to accept herself as she was, with no phony excuses given for her behavior. Since Tom's death two weeks ago they had been together a lot, talking. Harry told her about the affair he'd had with Tom before she came to Spain. She did not seem especially surprised or disgusted.

"It figures," was Alexis' only comment.

And she told him all about her infamous traveling days (of which the Raffles Hotel in Singapore was but one erotic stop-off), when by her own admission she was little more than a high-priced courtesan. Still, she evinced no regrets or shame for that previous life.

"I've been laid in practically every language, and I can still say 'Good evening' in fourteen countries, including Yugoslavia," she had joked. "So why complain? It was fun while it lasted."

They got off the elevator at the top floor of the Hotel Cartlon and entered the attractive dining room. The captain showed them to their table, which had a superb view of the port.

The wine steward shortly arrived with their bottle of Marqués de Riscal and poured some for Harry to taste. He nodded his approval. The steward then filled both glasses to the halfway mark.

"You haven't mentioned Jeanne," Harry said. "Only Ian. You were living in the same flat with Jeanne up until two months ago. What was her attitude when you said you were going to Paris?"

"I don't think she believed me."

"What? You never told me that!"

"My dear Harry, I haven't had a chance to tell you anything until Tom died. Before that you were too busy spying on Marguerita's private life. And before that you were too drunk to carry on a sensible conversation."

"That's true," he admitted. "But I'm sober now, and I'm not interested in Marguerita anymore. Let's get back to Jeanne. If she doesn't think you're in Paris, where does she think you are?"

"I have no idea. I put on a pretty good act about going to Paris, though. Maybe she bought it. I told her and Mrs. Cook that I'd be staying at the Ritz first, but only long enough to find a flat of my own. And I suggested that they write to me at the American Express office in Paris."

"That was kind of risky. Giving them the actual name of a hotel. They might have phoned."

"It was a chance I had to take. I couldn't very well pretend I was leaving for a city like Paris without a hotel reservation."

"What's happened to your mail?"

"I asked American Express to forward it to the post office in Alicante."

"How can you write back, though? Your letters would show a Spanish postmark."

"I made an arrangement with Renée, the Frenchwoman who's running the House of Thérèse. I send her the letters I want posted, and she mails them from Paris."

"It sounds like a neat arrangement."

Alexis giggled. "Renée always adored intrigue. She used to keep us in stitches recounting her latest escapades with titled ladies. They were always terrified their secret lovelives would reach their husbands' ears. As though their husbands cared."

"Speaking of husbands, have you received any interesting news from Ian?"

"He's upset because his canary has stopped singing. I also received a letter from Mrs. Cook saying that Jeanne was still missing. That was about a month ago. Maybe she's returned to the fold by now. Mail from London is so slow getting here, it has to go through Paris."

A waiter appeared at their table, carrying a plate of large grilled shrimps which smelled faintly of garlic and olive oil. He served Alexis and Harry and refilled their wine glasses.

"Missing?" Harry said. "What's this about Jeanne being missing?"

"That's one of the things I've been wanting to talk to you about. She disappeared from London several days before I left for Spain." Alexis peeled a shrimp. "I think she's gone to Pilgrim Lake."

Harry stared at the plate of aromatic shrimp, at the glass of red wine, at the bustling port of Alicante outside the window, at his sister sitting coolly opposite him. She looked perfectly normal, exceptionally attractive, and as fashionably dressed as always. But perhaps despite external appearances, Tom's death had unnerved her more severely than he realized. Perhaps she'd flipped out.

Jeanne in Pilgrim Lake! It was the most ridiculous, outlandish, ludicrous idea Harry had ever heard of. What would a rich, sophisticated girl like Jeanne be doing in a small provincial town like Pilgrim Lake?

"Did you know there's a lunatic asylum near here?" Harry said, laughing. "It's called Santa Faz. If you don't stop making nutty remarks, you're liable to end up there."

"*Dobra vece.*"

"What the hell does that mean?"

"*Good evening*, in Yugoslavian," Alexis said. "Now, can I get on with my story? Jeanne thinks that her father was framed. By us."

61 ❧

Except for Alexis and Harry being brother and sister, Jeanne didn't have a single fact to return and present to Detective-Inspector Langdale. And yet Jeanne could not help wondering about Kay. What did Kay have to do with Alexis and

where he was. Her old ice-skating friend from St. Moritz: the drummer in Tom's rock group.

From there it was a matter of luck. A matter of fate. Jeanne said a silent good-bye to Pilgrim Lake. This was where it had all begun, the unhealthy involvement between Alexis and Harry. As she began to walk back to the Windsor, she could only wonder where it was going to end, and how soon.

It could not be soon enough for Jeanne Jennifer Nicholson.

Christmas had come and gone, and it was now 1976.

Harry and I celebrated New Year's Eve at the home of some Spaniards we met in an Alicante nightclub. Because the club was crowded, four of us had to share a table, and something about the couple's sleek, somewhat jaded appearance drew us all together immediately.

Their names were Concha and Freddie (he had Americanized it from Fernando) Casal, and they owned a luxurious penthouse overlooking the city. When they invited us to a New Year's Eve party, we were surprised. Spaniards were not exactly famous for welcoming strangers to their home on such short acquaintance.

"You will enjoy yourselves," Concha said with a smile. "We put on a little show for our guests."

"What kind of show?" Harry asked.

"It is, how would you say, a flirtation with death?" Freddie said. "You will not be disappointed unless you have a distaste for the necrophilia."

We had no idea what we were in store for, although we later learned that the necrophiliac whorehouse was endemic to Spain. It seemed that Spaniards had a macabre fascination with night, darkness, death. Their idea of a typically sick toy was a pretty little doll which you wound up, then watched her writhe and die.

When we got to the Casals' penthouse, the party was going full blast, and on the surface it looked like any superanimated sophisticated gathering anywhere in the world. The people were fashionably, elegantly dressed. Diamonds, rubies, and emeralds flashed on women's necks, earlobes, fingers, plunging necklines. The men exuded prosperity and breeding. A bar was set up in one corner of the huge L-shaped living room, and waiters passed among the guests with trays of champagne and caviar canapés. Only Concha seemed to be mysteriously missing.

Shortly before midnight, Freddie led us and several others into a private room at the rear of the apartment where supposedly the fun was going to begin.

"I only invite the appreciative ones," Freddie said, smiling at Harry and me. "The others, they stay and enjoy themselves in the usual way. Music, dancing, drinking."

The room he took us into was totally black. The walls were covered with black velvet, and the only light was a flickering candle that stood at the head of an elaborately draped coffin. Inside the coffin lay a lovely young woman in a virginal white lace gown that came up to her neck. Her long dark hair fell in waves over her shoulders, but her cheeks were heavily, garishly rouged. It took us a moment to realize that it was Concha.

"It is how our women are made up for the embalming in this country," Freddie whispered to us.

For one foolish moment, I thought Concha was dead. Then Harry and I exchanged knowing, sardonic glances.

"Who wishes to commence?" Freddie asked, as if he were politely inviting someone to begin singing a Christmas carol.

A man in a black dinner jacket with a red silk lining stepped forward. He was about fifty, tall, with aristocratic features, and might have been a count whom one saw photographs of in *Vogue*, skiing with his distinguished family in Gstaad or sunbathing beside an exclusive villa in Marbella.

"Ah, *bueno*, Señor," Freddie said. "Shall we begin?"

The aristocratic man stripped quickly and climbed into the coffin. Even in the dim candlelight it was clear that he had a gigantic, glistening erection. Nobody in the room seemed to breathe. Carefully, almost modestly, he lifted Concha's white lace gown to reveal her naked body underneath. Her black pubic hair shone against her very pale thighs, which were placed demurely together.

The man spread her legs and lifted her up by the ass, higher and higher, until her long legs were poised in midair. Then he positioned himself over her, placed her delicate, white-satin shoed feet on his shoulders, and slowly, very slowly began to insert his enormous penis into her anus.

I frankly never thought it would go in, but it did, little by little, until there was none of it left to be seen, it was all inside her. During this slow but precise procedure, which took several minutes, Concha did not move, speak, gesture, or moan. She lay there like a cadaver, as though she were truly dead.

Then the man fucked her with what I can only describe as a kind of controlled frenzy. He was obviously used to this act, and it gave him immense pleasure to move his penis in and out, in and out, in and out of Concha's asshole, as she allowed herself to be taken, and the assembly of guests looked on solemnly, speechlessly.

But the heat and the beat were in the air. It was hot, and I now could see that Freddie had a glazed expression on his face and an erection which he made no attempt to hide. It bulged out from under his meticulously tailored dinner jacket, not as large as the aristocratic man's (from what I could see), but nothing to be ashamed of either.

Our eyes met, and I forgot about Harry, who was standing on the other side of me. I knew suddenly that Freddie and I were about to become lovers. Harry knew it too, for he gently squeezed my hand, as though to say: *It's all right, go ahead.*

But no words were exchanged, no words were necessary. I placed my other hand on Freddie's erection and felt it harden even more beneath my touch. Across the room, a beautiful woman in a scarlet chiffon gown had slipped it off her shoulders, so that her small pink-tipped breasts shimmered in the candlelight. Another woman who was standing next to her began to idly fondle the breasts with one hand and reach under the scarlet chiffon with the other. Yet their eyes remained on the aristocratic man and Concha.

Freddie gently touched my head at the nape of the neck, giving it the softest push forward. I got down on the thickly carpeted floor and opened his fly, took out his penis, put it in my mouth, and began to chew on it. Then I took it all the way in, all the way back up to my tonsils, as his balls dangled and banged against my face. His hands held my head, otherwise he did not make a move or a sound to indicate that anything unusual was going on.

Across the room I could see that the woman in scarlet chiffon was now having her breasts sucked by the other woman, just as I was sucking Freddie's cock. And yet we were all so quiet, so grave, so devotional. That was part of the enjoyment, having to hold back our cries of delight, our gasps, our pain, our joy, having to endure pleasure in total silence.

Harry had found a young blonde girl, not unlike Marguerita in appearance, but totally unknown to him, a stranger he was now undressing for the first time. She had moved over toward him stealthily, soundlessly, and with a glance made her desire known. But Harry merely undressed her until her couturier gown lay in a heap at her ankles, then he ignored her so blatantly that she could bear his indifference no longer and started to look around for another man.

But the other men, as though on cue, ignored her too. They all seemed to realize it was the game both she and Harry wanted: to make her desperate. She was a true beauty, with flawless skin and tendrils of golden curls about her face, but nobody would touch her. They wanted her to debase herself. She didn't seem to know what to do. She tried to approach the woman in scarlet chiffon and her female lover, but all they permitted her was a lingering kiss on their cunts. Then they patted her naked ass and murmured something in her ear.

She returned dutifully to Harry, who now appeared ready for her. Meanwhile, I could feel that Freddie was about to come in my mouth, and I opened it still wider to receive the flow of semen. It burst and spurt inside my throat, hot, salty, unending. Then his penis collapsed, he wiped it off with an immaculate white handkerchief, put it back inside his trousers, zipped himself up, and gazed dreamily at me, whispering his *piropos* (compliments).

Concha, in her coffin, still had not uttered a sound.

One of the men handed Harry something. I could see it in the dim light. It was a long black vibrator with a horizontal band made of diamonds, and when Harry turned it on it made the faintest buzzing noise. The blonde stared at it longingly, waiting for Harry to do something with it, but instead he handed it to her and made a go-ahead gesture with one open palm. Obligingly, she closed her eyes and began to run the vibrator across her nipples, her belly, her cunt, then she jammed it inside her and rotated it slowly, so that all you could see from time to time was a flash of the diamond band.

With her eyes still closed (as Concha's were), the blonde's body started to shake and shudder, she was trembling and clenching her teeth so as not to make a sound, although her orgasm had reached its zenith, around and around went the diamond ban until the girl stopped, spent, and leaned weakly against Harry. Sweat was pouring down her exquisitely made-up face, her beauty mark was running, her eyes were dancing as she smiled at Harry, who smiled back in complimentary reassurance.

Then he took her against the wall, a few feet away from the others, standing up, another woman holding him by the back of his knees for support, while another man kissed his balls. They were like a pyramid, the four of them, the blonde girl being fucked, the woman holding Harry's legs, the man sucking his balls, and Harry reveling in it all. But it was not finished yet, this pyramid.

For I took the discarded diamond vibrator and went over to join them, inserting it in the blonde's anus, so that she had Harry in front and me in back, and now the sweat was coming out of every opening in her body and she felt liquid, her short curly hair was damp and steamy, she swayed a little, and now she was ready to climax again. She jutted her ass out for me, thrust her pelvis against Harry, jutting back and thrusting forward to get the utmost benefits from both of us.

Harry's eyes and mine met over her head, they met and tangled with love in all the steamy, torrid heat. The girl's second orgasm was going to be even wilder than her first, it felt as though she was going to burst wide open as her climax continued and continued and continued in jerking, convulsive movements . . . and then it was over, we all moved away from her, all except Harry, who took her by the hand and gently kissed her on the mouth, and led her back to watch the finale in the coffin.

Concha was going to come.

Freddie had been waiting for this moment. His face was taut, expectant, he obviously knew all the signs that heralded his wife's orgasms, and I wondered if he thought she would be able to retain her monumental silence.

Now it started in the coffin.

The candlelight played upon Concha's ivory skin, her mouth tight with ecstasy, her hands clenched (the only sign of movement she had permitted herself so far), and it was suddenly apparent that she was coming. But instead of the convulsive shaking of the blonde, Concha merely opened her mouth wide and let out an absolutely boundless scream one so loud that all of Alicante could hear it and know that this woman had reached a long-awaited moment of ecstasy, this woman, this corpse.

The aristocratic man climbed off her, out of the coffin, and into his clothes. The woman in scarlet chiffon and her female lover were on the floor now, sucking each other, as Concha opened her eyes, pulled down her demure white lace gown, and picked herself up to join her husband and her guests, all of whom would continue to make love to whomever they wished, however they wished, for as long as they wished, in this black velvet, sepulchral room. Anyone who didn't want to stay was free to go and join the party at the other end of the penthouse. Several people quietly departed.

"Happy New Year," Harry said to me. "I love you."

"I love you, too."

Harry and I decided to stay. There were still quite a few men and women we were both attracted to, intended to explore. We had just started our long-awaited journey of orgiastic thrills. We were hungry and eager, unashamed of our desires, anxious to put them into action. We both knew that the more blatantly intimate we were with others, the more close we became to each other, the more we could love each other.

I began to remove the top of my two-piece sapphire gown. A man with blue eyes approached me, and whispered something in my ear.

"Yes let's," I said, softly.

Another woman had taken Concha's place in the coffin and was waiting for her first lover.

Harry had moved over to join a threesome of heads and arms and legs.

63 &

The orgies that Harry and I participated in, as well as our less flamboyant sexual escapades, only brought us closer together than ever before. Perhaps because we now could be truly honest about our diverse erotic longings, we could also be honest about our own special kind of love, which I'm sure the rest of the world would view as perverted, decadent, unnatural.

And yet to us, it was none of those things. Difficult as that may be to understand.

Harry and I loved and belonged to each other, relied upon each other, needed each other, could not imagine life apart from each other. We were friends, lovers, confidants, brother and sister, and in our own way, husband and wife. I knew that if anything should happen to Harry, I would want to die. He said he felt the same, that it would be inconceivable to go on without me.

"There is no substitute in the world for you," were his exact words.

"Nor you."

We had achieved an intimacy (in every sense of the word) that most people searched for all their lives. I believe that the desire to merge with one other human being lies buried deep inside all of us, but how many of us ever attain that almost impossibly precious and painful goal? Maybe that is why the world is filled with love songs, songs of yearning to find the one person with whom you do not have to put on an act, with whom you can truly be yourself. And Harry and I had done it.

Nobody else, no man or woman—however attractive, intelligent, sympathetic, tender, sensitive, charismatic—could possibly replace either of us. For only *we* shared the memories that went back so far, that festered so deep, that had seared into our souls and made us one.

Our long past, our childhood, our marriages, our murders, our travels (Paris, New York, St. Moritz, London, Spain), our passion for each other . . . these were secrets we held engraved in the heart. They were private, they would endure, they were not for sale, loan, or hire. And we held on to them with the tenacity of all lovers who are inescapably vulnerable to loss. Yet the only loss we feared, aside from death of course, was the law catching up with us and taking away our freedom, locking us up, separating us.

When I told Harry that I was afraid Jeanne had gone to Pilgrim Lake to try and check out our past, he asked why I hadn't stopped her.

"I couldn't," I said. "First of all, I wasn't absolutely certain that's where she had gone. It was just a hunch. She left Mount

Street while both Mrs. Cook and I were out of the flat. And even if I was certain, what could I do? Call the police and tell them what? That my stepdaughter had gone to America? It's not as though she committed a crime."

"You could have reported her missing. You could have said you thought she might be in danger."

"What good would that have done? Unless she actually was in danger of some kind."

"I suppose you're right," Harry admitted. "Anyway, you say she's back in London now?"

"Yes I finally got word from Mrs. Cook that she's home and has returned to university. The mail takes forever getting here. Renée is not exactly the soul of promptness when it comes to forwarding letters. Particularly since she seems to be off on a lot of holidays lately."

"Did Jeanne tell Mrs. Cook where she'd been?"

"Switzerland. She claimed that she got homesick for some of her old schoolfriends, so she decided to pay them a visit in Gstaad. On the spur of the moment."

Harry looked at me carefully. He was so handsome again, since he'd stopped that fiendish Pernod drinking.

"But you don't believe her?" he asked.

"No. If that was all Jeanne had in mind, she would have told me or Mrs. Cook, left us a note, something."

It was early evening and we were sitting in front of the fireplace, sipping a before-dinner sherry and toasting our toes. Actually, we were both recovering from rather hectic sessions the day before, with our lovers of the moment. And now it was pleasant to enjoy an evening off together. Or it would have been, if not for our mutual anxiety regarding Jeanne.

"Mrs. Cook writes that Jeanne is pressing her for my address in Paris," I said. "Why? Why is Jeanne so eager to find me all of a sudden? It can't be out of fondness. She hates my guts. So it must be something else."

"If Jeanne is pressing Mrs. Cook for your address in Paris, then she must feel certain that you *are* in Paris. That's encouraging, isn't it?"

"I guess so."

"What has Mrs. Cook told Jeanne about where you're supposed to be living in Paris?"

"The little false information I've given her. I wrote to Mrs. Cook approximately a month after I left London. I said I had moved out of the Ritz and was staying with a friend who did not have a telephone. I suggested that she continue writing to me at the American Express office in Paris, as my housing arrangements looked like they might be temporary."

"Then Jeanne has nothing to go on, really, No way to track you down."

"Not unless American Express gives her my Alicante forwarding address."

"I don't believe they do that sort of thing," Harry said. "It's not considered ethical."

"I guess you're right." Then why couldn't I shake off this horrible sense of anxiety, of impending doom?

"And I don't see how Jeanne could possibly trace *me*," Harry said. "Nobody knows where I am, including my solicitor. When I left England, I told him I'd be traveling around, seeing the world."

"That's what Tom told his friends, too."

Harry and I looked at each other, the same terrible question crossing both our minds: *had Tom been as discreet as the two of us?* He had had a much more careless, flippant nature, he was not accustomed to intrigue, camouflage, covering up his trail. He had lacked the practice and experience in such matters that Harry and I learned long ago. Tom had lacked a criminal mentality. That was why he was dead now.

Then I remembered the picture postcard Tom bought the day we visited the castle of Santa Barbara. He said he was going to send it to his friend the drummer, who'd moved to Los Angeles. I was so unnerved that afternoon because of Tom's intention to drown Harry (thinking I would be his accomplice), that I did not take the postcard away from him, as I normally would have done. And after Harry and I turned the tables on Tom, I forgot about the entire incident. Now I could only wonder whether Tom had actually gone ahead and mailed the card, unsigned, as he promised, with no return address.

My instinct told me not to say a word about it to Harry. If it had been mailed, there was nothing Harry could do except worry and fret. Anyhow, the drummer was more than nine thousand miles away from us (I tried to reassure myself), and not likely to get terribly excited about a picture of an obscure castle in Spain.

Harry lit one of the Alvaro Brevas that Tom had bought him as a birthday present. Its musky aroma filled the room. It was so serene here, with the fire going and the sherry giving us an appetite for dinner, so serene and peaceful, that it was hard to believe danger might be lurking outside these four walls.

"Even if Jeanne did go to Pilgrim Lake, by some unlikely chance, what could she have found out?" Harry asked. "Aside from the fact that we're brother and sister?"

"That would be all she needed to know in order to get Sarah's murder case reopened. Don't you see? The very fact that we lied to Scotland Yard about our relationship would give them fresh evidence. Evidence that was unavailable at the time Ian was tried for murder. It could be a legal lever to reexamine Ian's true guilt."

"I suppose so," Harry said uncertainly.

"Something else just occurs to me."

"What's that?"

"If Jeanne discovered that we're brother and sister, she'd go and tell Ian, who would then have to evaluate his entire position, his motives for doing what he did. He only confessed to Sarah's murder to protect Jeanne. Now he would realize what a fool he'd been. He'd realize that Jeanne wasn't the murderer, but that *I* was. That you and I had been working together all the time. That we weren't the casual acquaintances we pretended to be."

"That's serious stuff," Harry agreed. "But only if Jeanne went to Pilgrim Lake, as you seem convinced she did. Maybe all she did was run off with some guy she'd fallen for," Harry suggested. "She was all sexually turned on after Tom. She could have met someone at a pub or party and decided to go to the outer Hebrides with him for fun and games. That could explain her mysterious disappearance, couldn't it?"

I was hardly satisfied with the explanation. Jeanne's vanishing act gnawed at me. Something was terribly wrong. I didn't trust my stepdaughter. I knew her much better than Harry did.

"I hope so."

We were going to eat dinner in tonight. Faithful Marguerita had left a roast chicken and baked potatoes for us in the oven. They had only to be heated up. For starters, we were going to have homemade vegetable soup. All in all, it was going to be a very homey evening.

Even so, I had dressed up, put on a bright purple silk jumpsuit and my cherished ruby necklace. I wore the necklave every chance I got, I loved it so. The deep rich color reminded me of burgundy wine, of freshly spilled blood. I remembered the white, blood-splattered apron our mother

"I only want to show you something. A few documents. ?lease put the knife down, Alexis. I don't have a gun or nything. All I want you to do is look at a couple of birth :ertificates and some adoption papers."

"Adoption papers?" Harry said. "Who the hell was adopted around here?"

"You were," Jeanne said quietly.

"What?"

"You were really the son of Kay. Kay Maringo. Mark's sister. Alexis' late aunt. Kay died giving birth to you, Harry. Then Louise and Mark adopted you and brought you up as heir own."

"No! That isn't true! It can't be true! It's a bloody lie!" Harry was on his feet, raving. "You've come here to trick us into confessing. Alexis was right about you, after all. She was right all the time. I didn't listen to her, but I should have. You're a goddamned liar!"

Jeanne held out the papers. "Look at these if you don't believe me. Alexis was born only seven months after you were, Harry."

"Nine months," he said.

"Seven."

Harry's voice was shaking. "Even if Alexis was born seven months after me, as you claim, so what? She could have been premature. Women have premature babies all the time."

"So they do," Jeanne said. "But then why did Louise and Mark lie to you? Why did they pretend your birthday was in September? If you really were only seven months apart, why didn't they come out and say so?"

"How should I know? Maybe because it would have sounded a little fishy."

"That's right. It *was* a little fishy. It was an outright false- hood. You were born in November 1932. Louise Maringo was not your mother," Jeanne said. "She was your aunt by mar- riage. And Mark was not your father. He was your uncle. And you were not born in September. That's what they told you, but it's not true. Look at this birth certificate. It has your name right on it. Look at these adoption papers. *Look!*"

Harry took the papers and his face went white. I did not have to read over his shoulder to understand that what Jeanne had just said was the truth. The horrible, agonizing, in- credible truth. Harry and I had never been brother and sister,

as we were led to believe. It was a monumental lie, a monu
mental joke, and it was on *us!*

I sat there, trying to think, trying to be rational, trying no
to lose my grip on my zigzagging emotions, but the shock o
what Jeanne had just said triggered off a series of hideou
regrets. I wanted to cry, scream, die. Instead, I just sat ther
with my regrets.

We had what we wanted all along, but we didn't realize i
Nobody told us. Everyone lied to us. My mother, my father
Juliana. Liars, all! Liars, thieves, they had robbed us, ruine
us, they had turned us into barren murderers, sexual bank
rupts, emotional pretzels, they had destroyed us, the bastards
I was glad my mother was dead, glad my father was dead
Juliana couldn't die soon enough for me. I would be happ
to strangle her myself. I could feel my hands tighten aroun
her lying old throat. . . . The energy started to drain out o
me, to be replaced by a feeling of enormous, stultifying grie
Grief and loss. Harry and I were finished, our lives needlessl
wrecked. If only somebody had told us the truth, *we coul
have been happy.*

Suddenly Harry leaped out of the chair, scattering Jeanne'
wretched papers to the floor.

"WE'VE DONE IT ALL FOR NOTHING!" he shouted
"WE KILLED THEM ALL FOR NOTHING! FO
NOTHING! *PARA NADA!*"

"Harry." I touched his arm, but he was oblivious to me
"Please, darling. Sit down."

He did not sit down. He went on shouting.

"WE DID IT ALL FOR NOTHING. I KILLED PAU
LETTE AND ROSE FOR NOTHING. YOU KILLE
SARAH FOR NOTHING. WE KILLED TOM FOR NOTH
ING. THERE WAS NEVER ANY REASON TO KILL
ALEXIS, DO YOU UNDERSTAND WHAT I'M SAYING
ALL OF IT HAS BEEN FOR ABSOLUTELY NOTHING
NOTHING. NOTHING. NOTHING. NOTHING. NOTH
ING. NOTHING. NOTHING. NOTHING, NOTHING
NOTHING. . . ."

He collapsed, sobbing, in the armchair. Then he startec
laughing, a jagged clown's laugh. Then crying again. He
looked quite insane and it scared me. But Jeanne scared m
even more. For she was riveted to her seat by Harry's out
pouring of confession.

"Paulette and Rose," she murmured, dumbstruck. "My
mother and nanny. Oh, no. It's impossible."

"He doesn't know what he's saying. He's in a state of shock."

Her eyes went to the ruby pendant around my neck.

"My mother's necklace," she said. "Harry stole it after he killed both of them. Then he gave it to Sarah. I remember her wearing it in St. Moritz. Now you're wearing it. Oh, my God, this is a nightmare."

"Yes," I said. "It is."

"I knew about Sarah, but the others . . ." She shook her head in disbelief. "You killed them all, starting with my own mother. You killed Rose, Sarah, Tom. You fiends, you murderers, you maniacs!"

I flinched at her words, her accusations, the look of horror in her eyes. She was seeing Harry and me as though for the first time, and so was I. *Fiends, murderers, maniacs.* Was that all Harry and I amounted to? Were we filled with nothing but hate and revenge, with killing and more killing? No, I didn't want to believe it. That young girl I had thought of yesterday, the one buried deep within me, once again clamored to be free, to be given a chance. She deserved that chance, that life, even if I had to go to prison for it.

"Why are you looking at that knife?" Jeanne asked, frightened. "What are you going to do?"

"Nothing," I said quietly. "Nothing at all."

The hatred seemed to drain out of me, and Jeanne could feel it. It was like an evil force that I was discharging, tangible, terrible, and it was leaving me. I did not want or need it anymore. The carving knife that lay on the coffee table was meaningless now as a weapon. Nothing could prompt me to use it, not on Jeanne and not on Harry and myself, as I had briefly been considering.

The reason was very simple.

I wanted to live.

I looked over at Harry. He was no longer laughing hysterically, no longer sobbing, but had regained possession of himself. I wondered if he was thinking what I was: that one day, when all this lay behind us, we could finally be married. Man and wife. It was what we had wanted more than anything in the world, ever since we were children. True, certain states outlawed relationships between first cousins, but not all of them.

"Don't be afraid," I said to Jeanne. "It's all over. All the killing, all the violence. It's ended."

Across the room, Harry nodded in agreement.

"We thought you might show up here, Jeanne. We were ready for you. Well, almost ready. Finding out that we're not brother and sister is something Alexis and I will have to deal with in our own way, in our own time. It's a shocking realization, but it might turn out to have its . . . advantages."

His eyes sought mine. Yes, he had thought of marriage, too.

"As for what we've done," Harry went on, trying to reassure Jeanne of our peaceful intentions, "we know what the consequences will be, and we're willing to pay them. We're not going to run away anymore. We're through with killing and we're through with running."

"He's telling the truth," I said.

Jeanne seemed suspicious, though, distrustful. "I hope this isn't another trick of yours, Alexis, because you won't escape. And neither will you, Harry. The police are outside."

"I rather thought they would be," I said.

I walked to the window and looked out. There was Detective-Inspector Langdale and two of his men, accompanied by the Guardia Civil walking purposefully alongside them. They were coming to arrest us, lock us up, separate us. But Harry and I had been separated before and survived. We would survive this separation, too. Suddenly, I felt very tired and, oddly, very peaceful.

I turned and smiled at Harry, a smile that would have to last awhile. . . .

*   *   *

In July 1981, a strikingly handsome couple were sitting down to luncheon on the awninged terrace of the Eden Roc restaurant in Cap d'Antibes.

The terrace, which jutted out onto the dazzling blue Mediterranean, was a summer dining place for the world's most photographed people, who were so accustomed to seeing each other in close proximity that a certain bored cynicism had set in. They rarely, if ever, bothered to glance at anyone.

And yet now there was an almost imperceptible angling of heads in the direction of the two dark-haired newcomers . . . tall, sleek, tanned, still slightly wet from the water, he in a white terry coverup by Charvet, she in a white, ankle-length djellabah over her bikini. They raised their crystal goblets of Dom Perignon in a whispered toast, gazing deep, deep into each other's eyes. If they heard the muted comments about them, they appeared oblivious.

"... murder ... incest ... terrible scandal ... so delicious ... prison ... so decadent ... married, my dear ... in love ..."

Alexis and Harry sipped their champagne and smiled.

ABOUT THE AUTHOR

Joyce Elbert wrote THE CRAZY LOVERS while shuttling back and forth between Spain and London for a number of years. About this novel, she says: "Growing up as an only child, I always longed for an older, fabulous-looking brother. And that's why in THE CRAZY LOVERS, I invented Harry. He is the male counterpart of Alexis—sensitive, sympathetic, and sexy—exactly the kind of brother I would have chosen for myself."

Now back in New York, her hometown, she has just finished her eighth novel, a psychological thriller. An earlier novel, THE CRAZY LADIES, is available in a Signet edition.

More Bestsellers from SIGNET

- [ ] **TWO NYMPHS NAMED MELISSA** by John Colleton.
  (#E8848—$2.25)*
- [ ] **BETWEEN CLORIS AND AMY** by John Colleton.
  (#J7943—$1.95)
- [ ] **PLEASURES OF CLORIS** by John Colleton.
  (#J8197—$1.95)
- [ ] **REPLENISHING JENNIFER** by John Colleton.
  (#J8104—$1.95)
- [ ] **UP IN MAMIE'S DIARY** by John Colleton. (#J8318—$1.95)
- [ ] **KINFLICKS** by Lisa Alther. (#E8445—$2.50)
- [ ] **FEAR OF FLYING** by Erica Jong. (#E8677—$2.50)
- [ ] **HOW TO SAVE YOUR OWN LIFE** by Erica Jong.
  (#E7959—$2.50)*
- [ ] **THE RULING PASSION** by Shaun Herron. (#E8042—$2.25)
- [ ] **ALADALE** by Shaun Herron. (#E8882—$2.50)*
- [ ] **JUST LIKE HUMPHREY BOGART** by Adam Kennedy.
  (#J8820—$1.95)*
- [ ] **THE DOMINO PRINCIPLE** by Adam Kennedy.
  (#J7389—$1.95)
- [ ] **LOVE SONG** by Adam Kennedy. (#E7535—$1.75)
- [ ] **MEMOIRS OF FANNY HILL** by John Cleland.
  (#W7867—$1.50)
- [ ] **JO STERN** by David Slavitt. (#J8753—$1.95)*

* Price slightly higher in Canada

To order these titles,
please use coupon on
the last page of this book.

The Best in Fiction from SIGNET

☐ **ASPEN INCIDENT** by Tom Murphy.　　　(#J8889—$1.95)

☐ **LILY CIGAR** by Tom Murphy.　　　(#E8810—$2.75)*

☐ **BALLET!** by Tom Murphy.　　　(#E8112—$2.25)*

☐ **LOVE ME TOMORROW** by Robert H. Rimmer.
　　　(#E8385—$2.50)*

☐ **PREMAR EXPERIMENTS** by Robert H. Rimmer.
　　　(#J7515—$1.95)

☐ **PHOENIX** by Amos Aricha and Eli Landau.
　　　(#E8692—$2.50)*

☐ **FOOLS DIE** by Mario Puzo.　　　(#E8881—$3.50)

☐ **THE GODFATHER** by Mario Puzo.　　　(#E8970—$2.75)

☐ **THE SAVAGE** by Tom Ryan.　　　(#E8887—$2.25)*

☐ **SO WONDROUS FREE** by Maryhelen Clague.
　　　(#E8888—$2.25)*

☐ **FALL GUY** by Jay Cronley.　　　(#J8890—$1.95)

☐ **EYE OF THE NEEDLE** by Ken Follett.　(#E8746—$2.95)

☐ **DEATH TOUR** by David J. Michael.　　　(#E8842—$2.25)*

☐ **THE DOCTORS ON EDEN PLACE** by Elizabeth Seifert.
　　　(#E8852—$1.75)*

☐ **WINGS** by Robert J. Serling.　　　(#E8811—$2.75)*

　　　* Price slightly higher in Canada

To order these titles,

please use coupon on

the last page of this book.